BRIAN S. LEON

MAELSTROM WITHIN

THE METIS FILES: BOOK FOUR

Maelstrom Within
The Metis Files™: Book 4
Red Adept Publishing, LLC
104 Bugenfield Court
Garner, NC 27529
https://RedAdeptPublishing.com/
Copyright © 2025 by Brian S. Leon. All rights reserved.

---

1.   http://StreetlightGraphics.com

To my father, Henry V. Leon (1938-2019). I know these aren't the books you wanted me to write, but I hope they'll do.

And to my readers: Sorry for the delay. Life got in the way.

Out of every one hundred men,
ten shouldn't even be there,
eighty are just targets,
nine are the real fighters,
and we are lucky to have them,
for they make the battle.
Ah, but the one, one is a warrior, and he will bring the others back.
—Attributed to Heraclitus
in *The Cynic Epistles*

Chapter 1
Kona, Hawaii

The big fish took off on another blistering run, covering a hundred yards before I could even alternate the throttles for the two engines and spin the big boat to give chase.

"I keep losing line every time you turn the boat, Captain!" the tired angler shouted up at me from the fighting chair in the cockpit.

"I understand, but we can't chase the fish as easily going backward as we can going forward," I replied from the flying bridge. "We aren't fishing a tournament, so you're going to have to trust me."

"You think she's big enough?" the tanned and toned angler asked.

"Hard to tell until we get closer," I lied, trying to ignore him and focus on chasing the fish safely. The last thing I wanted was to wear out the gigantic fish and have her die on us.

My angler was a wealthy client and a friend of the guy who hired me to run the boat for him, so I couldn't just tell him to shut up and reel, like I wanted to. He'd come out to catch a grander to put on a wall in some mansion somewhere he probably visited once a year. I wasn't about to let him kill a big marlin for a trophy. I could tell by the fish's shadow when she first came up under the lure in the spread behind the boat that she was big. In the split second between when she struck the lure and exploded from the water, I guessed she was over a thousand pounds. The way she peeled line off the big reel with over forty pounds of drag on her, I knew she had to be well over the thousand-pound fish this guy wanted, but no way was I telling him that.

I had to gun the engines and chase her down at nearly twenty-five miles an hour just to keep up with her, and this was her fifth run in the forty minutes we'd had her on so far. She slowed, and I turned the boat so that the angler faced her dead astern and let him begin the rhythm of lifting the rod with his legs, pulling it with the bucket harness attached to the reel, then cranking down as fast as he could as he slid forward again in the chair. The fish erupted from the water, shook her sleek, broad head, then headed straight down. The marlin had to be close to four feet wide at the shoulders, meaning she was likely twelve hundred pounds at the least. And she was sounding for the first time. My angler was doomed, and I felt a smile grow across my face for the first time in weeks.

For the next thirty minutes, I turned the boat and changed the angle on the fish half a dozen times to try to bring her up and help out my angler. The fish was big, and she was not about to give up easily. I really didn't want to end up with the fish dead—either because it died during a prolonged fight or because we finally beat her. I preferred to tag and release her as we'd done with four other big females over the past week, but once this girl came up, the angler would have no doubt about her size. My mood began to sour, and to make things even worse, I kept getting flashes of Sarah's face. Agent Sarah Wright, the first woman I'd allowed myself to care for in over two centuries, worked for the Department of Homeland Security, and I'd condemned her to a fate worse than death. I kept seeing her in that comatose state, completely unresponsive, with tubes in her mouth and arms, her gray eyes closed. I shook my head involuntarily and felt bile rising up in my throat.

"Captain, did you hear me?" my mate shouted from down in the cockpit, next to the angler. He was pointing off the stern. "She's coming up right there."

We'd gotten to within fifty yards of her, and from my raised vantage on the flying bridge, I could see the flash of her giant flank under the deep blue water. *Big fish*.

I immediately climbed down the stairs from the flying bridge to take control of the boat from the cockpit steering station. I jammed the shift levers into reverse behind my back as I turned to face the back of the boat and keep an eye on the fish now that she was close. The big marlin made a half-hearted leap, clearly wearing out. If she was going to survive, she needed to be released soon.

"Ned, if you're listening," I whispered under my breath in a last-ditch effort, "if you could keep the tiger sharks off her ass, I'll buy you a freakin' keg of beer." I had no clue if my old friend Ned could even hear me, but he was a genuine Titan and onetime all-powerful sea god whose real name was Nereus.

"Whoa, she's definitely a grander, wouldn't you say, Captain Dore?" the angler asked, suddenly elated. "Honey, put the phone down and go get the big camera. I want you to film all this as we pull her in." The bikini-clad bottle-blonde woman, easily half his age, stumbled into the salon to get a bigger camera. The look on her face suggested she was entirely out of her element.

I jammed the throttle down harder than I needed to, and water shot up over the transom, soaked us all, and flooded the deck with a few inches of water.

"Yeah!" screamed the angler. "Let's get on her. Where's the gaff?"

"Momi, don't pull the gaff yet!" I shouted to my mate as he leaned below the gunnel for the big hook. "I'm not sure she's the one he's after."

"What?" the big Hawaiian kid asked over his shoulder. "Did you see the size of her? She's the biggest one I've seen this year. Bigger than the eleven fifty they got on *Sea Hunter* for sure."

"I think she's broad, but I don't think she has the length," I said, lying through my teeth. "We'll see. When you have her on the leader, I'll take a look. Meanwhile, just be steady."

"Aw, hell, Captain Dore," the angler said, wiping at his sweaty head. "She's got to be close, and she's big enough. Let's just take this one. I don't think I'll get another shot at one any bigger today, and I leave tomorrow."

I ignored him, watching my mate and the angle of the line on the water as the leader rose out of the water for the first time. Momi, who'd been working on fishing boats since he was twelve, took a few careful wraps of the heavy five-hundred-pound leader and lifted and guided the fish while I popped the boat in and out of gear just to keep us steady. Part of me hoped the big fish would go ballistic next to the boat and throw the hook, giving everyone a good show and a nice send-off without my help. It didn't happen. She came up easy. *Damn it.*

"Holy hell, skipper," Momi said, staring down into the water as he wired the fish. "Get the gaff—get both. You're gonna need to take a shot at her too."

Shit.

I pulled the boat completely out of gear and crossed the cockpit to Momi's side. "You get the gaff. I'll hold her," I said.

"Honey, honey, get this all on film," the excited angler said.

"Stay out of the cockpit," I said, growling. "If we stick her, all hell is going to break loose, and I don't want anyone getting hurt."

I looked down at the massive fish. She was broadside, sliding up easily as I lifted on the leader. She was beat, but her big eye kept moving in her head, and she wasn't washed out or bronzed, which indicated she was also far from dead. She was big—easily seventeen feet jaw to tail, probably close to twenty if you included the bill—easily twelve, maybe thirteen hundred pounds. I reached down as close to the water as I could and saw the hookset lodged precariously in the hinge of her jaw, but with the pressure I was putting on her and her lack of fight, it was never coming out on its own. I felt Momi show up behind me with the big flying gaff as he secured the line from the broad hook to a cleat under the gunnel.

"Hang on, Momi—she's right here," I said. "Give me the gaff and go get the other one."

The second Momi left to get the other gaff, I pulled on the five-hundred-pound monofilament leader with a sharp, violent tug, snapping it at the crimp near the big 14/0 hook.

"Shit!" I hoped my scream would sound like genuine disappointment. I made a show of lunging with the flying gaff as if attempting to free gaff the big fish but coming up empty. "Damn it."

"What happened?" the angler asked, rising up in the fighting chair.

"Line snapped," I said, dropping the gaff on the deck and holding up the chafed and snapped leader. "She was big, and she just wore out the line. I know we didn't get her in the boat, but technically since we got hold of the leader, she is officially a caught fish. And Momi was right—she might have been close to twelve. I'm really sorry, but that's what happens with big fish."

Momi stared at me from behind the angler, gaff in hand.

"Get them back out again," I said as I passed him to climb back up to the flying bridge. "We still have some time."

Chapter 2

No one spoke the rest of the afternoon, but I could see the irritation on the guy's face as he glanced up at me every so often. I could also see the confusion on Momi's face, though he said nothing even when he came to sit at the top of the ladder to the flying bridge to watch the lures.

As we came back into Honokohau Marina, only Momi spoke as he secured the big marlin lures, tidied up the cockpit, and prepared the dock lines. "It happens all the time on really big fish," he said, though I couldn't see the man or his too-blonde wife. "That's part of the reason you don't see more of them caught. Everything has to go just right. But at least you got to see a fish few people ever will. That's what we call a *blue moon* 'cause one that big only comes along once in a blue moon."

As we turned into the marina from open water, I saw Ned lounging in a chair by the thatched shed at the end of the dock. He had a beer in each hand and an ancient, sun-faded blue cooler under his feet. His garish shirt was a combination of reds and yellows that was fortunately mostly hidden by his massive bushy beard. He held a can up to me as we passed, and he gave me an exaggerated wink. *Drunken Island Santa Claus.*

Ned had followed me when I took off from San Diego a few months back. After everything that had happened with Sarah and my fight with the fallen Watcher Ramiel and his followers nearly six months before, I just couldn't get past it. I needed a break.

Three thousand years of protecting humanity from monsters and creatures it doesn't even believe exist, and I can't even protect the ones I care about most. What fucking good am I?

Ned and I didn't talk about much besides fishing, but he was always around. I even felt his weak Protogenoi presence offshore a few times. I knew he was worried about me. I didn't care that I hadn't heard a word from Athena, my benefactor and the source of my immortality, since I left the hospital in Pennsylvania six months before. Because of our relationship, I knew she knew exactly where I was and what I was feeling, and I assumed she was giving me space.

I had never taken off like that before. I was always the one everyone could count on—always.

Apparently not everyone.

I'd made Sarah a promise, and I couldn't keep it, so I was done.

As I maneuvered the forty-two-foot sportfishing boat around the marina to our slip, something, or rather someone, standing on the hill overlooking the charter docks caught my attention. It was a woman, dressed in a long gauzy white dress with some sort of white wrap draped over her shoulders and arms. Her face was hidden under a massive floppy white hat that belonged at the Kentucky Derby or a trendy beach, but her dress did little to hide her figure. The other thing she couldn't hide, from me anyway, was her aura. She was a Moroi—a vampire that fed off the energy of humankind.

And that was the third time I'd seen her in the past week.

I backed the boat into our slip as Momi secured her to the dock and connected the shore-power umbilical and the freshwater hose. I shut down the engines and went down to the cockpit. "Well, Captain Dore, we got a few, didn't we?" the tanned and toned angler said, holding out his hand.

"We did," I replied, shaking his hand, desperately wishing the guy would just leave. "Maybe next time, we'll stick a big one for you."

"Hey, technically, she was caught, right?" he asked, giving me a sideways glance.

"Not technically," I replied. "By International Game Fish Association rules, she was caught and released. I'll have a certificate saying as much sent out to you. We'll call her eleven hundred since we didn't weigh her, but I'd bet she'd have gone a few hundred more."

"Damn. Wish I'd have gotten to see her up close," he said. "How big would you say she was? I can still get a release mount of a fish roughly her size, right? It would look great at the house back in Florida, don't you think, hon? I'll have to move the tarpon, the grizzly bear, and the elephant tusks."

On the hill overhead, the vampiress moved around to watch us talk, her face still hidden by her giant hat. Something about her was familiar.

"Yeah, you can get a replica mount of the fish. I'd estimate her at close to two hundred inches at least, but that was the fish of a lifetime. You may have to settle for something smaller." I kept watch on the vampire as I talked.

Since I came out to Hawaii, I had been only periodically attacked by Lilith's Strigoi minions as part of our ongoing blood feud. They were always around, though. And after attacking Lilith's sisters Eisheth and Na'amah, along with Ramiel, at the Gates of Hell, I wouldn't doubt that I'd begun a blood feud with the Moroi and Succubi as well. But this woman was the only one of her kind I had seen, and so far, she was being aloof and passive.

The angler tipped Momi as the big Hawaiian helped him and his wife off the boat, and the kid turned back to me and nodded over his shoulder up the hill toward the woman in white. He mouthed, "Damn," and rolled his eyes. I laughed and turned on the hose to start cleaning.

"I'll get it, skipper," Momi said. "I do have a question about that big fish, though. I would swear she was all but in the boat when I went to go get the gaffs. What happened?"

"Ah, who knows, Momi?" I replied, heading into the boat's salon. "Big fish are smart and can get squirrely. She wasn't close to done. She was just biding her time, and I didn't react fast enough to drop the leader, I guess."

"You mean you actually had a few wraps on her when she broke?" he said, his eyes getting large. "That was five-hundred-pound mono, Skip. How did you not go overboard? I got a cousin who was killed the exact same way. He got all tangled up and jerked overboard. By the time we got him loose, he drowned."

I wasn't about to explain to him that I could have broken the leader myself as easily as he could break ten-pound test monofilament. "Just lucky, I guess. She rolled and it snapped so fast I never left my feet. Sometimes, better lucky than good, huh?"

"No kidding," Momi said with a laugh.

"I heard you boys lost a big one out there today." Ned's familiar, deep voice came from down the dock. "Good thing there weren't no sharks out there!" I could hear his flip-flops snapping against his feet as he walked. Then he belched. "Better out than in—ain't that what they say?" Ned stared purposefully up the hill at the woman in white for a good twenty seconds before she turned and left.

If I didn't know Ned better, I would have said he leered at her. I was more inclined to believe it was some sort of supernatural pissing contest. They could hose each other down—I didn't care. If she left me alone, I had no beef with her.

I could feel Ned glaring at me from the dock as I squared away my captain's log and checked my GPS numbers for the day. I was off the next day, my first day off in the past three weeks.

I would rather have been out fishing.

Chapter 3

By the time I finished up and stepped onto the dock, the woman in white was nowhere to be seen. Ned had disappeared as well, but I found him stretched out in the back of the beat-up old pickup I was using, snoring like a chainsaw trying to cut steel. I threw my gear bag in the truck's bed next to him, and it landed with a resounding *thunk* that didn't even disrupt the steady cacophony erupting from some primordial place deep within him. I drove to the Dolphin Spit Saloon in the strip mall just up the road from my temporary apartment to grab something to eat before calling it a night. Before I closed the car door, Ned was sitting up, getting his bearings.

"Oh, good, we're here," he said. "I'm parched, and I do believe you owe me."

"I suppose I do," I said, climbing the stoop to the dive.

"By the way, that energy thief has been watching you for two weeks now," Ned said, climbing out of the back of the truck with greater ease than I expected. "You got any idea why?"

"Two weeks?" I asked. "I've only seen her three times, including today."

"You ain't been payin' much attention to nothing lately, boy," Ned said, catching up to me. He fixed me with a hard glare as he walked past and opened the door without waiting for me. "I'm surprised Lilith's spawn haven't taken more runs at you as well. In your state, they might actually get you one of these days."

Whatever. He was already sitting at the bar when I finally walked in and sat next to him.

"So, like I asked, you got any idea why she's watchin' you?" he asked as the bartender set a beer in front of him.

"Probably has to do with that whole Ramiel mess," I said. "I went after both Eisheth and Na'amah in the process. Probably just one of Eisheth's lackeys."

"Nah," Ned said, finishing off his drink in one long pull. "If it had to do with revenge, she wouldn't be waiting. And there'd likely be more of 'em. I ain't seen none but her, dude. And if you ain't noticed, she's pretty weak too." He belched and wrung the dribbled beer from his beard with his hand.

"As long as she continues to leave me alone, she can do whatever she wants," I said, suddenly more concerned about what I was going to do with a full day off.

On the TV behind the bar, the newscaster was talking about yet another senseless shooting by a disgruntled person. *Of course we humans don't have to believe in mythical creatures—we make enough monsters of our own.*

"You know you're like a son to me, boy," Ned said, waving off the bartender. He turned on his seat to face me. "But if you don't get yer head outta yer butt soon, I'm afraid I'm gonna break your nose when I finally kick your ass. What happened to Sarah sucks, but it wasn't your fault. She'd tell you that to your face, and you know it."

"Maybe, but she can't, can she?" I replied. "And if you're going to harass me about it, you can just swim your ass back to San Diego or anywhere else you want, old man."

The bartender shot me a disdainful glower.

"You're right, dude," Ned said, climbing off his stool. "I believe I'm done here. Put it on his tab." He hooked a thumb at me as he walked out the door.

I didn't drink mostly because I didn't like the taste of alcohol, which was probably a good thing at that point. I didn't even remember getting back to my apartment, and I was stone-cold sober.

Given the blood feud I'd inadvertently started with Lilith and her Strigoi, I usually made it a point to be inside before sunset each night, and I tried never to be anyplace deserted after dark. I just chalked my behavior up to something instinctual, born of thousands of years of learning to survive in a world full of things trying to kill me. I really didn't care if they attacked me. In fact, most days, I would gladly welcome the fight. For reasons that were beyond me, the leeches usually left me alone in the early morning darkness as I walked from the parking lot at the marina down to the boat every day. The reason might have had something to do with the water or simply the fact that there was no place to hide for a surprise attack. Or it could have been that four thirty was just too freakin' early, even for monsters. Whatever it was that kept them from attacking me at the docks didn't hold true when I was alone outside my apartment in the dark.

Thanks to my argument with Ned, I was feeling particularly restless, watching the minutes tick by on my alarm clock instead of sleeping. After two hours, I'd had enough. I pulled on a pair of shorts and shoes, grabbed my pair of Dvergar-made tanto knives, and walked outside into the small parking lot adjacent to my building. It was pouring rain, but despite the deluge, it probably looked like I was going for a run. I even stretched a bit as I meandered toward the middle of the lot, aiming for a spot that would give me enough room to maneuver. I knew the leeches would be around. They were never far even if they didn't attack. And ever since my foray into their stronghold at Coronini a few years back, I'd killed dozens of them over this very specific and very stupid feud.

The time had come to add a few more to the tally.

With a knife in each hand, I raised my arms to the sides and waved, inviting any of the vampires that felt brave enough. "Whenever you're ready," I said into the downpour and rolled my head around to loosen my neck.

Through the rain, I watched the first pair scrabble out of the big banyan tree at the far corner of the parking lot like some kind of freakish squirrels. The tree was the most likely place for them to hide. In fact, I'd have bet at least half a dozen more were still hiding up in the branches, waiting to see what happened with the first of their kind to respond. Two more crawled slowly over the edge of the roof and down onto the walls of the building above my apartment like spiders. I felt but didn't see the greasy energy of other vampires close by. I flexed my fingers around the grips of my knives and waited in the warm tropical rain.

The first attack came from the pair from the tree. One bounded at me, arms and legs stretched out like four reaching claws as it leapt over an old, beat-up Chevy. The other crawled at me from under the car next to it like some sort of lizard, its fingernails and toenails audibly scratching across the pavement like steel against stone, even over the sound of the falling rain. I charged forward to meet the leaping vampire first, ramming one of my knives into its neck, impaling it and driving it backward and down so hard that the Dvergar-made blade went not only through the emaciated creature, but into the hood of the battered old Chevy, with the thump of rending steel. I brought my second knife down across the creature's bloated belly. The creature shrieked and thrashed wildly as its companion hit me from my right side, kicking at me with both of its back legs like a hopping frog. Slashing the one vampire across its belly burst its blood sac, covering everything, including me and the car, in a slick, foul-smelling, dark-colored liquid I knew to be partially digested human blood. Fortunately, the gore and the rain combined to make me slippery, causing the kicking vampire's attack to glance off my arm and ribs. Unfortunately, the creature's jagged, clawlike fingernails easily ripped at my skin, and I could instantly feel the burn of the lacerations.

I stabbed the impaled creature in its upper thigh and used both knives to lift it off the car and sling it at the monster that kicked me, just as it twisted its deformed body around for another attack. Both vampires writhed and turned as they collided, and I ran straight at them. I slashed downward across the torso of the uninjured one, immediately turning the stroke back into an upward jab into its chest with such force that I inadvertently threw it across the lot, where it landed on another car. A high-pitched whooping electronic alarm promptly split the air. The wounded creature in front of me turned and tried to scramble across the rain-and blood-covered parking lot back up into the big tree, but I managed to catch up and stomp hard on one of its legs, breaking the bone beneath my foot.

The other pair of vampires I'd seen along the roof emerged from among the parked cars behind me. I flipped the knife in my right hand around so that I was holding the blade, and I threw it backhanded down at the wounded creature under my feet, impaling it through the head and pinning it to the pavement. It thrashed wildly, and I stepped off its temporarily ruined limb. I reached under my arm to feel the ripped flesh under my right arm and winced at the touch of the injury. I could feel the scowl grow across my face as I faced the two newcomers.

The pair split up to flank me, so I picked the vampire on my left and charged. Surprised, the creature momentarily reared back and jumped, but its hesitation gave me the advantage. I dodged to my right as the creature swiped at my head with its clawed hand, barely missing. I snagged the airborne creature by its leg just above its knee and spun around to throw it at its partner. The collision carried the skeletal pair into the grille of a car just behind them with a heavy thud and the shattering of glass.

Something hit me hard from behind, sending me staggering into another car, knocking the breath from my lungs. Before I could turn, I felt a viselike grip on my left arm followed by a searing pain tearing across my back. I sucked in air, roared, and threw my left arm out wildly, trying to shake off the creature that held it, and I spun around. Through the rain running into my eyes, I saw a blur along the ground just as it hit my upper thigh. The surprise impact and the clinging weight on my left arm threw me off balance enough that I briefly lost my footing and fell to one knee.

Then something bashed me in the back of the head, causing me to see stars, and I felt a funny sensation in my head, like a clogged sinus suddenly releasing. In my dazed state, I thought I saw a dull flash of pale-blue light wash over the parking lot, but it could have just been the blow to my head—or a flash of lightning striking frighteningly close by. I threw my free hand up to cover my face just in case as the blaring car alarm cut off abruptly, but no peal of thunder ever followed. In the second it took for the feeling to pass, all the weight I felt holding onto my arm fell away, and everything went quiet except for the pattering of the rain on the concrete.

Blinking hard a few times while regaining control of my breathing, I saw three vampires lying motionless at my feet. Across the parking lot, several other figures lay motionless, including the thrashing monstrosity I impaled in the head. Then, one by one, three more fell from the big banyan tree like overripe fruit, each unmoving and lifeless as it flopped to the wet ground.

The hairs on the back of my neck stood up, and a chill went down my spine. It was similar to the feeling I got when Athena showed up, but with far less wattage.

An Old One is nearby.

Something about the sensation was familiar but not immediately recognizable. I scanned the parking lot in the scant light from the sodium security lamps along the building's facade, but I saw nothing through the rain. Likewise, nothing was in the parking lot across the street or along the street itself. Keeping a lookout, I made my way over to the impaled vampire and pried the knife from its skull then wiped it on my shorts.

"Whoever you are," I said quietly, almost to myself, "I'm not sure if I should be thanking you or preparing for you."

"You're welcome, Diomedes." The voice was female, sounding as if it was made by the falling rain itself.

I froze while I tried to peer into every dark corner again, searching for the telltale aura of one of the Protogenoi without success. After several minutes, I was convinced that whoever it was had left. I took the time to throw the carcasses of the seven dead Strigoi into the back of my truck and covered them with an old tarp. I would bury them in the pile of fish guts and bone "racks" at the processing building at the dock. Eventually, they'd be hauled off and ground up for fertilizer or used to bait traps, but not before they deteriorated into an unrecognizable mound of rotted flesh and shattered bones.

I went back up to my apartment and spent the rest of the night tending to the gouges over my ribs and along my right bicep. By the time I was done, the rain had let up, and the time came to head down to the boat—not because I had to but because it was something to keep me occupied.

Chapter 4

The next day, I didn't see or even feel Ned down at the docks either when we left or when we returned, but the woman in white was back—however, this time, her outfit was teal. Every time I noticed her, she would quickly turn away and disappear beyond my view. I decided if she was still there when I got to my truck, I was going to confront her just to provoke a reaction. She could attack me or leave me alone—either way. I just didn't care anymore.

She was gone.

I was finishing up my burger at the Dolphin Spit, trying hard not to think of anything, when a tingle ran up my right arm and down my spine as if someone with very cold fingers was lightly touching me. Before I could look up, someone sat down next to me. I saw the aura before I moved my head. To make matters worse, I felt like every eye in the room was staring at us—or me.

"Why are you watching me?" I asked without turning my head.

"I wanted to thank you." The honeyed voice was familiar.

I immediately turned to face her. It was the Moroi from the club where Sarah went undercover back in New York. She was the one beaten and left for dead on the street outside the building that Sarah's DHS team and I were staked out in. *She was the one watching me.*

Anger immediately welled up inside me, and I could feel myself start to growl, but then it dawned on me that her own people tried to kill her for helping me. She'd had nothing to do with Sarah's identity being uncovered. I took a deep breath, and I could feel my shoulders sink as I turned toward her. I recalled that we had discovered she was Hawaiian, and she was gorgeous. Her dark hair was longer than I remembered, and her preternaturally dark, predatory eyes seemed weary. And Ned was right: her aura was dim and weak. It barely even extended toward me, and I was less than a foot away.

"Thank me for what?" I asked, poking at the remnants of my food, no longer hungry.

"Getting me out of that place and away from those people back in New York," she said. She sounded genuinely grateful. "They think I'm dead, so I was able to start over. Sort of."

"Aren't you all connected or something?" I asked, not really interested but unsure what else to say. "Like, to Eisheth? I once heard that she could feel all her... offspring."

"We can feel everyone we've ever fed off of for some time, but yes, we can feel her, and she can feel us," she said, her voice becoming softer. "That's one reason I'm not feeding as much. I'm hoping I'm too weak for her to sense."

"One reason?" I asked, glancing sideways at her. "What are the others?" I almost made a nasty comment about her parasitic nature but didn't when I saw the fatigue etched on her face.

"You," she replied without looking up. "I know you think I'm a monster."

"Not you, exactly, but what you are," I said. "No offense."

"I can't help what I am," she said. "I didn't ask for this to happen to me. If the stories about you are true, then at least you had a choice to become what *you* are."

In my three-thousand-plus years, I'd never stopped to think about that. I had always just seen vampires as willing parasites. But she was right. She hadn't been born—she'd been made. Involuntarily. I sighed heavily, and the cuts along my back and ribs stung with the effort. I was tired of fighting. Some primal part of my brain raised a red flag, warning me that it could be a setup, some sort of ploy for revenge by Eisheth for what I did to Ramiel. But I didn't care anymore.

"I don't even know your name," I said.

"I've gone by lots of names over the years, but my real name was… is… Kailani Māhoe," she said. "I actually grew up not far from here. But that seems like a thousand years ago."

I laughed at her comment.

Then she laughed. "I guess you would understand that feeling," she said. "Well, I just wanted to say thanks. I know you have to get up early, so I'll go."

She stood up slowly and pursed her lips. Every eye in the room watched her as she headed toward the door, and for good reason. She really was gorgeous. I could see her aura creep out tentatively from her arms toward two men at the nearest table, who were watching as though hypnotized as she passed. For a second, she stumbled, and she grimaced slightly as she turned away, and the aura retracted. Instinctively, I moved to catch her even though she was ten feet away. I covered the distance before the two guys at the table next to her could stand to offer their help. My sudden presence startled one of them into knocking his chair over, then every eye was on me. Ignoring the stares of disbelief and confusion, I grabbed Kailani by one arm, my other arm around her waist, and her wispy aura immediately enfolded my hands. I felt warm as blood began to flow to them, and Kailani pulled herself free from my grasp and ran for the door with her head down. I followed her out into the parking lot.

"Wait," I said, "do you have someplace safe to stay?"

What the hell am I doing?

Chapter 5

Coming through the jetties at the entrance to the marina several days later, I was in a slightly better mood than I had been in weeks. As I turned the boat around the first dock, Ned was standing, hands on hips, glaring at me for the first time since we argued back at the Dolphin Spit a few days back. It didn't even dawn on me that he wasn't ensconced in his usual beach chair near the tiki-hut storage locker at the mouth of the marina. He was obviously still pissed at me, and I was still not ready to give in and apologize, so I ignored him. I should've known better than to ignore a pissed-off sea deity while on a boat, whether or not he was in self-imposed exile.

Suddenly, the bow of the old forty-two-foot sportfishing boat began to fall off to port as though being pushed. I cut the wheel to starboard slightly to try to compensate and maintain a steady course in the narrow channel between boats and docks. Then I realized I wasn't making any headway at all. Looking around to see if I was snagged on something, I saw Ned scowling at me from farther up the dock. I scowled back and goosed the big twin diesel engines in defiance. Still, I could make no headway into whatever current Ned was causing within the marina.

"Holy shit, skipper," Momi said from the cockpit down below. "You see the size of this tiger shark that's following us in? I've never seen one that big in here before."

I reluctantly glanced back to see what Momi was talking about. He was right. The sixteen-foot shark was massive, just hanging in the current two feet off my stern. I turned back toward Ned. His eyes narrowed in his weathered face, and he turned and headed toward my slip space. Suddenly, the boat shot forward, and I had to scramble to pull her out of gear and keep her from careering into one of the other boats.

Fucking squid's dick. Ned and I are definitely going to have words.

I pulled the boat into its slip on mental autopilot and farewelled our anglers, waiting for Ned to step up and open his mouth. I was itching for a fight. I knew that even the largest of our Forschner breaking knives, used to filet our biggest tuna, wouldn't even scratch the wrinkly hide of an Old One, but I was betting it would make me feel better.

I grabbed the big curved knife and hopped onto the dock in a move that would have been impossible for a normal person, and I stood there, waiting for Ned to get close enough. The incessant flopping of his flip-flops on the wooden dock only irritated me even more. He was shaking his head slowly, his mouth fixed in a heavy frown beneath his bushy beard. Still a few yards away, he stopped and jerked his head at me as though indicating something behind me. Confused, I craned my neck to check over my shoulder. Down at the end of the parking lot on the hillside above stood a winged woman wearing some sort of loose white dress. She held a short rod in one hand, and a sword hung from her waist. Her wings were a dirty brown. Her aura was unmistakable. She was one of the Old Ones, but like my friend Ned, she was weak. She had first appeared to me the day I left the hospital in Pennsylvania after my fight with Ramiel several months back.

Nemesis. Onetime goddess of retribution, she was a being whose sole interest was setting the balance right. *It was her voice I heard in the rain during the fight with the vampires.*

"What the hell is she doin' here, boy?" Ned asked in a disapproving fatherly tone.

"Hell if I know," I replied, throwing the knife into the wooden dock near my feet as I watched her. "She showed up at my hospital in Pennsylvania after that whole Watchers mess. She told me she could help me with Sarah if I helped her. I told her to take a hike." I rubbed at my face.

"That one is bad news, dude," Ned said in a hoarse whisper. "Trust me on this. She's got a one-track mind, and it don't go through the nicest places."

"Holy shit, skipper," Momi said from the cockpit of the boat behind us. "That chick is smokin' hot."

At that, Nemesis walked along the edge of the parking lot toward us. She descended the ragged cement staircase down to the docks like some sort of Hollywood movie star from the 1930s, and Momi let out a low whistle.

"Don't that kid see them wings?" Ned asked.

"Seriously?" I asked him in return.

"Well, shit, I wonder what the hell I look like to him," he said with a shrug.

"Like whatever the hell you want," I said. "I thought you knew that."

"Might have," he said. "I drink a lot, dude." He put a hand on my chest as though to hold me back despite the fact I wasn't moving. "Let me deal with her. She's older than me, and I was around long before Zeus was an itch in old Cronus's pants." He strolled off down the dock toward her, his flip-flops snapping as he walked. "Hey, cuz," he said, holding his arms out wide. "What brings you to Hawaii?"

"That fine ass wahine is that haole's cousin?" Momi asked, pointing from Nemesis to Ned while we watched the scene unfold.

"Maybe," I replied, "but I'm telling you now, it is not a story you want to hear. His family is dysfunctional in a way they write books and stories about."

If only he knew the truth.

Part of me wondered what sort of image she presented to Momi and any other mundanes that could see her. I knew that Protogenoi often played off human ideals and projected perfection, so I could imagine her appearance, but thanks to the many gifts Athena granted me in exchange for protecting the human race, I always saw right through the illusions, which wasn't always pleasant. In Nemesis' case, her thick dark hair and eyes really were attractive, though her expression was severe, and the wings were a bit much for my taste.

I bent down and grabbed the knife from the dock then hopped back into the cockpit of the boat. "Best we just let them talk," I said. "We got a boat to clean anyway."

"What the hell is up with you and him?" Momi asked as he began scrubbing the deck. "I thought you two were friends. Hell, at first, I thought he was your dad."

"We are friends," I replied, climbing back up to the flying bridge to finish my paperwork.

"Looked to me like you were ready to tear him a new one, if you know what I mean," he said.

"Ah, we had a disagreement the other night about how to properly fillet a fish," I said. "I was just going to show him."

"Yeah, that ain't what it looked like to me, but it sounds good the way you tell it, skipper," he said with a laugh.

Ned and Nemesis talked just out of earshot for less than ten minutes, then she ascended the stairs in the same flamboyant manner she'd come down then disappeared across the parking lot. The conversation was not loud, and neither made any gestures that suggested irritation or annoyance. Also, no flares showed in either would-be deity's aura. Then something struck me: Momi had no idea he had just witnessed two ancient beings once revered as gods conversing, and to me, it was just a Thursday, and fish slime was still on the gunnel of my boat. The fact that I'd had a vampire staying with me for the past few days didn't even register as odd anymore.

I wasn't sure if I was jaded or just didn't care. Gods, vampires, fallen angels, witches, ogres, and the Fae had been a part of my life for so long that I had no concept of what a mundane life even resembled. I envied Momi as he rubbed the small bone hook that hung around his neck, thanking Ku-ula for a good day on the water. His belief in the gods and goddesses of his people had largely been reduced to a tradition rather than actual worship. He had no idea that Ku-ula owned the small skiff at the end of the dock and was the guy who always offered us fish when he had a good day—or that he and Ned were actually very good friends.

Ned turned back around and shook his head slowly as he stared down at the dock, walking back toward me.

"What was that all about?" I asked, only slightly curious, given that Nemesis had apparently been watching me for months.

"Ah, I just invited her to take a long walk on a short pier," he replied. "I need a drink. You guys got anything on board, or do I gotta walk my ass all the way down the dock to my hut? Oh, and don't talk to her if you know what's good for ya, boy." He waved his hand in a quick motion like he was wiping off a table.

I just shrugged and went back to my paperwork.

"No, we don't have anything," Momi replied. "Sorry, Ned. So, she didn't want to fish with us, then? That's a crying shame. She was smokin'."

"Trust me, kid, that woman is a thousand miles of bad road, and you ain't got the shocks for it," Ned said as he headed down to his shack at the end of the dock.

I finally made it home a few hours later, and I felt Nemesis' presence before I saw her. She was standing in the parking lot across from my apartment. Given her wings, she almost resembled one of those angelic statues in cemeteries or at old churches.

Except she doesn't deliver forgiveness, only retribution.

Ned's comment to avoid her was unnecessary. I figured if she was here to exact some sort of revenge on me, she could have done it months before, when I was leaving the hospital in Pennsylvania. Rather, I figured it had to be another attempt to get me to do her dirty work. She was going to have a long wait.

Inside my small apartment, Kailani was sitting on the bed cross-legged, laying out tarot cards in front of her. She was wearing a ratty T-shirt and an old pair of shorts with her hair pulled over one shoulder. A smile spread across my face when I saw her. She was gorgeous, and her presence was a welcome distraction rather than the irritation that part of me expected after she all but moved in with me a few days before. She was so focused on the cards that she didn't even acknowledge my presence. I could see her eyebrows arch higher on her head as she flipped over a card—the Lovers, but it was inverted. While I never spent much time using tarot cards or other tools for divination, I knew that for those that did—and were in tune with their power—their meaning could be profound and even life alter-ing.

"Well, that can't be good," I said, dropping my captain's bag near the door with a *thump*. "Doesn't that indicate problems in a roman-tic relationship?"

"It can, yes, but it depends more on what you're seeking," she replied, flipping over another card: Judgement, also inverted. She cocked her head slightly as she eyed it. "Well, that's enough of that for now. Unless you want me to pull a card for you?"

"Sure," I said, flopping down onto the bed next to her.

She quickly shuffled the deck and then held it up for me. "Pick one," she said.

The Fool. Inverted.

"Well, what the hell is that supposed to mean?" I asked, slightly offended. "Isn't it supposed to mean I'm about to do something stu-pid?"

"It can, but what does it mean to you? Right now," Kailani replied, grabbing the card from me. She put the deck away before getting up.

"Yep. Definitely about to do something crazy," I said, grabbing her hand and pulling her back onto the bed next to me.

Chapter 6

Somewhere in the icy darkness surrounding me, a woman was screaming for help. It was a faint cry that almost sounded like a mewling kitten, but the second time I heard it, my skin went cold, and the hair stood on the back of my neck. *Sarah*. I began running. I had no idea where I was or which direction I was headed, but I felt something pulling at me. Sarah screamed again, that time from somewhere in the inky void in front of me, and I ran faster.

"Sarah!" I screamed, suddenly becoming confounded by the dimness.

My head swam. I slowed my gait, trying to regain some sense of direction. She screamed for help again, this time much closer and still right in front of me. I shook my head painfully and began sprinting again.

Somewhere at the back of my mind, a thought began to form. *What does Sarah need my help for?* I suddenly found myself almost stopped, lumbering around with leaden feet, barely able to move. Then I heard an indistinct buzzing like a swarm of angry bees, and Sarah screamed for help again, that time from my left. She appeared in the only speck of light visible anywhere I could see. She was standing on the top of a hill with hundreds of misshapen and deformed arms and appendages reaching up for her as she reached toward me. "Please, Diomedes, help!" she cried as the myriad of hands and tentacular appendages wrapped around her legs.

I felt myself scream until my throat hurt and my lungs ached, and I ran again. But the arms and appendages dragged Sarah back into the blackness. The faster I ran, the faster she was dragged away, all the while screaming for me to help.

I woke up with a shout in a cold sweat and found myself sitting straight up in bed. I was panting and needed a few moments to settle down and regain my wits. As my eyes adjusted to the muted light filtering in through the blinds, I saw I was still in the small apartment in Kona. Then I noticed the shape of a woman standing in the shadow next to the window. I could see her head turn in profile, and after a few more forced blinks, I saw the barest hint of an aura around her: Kailani.

"You want to talk about it?" she asked from the darkness.

"It was just a bad dream," I said, still trying to catch my breath.

"Another one?" she asked. "You were throwing off so much energy that I had to get up this time. I almost couldn't resist, like an alcoholic at an open bar. Bad." She didn't move from beside the window.

"What do you mean, 'this time'?" I asked. "I don't recall having any other nightmares."

"Every night I've been here," she said with a curt laugh. "But this one was really bad. You sure you don't want to talk about it? I know it's about that woman, Sarah. The one you couldn't save back in New York. You keep shouting her name." Her tone was flat and indifferent.

I could feel my temper flaring as my skin went from cold and clammy to hot. I didn't know if I was mad that I was having these dreams or that Kailani knew it. Maybe even both. I ripped the sheet off, grabbed my pants, and began dressing. "I don't want to talk about it."

Her head turned back toward the window as I grabbed my captain's bag and walked out the door.

The time was just after three in the morning, still a little early even for me, as I headed mindlessly down to the boat. I didn't know what else to do or where to go. I pulled onto the Kealakehe Parkway into the Honokohau Marina driving far too fast for the narrow road, desperately trying to push the haunting remnants of the dream out of my mind, along with Kailani's statement that it apparently wasn't the first.

It wasn't my fault.

As I came up to the only intersection on the all-but-deserted road at the top of the harbor, a figure suddenly appeared in the middle of the street in the old truck's headlights. I jerked the wheel hard to the right and skidded the truck through some shrubs and nearly sideways through the gravel parking lot before I managed to get the vehicle back under control just before heading over the riprap embankment down to the water. I slammed the gear shifter along the steering column into park and shoved the truck's door open so hard that I heard metal rend, and I charged across the dirt lot back to the intersection to scream at whatever moron was standing in the middle of the road at that time of night. My anger grew with each step as I followed the haphazard path my truck had taken, back to the road.

Approaching the intersection, I saw no one and nothing anywhere along the road. The scant moonlight didn't help, but nothing was visible. I stood, hands on hips, turning, trying to catch my breath and make sense of what had happened.

I swear someone—something—was there.

"What the fuck!" My head lolled back, and I closed my eyes as I exhaled heavily through my nose, one step shy of canceling my charter for the day. "If one more fucking thing goes—" Then I felt Nemesis' presence. "I told you to fuck off back at the hospital," I said, dropping my head without opening my eyes. "Hell, even Nereus told you to blow. You really can't take a hint, can you?"

"She's reaching out to you, isn't she?" Nemesis said from so close in front of me that it startled me into opening my eyes. I got a sudden flash of an image of Sarah being dragged away into darkness and quickly shook my head to clear it. When I opened my eyes, Nemesis was less than a foot away.

"You're one of those close talkers, aren't you?" I asked, glaring down at her. "'Cause that would just make my whole damn day, and it ain't even four a.m. yet. Back. The. Fuck. Up. Now."

Before I could blink, she was behind me, and I slowly turned around. "Pissing me off isn't the best way to get me to help you. You know that, right?" I began walking back to my truck, intent on leaving her behind.

"But *I* can help *you*, Diomedes," she said, suddenly right beside me, matching my pace stride for stride. "I can give you the power to free Sarah Wright's mind. What I ask in return is trivial for someone such as yourself. A mere trifle. Surely, ending Sarah's perpetual anguish is worth a few days in your long life?"

The vision of Sarah flashed in my head again. That stopped me, and I could feel my eyes narrow to slits as I faced Nemesis.

"You are pressing all the right buttons this morning, aren't you?" I said with a growl.

"Boy, don't you say another word to her," Ned said in a voice that carried from somewhere behind me as if transported by a howling wind. "And Nemesis, I thought I told you to leave him alone. We don't need the kind of trouble you're selling. I may be old and a shell of my former self in this world, but this close to this here ocean, I'm willing to bet I can muster enough strength to kick your spiteful ass if you make me." Ned suddenly appeared from behind the bed of my truck.

"I just assumed that Diomedes would want to save Sarah Wright now that he has some idea of her torment," Nemesis said with a shrug, her wings ruffling slightly to reseat themselves on her back as she did so.

Again, my vision of Sarah flashed through my head, and her scream for help echoed in my skull.

"Go sell your hate somewhere else," Ned said, his flip-flops snapping on his feet as he walked up next to me.

"Wait," I said, holding my hand up and giving Ned a sideways glance. "Are you saying that my dream tonight was some sort of a vision?" I narrowed my eyes at the onetime goddess of vengeance.

"I am not Morpheus," she replied, "but I can tell you that Sarah's mind is not peaceful. And I am being truthful when I tell you I can help you help her."

"Don't listen—" Ned said.

I held a finger up to stop him. "You can help me save Sarah from the state she's in? Fix her mind so that she can live a normal life again?" I took a few steps toward Nemesis.

She nodded. "All I ask is for your help with a task amenable to your finely honed skills."

"Boy, don't go down this road," Ned said, his voice low.

"Can she help me or not, Ned?" I asked, looking back over my shoulder at him. "Is she being honest with me or just jerking me off to get me to do her dirty work?"

"I don't know," he replied, "But I can promise you, even if she can, it won't be worth the price she'll ask of you."

"Okay, so what *exactly* do you need me to do that you can't?" I asked, directing my attention fully back to Nemesis. Her mouth slowly split into a wide grin reminiscent of the cartoon version of the Cheshire Cat.

"I would like you to bring *justice* to one of your kind who has abused his purpose and taken advantage of your fellow man," she said, turning away from me. "He should have died many centuries ago but instead has developed and twisted powers he should never have had and has profited greatly in the process."

"And by *bring justice*, I assume you mean *kill*," I said.

Nemesis only shrugged, once again ruffling the feathers on her wings.

"And for this, you swear that you will help me free Sarah from whatever is holding her mind captive."

"I so swear," she said.

"Fine. Tell me who you want me to kill, and it's done," I replied. "But if you fuck me on this or if Sarah comes out with even the slightest new personality quirk, I will find that damn chain that held Prometheus—that *Alysideus* whosits thing—and bind your ass for eternity to a rock just above low tide at the outflow of the sewage tunnel on the Tijuana River. And I, myself, will contribute to it daily, you understand me?" I turned back to Ned and pointed at him. "And I don't want to hear a fucking word from you. If this helps Sarah, then I'm going to do it."

I climbed back into my truck and had to pull the door so hard to close it that I pulled the interior door handle off. I tossed it out the window and started the truck. "I'll be back at the dock by four. You can tell me everything I need to know then, and I'll leave tomorrow."

Chapter 7

Over the course of fishing that day, I nearly ran over a floating log that had dozens of mahi mahi under it, missed seeing two marlin bites, and almost threw my angler out of the fighting chair and Momi overboard when I turned too sharply on a third marlin, which we lost when I ran over the line. All I could think about was the individual Nemesis was after. *I have to know who it is. Alive for hundreds of years, abusing ill-gotten power and wealth.*

No way could a human like that exist without me—or Athena—being aware.

Every human I knew who had a preternaturally long life had amassed inordinate amounts of money—except me and maybe one or two others—and that, at least, gave them access to power. I knew the Bhargava Rishi named Markendeya had lived for centuries, but he'd lived in isolation in a temple in northern India for at least the last two hundred years. Tithonus, a Greek from my time, was still alive but unlikely to be much of a problem since his immortality was a curse that allowed him to live forever yet still age. The last time I saw him, about five hundred years before, he made an Egyptian mummy look healthy and lively. I knew of others like the Wandering Jew, the Three Nephites, and supposedly even Galahad, the Arthurian knight who actually found the Grail, but none of them had caused any trouble that I was aware of—ever.

Still, I had dealt with others like Koschei the Deathless, who used magic to prolong his life and torment others along the way. My Fae friend Duma and I killed him years before, though. But numerous other alchemists and magic users had figured out ways to extend their lives, not to mention the odd cambion, like Merlin, who was still alive but imprisoned in a lost cave somewhere.

The real issue was with what Nemesis had determined to be her target's offense. She was a notorious stickler for balance—or at least anything other than an imbalance that favored any individual. She didn't care if your lot in life left you unrewarded, infirm, or destitute—just as long as you didn't get more than your share, as determined by her.

And that was the rub.

But if she really could help me break Sarah out of her mental prison and the price was to redress the balance that someone had tipped in their own favor, then so be it. I could be as black-and-white as Nemesis if I needed to be.

And Sarah needs me to be.

"Skipper, watch the piling!" Momi screamed, suddenly snapping me back to the moment. Luckily, the piling stood by itself as the tie-up point for the port-side bow and spring lines, so when I brushed against it, it just yielded without snapping off. Momi, on the other hand, nearly broke his arm trying to fend us off the wooden pole before I got the boat back under control.

The instant our anglers walked off the dock, Momi steamed up the ladder to the flying bridge with murder in his eyes. His steps were so heavy as he climbed that the forty-two-foot boat actually rocked. I had fished with the kid for weeks, and that was the first time I hadn't seen him with a smile plastered across his face.

"What the hell, skipper?" the big Hawaiian asked, hands on hips and his forehead creased so heavily that his hairline was drawn down to his eyebrows. His right arm was scraped up and bleeding from his brush with the piling. "Not only did you almost hit a twenty-foot log out there and fuck up what could have been a great mahi bite, but then you run over a line and lose us a big fish. Worse, you also cut off Kevin on the *Northern Lights* and Jeff on the *Humdinger*. They gonna be pissed at you for sure. Then you play bumper boats trying to dock," he said, holding out his bloody arm.

I had no recollection of cutting through the spreads of either boat, something that apparently registered via some sort of reaction that Momi noticed.

"Exactly what I'm talking about," Momi said, pointing at me. "Where the hell were you out there today? 'Cause it sure wasn't up here driving this boat."

I had no explanation that would make any sense to Momi, so I didn't say anything. Plus, anything I said would have just been an excuse anyway. After a few long, silent minutes, he just shook his head, clicked his tongue, and climbed back down the ladder.

"You best be thinking about how to apologize to Jeff and Kevin," Momi said as he descended to the cockpit. "And just take off. I'll clean up the boat. You gotta go get your head on straight." He mumbled nonstop as he headed into the salon. The boat continued to rock slightly as he stomped around, clearly agitated.

As I listened to him mumble, the skin on the back of my neck got hotter. Somewhere deep inside, anger welled up.

Who the fuck does Momi think he is, yelling at me like that? The ungrateful shit has no idea what I've saved him and all of his ancestors from over the past three thousand years. And right now, Sarah needs my help, so fuck him. And screw those other captains too. I do not need this shit.

I grabbed my gear bag and all but slid down the rails of the ladder down to the cockpit. "Tell the boss I got stuff to take care of. And you'll need to find someone to run the boat," I said without stopping to address Momi directly. I didn't even care if he heard me. I hopped easily from the cockpit up to the dock, covering the four-foot vertical distance as if it were a six-inch stoop. Then I took the steps up to the parking lot three at a time, searching for Nemesis the moment I had a good view of the open space above.

She was standing in front of my truck.

"Who?" I asked, feeling every muscle in my face tense into a scowl.

"He has gone by many names over the years, but you would know him best as the Count of St. Germain," she replied flatly.

"The alchemist," I said, instantly recognizing the name. "Fine. Any idea where he is right now?" I wasn't totally surprised at her intended target. It was rumored that the Count of St. Germain had been alive for thousands of years. Some thought he was the Wandering Jew, others that he was some sort of monster who fed off humans to keep himself alive. There were even those that believed he was an ascended master, keeper of all arcane knowledge of the universe. I had never actually met him, but I did investigate him back in the late 1800s in New Orleans. He was accused of murdering several women before disappearing. The locals thought he was a vampire. Nothing I discovered suggested he was any kind of vampire I knew of, but I never did find him. I knew he *was* a very talented alchemist who had amassed a fortune using his alchemical skills, and he was also a consummate scam artist over the centuries, but I never found any proof that he'd ever hurt anyone along the way.

"Naica, Mexico," she said.

"Once he's dead, you show me how to help Sarah," I replied. "That's the deal, right?"

"I give you my word."

I started the truck and spun the tires, spitting rocks and dirt everywhere as I tore off through the parking lot and onto the road. In the rearview mirror I saw Ned, a six-pack dangling from one hand, staring at the ground.

Sorry, St. Germain, it's not personal.

Chapter 8

I made it back to my apartment to gather the few belongings I didn't want to leave behind. Fortunately, Kailani wasn't there. But then neither were any of her things except a handful of tarot cards left on the bed in a pyramid spread: the Empress, the Fool, Strength, the Hanged Man, and the Wheel of Fortune, all inverted with the Empress at the top. Above them sat the Devil.

I didn't have time to contemplate what the cards meant to me. I didn't care. Besides, I didn't need them to know what I was doing was stupid and wrong and that I was asking for a world of trouble, trusting Nemesis. All I cared about was getting a chance to help Sarah, and I'd gone into battle with a lot less. I owed it to Sarah. I'd promised her I would protect her, but I hadn't. The least I could do was save her, and for that, I would make a deal with the devil himself. But he hadn't shown up. Nemesis had.

I don't recall much of the drive out to Umauma Falls on the north side of Mauna Kea crater. It was the only portal through the Ways I knew of on the Big Island, and I could get back to San Diego in minutes. My trip from the casino parking lot out in East County back to my house in Point Loma, on the other hand, took me considerably longer. Luckily, it was well into the evening, and a constant flow of cabs and other rideshare cars came and went in front of both the casino and hotel, so I just grabbed the first cab that I came to.

On the long ride home, I saw I'd missed a dozen phone calls and had at least half a dozen voice messages and a dozen texts on my phone. All of them were from the guy who'd hired me to run the boat in Hawaii. I rolled the window down and dropped the device out.

In less than ten minutes, I'd gathered my gear to go after St. Germain and was in my truck, headed east toward El Paso, Texas. I thought about trying to use the Telluric Pathways, but I wasn't adept or confident enough that I could get myself very close using the natural energy trails that crisscrossed the surface of the Earth without needing a car. All I knew about Naica was that it was south of Chihuahua and was the location of a series of mines that led into caverns holding the largest crystals known to exist in the world. It made sense that an alchemist would choose such a place.

The drive to El Paso took me just over ten hours, though it felt like a week as I drove into the blinding light of the rising sun. The West Texas border town was very different from the border town I'd lived in for the past few decades. San Diego started at the border but spread out from there. El Paso, on the other hand, embraced the border and grew around it. The metropolitan area began back in Las Cruces, New Mexico and spread all the way across the border into Juarez, forming what felt like one giant city. In all my long life, I'd never spent any real time there, and as nice as it might have been, I had no intention of spending any more time there than I needed.

I chose to cross the border at Bridge of the Americas Port of Entry. After half an hour of waiting, I began to feel the familiar buzzing in my head that heralded the presence of my benefactor, Athena.

"I don't want to hear it." By the time I said it, she was sitting in the seat next to me, dressed in a simple white linen suit with her fiery red hair pulled back into a loose bundle.

"I will not allow you to do this, Diomedes," she said, and the chill in her voice practically dropped the hundred-degree temperature in the cab of my truck by twenty degrees.

"Allow me?" I asked. "Funny, I don't recall asking for your permission."

"There is no honor in committing cold-blooded murder," she said.

"I've done worse for less noble reasons," I replied.

"No, you have not," she said, her voice softening to barely more than a whisper though it still echoed through my skull.

"I have to help Sarah. I promised her I would keep her safe."

"This is not the way, Diomedes," she said. "And I will not follow you down this path if you insist on taking it."

"I'm used to working alone."

"So be it," she said and was suddenly gone.

At the same instant, I felt utterly exhausted and weary in a way I'd never felt before. I could tell I hadn't slept in two days, and to make matters worse, every fiber in my being ached, pounded, or pulsed. My limbs felt like they weighed a thousand pounds, and resisting the urge to nod off took considerable effort as I sat in the hot car, waiting in the line to clear customs.

Five hours later, I drove into the city of Chihuahua and pulled off the highway at a coffee shop along Avenida Juarez for a rest. I was drifting in and out, fighting to stay awake while waiting for my food, when Duma dropped into the seat across the table from me. He made no noise as he did so beyond an exaggerated squeak of the vinyl on his leather pants. He was wearing a black T-shirt and black leather pants with his sunglasses pushed back into the shoulder-length pale-blond hair on his head. He placed a black-and-red motorcycle helmet, leather gloves, and a matching leather jacket on the seat next to himself. His dark clothing made the Peri appear even paler than normal.

"Damn," he said, staring wide-eyed at the ancient-looking booth, running his hand over the table. "What is this, Naugahyde? And is this tabletop actually Formica? Did we go back in time somehow?" He rubbed his hands together as though dusting them off then picked up a napkin and rubbed them some more before dropping the wadded paper onto the table in disgust.

"What are you doing here?" I asked, startled into a state of extreme awareness. I noticed I was blinking hard and frequently.

"Nice to see you too," he replied, glancing around the little roadhouse coffee shop with his face all scrunched up. He stopped and stared at two truckers sitting at the counter for just a moment, then his eyes traveled back to me. "You look like shit, by the way. Have you slept in the last month? And something else is different about you, too, but I can't quite put my finger on it. You stink a little too. Like corn chips or old socks."

"Thanks," I replied. "So, what are you doing here?"

"Just enjoying the open road, D. Trying not to let my only friend do something really stupid," he said. "Well, at least not without me anyway. So, what *are* we doing here?"

"*We* aren't doing anything," I said. "*I* got something I need to take care of." I took a bite of the hamburger I realized had been sitting in front of me and practically spat out the cold, clammy meat. "And how *did* you find me anyway?"

"Fascinating story, actually," he said, waving a hand like the showman he was. "There I was on my yacht, anchored off Ibiza with two Russian supermodels, when all of a sudden, this Santa Claus–looking beach bum crawls out of the ocean and up onto my swimstep and walks right into my salon, dripping wet."

"Ned," I replied, dropping my head, which in turn pulled the muscles in my neck. "Ow."

"D, you gotta get some sleep," Duma said with a snort. "If I didn't see that big freakin' eyesore of a truck you drive in the parking lot, I would have sworn by looking at you that you walked here."

"I'll sleep when I'm finished..." I could hear myself saying it, but it felt like it was coming from someone else. "Gotta help Sarah."

"La cuenta, por favor" was the last thing I heard before I passed out.

Chapter 9

"Diomedes, please..." Sarah's pained voice came from somewhere out in the blackness around me. It seemed to be coming at me from all directions. She just kept calling my name, and the more I chased her voice, the softer it became.

Then came an earsplitting, bloodcurdling scream. I woke up in a pitch-black room in a panic, sitting straight up in bed. My head was pounding, I was in a cold sweat, and I was breathing rapidly. I had no idea where I was. The only thing I could see was some sort of red light glowing in front of me. Part of me began to think back to the dark, dank cell the Unseelie Court held me in a few years back, but I managed to shake the vision and control my breathing. I was warm and sitting on something soft. I blinked hard a few times and realized the red light was some sort of clock.

Realizing I must have been on a bed, I tried to get to my feet, but I got so tangled up that I ended up falling, bouncing off some sort of hard edge, and landing on the floor, hard. I heard a door open, and a light came on.

"I can't leave you unattended at all, can I?" Duma said.

With the lights on, I could see I was in a reasonably nice hotel room, lying on the floor between two beds. The blackout curtains were drawn across one wall. I could hear one of the beds creak and squeak as Duma sat down on it. After a moment, I took a second to gather my wits and got to my knees then my feet.

"You okay there, pumpkin?" Duma asked with a lilt in his voice.

"Fuck you," I replied and sat down on the other bed. I was still dressed in the same clothes I'd been in since I left Hawaii.

"You think just because we're in a hotel room together, that's the way things work?" he said.

"How long has it been?" I asked.

"Since I checked you in here?" he asked. "Relax—it's only been a day. You any closer to telling me what you're up to?"

My head still hurt, and I wasn't in the mood to talk, but I knew Duma well enough to know he would just badger me until I told him what he wanted to know.

"Helping Sarah," I said.

"Yeah, you said that back in *la cuchara grasienta*," he said, standing up and crossing his arms over his chest. "How exactly do you plan on doing that?"

"I made a deal with someone who said they could," I replied, rubbing my temples with both hands.

"Ah, and in return, what do you have to do for them?" he asked.

"Kill someone."

"Oh, shit, is that all?" he replied. "I thought it was going to be something difficult. Your friend Nereus made it sound all dire and extreme." He waved his hands around for effect. "'Something you might not come back from,' I believe he said, to be exact." He threw air quotes up as he said it.

If anyone else said that to me using his tone and gestures, I would have assumed they were being sarcastic. Duma was being serious.

"Tell you what," he said, "you tell me who and where, and I'll run out and pop them and be back before you know it. I owe you for letting them get Sarah. And I owe her, too, so let me do this. It'll be easy-peasy."

"'Preciate it, Duma. I really do," I said. "But I gotta do this one myself just to make sure the Old One I made the deal with doesn't renege."

"Yeah, that ain't you, D," he replied, cocking his head to one side. "How long we known each other? Few hundred years or so? And not once have I ever seen you kill someone for payment. Honestly, I don't think I've ever even seen you kill someone that didn't really deserve it. And I mean by your standards, not mine. This thing must really have you messed up."

I just shrugged. "I've killed thousands of creatures—even people—to protect the human race. This is the same thing. I kill this person, and I save Sarah. It's that simple," I said while staring at the wild pattern in the carpet.

"Can I ask who has the red dot painted on their forehead?" he asked without a hint of judgment.

"Count of St. Germain, or whatever he's calling himself these days," I said.

"The alchemist?" he said. "Damn, mind if I get something from him before you do? He made my scrying pendulum—you know, the black diamond one—and if he's going to be dead soon, I probably ought to pick up a backup just to be safe. He's a genius with crystals."

Again, I would assume anyone else was joking—not Duma.

He exhaled heavily. "Well, at least that explains why you're down here in Mexico," he said, not really talking to me so much as talking to himself out loud. "Tell you what, I'll go with you anyway. You know, just in case."

I still felt worn out, but I was rested and not as weary. "Where are my keys?" I asked, standing up.

Duma pointed at the dresser next to the TV. By the time I crossed the room, grabbed my keys, and headed to the door, Duma was on my heels, pulling on his jacket. I felt like I was moving in slow motion. Duma had always been faster than I was, but not by much. This whole thing had me off my game.

Duma had loaded his bike into the back of my truck and strapped it down. For the briefest of moments, I contemplated leaving him in the parking lot rather than dragging him any further into my mess. While I knew that, as a Fae, he didn't have the same type of emotions that humans had, I knew from our long friendship that he'd developed something akin to them. I could tell he held himself almost as responsible as I did for the mess with Sarah. And Duma was better at wet work than I was.

The drive down Highway 45D to the San Pedro road took two hours, then we followed the turnoff to Naica at the little farming town of Rancho Campesina. The minute we hit it, I could feel every eye we passed watching us as we pulled off the highway. Maybe the reason was that my big truck was newer than most in that dusty little town or that we had an extremely bizarre motorcycle strapped in the bed or that Duma kept waving at everyone that made eye contact. Or I could have just been paranoid.

"Pull over and let me get my bike down once we get outside of town," Duma said, waving at an older man who turned to watch as we approached and then as we drove past.

You'd think my truck was painted hot pink.

"These townies all work for St. Germain and that mining company he owns in Naica. They don't like outsiders."

"You've been here before?" I asked, pulling over onto the shoulder of the narrow two-lane road.

"Sure. Bunch o' times," Duma replied, pulling his helmet and gloves out from the back seat of my truck. "Guy's pretty paranoid, but for good reason. It's a straight shot about twelve miles straight down this road. Take your time. I'll meet you at the arch."

"The what?"

"There's some crazy welcome arch just on the outskirts of town. You can't miss it," Duma said, making an arcing motion with both hands. "Now, help me get my bike down."

"How'd you get it up there by yourself?" I asked, knowing Duma did not share his brother Ab's strength.

"Truckers," he replied, hopping into the bed in a single fluid motion without so much as a metallic *dink*.

I opened the gate and climbed up, a simple action that took me more effort than I would have expected. Duma was unstrapping the funky bike, which looked more like a skeletal framework than a normal motorcycle. Knowing Duma, it probably cost more than some houses. I grabbed the bike, expecting to roll it easily back to the gate then lift it down. Once Duma released the last tie-down and the weight of the bike hit me, it nearly knocked me over, and Duma had to reach out to help.

"What the fuck, D?" Duma said, his brow creased and pinched over his nose. "This bike cost three times as much as your truck. Take it easy with it, wouldya?"

I had no idea what had happened. *I should be able to lift the bike easily, let alone prop it up.*

"Something wrong, D?" Duma said, giving me a side-eye as he pulled his gloves on.

"No, I'm okay," I replied after a pause.

"Okay, step back. I'll get the bike down without hurting it," he said. "Can't say the same for your truck, though." He smiled broadly then pulled his helmet on.

I hopped down with a thud that jarred every joint in my body, and pain shot through my knees and ankles. I nearly fell as I tried to straighten up. Duma started up the bike with a throaty roar, gunned the engine several times, then popped the clutch, and the bike suddenly lurched up onto its rear wheel. In a practiced move made even smoother by his preternatural reflexes, he spun the bike around in the truck bed on its back wheel, dropped the front wheel a bit, and gunned the engine. The bike flew out of the back of the truck, and Duma landed it expertly ten feet away, threw the bike into a slide, and turned it back around. He pulled up next to me and popped up the visor of his helmet. "See you at the arch in a few minutes," he said, reaching under the back of his jacket to pull out a Glock .22. He checked to make sure a round was chambered then returned the gun to its hiding place on his waist. Then he winked, slammed the visor down, and gunned the engine of the freaky-looking bike, spraying rocks and dirt everywhere. He was down the road and out of sight and earshot in two blinks of an eye.

I closed the truck's gate and hobbled around to the driver's side door. As I climbed into the cab with more effort than it should have taken, a thought occurred to me: *Athena said she wasn't going to help me. Did that mean she had taken back my speed, strength, and other abilities?*

Suddenly, I found myself becoming very angry. I realized I was gripping the steering wheel so tightly that my knuckles turned white, but rather than bending the steel core and cracking the plastic coating, my fingers simply ached. I tried to shake the wheel, but rather than tearing it loose, I simply rocked the truck back and forth in a fit of impotent rage. I punched the center of the wheel repeatedly, causing the horn to sound continuously and reducing my knuckles to a bloody, swollen pulp. I slammed the center of the steering wheel one more time with my left hand, and the horn, thankfully, went silent. I closed my eyes, feeling the pulsing ache grow in my swollen right hand. That was the last thing I needed right then.

Fuck it. I've been a soldier for three thousand years. I don't need Athena to help me kill someone.

Chapter 10

I started the truck and took off down the road, flexing my right hand to keep it from stiffening as I drove. Twice, the horn sounded, though in a brief high-pitched squeak rather than the throaty honk it should have been.

A few miles down the road, the arch welcoming me to Naica rose up over the road through the waves of heat that radiated up from the ground. I pulled over just before I passed under it, rolled down my window, and turned the truck off to wait for Duma. As I sat, I examined my battered hand, feeling it pop and snap with each flex.

So, this is what it feels like to age?

The lightest of breezes washed through the cab of my truck, and the dry heat of the Chihuahuan desert felt good, so I closed my eyes and allowed my mind to wander toward things normal people did—mow their grass, clean their house, shop for groceries, gripe about their bills, and take kids to school and baseball games. It sounded boring but pleasantly so, I suppose. I had no idea if I could stand it, but the first thing I was going to have to do was get a real job. Being a fishing guide was fun, and the daily view out of my office window was incredible, but the pay sucked.

If only I had planned and saved for a retirement over the past three thousand years.

The high-pitched scream of Duma's motorcycle caused me to open my eyes as he neared then goosed the throttle on his bike and spun it around on the hot pavement, sending smoke and the acrid odor of burning rubber everywhere. He pulled the bike right up alongside my truck, turned it off, and flipped up the visor on his helmet. Despite the temperature being well over a hundred degrees out in the midsummer morning sun, he didn't even seem to be sweating in all his leather gear.

"I don't think he's here," Duma said, crossing his arms over the handlebars of his bike. "You wanna camp out or go home?"

"Neither," I replied, glaring down the road toward Naica. "Someone here has to know where he is. We find out, then that's where I'm headed."

"You okay there, D?" Duma asked. "Something about you just ain't right. I mean, I'm all up for some wholesale bloodletting, but you usually lecture me about that kind of stuff, tell me about how it's not civilized, not something that should be done for fun, blah, blah, blah, blah, blah." Duma waggled his fingers and thumb like a quacking duck. "Plus, I dunno, but you just seem... off."

"I'm off the reservation on this one, Duma," I replied, turning my head away so that I wouldn't have to see his eyes when I said it. "Way off."

"No shit. And water is wet, and fire is hot," he said. "Well, most fire is hot anyway. I figured that out back in Chihuahua. Still, something about you... ain't you."

"Athena didn't want me to do this and refused to help," I replied.

"So? She never helps," he said with a shrug.

"At all."

"Yeah, and..." He stopped, and his brow knit up behind the opening in his helmet. "You mean she took it all away?"

I nodded.

"Your speed? Your strength... your... immortality?" he said, his eyes widening with each attribute.

"I'm thinking so, yeah."

"Oh, this is real bad, man," he said, shaking his helmeted head. "If anyone finds out, it'll be open season on you, D."

"It's always open season on me," I said with a scoff. "Why should this make it any different?"

"'Cause now, you can't go toe-to-toe with most of the things that'd come after you," he replied, throwing his hands up. "I'm going to have to call Ab for backup, or you won't make it back to Chihuahua alive, man. I'm telling you."

"What? Stop being so dramatic," I said.

"Oh, you think I'm exaggerating?" he asked. "Really? This town is run by the Count of St. Germain, probably the greatest alchemist the world has ever seen. The guy is a wiz with crystals, energy manipulation, and transmutation of elements, not to mention he's privy to information and knowledge that no one else seems to know. His clients include kings and queens across time, dictators, presidents, rulers, military leaders, and individuals of almost any race you can think of and a few dozen even you've never heard of, and they all come *here* to visit him. I'm telling you—normally, it's like the Wild West, and there are times even Ab and I won't go in because of who's in town. Still think I'm exaggerating? You're lucky St. Germain isn't here, because the town is empty as a result. I'm not saying—I'm just saying..." He leaned back on his motorcycle and crossed his arms over his chest.

After a few seconds of silence, he spoke up again. "Hell, without your speed and strength, there are probably a few human residents in town that could kick your mortal ass." He rocked his head side to side as he spoke as if weighing options. "Exaggerating, my eye. Hell, *I* might just kick your ass."

"Okay, so it's a dangerous place," I said in a low, even voice. "But if this really is his town, then somebody in there has to know where St. Germain is, and he is the key to helping Sarah. So if that's where I have to go, then I don't care how dangerous it is. I'm going. With or without you."

"Okay, relax, D," Duma replied. "Sheesh. Just making sure you can make an informed decision." He shrugged then started his bike.

Chapter 11

He took off down the lonely road at a snail's pace, which must have been killing him. I followed in my truck. We made it into Naica, and I kept right on Duma's rear wheel until he pulled over next to the town square. All eyes were on us. No furtive glances or surreptitious stares—everyone stopped what they were doing as we passed and openly watched our every move. I got out of my truck and walked around to lean against the bed, and Duma joined me, setting his helmet on the edge of the bed. A few blocks to the northeast I could see the edge of town and the desert beyond. In the other direction, I could see the foothills and the complex that had to house the mining operation.

"I'm going to guess that's where he normally is?" I said, nodding toward the fenced compound of metal industrial buildings at the base of the hills.

"Yup," Duma replied and pursed his lips and raised his eyebrows briefly before putting on a pair of sunglasses.

I was sweating, and everything was annoying me. Finally, tired of being stared at, I walked to the rear passenger side door of my truck and got out my gear bag. The first thing I pulled out were my swords—the substantial Kopis-style blades given to me by Athena and made by Hephaestus. I'd used them to hack through armored vehicles and trolls with equal ease, and normally they felt as light as feathers in my hands. Now, they felt clunky.

I pulled one of the blades free from its scabbard, exposing just a few inches of its metal, not sure exactly what I would see. Some part of me knew they wouldn't resemble the pristine, almost glowing blades I was used to seeing. Without my connection to Athena, the things would be no more useful to me than any other swords. I didn't expect, however, to see the metal so tarnished and almost blackened. For an instant, I felt like I was looking at my own soul. I threw the swords back into my bag then tucked one of my tanto knives into my waistband under my shirt. Then I pulled out my Sig Sauer P226 Navy, checked to make sure the magazine was full, chambered a round, and slid it back into its holster then repeated the process with my Glock 19 before strapping it to my thigh. Like my swords, I knew my cuirass wouldn't afford me the protection it had for the last three thousand years, but it would be better than nothing, so I pulled on my tactical vest and filled the pockets with spare magazines, slid the Sig into its holster, and put my other tanto knife into its sheath on my shoulder.

Duma watched me with the practiced disinterest of someone intimately familiar with gearing up for combat. I could tell that, even with his pure-white eyes, he alternated between watching me and the townsfolk that were watching us.

The last thing I did was pull out my FN-SCAR-H assault rifle and check its magazine, then I ran my arm through its sling to let it hang across my chest at the ready. For the first time, I felt the weight of everything I wore, and it was oppressive. The cuirass dug into my shoulders at my neck, and the drop holster that held my Glock on my thigh felt tight and restrictive. Overall, I felt heavy and clumsy—almost uncomfortable.

"You ready?" Duma asked, scrutinizing the people around the plaza rather than paying attention to me. I knew what he was doing, and I probably should have been a bit more focused than I was.

I rolled my shoulders to try to make my cuirass more comfortable. "Yeah. Any threats?" I asked.

"Not yet, but it's a long three blocks before we get to the gate out-side the facility," he said, his head still on a swivel. He walked down the street toward the mine, and I fell in step behind him. Some of the townsfolk from the plaza began to follow us at a distance, and we picked up a few more stalkers as we walked. By the time we made it to the fence surrounding the mining complex, a dozen men and women were standing across the street behind us, requiring us to keep our backs to the gate. Most of them had guns either on their belts or un-der their arms, but nobody appeared to give off any sort of magical or supernatural energy. Then I remembered I could no longer see that even if they did. For all I knew, they could've been anything from Old Ones to Parans to simple humans—like me.

"*La mina está cerrada,*" said a man with a bushy handlebar mus-tache and a ratty old cowboy hat from across the street. "It is closed." He pointed at the gate for emphasis.

"Do you know where the owner is?" I asked, addressing the man who'd spoken, as well as the crowd. The fact that no one seemed fazed by my armament registered as a concern in the back of my mind. If things got dicey, I needed to make the first move and make it decisive and overwhelming.

No one spoke or moved. The tension became palpable.

"*Dónde está el jefe?*" Duma asked, taking off his sunglasses and hooking a thumb over his shoulder at the mine behind us. "*Estamos aquí para hacer negocios,*" he said, pulling a thick wad of cash from inside his jacket.

"*La mina está cerrada,*" the man with the bushy mustache said again.

Duma cocked up one side of his mouth in disappointment, sigh-ing heavily, and if his eyes hadn't been solid white, I'm sure the roll would have been obvious.

He put the wad of cash back into his jacket and, in one fluid and incredibly rapid movement, had one of his big kukri knives out and down by his side. I had no idea where the knife came from, and its sudden appearance surprised me. I felt like I was moving in slow motion.

A screech of tires and the rumble of a large engine drew the attention of everyone on the street. A heavy black pickup truck of some kind, with oversized tires rigged for off-road conditions and a covered bed, roared into the street between Duma and me and the crowd and stopped with a lurch and a squeal of rubber on the hot pavement. The instant the truck stopped, the passenger side door flew open, and a bearded man dressed in tan fatigues, a tactical vest, sunglasses, and a ball cap climbed out. Instinctively, I raised my assault rifle to a combat-ready position with my finger on the guard above the trigger. Duma held his hand out, low and to the side, then wiggled his index finger back and forth. I tried to relax.

"Duma," the khaki man said. Then he turned toward the gathered crowd on the other side of the truck. "*Nada que ver aquí*," he said, shooing them away with the wave of a hand. "Vamoose."

Reluctantly, the crowd dispersed, and he turned back to face Duma, thumbs hooked nonthreateningly at the shoulders of his tactical vest. The only weapon I could see on him was a sidearm at his hip.

"Nils," Duma replied as Nils smiled back. "Looking for your boss."

"Well, I didn't think you came for the scenery," Nils said in a heavy accent that had to be South African. He eyed me sideways then focused on Duma. "He's not here."

"We need to find him," I said.

Duma slowly turned his head to look back at me over his shoulder. His white eyes were wide, and his mouth was a tight line.

"Do you, now?" Nils replied. "And who might you be?"

"I'm—"

"He's with me," Duma said.

"You look familiar," the mercenary said. "Have we worked together before?"

"Not likely. You a Recce?" I asked, referring to the South African Special Forces.

Nils nodded. "You SF?"

"Teams," I said, staring hard at the man, trying to determine how much of a threat he really was. Two days before, I wouldn't have given him a second thought, but now, I had to rethink everything because I had no idea what I was capable of without Athena's gifts. With my rifle at the combat-ready position and his hands idly on his vest, I knew I had the drop on him, even in my current state.

Then a behemoth of a man climbed out of the back of the truck, and the vehicle visibly rose on its suspension. Moving stiffly, the man was dressed similarly to Nils but clean-shaven, bald, and completely unarmed. He was easily seven feet tall and built like Duma's massive brother, Ab. He walked by rocking side to side with each step, as if his knees didn't work properly.

If it comes down to it, I can put a few rounds in Nils's chest then hit the giant in his knees and finish Nils off.

"*Tafsik*," Nils said, glancing over at the monster, who immediately came to a halt a few steps out from the truck.

At first, I thought that might be the giant's name.

"He keeps making those things bigger and bigger," Duma said, raising his eyebrows. "If only he could make them move half as well as they can take a hit."

Nils shrugged a shoulder in response. "He's big and dumb and only understands Hebrew, but he's a tank. I don't know where the boss finds them," Nils said.

Then, despite Nils's comment suggesting he was just a big human merc, I realized the giant must be a golem, one of St. Germain's specialties. That meant *tafsik* was the Hebrew word for "stop," and Nils had no idea what this thing was. Normally, I would be able to see the magic surrounding it and see through the glamour that made it appear human. The realization made me break out into a cold sweat, and I could feel my heart racing.

I am simply human.

I hyperventilated and had to fight to control my breathing using a trick I learned in the Teams.

Nils and Duma watched me.

"You okay?" Nils asked, dropping his left hand to the sidearm on his hip.

Duma rotated his head slightly sideways to watch Nils. I regained control of my breathing but had to deal with the resultant lightheadedness. I took a few deep breaths to steady myself again. I was getting angry.

"Where's St. Germain?" I asked, shifting the rifle in my hands.

"Who?" Nils asked, cocking his head back and grimacing at the name.

His reaction seemed genuine.

"Your boss, St. Germain," I said, becoming more agitated.

"Uh, friend, the owner of this mine is a company called Industrias Peñoles, and it's run by Raul Baillares," Nils said. "My boss is the mine foreman, and his name is Fayol. Henri Fayol and not Germain."

I had to stifle a laugh.

"What's so funny, frogman?" Nils said, hand still on his sidearm at his waist. He took a small step forward.

"Whoa, whoa, whoa," Duma said, stepping closer to Nils with both hands up though he still held the kukri in his right one. "Nobody is laughing at anybody, right? It's all cool here. Clearly, my friend here is a bit out of it..." He glanced fixedly at me for a second then turned back to Nils. "But we are looking for Fayol, yes. It's a matter of great importance."

"Always is with you, Duma," Nils said, stepping back. Maybe he took the step to put more distance between him and Duma or perhaps because the situation was diffusing. "But like I said earlier, he's not here."

"Well, where is he?" Duma asked.

"I'm not at liberty—" Nils started.

I screamed and opened fire on the golem, and Nils dove for cover in front of the truck, and Duma ducked down on one knee. The big 7.62mm rounds blew parts of the creature's outer casing away in chunks until the glamour disguising it wavered and disappeared. What stood before us was a massive, featureless clay hulk with chunks missing from its torso, showing a bright yellow metal underneath. And it never moved.

"Holy shit, D!" Duma shouted. "You done, or do you wanna shoot up the rest of the town?"

"I don't have time for this shit, Duma!" I roared. "This guy knows something, and he's going to tell me now, or I'll rip him and everyone in this town apart!" I ejected the spent magazine, inserted a new one, and opened fire again, advancing and spraying the side of the truck, working my way toward Nils.

"Diomedes, stop!" Duma shouted, suddenly next to me, one hand on my forearm. "I'll get him to talk, but not like this." Suddenly, Duma was just gone, and within the next heartbeat, I saw him in front of the truck, looking down at Nils's prone form in a ball on the ground. He had a gun in his hand that wasn't his. He pointed it at the driver of the truck, who was hunched over the wheel with his head ducked, and motioned for him to get out.

I stepped forward to the open passenger door and aimed the big assault rifle at the man, who held both hands out. "Out, or I will shoot you," I said. A big revolver was resting on the passenger seat next to him. He clumsily clawed at his door, opened it, and almost fell out.

"You got him, Duma?" I asked, watching the driver through the open doors.

"Yeah, but thanks to your tirade, we need to get out of here—and fast," Duma said. "That isn't St. Germain's only golem, and he has... other... employees too." He jerked his head toward the golem I shot up. I knew it was far from incapacitated, but without a specific command, it wouldn't act.

"Make sure Nils doesn't open his mouth," I said, walking around the front of the truck. I didn't want him shouting commands to the golem. I saw Nils wasn't moving. "Did you kill him? Dammit, Duma, I needed him to talk."

"No, he's not dead, just unconscious," Duma said. "But I'll guarantee Nils doesn't know a damn thing."

Taking advantage of our conversation, the driver bolted and ran down the street away from us, and I raised my rifle to shoot. Duma caught my arm and stopped me before I could get the rifle into position. I shot him a withering stare and tried to jerk my arm away, but I couldn't.

Damn. Duma is stronger than me as a mortal.

His eyebrows shot high on his forehead as we came to that revelation at the same time.

"You done, cowboy?" Duma asked, letting my arm go. "You *really* want to know just how fucked up this situation is? You realize not only am I stronger than you now, but I—me, the bloodthirsty bane of the Fae—just stopped you—a man of honor and decency—from shooting an unarmed man *in the back as he was running away*." He waggled Nils's gun around as he said it then threw it on the hood of the truck with a heavy *clunk*. "That's fucked up. I'll say it again, in case your ears are still ringing from all that random gunfire: Nils. Doesn't. Know. Shit." He said the last part loud and slow. "Do I need to repeat that?"

At first, I didn't respond. I couldn't. I had no idea what to say and no way to justify what I'd done, but anger continued rising in my chest.

"Why the fuck did you stop me?" I finally asked, growling and pushing past him to walk back up the street toward my truck. "Now how the fuck do I find St. Germain?"

Duma was beside me in an instant, wiping his hands as if to clean dirt off them. "No clue, but we should get out of here fast. You know, like, you should run. I'll try to walk slow enough not to leave you behind." He grinned a wide smile that showed a lot of perfect teeth.

For a second, I contemplated knocking a few of them out, then I realized he was too fast for that.

Or I'm too slow in my current state.

I began to jog then broke into a steady trot. By the time I reached my truck a few blocks later, I was surprised at how hard I was breathing and how fast my heart was beating.

All the times in my past I lamented being a simple mortal again... Being simply human sucks.

Duma started up his bike. He didn't bother with his helmet but did put on his sunglasses.

"You got gas?" Duma asked.

I nodded in response as I threw my rifle onto the rear bench in my truck's cab.

"Good. We go straight for the border—no stops. I'll push ahead and wait for you on the side of the road from time to time. Don't stop. You got me?" He peered over his sunglasses at me for emphasis.

"Yeah, don't stop," I said. My brain registered what he said, but all I could think about was how I was going to locate St. Germain—and save Sarah.

Chapter 12

Duma and I went through customs and across the border in El Paso separately, assuming Duma crossed legally at all, and we met up again at a truck stop on the west side of Las Cruces. By the time I arrived, I found Duma leaning against the side of a boxy flat-black Mercedes SUV, his skeletal brushed-aluminum bike parked next to it. I pulled into a spot on the passenger side of the Mercedes and got out.

"D!" a familiar booming voice shouted across the expansive parking lot, easily carrying over the sound of a dozen semis idling nearby and the adjacent interstate.

I turned to see Abraxos, Duma's massive brother and one of my closest friends and allies. The stupid, genuine grin on his face made me smile despite myself. He was carrying a giant fountain drink in one hand and a large bag of pork rinds in the other, though they appeared much smaller in his massive hands. At nearly seven feet tall, almost everything appeared smaller next to him.

"There is no way you are eating or drinking that shit in this car," Duma said to his brother as he neared.

Ab's face retracted slightly as if he'd been punched, and his brow knitted heavily. "I won't spill a drop," he said, raising the giant cup in protest. "Besides, I put the waterproof seat covers on and changed out the floor mats to the rubber ones."

"Fine, but pork rinds?" Duma said with a sneer.

"Traveling food, bro!" Ab replied.

"Did you get me any?" he asked then disappeared from next to the truck, suddenly reappearing behind his brother with the bag in hand.

I never realized how complacent I'd become. Duma always moved fast enough that he seemed to be a blur, but as a mortal, I understood why the legends suggested his race could fly. Athena's gift of speed clearly affected more than just my muscles, but also the nerves and even my brain and eyes, to let me keep up with the increased velocity.

"You speedy little shit," Ab said, shaking his head. "Come on, man, get your own."

Duma popped the bag open and began to munch. Ab just shook his head.

Once Ab was close enough, he held out his hand, and I grabbed it. He pulled me into a brief hug, and I felt like a rag doll being tossed around.

"Sorry, D," Ab said as I bounced into him. "Guess I caught you off guard."

"Nah," Duma said, strolling up next to us. "Dipshit went and pissed off Athena. He's *mortal*. That's why I called you. If anyone finds out, it'll be open season."

"What?" Ab said, his white eyes growing wide as he stood a little straighter, his head cocking slightly to one side. "You're kidding me, right?"

I shook my head.

"What'd you do to piss off her high and mighty highness?" Ab asked.

Duma snorted derisively.

"Long story," I replied, not really interested in going into an explanation.

"Basically, he decided to abandon his moral code to help Sarah," Duma said.

"Well, shit, let *us* do whatever it is, then," Ab said. "That way, you can go back to working for Lady Resting Bitch Face, and Sarah will be good again. Win-win." The big Peri shrugged his massive shoulders. "Otherwise, something's going to find out you're just human and come after you, D. I can think of at least two dozen creatures that have beefs with you right off the top of my head. I mean, Duma and I can help, but we can't protect you forever." He motioned to Duma and himself with his drink then shook his head.

"Thanks, Ab, but this is on me," I said.

"Do you understand the concept of the blood oath we took when you saved us from Rubezahl?" Duma asked. "Like it or not, we're with you on this one, at least till you can take care of yourself again. Hell, you know I'm stronger than him now, Ab?"

"You? Stronger than Diomedes?" Ab asked, his head and shoulders dropping. "Your runty ass? Seriously? Oh, this is really bad. D, maybe you should ride with me. That way, I can carry you when you get tired and open the doors for you." He laughed as Duma snorted. It was the same kind of brotherly ribbing Ab and Duma gave each other all the time.

I wasn't in the mood for it.

I swung to punch Ab in the stomach, but before my fist made it halfway, the giant Peri swatted my hand down and away, knocking me off balance. So instead of hitting him, I stumbled into Ab's chest face-first.

"Oh... shit! Wow, you are weak *and slow* as a mortal, aren't you?" Ab said. "I'm faster than Diomedes. I. Am. Faster. Than. Diomedes." Ab threw his arms up in victory and beamed as he turned to gloat to an audience that didn't exist in the mostly empty parking lot.

"Kiss my ass," I said.

"We should get back on the road," Duma said, handing the bag of pork rinds back to Ab. "I'll ride with D in his truck. You follow." He pointed at Ab. "Help me get the bike in the back of the truck.

I'd ask D for help, but…" Duma bent exaggeratedly to one side as he walked toward his motorcycle.

I didn't like being ribbed, and I liked the fact he was right even less. Normally, I would easily have been able to pick up a five- or six-hundred-pound motorcycle if I needed to. Ab hoisted the bike over the side of my truck with no more effort than if he was lifting a bag of groceries. Duma quickly strapped it down, and we were back on the road.

"So, any idea how we're going to find St. Germain, now?" I asked.

"Nope." Duma stretched out across the back seat of my truck. "But the closest, safest place to figure it out right now is your house. So home, James. My ass hurts from riding that bike for so long, and I'm going to nap."

He was probably right, and frankly, I didn't want to talk anyway.

Thirteen hours later, just as the sun was rising, we pulled up into my driveway in the Roseville area of Point Loma, and I hit the button to open the garage door. For some reason, it didn't feel like home, but given my thirty-two hundred years of life, every place felt temporary to me. For the time being, and maybe for the rest of my mortal life, that would be home. Right on cue, Duma woke, yawned, and stretched while I gathered my gear.

"Oh, we're here," he said, actually managing to sound surprised. "You should have woken me. I would have driven some."

"We stopped twice for gas," I replied. "You never budged."

"Wake up, dipstick," Ab said, carrying a duffel bag over one shoulder and knocking on Duma's window.

Something bothered me, but I couldn't put my finger on it. I'd long since learned to rely on my gut, but part of my brain was saying I was just being hyperparanoid since I was no longer immortal. Still, I'd rather be alive and paranoid than dead and dismissive. I pulled one of my Sig Sauer P-226s from my gear bag, made sure a round was chambered, and walked into the house through the door in my garage that led to the kitchen.

Chapter 13

Inside, I dropped my gear bag and raised the gun in front of me in a combat high position and flipped the light on.

"Oh good, you're finally home," said a man in a calm, almost friendly manner.

He stood up from my easy chair next to my fly-tying desk and checked his watch. He was well-built, dressed in jeans and a button-down shirt with the sleeves rolled up, revealing heavily tattooed forearms, and he had slicked-back salt-and-pepper hair and a short gray beard with a black mustache. He had an aquiline nose and bright, widely set eyes under thick dark brows that stood out because of his mostly gray hair and beard. He held a phone in one hand but was otherwise unarmed.

"Who are you, and what are you doing in my house?" I asked. "And it better be good, or I will shoot you. Twice."

"I have no doubt, Diomedes," the man said. "Ah, hello. Duma. Abraxos." He nodded slightly as the pair came in behind me.

"Well, I'll be," Duma said, walking up next to me. "We were just looking for you."

"I am aware," the man said. "I felt it might be more prudent if I found you first."

"St. Germain?" I asked, lowering the gun ever so slightly in surprise.

"At your service," the man replied with a forward cant of his head.

I roared and ran forward, but instead of shooting St. Germain, I tried to bring my gun down across his head once I got close enough. I missed and tried to backhand him. Again, he stepped back at just the right moment, and I swung past him. Two more times I swung, and both times I missed at the last second. He wasn't fast, but he seemed to *know* what I was going to do. After a few more fruitless swings, I was getting winded. St. Germain watched me with sad eyes and a slight frown, almost as though he felt sorry for me. Out of breath, I stopped and screamed, which tired me out even more. Breathing heavily, I raised the gun and aimed it at him from less than a yard away.

"Let's see you dodge this," I said between breaths.

"Wait," he said, holding up one hand. "I know you've been sent to kill me, but do you really know why?"

"I don't care why as long as it helps me save Sarah," I said, getting my breathing back under control. My gun arm felt like it was trying to support a hundred pounds.

"I promise you whatever Adrestia told you was a lie," he said, his expression serious but not fearful.

"No!" I shouted, reasserting the gun, trying to reposition my arm without lowering the weapon.

"Hear me out, Diomedes," he said, raising both hands to calm me. "If after that you don't believe me, I will let you carry out your business. I will not resist."

"D, you should probably listen," Duma said behind me.

I was tired of being told what to do and who to listen to. With one last effort, I lurched forward to hit St. Germain across his temple with my gun. He did not flinch as my gun connected. At the blow, he slumped back against my fly-tying desk, and I swung at him with my free hand, knocking him off the desk and onto the floor. I staggered over, knelt down over his prone form, dropped my gun, and began to swing.

"D!" both Ab and Duma screamed behind me as I beat the man.

I managed to swing only a few more times before I became so exhausted that I could barely lift my arms. Staring down at St. Germain's bloody face, I reached for my Sig, placed the barrel against his forehead and took a few deep breaths to steady myself. My eyes never left St. Germain's, and never once did he try to stop me or even fight back. No hatred or fear showed in his piercing gray eyes—the same eyes Sarah had—he simply gazed back at me. I tried to squeeze the trigger, but I couldn't. I roared in his face, but he remained motionless though his eyes remained clear and bright in his pulpy, swollen face.

I screamed again, panting heavily, then I slowly stood up, still aiming the gun at him. I towered over St. Germain, and he remained still, watching me, the whites of his eyes stark against his swollen face, his silvery beard stained with blood. The only thing I saw was compassion—no distress, no animosity, just understanding.

I flashed back to the battlefield at Troy over three thousand years before. Covered in blood from battle, I'd roamed the field, searching for any Trojans brave enough to fight me. They feared me and avoided me like a plague. As I wandered, I dispatched any Trojans left dying or severely injured until I came across an old man—a Trojan far too old to have been fighting—sitting on his haunches, winded, with his sword lying at his side. I raised my sword to strike him, but he held up his hands and asked for mercy. Something in me made me stop mid-strike.

"I know who you are, Lord Diomedes," the old man said. "Indeed, all Trojans know and fear you, even one as old as me. I understand that there is glory in killing the strong and valiant, but killing an old man like me gains you nothing. Let me live. Let me live so that when you are old and gray, you can live with yourself. I beg you."

I remember hearing his words. I remember hearing them then dismissing them just as quickly. He was a foe—an enemy in war—unarmed and old or not. And I remember what I said to him that day: "Old man, I expect to grow old, but as long as I can lift my sword, I will not let a single foe escape alive. The brave man makes an end of every foe." Then I killed him.

Not a day went by when my words to old Ilioneus didn't haunt me. Despite that, I still stand by them and believe that, in war, one can never leave an enemy alive. *In war.* But this was not war. And *this* man was not my enemy. To my knowledge, he had never actually done anything proven to hurt anyone. Yet if I could bring myself to kill him, I could save Sarah.

I'd killed thousands over my lifetime. I could kill one more.

"But at what cost?" Sarah's voice echoed in my head, and hot tears streamed down my face.

Focusing through tears, I tried again to pull the trigger, remembering all the horrible, inhumane things St. Germain had been blamed for—from accusations of being the cursed Wandering Jew who insulted Jesus on the cross, to the brutal murders as the Sultan of Rue Dauphine in New Orleans—but his gray eyes, Sarah's eyes, haunted me. I just couldn't do it. I couldn't bring myself to kill an unarmed man for no reason, no matter what was at stake. Again, I screamed then threw the gun at the far wall and fell on my butt next to St. Germain, exhausted.

"If you truly think killing me will save Sarah, then I will gladly allow it," St. Germain said through ruined and swollen lips. "But I think you know better. And I really can help you save her."

"How?" I asked, not really interested in an answer. "Nemesis says she can. You say she can't. Now you say *you* can. I don't believe either of you."

"I promise you two things, Diomedes," St. Germain said. "First, I can help you save Sarah. I believe it's a matter of... simple transference." The alchemist gestured with both hands, moving them from one side of his body to the other in front of himself to illustrate his point. "And I have the tools and knowledge to accomplish it."

Duma's eyebrows rose high on his head while the corners of his mouth turned down. Ab yawned.

"Simple, huh?" I asked. "What's the second thing?"

"It will not be easy," he replied.

"You just said it was a simple process," I said, rolling my head.

"Oh, the process of transference will be," he said with a shrug. "Getting the energy we need to transfer is entirely different."

"Why, what is it? Some kind of highly radioactive material?" I asked.

Duma had to stifle a laugh. "You been alive, what, three thousand years, seen all kinds of crazy shit, and you still think in such mundane terms." He shook his head.

"Screw you, Duma," I said.

"Actually, he's right, Diomedes," St. Germain said. "And nuclear energy would be easy to get by comparison."

"Okay, then, what kind of energy do we need? Crystal power?" I asked.

Again came the sniggering, including St. Germain's that time. I just shook my head and stared at the ground with my hands on my hips. "You guys are starting to piss me off again."

"Save it, Diomedes," St. Germain said. "You're closer this time, though. Only you'll be using crystals to hold the energy. But you'll be collecting it from Eisheth."

"And there it is..." Duma said.

"You mean Eisheth, progenitor and Queen Mother of the entire Moroi vampire strain?" I asked, fighting the urge to fall down and throw up at the same time. "Lilith's sister. You know, the vampire bitch who's already pissed at me for killing *one* of her brood and trespassing a few *years* ago?"

"You sure do get yourself in some fucked-up spots, don't you, D?" Duma said. "All for some girl."

"I swear—" I began, pointing at Duma.

"And she's the reason I'll be right behind you, D," Duma said, holding up a hand to stop me. "I owe her."

"Well, fuck it," Ab said. "I'm in. I like Sarah, and I ain't been in a good fight in weeks. I like hitting Moroi. They're kinda resilient. Like rubber balls. They don't just fall over when you hit them." He rolled his massive shoulders and pumped his fists.

For a second, I felt it was possible. Then I remembered I didn't have Athena on my side anymore. I was simply mortal. I sat down heavily on my couch. "I have no idea what good I'll be now," I said without raising my head.

"Shit, D," Duma said, "did being mortal stop Sarah from raiding Medea's stronghold with us? Did it stop her from going undercover into *their* world? Do you think it would have stopped her from doing *this*? And you got three thousand years of experience that she didn't have. Maybe she's the one Athena should have talked to."

"Yeah, and we got St. Germain here to go with us," Ab said. "And you know everything, right?"

"Uh, well, I know enough to know that I'm not going with you guys to find Eisheth," he said. "I'm a thinker, not a fighter."

"Do you at least know where she is?" I asked.

"Aw, hell, D," Duma said, "Everyone knows she has places in Shanghai, Los Angeles, and a dozen other cities around the world. Problem is she could be anywhere."

St. Germain bobbed his head. "Yeah," he added, pointing absently at Duma.

"Oh, then where the hell do we look?" I asked, throwing my arms up in frustration.

"While it's true she could be almost anywhere, I'd suggest you start your search for her in Transnistria in Moldova," St. Germain replied.

"Moldova," I said. "Of course. Where else would a vampire keep her summer place?"

Chapter 14

"Okay, so say we eventually track Eisheth down. What exactly do I need to collect from her, and how and where do I put it?" I asked.

"Well, the how and where is pretty easy," St. Germain said. "I'll give you a talisman made of several crystals attuned to the energy you'll need. They'll absorb the energy automatically if you can get close enough."

"That sounds too easy," Duma said. "What's the catch?"

"A being like Eisheth isn't going to give up her energy willingly, now is she?" the alchemist replied. "And the fastest way for the crystals to absorb the energy will be in direct contact with her skin, at any of the chakra points."

"You have got to be kidding me," I said.

St. Germain shrugged and frowned. "You could do it without contact, but the amount of energy needed would take hours, if not days, to be absorbed. It'd be like trying to download a high-def movie over dial-up internet."

"Okay. At least I understood that comparison," I replied. "So, we gotta place the crystals on her skin. How long will they take to absorb the energy if we can do that?"

"No more than fifteen minutes, tops," St. Germain replied, waving his hand in a short chop, as if his answer was supposed to be good news.

Duma, Ab, and I all let out a collective groan. "What if we just kill her?" Ab said. "Can't we collect it from her as her life force dissipates?"

"No, no, no," St. Germain said, shaking his head violently. "That could overcharge the crystals and cause them to shatter. Too much, too fast. Plus, she's connected to every other Moroi on earth and all that could be released as well. There would be no way to control exactly what you pulled out. The crystals I give you will be specially tuned to absorb the life force from Eisheth that she took from Sarah. You don't want fragmented energy from others getting pulled out along with hers. That would be bad. Trust me when I tell you that multiple souls trapped in one body is the making of a monster."

"Got it," I replied. "So we just need her incapacitated for at least fifteen minutes."

"She's going to be pissed," Ab said.

"Fifteen minutes? Like that's going to be easy," Duma said with a sneer. "I'm sayin' if we get *this* monstrosity down for fifteen minutes, I'm going to shave her head or draw a mustache on her or something 'cause otherwise, no one is going to believe us. And if she's going to be pissed at us, we might as well give her a good reason. Besides roofying her and giving her an energyectomy, I mean."

"We should kill her after," Ab said matter-of-factly.

"Not a bad idea," Duma said with a nod.

I thought about that for a second. I despised the various vampiric races more than any others, mostly because they viewed humans as little more than a food source and a host program. In truth, the only reason I hadn't killed her or her sisters yet was because I'd never been close enough. And in my current mortal state, I was going to need every dirty trick in the book just to get close to her. Killing her might just be the only way I could make it out alive and save Sarah. Besides, if she was the one who did that to Sarah, then she would pay for it with more than her energy.

I looked at Ab. "If you want her head as a trophy when we're done, then take it," I said.

Ab and Duma turned to each other and stared for a long moment then simultaneously turned back to me, their eyes wide. Then Duma's brows shot up on his forehead.

"Oh, hell yeah," Ab said. "We gonna be famous." He started to do a little dance, flexing his gigantic arms as he moved.

"You guys already are," St. Germain said. "Well, *in*famous anyway."

"It all adds to the legend that is us," Duma said, a bloodthirsty, predatory grin forming at one corner of his mouth.

"Yeah, well, just make sure she's alive when you place the crystals on her," St. Germain replied. "I've no love for her or her sisters or any of her kindred either. They are part of the evil that grips this world we live in, and their kind's removal from it can only make things better for all of us."

"So, where are these crystals we'll need?" I asked.

"Still growing in my garden back in Naica," he said. "They're not quite large enough yet. Then I need to make a visit to Hart Island and see Sarah. I'll need a week tops."

"Good. That will give us some time to track her down," I said. "I assume you two have connections in Transnistria? Oh, what the hell am I asking? Of course you do."

Duma glanced at his brother, and they both just shrugged. "That place is like Disney World for smugglers, D," Duma said. "We… may have a few contacts there."

Ab snorted.

"I don't want to know," I replied, holding up a hand to stop him from continuing. "I want to talk to Athena, then we can get going."

Half an hour later, I was walking into the Metis Foundation offices in the funky old Victorian on the corner of 13th and Island in downtown San Diego. As usual, parking was a pain in the ass, which only added to my already heightened level of agitation.

Inside the door was yet another new receptionist behind the unassuming wooden desk. That one was a bookish young woman with black hair pulled tightly back into a ponytail, wearing bright-red glasses and a white shirt opened at the collar just enough to reveal some serious tattoo work on her neck and shoulders. Suddenly, she appeared less bookish.

"Can I help you?" she asked as I turned to go up the stairs on the right like I'd done a thousand times before.

"Oh, um, Steve Dore to see the big cheese," I said, stopping at the bottom of the stairs.

"One second, please," she said, lifting the receiver from its cradle on her desk. She spoke in a very hushed voice, but I heard her say my name, and she continued to eye me skeptically as she talked. The second she hung up, Athena's office manager, Breygivila, a striking female elf, opened the door at the top of the staircase.

"Come up, Mr. Dore," she said in a curt and clipped tone.

"How the hell are you, Brey?" I asked as I ascended the steps. "And what the hell is with the Mr. Dore shit? Oh wait, this is about my feud with Mommy, isn't it?"

I crossed into the office, and the door shut silently behind me. The room felt cold. It always felt a little off and normally buzzed with energy, but all I noticed was that it was cold—and plain. The walls, which I was convinced were made of some kind of living material that could change color and texture at will and were most often clear from the inside, allowing Athena and Brey to watch over the bullpen below, just looked like simple drywall construction painted a flat white.

"Wow, is this really what this place looks like to mundanes?" I asked. "How utterly boring."

"She isn't here," Brey said, "and I don't think you should be either."

She was being colder than normal. Because she was an elf, I was used to her being devoid of human emotion, and I normally reveled in ribbing her in what has been a long-standing yet fruitless attempt to get a rise out of her. But I could tell she was trying to keep me at a distance.

"I could tell she wasn't here—" I began before I realized I wouldn't be able to feel her presence anymore unless she wanted me to. Our connection was gone. I was simply a mortal again—after nearly thirty-three centuries. I stopped and I dropped my head and stared at the drab tan carpet. I realized I'd never paid enough attention to what it really looked like when I could see it, but now, I couldn't help noticing it was just plain ugly.

"Isn't the floor actually some kind of highly polished wood?" I asked Brey without looking up. "I don't think I ever really paid attention before."

"The floor, like the walls, are neither wood nor any other material normally used for construction. And I do not know how it chooses to present itself to you now, Diomedes."

I swear if I didn't know better, I would've said her voice developed the slightest hint of sadness as she spoke.

"But she is not here, and you should not be here either," Brey said. "Not under the circumstances."

"I wanted to let her know I didn't kill St. Germain and that I'm going after Eisheth," I said, hands on hips. "Then I'll figure out some way to deal with Nemesis or Adrestia or whatever her name is this century."

Brey nodded ever so slightly. "Adrestia goes by many names, but I will relay your message," she said then cleared her throat slightly and broke eye contact.

"I'll leave," I said and turned toward the door. "I'm sorry if I disappointed you, Brey," I said as I opened the door. I stood there for a few seconds, waiting to see if she would respond. When she didn't, I headed down.

"She continues to watch you, Diomedes," Brey said in a soft voice after I took several steps.

I paused for a moment.

"But please be careful. You are a good man. Remember that."

I nodded without looking back then left.

I honestly had no idea what I was going to tell Athena that she didn't already know. Maybe I needed to explain things to her because it was just force of habit. Even though our past connection gave her the ability to read my thoughts, she stayed out of my head for the sake of my sanity and a sense of autonomy. As a result, I was so used to debriefing her on every move I made that doing something like this without her input was foreign to me—ever since she guided me on the battlefield at Troy and helped me best Ares, and for countless foes since.

Maybe I was hoping Athena would forgive me and give me back my strength and speed because, frankly, being a mundane in the world and knowing what I know about it scared me—more than a little. I was used to being the one that kept the boogeyman at bay. And now, without her help, I was about to do something I hadn't had the guts to do when I *was* strong and fast enough to attempt it, all because I did something I'd sworn to myself I would never do again: care for someone. And that got her hurt. Worse than hurt, actually—far worse. And mundane or not, I could not live with that.

Chapter 15

By the time I got back to my house on Point Loma, Duma had already gone. Ab was waiting for me, though.

"Get your gear, and we'll take off," Ab said as he lounged across the couch in my living room. "We'll meet up with Duma outside Odessa then head to Tiraspol, where Eisheth has a place."

"It'll only take me a few minutes," I said, walking into my bedroom and into the special closet I used as my loadout room.

"D, you gotta prepare yourself for what we're likely to encounter there!" Ab shouted down the hallway.

"I get it, Ab," I replied. "I realize I don't have my strength or speed anymore, but I've still been a soldier for three millennia."

"Nah, man," he said. "Well, yeah, that will be an issue, but the bigger one is the type of operation that Eisheth is known to run out of this region. You won't like it, and you aren't in a position to do much about it now is all I'm saying."

I tuned Ab out for a few minutes while I tried to decide if I should bring my swords and cuirass. Without my connection to Athena, they were hardly more effective than they appeared. I still knew how to use them, but I'd come to expect to use them in certain ways and to rely on the fact that the cuirass was impenetrable. I decided that I would bring them just because they were familiar, and I didn't want to start doing things that I wasn't used to doing. My gear bag was heavy and awkward to carry down my narrow hallway. I dropped it with a heavy thud that resonated within me far more than normal. Ab turned his head toward me and blinked a few times.

"So, what was all that about me not liking what we're going to find?" I asked.

"Well, Eisheth runs some of her smuggling out of Tiraspol," he replied.

"Yeah, I know it's a smuggler's haven since the fall of the Soviet Union," I said. "Lots of illegal activities in the Transnistria region. Drugs, weapons, money—"

"Humans," Ab said.

That stopped me. I knew a few places in the world were known for human trafficking. I might even have known that Transnistria was one of the worst, but I always just assumed it was a human issue, one that I conveniently ignored for the sake of my own sanity. I should have known that nonhumans would be involved in human trafficking. It made sense. And the fact that Eisheth was in-volved—Queen Mother of the Moroi vampire strain—made even more sense. It gave me all the more reason to hate her. The hair on the back of my arms and neck stood on end, and the skin on my back became hot and prickly.

"This area is one of the worst places in the world for human traf-ficking, D," Ab said, sitting up on the couch. "Eisheth uses the local Ukrainian mob to do her dirty work, but it's all her operation. We're likely to run into dozens of women, kids, and even some men being kept for sale, and we won't be able to save them. You get that, right?"

I didn't respond. I couldn't.

"How did I not know this was happening?" I said finally, my voice cracking.

"It's a big world, D," Ab replied. "And Eisheth is ancient, even by your standards, and far more versed in hiding her interests than you or I will ever know. But we aren't equipped for a full-scale assault on her. We need to get in and get out as quickly as we can. Like that North Korean thing with the Hanner Brid. In and out."

Despite his enormous size and penchant for destroying things, I always marveled at how levelheaded Ab could be, especially when compared to his hotheaded brother. The problem was, right then, I felt more like Duma than Ab even though I knew the giant Peri was right.

"For Sarah, right?" he said.

I could feel my heart sink even further, and my arms suddenly felt like they weighed a thousand pounds each. "Yeah," I replied.

Ab got up and walked over, clapped me on the shoulder, then grabbed my gear bag and slung it effortlessly over his shoulder with the practiced ease that I was used to.

For Sarah.

Travel through the Telluric Pathways was never straightforward for me, but it was always manageable. That time, as a mundane human, I was overwhelmed. Colors flashed at me so fast and bright that I could barely keep my eyes open, and the sounds were a cacophony of blaring noises that blended in a deafening roar. The smells were so intense that I felt I couldn't breathe, and when I did, I wanted to throw up. My nose and mouth were awash with the scents of food, garbage, decay, pollution, flowers, earth, ocean, chemicals, and a thousand other unidentifiable smells intensified and combined. Even the sensations of hot and cold on my skin changed so rapidly that I began to lose all sense of temperature beyond being uncomfortable. Just as I began to hyperventilate, Ab pulled me through, out into a warm, humid night in the middle of a wheat field with a sizeable but old city in front of us. From my normal jump point through the Ways outside a casino east of San Diego, Ab and I had made it to Odessa on the northwest coast of the Black Sea in under thirty minutes.

It was the longest half hour of my life.

I fell to my knees and started shaking, sucking in the fresh, humid, earthy air like I'd just surfaced from deep water after holding my breath for five minutes. Then I threw up.

"Damn, D," Ab said, staring at me in abject horror. "Even Sarah didn't react that badly when she went through the Ways her first time. Stop, or you're gonna make me puke too." He gagged and held the back of one fist over his mouth.

"Yeah, yeah, I'm okay," I said, wiping my mouth as I got to my feet.

We crossed the fields, thick with winter wheat close to being ready for harvest, through some low scrub brush and out onto a narrow but well-worn dirt road. Lights from small villages shone from just about every direction around us, but Odessa, to the south, was the largest source of light noise in the sky. Within a few minutes, I heard the heavy rumble of a large, powerful engine and saw the glare of headlights with a row of smaller irritatingly brilliant LED spotlights above as the vehicle approached up the dirt road from the south.

The truck was massive but had no shine whatsoever to its body, except a little glare off its windows. It didn't sound like a truck—it sounded like a racecar, only deeper. The driver's side door opened, and an unmistakable slim, pale figure emerged.

"Get in," Duma said.

"What is this?" I asked, climbing into the back of something that was a cross between a tank and a Suburban. "Some kind of tank?"

"EM-50 Urban Assault Vehicle," Duma replied from the front seat.

"Funny," I replied.

"Nah, it's a Dartz Prombron Black Shark, custom built," Ab said after throwing my gear bag into the back and climbing into the vehicle from the passenger side opposite Duma. The car didn't even rock as the big fairy did so.

"Basically, it is a tank," Duma said, "not only armored, but she'll do over a hundred and fifty when I punch it. We may need it, too."

Normally, I would've taken that kind of comment in stride, but for some reason, it gave me the chills.

"We're headed to Tiraspol," Duma said. "It's less than seventy miles away, but we'll have to cross the border from Ukraine into Transnistria. Easier to do that from Ukraine than from Moldova. There's a small canvas bag on the seat next to you. When we stop, just hand it to me."

I looked at the bag. The interior of the car was lit up by red lighting along the door panels, which cast an eerie glow over the bag, and I could see stacks of US currency inside. I guessed about fifty thousand dollars. I knew a shadowy world existed alongside the one I protected mankind from, but this one, the underground one where people bought and sold guns and drugs and even other people and paid each other off with large bribes, I was largely ignorant of. I wasn't just a fish out of water. I was a fish floating around weightless in space.

Chapter 16

We crossed the border into the breakaway state of Transnistria through the Ukrainian town of Limanskoye along the E581 Highway. Duma presented the bag instead of credentials at the lonely outpost, and within minutes, we were waved through, no further questions asked and no paperwork filled out.

Even with everything I've spent my life protecting humanity from, I can't help but think that humanity's worst enemy is itself.

"We'll head down south of Tiraspol a bit, to the village of Caragas," Duma said, finally breaking the silence. "It's far enough out that we won't draw the attention of Eisheth's people when we arrive. We won't have long before somebody mentions a few foreigners showing up, though. This ain't exactly a tourist town, if you know what I mean."

When we reached the city of Tiraspol, we turned off the E581 onto the R27 and continued for another half hour through a quaint hamlet, where we pulled in behind a small ramshackle house and into an open garage bay next to a diminutive, squat Soviet-era sedan.

"What the hell is that?" I asked, trying to place the ugly car among Duma's other high-end vehicles.

"It's a Lada Riva," Duma replied. "It's a piece of shit, but it fits in here better than the Dartz."

"I can't even fit in the damn thing," Ab said. "Russian piece of junk. They should stick to making weapons and leave the cars to the Germans and Italians." He grabbed my gear bag out of the back of the big SUV, along with two other massive duffels, carrying them like grocery bags. Duma grabbed two black heavy-duty, durable plastic briefcases out of the back, and I made myself useful by shutting the gate on the SUV.

"What's the plan?" I asked as we entered the small house.

"Compound is a few miles up the road, closer to Tiraspol," Duma said. "But we need to lay eyes on it to see exactly what we're dealing with first."

The inside of the tiny crumbling structure was austere. It was a single room with four cots along one wall, with a small wood-burning stove and a sink on the other. The one other doorway led to a small bathroom. It had no door, only a sheet draped across it. It had no other furniture and no signs of an armory or even a single knife embedded in a wall.

"Okay, so where's the rest?" I asked, taking in the empty structure. "In the floor, out in the yard, where?"

"Hell if I know. It's not our place," Duma replied. "We just arranged to use it. We brought everything with us." He pointed offhandedly at the duffle bags as he set the briefcases down then opened one to examine the contents.

Inside was something that resembled a four-armed mechanical insect about the size of a small bird—a drone. Duma noticed me watching.

"Probably best if I go by myself for the first look," he said, putting small propellers on each of the arms. "This one has a standard camera, but that one has infrared and low-light capabilities." He nodded toward the other case.

"Aren't those things loud?" I asked, recalling the only times I'd ever seen them used over the landing where I kept my boat, buzzing like a swarm of angry bees.

"Commercially available ones are very loud, yeah," Duma said. "These are not commercially available. I'll skulk around and get the lay of the land tonight, then we can go over the footage and decide our next step. Make sense?"

"Yeah," I replied. "I hate being left out, but I'd only hold you back while you skulk. Just try not to kill anyone, please? At least not yet."

"Strictly eyes and ears tonight. Gotcha," he said, giving me a mock salute. "But I'm bringing these just in case." He pulled one of his favored kukris out from under his jacket at his waist.

"You want something bigger?" Ab asked, pulling one of his preferred automatic Jackhammer shotguns from one of the gear bags.

"Hard to skulk with something like that over my shoulder," Duma replied.

"Fuck skulking," Ab replied, slamming one of the circular magazines into the heavy weapon. "I say we just go knock on the door and see who's home."

I walked over and patted Ab's shoulder.

After a brief check of the drones and associated gear, Duma took off, and I was more than a little relieved that my friend Geek wasn't there, controlling the tech stuff. The explanations and descriptions would have been endless and detailed—and boring. I still found it hard to believe that a former rugby player, Royal Marine, and SBS door-kicker could be such a geek. But he was as good with a computer as with a gun. Outside, I could hear Duma cursing as he started the dumpy little Lada up out in the garage. Ab and I both laughed as the out-of-tune engine revved, sputtered, and finally caught.

Five hours later, Duma returned, his white eyes set hard, along with his jaw.

"It ain't good, D," Duma said, setting down the cases.

"How bad is it?" I asked.

The pale fairy opened one of the cases and pulled out a laptop, propped it open, and played the footage he'd recorded with the drones. I watched for several long minutes, and no one spoke while it played.

Three buildings were inside a walled compound, with a dozen shipping containers regularly spaced in one large open area behind the structures. Two of the buildings were significantly smaller, but the third was some sort of old manor house made of multiple parts probably added as needed over the centuries. The shipping containers were placed like trailers in a trailer park, spaced about ten feet apart in a row. Not much was visible on the regular camera view, but then Duma switched the feed over to the IR/night vision camera. First, we watched the night vision imagery. With everything washed in whitish hues from stark white to dark gray, figures immediately popped out in the darkest corners of the compound. Two large dogs even came into view. All in all, I counted six guards and two dogs outside the buildings, though they stayed put rather than patrolling the area.

"I'm assuming they have cameras covering pretty much every aspect of the space, which is why these guys don't move," I said.

Duma just nodded and switched to the IR view, and the image came alive with colors. The large manor house became a variety of reds, yellows, oranges, blues, and greens. Duma hit a few buttons on the keyboard, and the image changed slightly. Immediately, several of the wings of the building became crowded with red figures—several dozen at least, all prone, lying tightly packed next to one another.

We continued to watch in silence. I counted fifteen figures outside the half dozen rooms, which held a total of an additional thirty-two figures, all prone. Each room had what appeared to be one guard posted outside, while the remaining nine figures moved about randomly throughout the structure. Also, two more large dogs were posted in another room. Two of the fifteen figures stood out because they were orange instead of darker red like the rest, but I just chalked that up to wall thickness or clothing rather than being inhuman because they otherwise moved and acted just like everyone else. Outside in the shipping containers, nothing gave off a heat signature that suggested anything alive was within them.

"So, fifteen guys inside, six more outside, and four dogs protecting, what, thirty-two prisoners of some kind?" I asked. "Plus, cameras covering every space outside and probably inside as well. Am I reading this right?"

"Best I can tell, yeah, that's what I saw too," Duma said. "But those two aren't human." He pointed at the two orange figures I dismissed as anomalies. "And those prisoners are women, D. Some might even be kids."

I could feel the muscles in my jaw tighten, and I squeezed my fists so hard that my knuckles hurt. Then I realized I wasn't breathing either.

"Any sign of Eisheth?" I asked, finally inhaling and exhaling deeply.

"I didn't see her specifically," he said. "And to be honest, I don't know how she'd appear on FLIR. Those two are definitely Moroi—they usually show up as slightly cooler-than-normal humans like that, maybe low ninety-degree temps rather than high nineties, like normal humans. Eisheth is different, though. One of those *could* be her, but I can't say for sure. I'd think her heat signature would be very different. If I had to make a decision, I'd say she isn't here, so let's not waste our time."

"Shit," I said, trying to decide what to do. Duma was likely right—Eisheth wasn't there. But I couldn't just leave those women to some unknown horrific fate.

"D, we don't have the time or resources to do what I know you're thinking," Duma said.

"Do what?" I asked, confused for a second.

"Oh, no," he said. "I know you. Mortal or not, you're going to want to go save these people."

"Well, we can't just leave them there," I said.

"D, you gotta realize that even the local police around here work for these thugs. Every house around is paid to be eyes and ears. Hell, even the local government is in on it to some extent," Duma said. "We ain't equipped for this—especially with you being, you know, mortal and all." He gestured at me, waving his hand up and down. "Besides, Eisheth probably isn't even here—and she's the target, re-member?"

"Maybe one of those Moroi in there will know where Eisheth is," I said. "And mortal or not, I still have over three thousand years of training and experience. We just have to take them by surprise. Use the guerilla tactic of Violence of Action to our advantage and hit them fast and hard. Make them think the three of us are more like fifteen or twenty."

Ab grunted behind us. "That's my specialty."

"Going in there is bad enough. Anything more is suicide, D, plain and simple," Duma said, shaking his head and sitting back on his heels.

"You're telling me that you and Ab can't rip this place to shreds?" I asked, goading the bloodthirsty Peri.

"Well, of course we could, but you always rein us in, tell us not to kill everything that moves—especially humans," he said.

"Well, now, I'm telling you we need to go in there, and you two need to do what you do best. Just leave the prisoners and one of those Moroi alive so we can question them," I said. "If you think you can pull that off. We are talking over twenty guys and four really big dogs." I sat back and spread my hands apart, cocking my head in doubt.

Duma and Ab both snorted in unison, underlining their broth-erly connection.

"Whaddya think, Ab? You saw the layout. Seven, eight minutes tops?" Duma said.

Ab rocked his head back and forth a few times. "I'm thinking closer to seven than eight. But what do we do with all those prisoners? This place is surrounded by paid informants, policed by crooked cops, and controlled by corrupt politicians, and this entire region is neighbored by unfriendly countries that couldn't care less about human trafficking. We'd have to get them hundreds of miles away before they'd be safe. It's a logistical nightmare."

Duma motioned exaggeratedly at Ab with his last comment.

"*Nightmare* is an understatement," Duma said.

"But I do like a challenge," Ab said, practically growling in anticipation.

"That would put you in the minority here, Duma," I said.

"Yeah, the only one with a brain," he said, shaking his head. "You guys are nuts. But hell, I'm not letting you guys go in alone. Especially if you're removing all the stops."

"Now we just have to figure out how to get those prisoners out of here," I said.

Chapter 17

I stared at a map of the area around the compound and an aerial image of the buildings from one of the drones for a while. The north side of the compound was bordered by a railroad track then an open field for quite some distance. The south side was bordered by a road that curved around the area and to the west, which was where the only entrance was located. The eastern edge abutted a few homes. The opposite side of the roadway on the south was lined with similar small homes as well. The one road past the compound was so narrow that for two cars to pass each other, one would have to pull over.

Electricity was supplied by ancient lines strung along rickety poles placed every thirty yards or so. That could prove useful, but I had no doubt that the compound would have a secondary or even a more reliable primary source. However, taking it out might just give us a few seconds to operate in the dark before the alternate source kicked in.

Whatever we were going to do was going to have to be surgical in its precision and swift in its execution. We would have to be in and out in minutes. But even if we managed to get the thirty-plus prisoners out safely, we still had the issue of transporting them from Transnistria to someplace safe. With Ukraine to the east, Moldova and Romania to the west, Belarus to the north, and the Black Sea to the south, we were hundreds of miles from the nearest potential safe haven.

"Can we take out the electricity to the area?" I asked.

"Sure," Duma replied. "Just pop a small charge on the base of one of these power poles. As old as they look, a good shove might even be enough. But you know they'll have backup, assuming they aren't on some sort of separate power supply to begin with."

"Yeah, I thought about that, but at least it'll keep the rest of the area quiet while we work," I said. "What we really need is a big transport helicopter—something like a Chinook," I said. "We can land it right there in that field to the north, pop a hole in the wall, and load everyone up and get them out. We can grab our vampire and sneak out in a different direction. You guys know anyone with a big helicopter they aren't using, and a back door into the Ways?"

"Well, yeah," Ab said. "I know this guy up in Belarus. He runs an air ambulance. Has an old Soviet Mil Mi-26MS. That thing will hold sixty passengers, including stretchers if necessary. I'm sure he can get some paramedics to help him too. But where would we land them? They can't go back into the Ukraine, and Belarus and Romania aren't much safer."

"We can land them near Debrecen in Hungary. It's about four hundred miles due west on the other side of Romania," Duma said. "You remember Gheorge, the smuggler who took us down the Danube to vampire town when we were chasing the Hanner Brid?"

I nodded.

"Well, he's got connections," Duma said. "If we can get them there, then he can get them out to someplace safer."

"I got enough Semtex to rig some shaped charges to blow a hole through that north wall," Ab said, pointing at the image. "It won't be loud, but in a sleepy little village like this, it'll still be audible."

"Then that will be the last thing we do, once everyone is safe in the courtyard," I said. "We should also rig some roadblocks to slow up any police or militia response." Both Duma and Ab nodded their heads. "So, assuming we can do all that, then here's the plan: Duma, you go in first, fast and hard. Anything that's alive in the courtyard needs to be eliminated. Then you meet up with Ab at this door to the main building. Ab, you're the breach team. You guys need to take out everyone you can, leaving one of those Moroi alive for us to question. I will follow and deal with the occupants in these six rooms." I pointed at the glowing IR image that showed thirty-two people in small spaces within the main building. "I'll get them into the yard, then we blow the wall and get them onto a helicopter and out of here. Then we load up with our vampire and get our asses gone too. Make sense?"

"And Plan B?" Duma asked with a sneer on his face.

"Plan B is do anything we gotta do to make Plan A work," I said. "But there is no scenario where anyone gets left behind, you guys understand?"

"I'll contact the guy with the helicopter and get the explosives ready," Ab said.

"Uh, I'll sharpen my knives," Duma said, one corner of his mouth ticking up to reveal just enough of a tooth to make him look predatory.

He could be one scary son of a bitch.

The only thing for me to do was check my gear and wait until everything was in order.

Ab made the arrangements for the helicopter within a few hours, but nothing could happen until the following night. He let me know that our little operation was going to cost a significant amount of money to pull off, bribes to file fictional flight manifests and illegal border crossings notwithstanding. Both he and his brother knew I would never be able to pay them back, but I knew they would never expect it.

Frankly, I was sure they had more money squirreled away than the five wealthiest humans in the world combined. What I knew for sure was that the brothers had at least twenty safe houses around the world, Duma had a car collection worth millions upon millions, and their armories could supply a decent-sized militia in a sustained battle for months if necessary. And no matter what the underhanded endeavor, they always knew a guy.

Chapter 18

The next morning, Duma and I took a leisurely drive in the So-viet-era relic back through Transnistria and past the compound at the northern edge of town. Whether it was paranoia or maybe due diligence, I wanted to lay eyes on the place before we stormed the walls.

The outer wall was easily ten feet high and topped with con-certina wire. Two of the buildings were tall enough to be seen over the wall: one was three stories, the other two. I could see only the roofs of the rest of the structures within. The only gate in the wall, along the western edge, was a massive solid metal construct rigged to slide open on a heavy track. I spotted surveillance cameras inside the gateway, at every corner along the outer wall, and along the eaves of the higher floors within. However, powerlines crossed over the wall along the eastern edge of the compound and connected to the tallest building inside. Not that I expected it, but I heard no sounds coming from inside.

We drove up the road a bit farther then pulled over at the far side of the field that bordered the compound to the north.

"Breaching that gate will be a mess," I said, staring in the side-view mirror at our intended target.

"Why the hell would we breach it?" Duma asked. "We'll go over. It'll be quieter. That way, the only explosion will be cracking a hole in that wall right there." He pointed at a spot in the broad structure adjacent to the tallest building within.

"You're forgetting that I can't jump like I used to," I said.

"No, I'm not," he replied. "Ab can pitch your scrawny butt over like a sack of flour."

"Fat chance. I'd probably end up with a broken leg, if not two," I said.

Duma was smiling as though to stifle a laugh. "Relax. We'll go over then toss you a rope. You can drag your own ass over it at your leisure. I'm thinking we go in right where we intend to blow the hole to get out. It's less visible to the neighbors, and only three cameras are mounted along that whole wall."

"There are power cables running to the house," I said. "With luck, if we take those out, maybe we'll have a sixty-second window before their generators kick in. That'll give me and Ab time to get in. Meanwhile, I'm assuming you'll have already dispatched everyone inside?"

"Sixty seconds?" he said, eyeing me sideways. "What'll I do with the remaining twenty-five?" He smiled as though trying to pass his comment off as a humorous boast, but something about his eyes suggested he was being serious. I knew he was blindingly fast, but even at my best and with Athena's gifts of speed and strength, I guessed I would've needed three minutes to take out that many targets, assuming they never moved. Call it five for good measure.

"No way you're that fast," I said.

He just smiled at me the way people do when someone says something blatantly silly. "Wanna bet?"

"Not particularly," I said. "Just take your time and make sure you do it right. Remember, this is for Sarah, but there are a lot of other lives we can help while pulling this off."

We sat quietly for a few more minutes. I continued to stare at the reflection of the compound in the rearview mirrors.

"Let's head back before we draw attention to ourselves," Duma said, starting the old jalopy up with a sputter. "Piece of crap."

My plan was to wait until the witching hour, three in the morning, to make our move. Routinely, that was the quietest time of the night no matter where in the world you went. The only problem was that night, the compound was bustling with people and was lit up like downtown Manhattan on New Year's. Duma broke out the drone and sent it up to get us a bird's-eye view of the landscape since it was crawling with people. While we surveyed the new situation, Ab rigged the charges on the power lines and set up a way to create roadblocks along the street.

The little camera revealed another two dozen people, mostly congregated around the storage containers in the back. More precisely, eighteen men were standing in line outside the containers with six armed guards in two groups of three, keeping watch over the whole thing. Switching to the IR drone showed four people in each of the dozen containers—two at each end, clearly engaged in sexual activity.

What a freakin' mess.

"We got bigger issues, D," Duma said, pointing at two figures on the brightly colored screen. "These two are likely Moroi." They were part of the armed six-man team keeping watch over the situation.

Armed vampires. Even better.

The only upside to the whole thing was that those containers were at the far end of the compound, which gave us a marginal shot at catching them by surprise, overwhelming them, and getting on to the rest of the buildings without raising too much of an alarm.

"All these guys need to go," I said. "You hear me? I'm assuming those men are lining up to take their turns with some of the prisoners. The women are the only ones to be spared. Got me?"

"Loud and clear, boss," Duma replied.

Ab just nodded.

"Duma, you and I go in from the rear and work our way forward. Ab, you go in the front of the containers here," I said, pointing at the wall in an area around the container nearest the buildings. "Work your way toward us, and keep anyone from getting past you. Top priority is anyone with a gun then anyone that offers resistance. If they surrender, leave them be. We'll lock up the ones that don't fight in one of the containers then move on to the main house. I'll get the girls inside the containers out then join up with you guys in the house as planned. It's gonna suck, but we don't have a choice."

"Suck for who?" Duma asked, glancing at his brother, who just rolled his massive shoulders and smiled.

"Me," I replied. "I still gotta get over that concertina wire in a hurry."

"Hop on, D," Ab said, hooking a thumb at his back. "I got you."

It was going to be all kinds of humiliating, but I didn't have much choice. I had to get in quickly.

I hopped up and wrapped my arms around Ab's massive neck like a kid hanging on to his parents at the end of a long day at a theme park, and Duma's teeth glinted in the ambient light. He was going to dine out on this for weeks.

"Shut up, dickhead," I said, making both of them break out into muffled laughter. "Let's just get on with it."

Duma made the jump first, then Ab went over. His gracefulness always surprised me because of his size. He wasn't as fluid as his brother, but he was better than any human gymnast by far. We landed, and I caught up with Duma, and Ab went toward the front of the row of containers. I had the stock folded down on my FN-SCAR-H to make it easier to maneuver in the tight confines, and I also had fitted it with a suppressor to keep the sound down.

The large 7.62mm rounds would have more than enough stopping power. I carried my swords as I always did on my back even though they wouldn't be as useful to me as they once were, and my once-impenetrable cuirass was under my tactical vest. I was going to need every advantage I could get, especially with two and maybe as many as four Moroi on the premises.

Duma moved slowly around the last container, watching carefully for the armed guards. I was just too slow to keep up with him and would simply get in his way, so I resigned myself to mop-up duty. And I hated it.

In an instant, he disappeared from in front of me and reappeared twenty feet away, blood dripping from his favored kukris. Like dominoes that didn't know they were supposed to fall, three men between us wavered slightly then fell first to their knees then to the ground, the dirt turning even darker around their heads. I didn't even have time to raise my weapon and advance.

I turned the corner with my weapon in a combat high position and targeted the four men standing in line then quickly motioned toward the ground. Immediately, their hands went up, and they all dropped to their knees then lay down without saying a word. By the time I glanced up, Duma was gone, off to the next container. I stepped over the prone men and into the storage container. The interior was divided by curtains and dimly lit by a series of faint lightbulbs suspended from a wire strung along the ceiling. The place smelled like sweat and sex, with an overwhelming odor that I could only describe as fear.

I ripped the curtain closest to me back only to find the stall empty, so I moved farther in. At the next opening, I pulled the curtain back just enough to see a man with his pants pulled down around his legs, thrusting on top of a woman who was listless and probably drugged. Without hesitating, I shot him twice in the upper back, and he went as still as the woman he was straddling. She was so out of it that she didn't even make a sound when I dragged his body off her. His dead weight surprised me. The woman was far too stoned to think or even reason with, so I left her and moved farther into the container, finding nothing.

I repeated the process at each successive container, shooting four more men with only a few of the women coherent enough to understand I was there to help. At the fourth container, I met up with Duma and Ab with a small group of women between them. Ab was also carrying two more—one under each arm—with no more effort than holding sacks of groceries.

"There are several more women in these containers, but they're too drugged up to move on their own," I said.

Duma immediately began speaking Russian to the women with him and Ab. I understood enough to know he was telling them to gather up any other women and keep them quiet until we came for them. All totaled, there were seventeen. I hoped that meant only fifteen were left in the main building. We took a few more minutes to lock the johns up in one of the containers then moved on to the main building. So far, we'd managed to be quiet enough that no alarms had been raised. And I could only assume that either Ab or Duma had dispatched the Moroi we saw among the guards.

Next, we could get on with Plan A—sort of.

Chapter 19

I ran as fast as I could to keep up with the brothers, failing miserably, and arrived just in time to see Duma flip a switch on a small handheld remote detonator and to hear a muffled thump as everything went black, followed by a tremendous crash as Ab kicked in the front door of the big manor house. Duma disappeared, and I followed Ab down the hallway. I was coming out of the fourth room that was supposed to hold prisoners, having found it empty as well, when I ran into the brothers, looking smug and satisfied with themselves.

"Did you find the Moroi?" I asked, noticing they had no prisoners.

"Not yet," Duma said, wiping at his mouth with the back of his hand. "We saw Eisheth, but the little shit eluded me."

"Got away from *you*? Seriously?" I asked. "Fine. Well, one of you go track her down, the other go get those women to the extraction point, and I'll finish checking and clearing these rooms and meet you outside within a few minutes."

They nodded and took off, and I resumed my search.

Entering the next room, I knew something was off right away. The smell was overwhelming in the dank darkness—a combination of body odor, urine, blood, and offal. It reminded me of an old-time slaughterhouse. Despite the smell, no bodies were in there, but the floor was slick with a dark coppery liquid, the mattresses strewn haphazardly about were covered in a deep crimson, and the walls were smeared with it as well. Whatever happened in there hadn't happened long before.

I backed out and headed for the next room, pushing down the dark, dimly lit hallway. It felt claustrophobic, more like a cave than a hallway, and the smell of blood hung thick in my nose, gagging me. I was starting to feel lightheaded, too, and I suddenly realized that was the adrenaline. I guess Athena's abilities also allowed me to deal with the rush associated with that kind of activity a bit better. That was a feeling I hadn't felt in a very long time—the surge of energy, heightened reflexes, and acute senses of the first real kick of adrenaline, followed inevitably at some point by the sudden letdown as the chemical boost dissipated. Clearly, I was on the downward slide.

I pushed into the next room and was immediately met by a wall of odor that stopped me dead in my tracks. It was like the last room, only magnified. My eyes began to water, I couldn't stop my gag reflex, and I began to retch. Then my eyes adjusted to the darkness within, and I saw bodies piled up like dirty rags, everything awash in a coppery crimson color in the dim light from the single pathetic bulb.

I jerked back and, in my reeling, caught sight of another monstrous figure coming out of the shadows from up the hallway. My addled brain immediately thought, *Ab,* but something wasn't right as I noticed the figure's bulk came from wings, spread as much as they could be and scraping against the masonry walls with a metallic grinding as the figure advanced. Then something shiny flashed at me from within the shadowy form, and I barely had time to react. My movement was more of a fall than a controlled action, but before I hit the ground, something grabbed me from behind and pulled me farther back out of harm's way and lifted me back to my feet.

My head was spinning.

"I don't know what that is, but we need to run, now!" The female voice behind me was familiar.

Something in my brain kicked in, honed by thousands of years of training, and I reached for my swords—my useless swords. I immediately got into my stance, ready to face whatever the creature was, and was surprised to see the monstrous winged form had shrunken to that of a startlingly beautiful blonde woman, albeit one carrying a sword.

"You should have kept to our bargain, Diomedes," the figure said, practically purring. "Now that you're mortal again, I would say that it's time to redress the balance of all the injustices *you* have inflicted upon the world."

"Nemesis," I said more than asked, trying to understand what was going on. Then I realized I no longer had the ability to see through her disguises—she could appear to me as whatever she wanted.

No sooner did I say her name than she leveled a backhand slash at me, arcing from overhead, her blade slicing through the masonry ceiling as if it were hot butter. Instinctively, I threw my swords up to catch the blow. To my surprise, the blades held, but the incredible force of the impact dropped me to my knees and off-balance, and I almost fell flat on my ass. Again, the blade came at me, slicing through the air, knocking aside my feeble attempt to parry as if I were a child sparring with a master. I couldn't move fast enough to make an offensive stand, and Nemesis just kept batting my swords away, playing with me.

"There she is." Ab's voice came from somewhere down the hallway behind me. "Who the fuck *is* that?"

"*Now* who did you piss off, D?" asked Duma.

Again, Nemesis just swung her long blade, batting my swords aside.

"Fuck, I knew I shouldn't have come here," said the female with the familiar voice immediately behind me, followed by a moment of clarity and recognition on my part.

"Kailani," I said, desperately trying to maintain enough focus to not get killed by Nemesis.

"Yeah, who did you think it was?" she replied. "And who is Nemesis, and why is she trying to kill you?"

"Not the right time, not the right time!" I screamed while trying to muster enough strength to effectively block one of Nemesis' blows.

"Enough of this," Nemesis said. "Your friends will die also, in payment for your transgressions, just like *all* the women here you so desperately wanted to save."

"You did this?" I asked, horrified and desperately wishing that Athena would give me the strength to stand up to this would-be deity.

Something in me began to burn, and I managed to deflect her next passing blow—meant to throw me off, not hit me, and I swung with my remaining sword, striking her across one arm with as much force as I could muster. It was like hitting stone. The blow jarred my arm and just caromed off without leaving so much as a scratch.

I was fucked.

The goddess of retribution screeched and stabbed at my chest so quickly that I couldn't react. The blade hit my vest and the cuirass underneath but didn't penetrate like I expected. Instead, the impact of the blow threw me backward into Kailani and knocked us both whirling. I was surprised and stunned, not to mention tangled up with a reluctant vampiress.

"Stay down, D!" Ab screamed.

Without questioning what was coming, I flipped onto my stomach, scrambled to Kailani, and covered our heads with my arms. Half a second later, a thunderous *whump* was followed by a small but powerful explosion just behind me. The heat from it washed over me and stung the back of my neck and my exposed forearms. Everything went silent, and my ears rang. Even through my tightly shut eyes, the light from the conflagration made me flinch.

The next thing I knew, I was being picked up by the back of my vest like a sack of rice. I could hear voices, but the ringing in my ears made it impossible to discern what was being said. With my feet under me, I turned to see Ab waving at me as if urging me to round third base and head for home. I could see his mouth moving, but I had been in that situation so many times that reflex took over, and I ran, swords still in hand. I didn't stop to look for Nemesis behind me or even to see what had happened. The only thing that went through my mind was "retreat to cover."

Running at my new full speed, I bolted into the cool night air outside the building and tucked into a feetfirst baseball slide to take cover behind some wooden crates. The ringing in my ears subsided, and I risked poking my mortal noggin out from behind the crates. Smoke was billowing out of the doorway. Then all at once, the sounds of the world around me came flooding back.

"What the fuck?" Kailani screamed from inside the doorway. "Let me go, you freaks!"

An instant later, Ab and Duma came out, restraining Kailani, each holding one of her arms. Apparently, she was the Moroi they'd been chasing.

"What the hell are you doing here?" I asked. "Forget it. Ab, Duma, get her out of here, but don't hurt her. We still gotta deal with Nemesis," I said, motioning back inside the building with one of my swords.

"She's gone, D," Duma said, struggling to maintain hold of Kailani. "Disappeared when Ab shot her."

"Dammit," I said, watching them struggle to restrain Kailani, who was wiggling like a thrashing marlin being dragged out of the water and onto the deck. She broke Duma's grip and landed a solid blow to Ab's jaw and kicked Duma at least twice, barely missing his groin both times.

"Can't I just stab her until she loses consciousness?" Duma asked, fighting to regain his grip on her arm.

"Let me go, or I'll kick you until you lose all your teeth, pretty boy," Kailani said, spitting nails.

"Let her go, but we gotta get the hell outta here. Now," I said. "And that means you too." I pointed at Kailani.

Ab and Duma reluctantly let go of her, and Duma immediately moved to protect his groin while Ab jerked back as Kailani regained her composure.

"You know her?" Duma asked as I caught up to them.

"Yeah. Duma and Ab, this is Kailani. Kailani, this pretty boy here is Duma, and that's his brother, Abraxos. They're Peri—Anseelie Fae," I said. "And yes, she's a Moroi. Now, let's get the hell outta here. Before Nemesis comes back."

"Holy fuck," Duma said with a gasp. "She's the one from the club where Sarah got taken."

"Not now, Duma," I growled, pushing his shoulder hard to get him to move.

Chapter 20

At the back of the large house, the women we freed were all gathered near the wall, and in the near distance, I could hear the heavy beating of helicopter blades. It wasn't exactly stealthy, but it didn't matter anyway after Ab's attempt to blow up Nemesis and charbroil me. Off in the distance, back toward town, sirens were wailing. If Ab had done his job, they would never make it in time to stop us.

We cleared the women from around the wall, blew the shaped charges to open a passageway through it, and waited until the big Soviet-made Mil Mi-26 landed in the field fifty yards away. The second the helicopter's tailgate opened, we ushered the women out and herded them across the open ground. To my surprise, four paramedics were standing by to help with the injured. Once everyone was on board, Duma, Ab, and I took off for the Dartz left on the side of the road less than half a mile away and left the helicopter pilot and his rescued passengers to their arduous four-hundred-mile flight at treetop level into Hungary.

"Come on!" I yelled to Kailani. "You're with us."

"You mean we're not taking the helicopter?" she asked.

"No, we have a different exfil plan. And now, you're with us," I replied.

She rolled her eyes but fell in behind us as we ran. I could tell everyone was holding back as we ran, likely to not leave me behind. I made it to our car slightly winded. Duma gave me a sideways glance and quick, disdainful shake of his head as I tried to gain control of my breathing. Once we were in the heavily armored Dartz, rolling along at a hundred and fifty miles per hour, with Transnistria safely in our rearview mirror, everyone breathed a little easier.

"Our exfil plan is through Belarus," Duma said. "There's a place through the Ways just over the border, and we can make a quick jump to someplace far, far away."

"What about the car?" I asked, assuming Duma would have somebody come pick it up or something.

"Torch it," he replied. "The rest of the explosives are in the back."

I was surprised at his response.

Ab shook his head and clucked his tongue disapprovingly. "You know how many of these things you go through?"

"I haven't kept a specific count, no," Duma replied. "Why? Do you?"

He held up four beefy fingers. "And that's just in the last year alone. I'll bet they have a new one ready to go for you, don't they?"

"Maybe," Duma said petulantly. "Shut up."

"What the hell were you doing at that compound?" I asked Kailani. "I thought you were trying to stay out of that stuff."

"I was," she said, turning to stare out the darkened window at the landscape cloaked in blackness beyond. "I got the feeling you'd end up there at some point, though, so I've been lying low and waiting. I wanted to help. I'm guessing you're going to need to find Eisheth, and I know where she's likely to be."

"You trust her, D?" Duma asked, making eye contact in the rearview mirror. His brows were knitted tightly across his forehead.

I stared hard at Kailani for a minute before I responded. "Yeah, I do."

Chapter 21

We made it across the border into Belarus, thanks largely in part to another massive bribe at the border. Once Moldova was a tiny speck in the rearview mirror, tensions began to ease within the car—at least my tension. I'm not sure Duma or Ab's blood pressure rose a single millimeter—ever. For all I knew, they didn't even have blood pressure to raise as we humans knew it.

"So, D, it would appear that Her Muzzled Rump-Fed Moldwarpness has really forsaken your ass," Duma said without a hint of humor in his tone. "Just askin' 'cause lookin' after you is going to be seriously tough."

I just stared into the rearview mirror, seeing a small part of my face in the reflection mixed with the inky darkness that surrounded us. My arms and neck burned and ached every time I moved.

"So... where are we headed?" He said after another silent minute.

"You said you know where Eisheth is going to be," I said, turning to Kailani.

"Well, sort of, yeah," she said with a shrug and a tilt of her head. "If she wasn't here, then she should be at her place in Shanghai."

"You mean the Riverside Triumphal Arch in Pudong?" Duma asked, the pitch of his voice rising.

Kailani just nodded.

"Well, fuck," Duma said, trading a look with Ab that conveyed something even more serious than his statement. "Maybe we should just sneak back into Coronini or go back to Poveglia, D. You planning on making a tour of all the great strongholds of the world's nastiest creatures? 'Cause if you are, I'll just shoot myself right now and get it over with. Whatever luck you keep dipping into is bound to run out eventually. Especially now. Lemme ask you something. Do you actually *try* to make things harder each time?"

"I choose to believe that luck presents itself as opportunity when you are well prepared," I said. "So we'll just have to make sure we cross all our t's and dot all our i's. Just like we always do."

"You mean you *actually* do plan for all this shit to happen?" Duma said with a laugh. "Crazy villagers with pitchforks, Belphoebe's crazy ass tracking us down, me being betrayed by a Hulder... bitch." He spat the last word out like it was poison. "And Sarah?"

"Low blow, Duma," I said. "I was hoping I would be fast enough, strong enough—"

"Not what I meant," Duma said. "It was as much my fault as anyone's. I'm just saying sneaking into the high-rise penthouse apartment of the Queen of the Moroi in the middle of Shanghai is not exactly going to be a swim up the Danube, my friend."

His reference to our chase of the half-demon half-fae hitman that framed me for murder a few years back wasn't lost on me. That one nearly got me killed by any number of beings all just aching for the excuse. And it had started a blood feud with the *other* strain of vampires—the Strigoi. But such was my life. And if I needed to storm the very gates of Hades to save Sarah, then that was damn well what I would do, mortal or not.

"I'll work it out or die trying," I replied.

"You mean 'we,' D," Ab said.

"How well do you know Eisheth's place in Shanghai?" I asked Kailani.

"Not well," she replied. "I mean, I've been there. I know it's the entire top floor of Tower One. I can give you the layout of the rooms I've been in, but that's about it. I don't know anything about the building's security or even her own private security—other than she has them in the apartment."

"So, we need to get plans for the building and lay eyes on it somehow," I said, noticing yet another sideways glance between Duma and Ab. "What's going on up here?" I asked, leaning forward between the front seats. "I've seen the glances every time we mention Eisheth's apartment. What aren't you two saying?"

"Nothing. And, uh, hey, what about that godling that was kicking your ass back in Transnistria?" Duma asked. "Is that an ongoing concern, too, because I'd hate to think we were dealing with only one impossible task at a time here."

"That was Nemesis, the one from our conversation with St. Germain, but unfortunately, I do believe she will be a proverbial fly in the ointment unless I can deal with her first," I said. "And I am definitely going to have to deal with her—mortal or not. And if you two know something about that building that you're not telling me, I'll add you to that growing list as well."

"It ain't nothing big," Ab said with a shrug of one of his big shoulders. "We own the floor a couple down from Eisheth's in Tower Two. We tried to buy the top floor, but all they told us was that some corporation bought it before the place was even built. That and the two floors below it. We had to settle for third floor down from the top in the middle tower facing Tower One. Even we didn't even know for sure it was Eisheth's place until now. Honest, D."

"We poked around a bit," Duma said, "And believe me when I say it's locked down tight as a... It's pretty tight." He stared at me hard through the rearview mirror. "We don't even know who's above *us*. Seriously. You want to know how good security in those buildings is, then believe me when I say that until your vampire friend here confirmed it, Ab and I had no concrete idea who lived there, and it's just across from our place. *Our place.*"

"I get it, Duma," I said, leaning back into my seat. "We still have no choice."

"There might be one other option," Kailani said, still staring at her reflection in the darkened window.

"Oh," I said.

"Other options are good," Duma added.

Ab turned and nodded vigorously, pointing at his brother.

"Her place in LA—the Mondrian Hotel," she replied.

"Are you serious?" Duma asked, his white eyes widening as his eyebrows climbed high on his forehead.

Ab let out a low multitone whistle.

"What's the Mondrian Hotel?" I asked, feeling awkward and anachronistic, as usual. No weapon existed on this planet that I hadn't or couldn't master, but I was at a total loss when it came to things as simple as social media and what was "in."

Duma snorted as Ab smiled a bit. "It's, like, only one of the trendiest places in LA. The normal guest list would make the Academy Awards seem like second-tier stars. It's what I want my place in Miami Beach to be like. You remember that place, right?" Duma turned his head to glance back at me.

"Yeah, the Laplander or something," I replied. "Too much white tile and uncomfortable furniture." I recalled the place where he and I had planned our assault on North Korea to get the Hanner Brid. Short of its ocean view, I couldn't think of a single redeeming feature of the neon monstrosity.

"Clevelander, D. The Clevelander," Duma replied. "You're hopeless."

"You own the Clevelander in Miami Beach?" Kailani asked, turning, her face scrunched up in astonishment.

"Yep."

"Well, *we* own it," Ab said. "I'm the silent partner."

"I thought that place was owned by some Italian guy named Fermini or something," Kailani said.

At that, Duma broke into a flawless Italian tirade that I promptly tried to ignore.

"Give it a rest, Duma. We get it. And it's a nice place. If you like pink neon, white marble, and loud music," I said.

"Don't forget lots of beautiful people wearing very little clothing," Duma added, waggling his eyebrows.

"Fine, so what about this Mondrian place?" I asked.

"Eisheth owns it and spends a fair amount of time there," the vampiress replied. "In fact, if she's not in Shanghai or Tiraspol, I'd bet she's there. And I will guarantee you that she *will* show up there eventually."

"Yeah, but that's smack-dab in the middle of Hollywood, on Sunset Boulevard, and I imagine that her being the queen energy leech—no offense—she wouldn't show up when the hotel was empty," Duma said, his forehead creased. "Security might be less... secure... but we'd almost end up being the main entertainment for the evening. That place is crawling with people when it gets going. You remember the Clevelander, D? Picture that, only magnified, like, a hundred times. Not to mention all the other stuff that happens up and down Sunset Boulevard on a nightly basis."

"So, at first blush, you think taking Eisheth in Shanghai would be easier?" I asked.

"Whoa, I know I didn't say that," Duma replied. "Look, my first reaction is the place in Shanghai is a fortress, but that also works in our favor. The place in LA is a zoo with no locks on the doors. Six of one, half dozen of the other, the way I see it. I'd be more than happy to sit at the Mondrian for a few weeks to check it out to make sure, though."

"Not that it matters, but I have a place in Silver Lake, just down from the Mondrian," Kailani said. "And I've spent a lot of time at the Mondrian."

"I'll tell you what, Duma: you and Ab head to Shanghai and recon that situation from a tactical standpoint. Find out everything you can. I'll head to LA with Kailani to check out the situation at the Mongolian," I said.

"Mondrian. Mondrian. Not Mongolian. Sheesh, D. Or—and I'm just spitballing here—I could go to LA with... Kailani, was it?" Duma said, watching me in the rearview mirror. "D, you could go with Ab to China. Whatcha think?"

"I think you should stick to cutting throats and let me think up the plans," I said.

"Yeah, said the battering ram. Fine," Duma said with a frown. "Ab, remind me to get some heavier body armor for this one. It's gonna get messy."

Chapter 22

I'd done a lot of awful crap in my considerable lifespan, seen some nasty stuff, and literally been through hell, but nothing could've prepared me for the tedium, frustration, and discomfort of transcontinental commercial air travel or the huge lines at customs—except maybe the special torture that is traffic in LA. The hour that it took to make it from LAX to Kailani's place in the Silver Lake neighborhood just east of Hollywood because of construction and traffic during the middle of the day made the previous nineteen hours of planes and airports seem fleeting. How people in LA did this on a regular basis without constant psychotic breaks was beyond me. Luckily, thanks to Duma's less-than-legal connections, my passport wasn't even questioned.

Kailani's place was near the reservoir that gave the area its name. The drought that had plagued the state for years had all but dried up its namesake, though. Her place, which I expected to be a simple small house, was actually a large two-story Mediterranean-style building that resembled a medieval castle, with white stucco and a red-tile roof—on a corner of Castle Street, no less. Even the massive wooden front door gave the impression of a drawbridge rather than a door.

"Cozy," I said, mostly to myself, feeling exhausted.

The interior of her home was remarkably simple, compared to the facade.

"It's home," she replied flatly. "I've owned it for the last sixty years. Well, if we're going to the Mondrian, we're definitely going to have to get you some new clothes." She eyed me as though I was wearing a powder-blue leisure suit complete with ruffled shirt.

"Sorry I didn't pack anything for a party," I replied. "But I'll have you know I do have more stylish clothes at home. In San Diego, I mean."

"Mm-hmm," she said, walking upstairs. "I'm sure you do. Probably even have a shirt with a collar and everything."

"Well, of course," I said, wounded by her tone, which suggested I had no fashion sense at all. I walked over to the foot of the stairs to shout up them. "I even have a tie. I think." I said the last part mostly to myself. Then I heard her shower start up.

I had no idea what to do. Most of me was simply tired, but part of me wanted to go up, and part of me was scared to death—of what, I had no idea. We'd had an intimate relationship for weeks up until she left. I couldn't blame her for leaving. And I missed her. The problem was I didn't know if I missed her or the idea of her—someone, anyone to be close and share a connection with.

I stood there at the bottom of the stairs, deep in my thoughts about Kailani—and Sarah—until the high-pitched whine of a hair dryer brought me back to reality. A few minutes later, Kailani walked to the top of the stairs, dressed in a simple tan skirt and top, running her hand and a brush through her still-damp dark hair. She looked at me for a moment. I stared back, unable to blink. In that moment, my chest hurt—not because she was beautiful but because a connection was there. At some level, we were the same—once human but now something different. And we didn't fit in anywhere, probably not even with each other. But in our shared marginalization, we shared a common bond. And she *was* beautiful and fearless. I found it ironic that for eons I would have seen her as little more than a monster to be destroyed, and she would have seen me as the monster who destroys her kind without remorse. In truth, we weren't that different.

"You should probably shower. I have a friend who makes bespoke men's clothing. I'll give him a call and see if he can squeeze you in for an emergency," she said.

I didn't respond. I just continued to stare.

She descended the stairs halfway then stammered and cleared her throat. "There are towels on the vanity in the bathroom," she said, her voice husky.

"I, uh, okay, thanks," I replied, heading up the stairs. We passed each other awkwardly on the narrow staircase without making eye contact.

The upper floor was just a big bedroom with a massive closet to one side and a cavernous white marble-lined bathroom to the other. I began to undress, still feeling a bit out of sorts.

"You know, no one has looked at me that way in a long time," Kailani said from somewhere behind me. "Like I was real, like you were looking at me, seeing me—not a vampire or even an attractive woman. I... just wanted to tell you that. I'll... uh... let you shower."

I tried to say something, but nothing that ran through my head sounded appropriate or even good enough, so I kept my mouth shut.

We arrived at a quirky work/loft space just off Melrose Avenue between Los Angeles City College and the 101 Freeway. Kailani strode into the alleyway behind the building and straight through a doorway. She wasn't walking preternaturally fast, but her long legs made for giant strides. I had to focus to keep up without moving so quickly that I drew attention to myself. Inside the loft space, we walked into an open area with dozens of fabrics on rolls hanging from the walls, brightly lit tables covered in pieces of material being sewn by hand and machine, and stacks of folded clothes. A small group of people stopped to see who'd come in.

Forty minutes later, I was measured, the tailors in the shop went to work, and I was told they would need at least twenty-four hours to finish, given that everything was being custom sewn based on my measurements. It also meant they would work on nothing else but my clothes for the next day. I could only imagine the relationship Kailani had with those guys to garner such treatment, let alone the cost for clothes like those.

I found Kailani outside on her phone. Her lips were pursed into a tight colorless line across her face, and the set of her brow was hard.

"Well, I can get us into the Mondrian tonight, but I don't think she's going to be there," she said, taking a deep breath. "Which is good and bad. Good because it means that I won't cause you trouble by showing up with you, but bad because it means she's likely in Shanghai. I assume you won't have an issue dealing with any other Moroi that will be at the hotel, should the need arise? And that you can be discreet doing so?"

"Discreet is my middle name," I replied, trying to look capable and competent somehow. She just rolled her eyes and shook her head. Apparently, I didn't pull off the look.

At my request, we drove past the Mondrian just so I could get a feel for it. It was a massive blocky white structure dotted with twelve floors of long silvery windows, which gave me the impression of one of those DNA tests they show on educational programs, only turned sideways. I could see no balconies. The western facade was adorned with an advertisement for some TV show that took up the entire face of the building, however. It *was* LA, after all. The entire structure was otherwise unremarkable from the street, and the neighboring businesses were all either bars, clubs, restaurants, or other hotels. Sunset Boulevard was busy but not crowded at that time of day, though it gave every impression that, at night, it was everything Hollywood was famous for. The very thought of the throngs of people and who knows what other kinds of human-looking creatures trying to mingle, hobnob, network, and otherwise socialize—not to mention hunt—made my skin crawl.

That was definitely not my world, and I had largely avoided LA and Hollywood for decades. Everyone who knew about the existence of Old Ones and Parans was aware of the fact that the city had a sizeable population of nonhumans, but the city thrived on a different kind of carnage than was normally my purview. So as long as everyone played nice, I just let things go. Sure, things popped up from time to time, but in that town, scandal and crazy went hand in hand and were easily dismissed as "typical Hollywood." Most of the worst the city had seen were all human-based anyway—including the Manson mess, the Black Dahlia, the Hillside Strangler, and countless others. When organized crime started to move in during the early years, however, those activities weren't limited to humans. All manner of beings wanted a piece of the exploding city, and the police were just as corrupt as the gangsters and monsters. It made the Wild West seem tame at times, but as soon as the government got involved, the nonhuman elements faded from the limelight.

Faded—but didn't disappear.

I gave Kailani a sideways glance, trying not to appear judgmental. "Look, I know the Moroi have had a hand in LA for decades. And the film industry too. Including driving the development of the porn industry in the seventies," I said as we drove. "So the fact that the Queen of the Moroi operates one of the hottest nightspots in all of Hollywood is no surprise. It makes sense that you Moroi choose heavily populated areas where you can feed inconspicuously just by being in proximity to your food source. No offense."

Kailani had made it clear that she'd apparently been around there for most of the energy vampires' tenure in the city.

"Out of curiosity, how much *does* Eisheth actually control around here?"

She inhaled and exhaled audibly. "Not as much as she used to, believe me," she said. "Back in the thirties and forties, she had her fingers in two major film studios. I even heard rumors she was involved with that mouse cartoonist guy at one point when he was building that park. She was big in the adult film stuff until the early nineties, too, but now, she mostly runs clubs and a few hotels, both here and in San Fran as far as I know. It's all technically owned by holding companies and dummy corporations and such, but it's all her behind the curtain. And no offense taken, by the way."

I nodded, mostly to myself, realizing how my comment sounded. Feeling stupid, I tried to get back to my questions. "Ah, so what should we expect for security and other... less human elements?" I asked after clearing my throat a few times.

A smile just ticked at the corner of her mouth. She was enjoying my discomfort a bit too much.

"Most of her security is human because most of the guests are human. A few unexplainable things add to the mystique, but too much puts people off. The head of her security team will be Moroi, but I'd expect at least a few of Na'amah's offspring as well. Beyond that, there could be a few Fae of either Court and possibly even an Old One if the party is particularly wild. I've seen Bacchus, Eros, and even Aphrodite at more than a few of these things. Though they'd be more likely around the time they give out all those awards. Point is, you never know."

Chapter 23

We picked up my bespoke clothes the next day. The waistcoat was a little tighter than I expected and left me no room whatsoever to carry a gun. I didn't even have a place to hide a knife. I would just have to make do without a weapon that night, which made me even more uneasy than I already was. *Talk about feeling naked.*

Kailani took nearly two hours to get ready, and when she finally appeared at the bottom of the stairs, she was a bundle of nerves. She was also drop-dead gorgeous in a tight-fitting red Japanese kimono-type gown, complete with matching gloves and heels that had to be five inches high, accentuating her long legs. For a second, I forgot to breathe.

"What, don't I look okay?" Kailani asked nervously.

I hadn't realized I was staring.

"Um... what?" I asked, trying not to stammer. "No, you look good. Ah... great. I mean beautiful." Damn, did I suck when it came to women. "You look beautiful."

She smiled and smoothed her dark hair, which she wore pulled back tightly into a bun and pinned by what looked like bright red-and-gold chopsticks. She was nervous. I couldn't imagine why. Surely, she'd done that kind of thing hundreds of times before.

"With you dressed like that, no one will even pay the slightest attention to me at all," I said, making her smile and turn slightly away while she smoothed her dress down. "I feel underdressed."

"Thanks, but you look great," she replied. "They outdid themselves."

"No, not the clothes," I said, reaching around to grab at my lower back along my waistline, desperately trying to determine if I could jam some sort of weapon in there at all without it showing too obviously. "This outfit doesn't leave me any room for a gun or even a knife."

"Oh, well you'll just have to pummel them to death if the night gets too wild," she said, rolling her eyes. "Come on, let's get going before you rip something."

"Are you carrying anything?" I asked, mostly out of paranoia.

"Where would I put it?" Kailani replied, holding her arms up to display the tightness of her dress.

"I don't know. I figured you're more used to dressing up like this than I am," I said. "I thought maybe you, you know—"

"Don't be ridiculous, Diomedes," she said then turned on a practiced heel and headed out the door.

"Ridiculous?" I said, chasing after her. "I've seen Belphoebe of the Unseelie Court pull no less than two weapons while she was stark naked. *Two*." At that point, even I realized I'd stepped into something deep and had just better shut up.

The drive to the Mondrian was cold and quiet. We pulled up in the driveway of the hotel and were quickly met by a pair of valets, each attacking a door like seagulls swarming the bait I dumped at the end of the day. I climbed out paranoid that I was going to rip something as I twisted and turned. The second Kailani rose from the car, all eyes shifted to her. Surprisingly, nobody appeared to recognize her, though. A few paparazzi were hanging around, snapping photos, presumably just in case someone of note showed up. A few pictures were taken of Kailani, but no one paid much attention to me, which was fine. A long queue stretched around the corner outside the hotel under an archway labeled Skybar. We bypassed the line and headed inside the hotel. Kailani moved with elegance, grace, and speed. I had to make an effort to keep up with her, which irritated me. We headed straight to a nondescript private elevator in the back of the lobby. When the doors opened, Kailani flashed a gold card at the operator, and we were joined by a young man and three women—at least, I hoped they were humans.

The second the elevator doors opened, the sound of club music hit me like a mace to the chest, driving the breath from me for a moment. Again, we brushed straight out through a set of doors flanked by a pair of uniformed men that looked more like doormen than bouncers, though they were wearing earpieces. We walked out into a sunken courtyard with stairs up to the pool deck and some sort of small thatched-roof structure, which I assumed would be a bar under normal circumstances, off to our right.

Actual trees, strung with lights, had been planted in the wooden deck surrounding a brightly lit pool, and the small thatched-roof building was covered by bright-pink bougainvilleas. The pool deck was open on two sides and bounded by the hotel on the other two. The two open sides had unique fake walls with a series of large windowlike openings in them, offering a view south toward Los Angeles itself. The DJ was situated on a raised stage at the crook of the two fake walls. Another set of stairs on the far side of the pool led down, and I could see people strolling up, presumably lucky enough to be chosen from the queue building down on Sunset Boulevard below.

The crowd, maybe two hundred strong, I assessed as mostly human with a sprinkling of Fae and other creatures—mostly based on movements and an occasional odd body feature that I recognized. I was sure at least three Moroi were there—a male and two females—because they moved too fluidly and touched almost every person they passed. In my experience, that was how they fed discreetly in large crowds. At least one gorgeous woman—most likely a succubus—was holding court over an unusually rapt group of young human men with features that all could have been chiseled from marble. Mixed in was at least one male elf making his way through the crowd as well. As my gaze traveled back around, I noticed Kailani had begun to attract attention, and young men and women began to swarm like sharks in a chum slick. She knew it, though, and apparently, she saw me noticing the growing tide of attention. One side of her mouth ticked up slightly into a knowing smirk, and she pursed her lower lip ever so slightly and shook her head. I could feel the back of my neck get hot, followed by my chest, and the next thing I knew, I was looking for someone to punch.

What the hell? Is this jealousy?

I turned away, my field of vision narrowing to nearly a pinpoint when something—or someone—caught my attention: an attractive blonde with very long hair down her back. Her features were pretty but severe, and she wore a lot of well-applied makeup, and from the way she moved, she clearly wasn't human, but something was familiar about her. I watched intently as she weaved among the people, looking them over like some sort of buffet.

Her ears were slightly pointed like an elf's, and she moved with the smooth, preternatural grace that only the Fae and a few other creatures could. She wore a very short white knit dress that barely contained her chest and hid very little of what was actually covered. Her long pale hair covered more of her than the cloth did. While I was trying to place her, something briefly parted the long blonde locks around the middle of her back and sent a ripple through her hair that was counter to her body's movement.

It was the tip of a cowlike tail. She was a Hulder. *Fuck. She's* the *Hulder—the one that betrayed Duma back in New York.*

Chapter 24

Someone grabbed my wrist with such force that it not only stopped me but also caused me to jerk around. The grip itself wasn't tight, but it was solid. I hadn't even realized I was walking. I shook my head and looked from my wrist to the person holding it, Kailani. The earlier jealousy and the anger at what that Hulder had done to my friend collided, and I felt a growl grow in my throat.

"Let me—"

"I figured she'd be here," Kailani said. "Don't forget she betrayed me too. But as much as she deserves it, you can't just go over and beat the crap out of her. So just calm down for a second, and play this smart. She's going to shit a kitten when she notices me anyway."

"Then try to play it down a bit so she doesn't notice you, and let's see what she does," I said, feeling the muscles in my shoulders suddenly release and the blood return to my fingers as I relaxed my fists.

"Likewise, Rambo," she said, giving me a half smile that played through her eyes as well, reinforcing the fact she was, in fact, on my team.

"Rambo was a wimp," I said, slowly pulling my arm away from her hand as I tried to melt into the crowd.

I slowly worked my way to the bar, attempting to sidle up to it the way I assumed everyone else here would, and tried to get the attention of the bartender. For the first two minutes, I thought he was just busy. After the fourth minute without service, I wondered if I was invisible, especially with all the women around me getting served. For a moment, I thought about reaching over the bar and snatching his shirt, but as I contemplated it, I saw the Hulder lounging on a chaise next to a young man whose face I recognized from TV. Then I saw Kailani, surrounded by a small throng of men, all desperately trying to get her attention. Our eyes met for an instant, and she shifted her eyes and jerked her head slightly toward the Hulder, then she laughed, probably at something someone around her said. It was fake, but it was enough to fire up the fervor of everyone near her. I sighed heavily and turned my attention back to the Hulder.

While I watched, leaning an elbow on the bar, still drinkless—not that I cared—someone walked right in front of me, partially blocking my view.

"Bartender, I'd like a gimlet, please," said the woman who blocked my view. "A ratio of eight to two to one of gin, Rose's lime, and a splash of soda would be the most proper way, I believe. I would prefer Nolet's if you have it."

Who orders a drink that precisely? I glanced at the woman to see what type of person would be that uptight. The pale blonde hair was loose around her shoulders, and the soft blue dress she wore barely covered her shapely form. Then I noticed the pointed ears.

"Stop staring, Diomedes," she said, slowly turning to face me once she had her drink. "The drink's on him," she nodded at me as I saw the solid dark color of her eyes.

"Brey," I said, almost unable to believe my eyes. "Holy—"

"Close your mouth and act civilized, please," she replied. "I am not a piece of meat."

"But... what are you doing here?" I asked, stumped by the fact I had never, ever, seen Brey outside the Metis Foundation offices, let alone dressed in anything but conservative business attire. I knew she was typically attractive for her race, but I'd never thought of her beyond being Athena's right hand.

"I do have a life outside of the Metis Foundation, Diomedes," she said. "But it has been some time since I've been to the Mondrian, I'll admit. San Diego's nightlife by comparison is dull, and I needed to blow off some steam, as you might say."

"You? Blow off steam?" I asked, suddenly skeptical.

Brey lived in a constant state of tension. She thrived on it. Something was off.

"Athena sent you, didn't she?" I eyed her sideways.

"Not entirely, no," she replied.

"Um, buddy," the bartender said behind me. "That'll be forty-five bucks for the lady's drink?"

"Wait, what? How much?"

"Nolet's is expensive gin, chief," the bartender replied in a condescending, disaffected tone. I was too distracted by Brey's appearance to care.

"You are not a cheap date," I said, pulling cash out of my pocket.

"You are correct in that I am not cheap, but I am not your date," she replied.

"It's just an expression, Brey."

In truth, her presence put me at ease, mostly because our usual banter was always brother-and-sister playful, at least on my part.

Behind her, some guy ran into another guy and spilled his drink on him when he stopped to admire the elf. For a moment, I thought Brey might make a derisive comment about the guy's behavior or maybe even his intelligence. Instead, she watched him with the same expression half the people here were looking at the other half with. Human or Fae, lust was lust. The poor guy was so embarrassed he stumbled off as fast as he could move, and Brey turned her attention back to me.

"Seriously," I asked. "That guy? And no comment about his inability to walk and think at the same time or his pathetic human dexterity or some such?"

"On the contrary," she replied. "I am not seeking a conversation. And he was very pretty and young. And among your species, young men have greater stamina."

"Okay, TMI, TMI, TMI," I said, covering my ears. "Now, I will never get this image of you out of my brain."

"Flattering, but you and I work together," she said matter-of-factly. "A sexual relationship—"

"Whoa, stop right there," I said. "Not what I was thinking. Crap, you're like my sister, Brey!"

"Not biologically possible, but I follow the logic of your sentiment," she said. "I am fond of you as well. In a familial sense."

Across the way, the Hulder was still speaking with the TV star, leaning in very close and stroking his arm lightly. And I got an idea. It wasn't nice, but I didn't care. That Hulder nearly killed Kailani and Duma. She's lucky I didn't kill her here and now.

"Brey, I have a favor to ask."

"No, I will not have sex with you," she said.

"Well, that's enough of that," I replied. "Again, not what I was thinking, Brey. Seriously."

"Oh, then what?"

"You see the blonde over there by the pool in the chaise lounge?" I said, pointing with my chin.

"The one in the see-through white knit outfit and not wearing underwear?" she asked. "The Hulder?"

"Yes, and aren't you the pot calling the kettle black?" I replied.

"But you cannot see through my dress," she said. "Besides, Hulder are Unseelie, and she is what I believe would be called a 'skank,' no?"

I laughed. "I don't know about that, but I do know she is not to be trusted. She nearly got two of my friends killed. Look, all I need you to do is go over and steal her current target."

"Won't that upset her?" she asked, appearing to be honestly confused.

"I hope so," I said. "I hope it will piss her off so much that when you lead that kid back inside the hotel that she'll follow, and I can corner her."

"Why would I lead that young man into the hotel?" She asked, again confused. "Oh, wait, I understand. It's a ruse to draw the Hulder into a trap. The boy is bait."

"Uh, yeah. You think you can do it?" I asked.

"You're asking if I think that I, an elf, can lure a human male away from a Hulder?" she said. "Hmm. I am unsure. Hulder are more sexual creatures than we elves. While I do feel I am more attractive than she, she may be able to employ wiles in which I am not well-versed. My breasts are larger, and my hips are wider, suggesting I'd make a better breeding partner in biological terms."

"Uh, yeah, sure," I replied. "I have faith in you, Brey."

"Perhaps you should get your vampire friend to act as the lure," Brey said. "She is far more accomplished at such matters, I am sure."

The fact that she knew about Kailani threw me. It shouldn't have, given her relationship with Athena, and I wasn't trying to hide my relationship with Kailani. Still, I felt a sudden pang of guilt about Sarah and what I was doing with Kailani.

"There's a problem with that scenario," I said. "They have history. In fact, the Hulder tried to kill Kailani the last time they saw each other."

"All the more reason why it would work," Brey replied. "She'd make an ideal foil."

"No, I need this to be a surprise. If she sees Kailani, she may realize something's up and bolt or raise an alarm. Better if her boy toy is poached by someone she doesn't know."

"Logical," she said. "I will do my best."

Brey sauntered over to the Hulder and the TV star with purpose. Heads turned as she walked, hips swaying, and I couldn't get over the fact that she was the same Brey from the office that I'd known and teased for the past fifty years. I felt like I was watching an entirely different person, or elf. *Damn*. There wasn't enough eye bleach in the world to make me forget what I was seeing. It was indeed a sight to see, but I felt like I was watching my sister and realizing she was actually hot. *Ugh*.

Chapter 25

After taking a moment to recompose myself, I somehow managed to get Kailani's attention. Once I did, she shot me a terse stare, and her eyes traveled from me to Brey and back several times to get her point across. I shook my head and gave her a thumbs-up then jerked my head toward the solitary doorway leading back inside the hotel.

I worked my way through the crowd, resisting the urge to just shove everyone out of the way, partially driven by the weirdness of seeing my *sister* trolling for guys and partially driven by seeing the Hulder that set my friends up. First, I had to get my hands on her, though.

I made it back into the hotel and waited until Kailani ambled through the doors. She saw me immediately, and I motioned to follow me down the hallway.

"Who was that?" she asked tersely.

"Would you believe me if I told you it was a friend from work?" I said, trying not to laugh. Sometimes the truth is just so absurd.

"Work? Seriously—"

"Cross my heart and hope to die," I said. A smile was spreading across my face. "Better still, she's going to steal that Hulder's current focus and lead them in here so we can grab her."

"Can we trust her?" Kailani asked.

"With our lives, yeah," I said.

She frowned and shrugged in acquiescence, and we waited.

"So, you're telling me that woman works for you at that foundation?" Kailani asked after a solid five minutes of silence.

"Not *for* me, but yes. And she's not exactly a woman," I replied. "She's an elf, and she's Athena's right hand."

"Well, she's still female, and she's gorgeous."

I glanced sideways at Kailani so that she wouldn't see me looking at her. She had her arms crossed across her chest and was shifting her weight from one foot to the other as we stood there. I knew the feeling exactly: insecurity, probably mixed with a little jealousy. It made me feel smug that I knew what I was looking at. In no way did my smugness have anything to do with the fact Kailani felt it for me.

After another silent five minutes of watching people come and go, stumbling around and avoiding us, Brey emerged through the doorway in what felt like slow motion, one inch at a time, boy toy in tow. She stopped once they were inside the doorway, glanced down each of the hallways until she saw me, then headed toward us. The boy toy followed like a puppy, plodding along happily as if he had good sense, clearly under the impression that his evening was about to get really interesting.

I had no intention of disappointing him.

Brey walked right up to us and stopped, and the quiescent but expectant look on the boy toy's face turned to one of genuine surprise and concern. He pulled his hand from Brey's and stood stark straight as if slapped. Then he saw Kailani, and an evil grin grew across his face.

"Not on your best night, hotshot," I said, grabbing him by his shirt front. "Now, sit still and be quiet, and you'll have plenty of time to get back out there and find your happy ending tonight." With a noticeable effort, I shoved him into the corner behind us and pushed him so that he all but fell down on his own. He cowered in the corner without saying a word, probably too shocked to think straight—maybe not even smart enough.

The moment I turned around, the Hulder came through the doors with a stride that implied a predatory purpose. She saw Brey, but before she recognized Kailani or me, we sprang, Kailani moving as fast as she could go, me trailing behind. *Way behind.* Kailani grabbed the Hulder, spun her around, and shoved her down the hallway at me, and I pinned her arm behind her and walked her toward the boy toy. Brey, Kailani, and I surrounded her as the sudden realization of who we were hit her. Her brow went from heavily creased and tented over hooded eyes, rife with anger, to shooting high onto her forehead with her eyes wide with recognition. Her mouth even dropped open.

"Hi," I said. "Long time, no see."

"Remember me, Rebekah?" Kailani asked, slapping the Hulder hard across the face. The Fae's pale skin turned a light blue in the shape of a hand across her cheek, and a bright-blue liquid dribbled from the corner of her mouth. "If I recall, you like the rough stuff."

Before Kailani could hit her again, I grabbed her arm and held on with all my strength to stop her. "Whoa, whoa, whoa. There'll be plenty of time for that later," I said as the female vampire pulled her arm roughly and easily from my grasp. "First things first. We need some information about Eisheth's whereabouts. And if you're helpful, I'll turn you over to her"—I hooked my thumb at Kailani—"instead of my good friend Duma. I'm sure you remember my Peri friend you tried to kill back in New York I say 'tried' because he survived, by the way, and I know he'd just love to see you and rekindle old acquaintances and such."

Without saying a word, the Hulder—apparently named Rebekah—spat blue blood all over my new waistcoat. I rolled my eyes in frustration and punched her in the face. She collapsed backward against the wall, banging her head, and slid down into a heap.

Apparently, some Fae are more delicate than I would have thought.

"Hey, what do you think you're doing?" the boy toy said, almost squeaking, immediately shooting to his feet in a feeble attempt at chivalry. He cleared his throat and pulled at his pants, trying to screw up his courage for further action.

"Shut up, kid," Kailani said, her eyes suddenly alive and pure black.

With the sudden change in her countenance, the boy toy staggered back until he hit the wall, and his eyes flitted around, surveying his situation. "But I'm—" he tried to say.

"Shut it," I told him then turned back to Brey. "We need someplace to talk to her," I said. "Brey, can you get us a room or something?"

"I already have one," she said, digging in her clutch and producing a key card. "Upstairs."

"Convenient," Kailani replied.

Brey glared back in confusion, completely missing the sarcasm.

Chapter 26

From somewhere outside on the deck, the all-too-familiar staccato of automatic gunfire cut through the bass and thump of the dance music, which abruptly stopped with a screech. High-pitched screams followed, interrupted by multiple short bursts of gunfire. Within seconds, people were slamming through the glass doors into the hotel and the hallways, screaming, "Shooters!" and "Guns!"

Nothing is ever simple.

Gunfire mixed with screams of both fear and agony.

I ran back to the nearest window to see what was going on. Outside on the deck, it was mass panic. People were running for the doors into the hotel, shoving and knocking others out of their way. Over the crowd of people trying to escape, I could see four heavily armed figures, two of whom were firing assault rifles into the air to incite more panic.

As I tried to get a full lay of the situation, something drew my attention to the smallest of the four gunmen. As if on cue, he turned and stared through the crowd, directly at me, making definite eye contact across the panicked mob. It was so specific that it startled me, and I jerked back slightly. Then the gunman lifted up his mask and smiled, and for the briefest of moments, the figure shifted into Nemesis. I blinked hard, and by the time I reopened my eyes, the gunman appeared as before. Then he winked and smiled again and pulled his mask back down.

"Fuck. Brey, you need to get these people out of the hallway and someplace safe before they stampede each other. And try to call nine-one-one if you can," I said.

She nodded and hurried off, weaving through the fleeing crowd with a fluid ease only possible for one of the Fae. "Kailani, I need you to get the Hulder someplace secure and stay there."

"What are you going to do?" she asked, her eyes heavily creased at the corners and her eyebrows tented on her forehead.

"Something really stupid. I have got to end that bitch."

"Wait, what?" Kailani asked.

I pushed my way through the crowd trying to fight their way into the hotel. I was like a salmon swimming upstream through winter molasses. I was elbowed, stepped on, kneed, and slapped at least a dozen different times by the time I pushed through, barely making it. All of that just served to piss me off even more. The entire time, I could hear random gunfire from just outside over the screams and shouts of scared and panicked people.

Once on the deck, I moved to my left among a row of small trees and tables that overlooked both the pool and the sunken patio. Three bodies were floating face down, the brightly lit teal water turning crimson around them. Another half a dozen people were lying on the deck, unmoving, while at least another dozen prone people were crawling and pulling themselves along, many trailing blood as they clambered for safety. People hid and took cover behind anything and everything, even other people. The four gunmen were the only ones standing, and I could now see three carried heavy assault rifles and were dressed in body armor. The smallest one—the one I was sure was Nemesis—was armed with an automatic pistol, and he pointed and screamed at the other gunmen as if in charge.

One of the shooters stood at the top of the stairs leading out to the main sidewalk entrance below, while another walked slowly and deliberately into the pool-house bar across from me. Fortunately, the mass of bodies trying to push into the hotel through the deck entrance was ignored for the moment.

The gunman in charge glanced over his shoulder at a shooter changing out his magazine and jerked his head toward the crowd at the doors and pointed at them. The third shooter on the deck was being slow and deliberate as he changed out a back-to-back banana-style magazine, then, at the direction of the lead gunman, he strolled toward the mass of people trying to fit through the doors into the hotel.

It was going to be a bloodbath if I didn't stop him immediately. Like the others, that shooter was wearing some sort of body armor on his torso, and once he had the rifle reloaded, he pulled an automatic pistol from a holster on his left hip. I couldn't tell by their encumbered movement if any of them were anything other than human, but the fact they were using guns suggested they were more than likely mundane.

Back at the doorway into the hotel, things had bogged down. The sounds of more automatic gunfire split the air from inside the poolside bar, followed by more screams. I didn't have time to figure out a plan or worry about being mundane. I suppose I should've been more concerned about helping the people, but I was focused on Nemesis. I didn't know what I could do to her as a human, but I was still a highly trained soldier.

I jumped the railing down to the sunken patio and bolted across to tackle the strolling gunman as he leveled the heavy assault rifle at the bottlenecked and panicking crowd. Just managing to blindside him before he noticed me, I hit him hard enough to knock him off his feet, and we tumbled across the fake grass until we hit a wicker chaise lounge. I pushed myself up, grabbed him by his vest, and slammed his head into the ground—repeatedly, until blood pooled under his head. I didn't have time to be gentle or worry about the fucker's rights. I still had two other gunmen and Nemesis to deal with.

The instant I felt the first gunman go limp in my hands, I pulled his rifle free and brought it to bear on the shooter blocking the main entrance stairway and keeping watch on the street down below. Relying on skills developed over centuries rather than strength and speed, I put two rounds into the gunman's shoulder and two more in his hip, knocking him to the ground and sending his rifle skittering across the deck. He rolled over clumsily and tried to pull a pistol from a holster on his hip, but I put two more rounds into his head before he could finish.

I quickly turned to my right and saw the lead shooter I was sure was actually Nemesis, pistol in hand, standing on the pool deck, less than twenty feet in front of me. Gunfire erupted from the enclosed cabana bar behind him, followed by screams of panic and terror.

I drew down, ready to open fire on him when, in the span of a single step, the shooter once again shifted from a masculine figure dressed in fatigues to a feminine figure dressed in white robes with dirty brown wings folded behind her, back to the fatigue-clad gunman. When I refocused on him, he was staring directly at me. In my momentary hesitation, the gunman lowered his pistol and took a few steps toward me.

"There you are," he said.

"Nemesis?" I asked, trying to make sense of what I'd seen. I wasn't used to being uncertain.

"I told you I would make you suffer," the gunman said.

Nemesis.

"What the hell did these people do to deserve this?" I screamed.

"This is your fault, Diomedes," Nemesis said in a low, calm voice as her persona walked to the edge of the deck.

"If you've got a beef with me, then settle it with me," I said. "Just you and me. No innocent bystanders."

"Like you, these people are *not* innocent," she said, gesturing at the carnage around us.

Every survivor was watching us.

"But they are under your protection, and so they will suffer to make you suffer until you realize that you are an affront to the natural order of things in this world. All I asked for was one simple task, but no..."

Gunfire erupted from the cabana bar again, followed by prolonged screams of panic and pain. And then a body came flying out of the poolside bar and landed like a rag doll on the pool deck a few yards to Nemesis' left, rifle clattering across the fake turf. The goddess of retribution started at the sound and turned to see what had caused the commotion.

That was my window.

Chapter 27

Dropping the rifle, I raced up the stairs to the pool deck and tackled Nemesis. To my surprise, she went limp, but I didn't stop to analyze the situation. I knelt over her prone gunman form and grabbed her by the armor-plate-carrier vest her visage wore and raised her head slightly off the ground. She didn't even try to resist but simply smiled at me. That pissed me off even more. Without a second thought, I began punching. I knew, as a mortal, I could do almost no damage to her. Heck, even with Athena's help, I would've needed one of my supernatural weapons to really injure her, but that didn't stop me from swinging with everything I had.

From somewhere in the distance, I could just hear the muffled sounds of people screaming again, which only served to anger me even more. I continued to punch, but Nemesis' smile didn't diminish. I could feel the disconnected rumble of a growl in my chest as I swung. Then something dawned on me. I glanced back at the two gunmen I'd killed. *Humans. Just humans. What if she was controlling them, and I'd killed innocent, deceived humans?*

"Are these men under your control?" I asked, growling through clenched teeth. "Did you trick them into doing this?" She smiled again, and I began punching again, more frenzied, howling with each blow.

Then, over my bellowing, I heard someone calling my name—not Steve, but Diomedes. A hand lightly grabbed my shoulder, and I rose up and spun around, ready to attack whoever had grabbed me. Kailani was staring at me, her eyes solid black and wide. I jerked back.

"Now! Get out of here before the police get here," she was saying. "Please, go now. I'll take care of her, but you need to get out of here. What the hell were you thinking?" She began pushing at me, shoving me off Nemesis.

What?

"Everyone is watching you, Diomedes," she said, shoving hard at my shoulder. "Get out of here right now."

My eyes traveled to the faces of the survivors around the pool. All of them were fixed on me. They were horrified, but I didn't know if it was at me or the senseless carnage they had witnessed. Then I noticed the cell phones aimed at me.

This is not good.

Slowly, I raised myself and began to stagger around, hands stiff and swollen, trying to regain my bearings, searching every horrified face, each fixed on me as if I was one of the shooters I'd saved them from. I shook my head. Kailani knelt over Nemesis, tending to her as if she was an injured person. Suddenly, she stood up and faced me.

"She's not human," Kailani said with her inky eyes wide.

"No shit," I replied. "That's Nemesis. She's behind this." My eyes traveled across the carnage, including the two gunmen I'd killed. For a second, I couldn't breathe.

"Well, it *looked* like you were beating the crap out of an innocent woman," Kailani said. "But her energy is definitely not human. You'd better just get the hell out of here."

On the ground, I saw Nemesis in a flash under her gunman visage, smiling at me with perfect teeth through undamaged lips. She didn't even have a blemish on her face. Without my swords or the Pelian Spear, and without Athena's help, I could do nothing to an Old One. And I was the only one there who knew who she really was. Everyone else just saw me beating some person. *And I'm sure she's manifesting the visage of a severely beaten person.*

As the world coalesced around me again, I could hear sirens increase in volume and number around the building, and somewhere in the near distance, the beating of helicopter blades rattled like a continually backfiring engine. Kailani was right. I needed to get out of there fast.

"Go," Kailani said in a terse, low voice, "Now. Meet me at my place when you can." She pointed toward the building's south facade, the one with the faux walls overlooking LA's skyline.

Then I recalled Rebekah. *If Kailani is here, then who's watching her?*

"Where's Rebekah?" I asked, taking stock of my surroundings.

"I had to let her go," she replied. "I thought you could use my help, so I made a decision. I'm sorry."

Anger filled my brain, and I could feel it welling up in my chest.

"Dammit! She was our best shot at finding Eisheth," I said with a growl.

"We can argue about my decision later, but right now, you really need to get out of here," she pleaded, her eyes wide and her eyebrows tightly knitted on her forehead.

The sirens were louder. She was right. I screamed, took a deep breath, then jogged over to an overturned table beneath the series of fake windows along a faux wall and surveyed the buildings and streets below. I was only a few stories up, and the alley below was narrow but already glowing with flashing red and blue lights as police cars and SUVs pulled in. Guns drawn, cops swarmed the alley, approaching apparent victims. Across the alley, less than twenty-five feet away, was the brown shingled roof of an apartment building two stories lower than where I stood. It would have been an easy jump for me before, but now, it was going to hurt.

The sirens continued to screech, and cops poured over the outdoor space on the rooftop behind me. I stepped back, took a few quick breaths, steeled my nerves, then ran for the window opening and jumped. Miraculously, I covered the distance, and while I tried to tuck and roll as I hit, the impact drove my knees into my chest and forced the air from my lungs before I tumbled uncontrollably down the apartment roof and flopped into the swimming pool below. Catching my breath took a few long moments, and I was grateful the pool wasn't so deep that I couldn't stand up. I forced myself to get moving again, clambering out of the pool clumsily on ankles, knees, and hips that were all screaming in pain but fortunately unbroken. I limped and crept along alleys and around buildings as quickly but quietly as I could go without drawing attention to myself. Slowly, the sounds of sirens and helicopters faded behind me, and I eventually found myself on Melrose Avenue, which I knew ran east almost all the way to Silver Lake, so I just walked—gingerly.

The time was very late as I walked past Pink's Hot Dogs, which was doing a brisk business despite the time of night. I eventually made my way past Paramount Pictures and Raleigh Studios. By the time I got to the 101 Freeway, my phone rang. It was Brey.

Thank the gods they make these waterproof now.

"Brey, is everything alright?" I asked. "Did you make it out okay?"

"Yes, Kailani and I are fine," she said. "I found her and called one of our assets in the LAPD, a Perelesnyk named Stefan. His race is particularly adept at convincing humans to do simple, agreeable things. He collected all the cell phones and is, how shall I say... leading... some of the statements about what happened. Eleven people were killed and twenty-four more were injured, six seriously. The carnage would've been much worse if you and Kailani hadn't acted. Three of the gunmen are indeed dead and accounted for, but the fourth is still at large. Diomedes, they think it's you. They think you escaped after beating up a woman, who also happens to be unaccounted for."

"That wasn't a woman," I said. "It was Nemesis. She was also the fourth gunman."

"That's what Kailani was saying. I will do everything I can to make sure your involvement is obfuscated as much as possible, but please maintain a low profile for as long as you can," the elf said. Her voice seemed to betray the slightest hint of concern as she spoke. "Oh, it appears the Hulder is gone, by the way."

"Will do," I said. "And I know, but thanks. Any way you can let the boss know I need her help to finish this mess with Nemesis and help Sarah? I'm not sure how effective I can be without her support."

"Given your prior connection, I am sure she is well aware of your intentions. She does not approve of your course of action, and you are not behaving as yourself, so I doubt it. But please endeavor to keep yourself safe, Diomedes," she said, then the phone clicked off.

As I walked, I thought about Kailani letting Rebekah go. Duma was going to be pissed that she slipped through our fingers. And I was pretty damn sure that the Hulder would head straight to Eisheth with the information that we were after her. The fact that she knew made no difference. I would get to her. Then a sudden realization hit me: Kailani helped me. To help me, it meant she'd had to feed again. She'd sacrificed everything she'd been hiding from to help me.

I stared down without really focusing on anything until I noticed the dark-blue stain on my waistcoat where Rebekah had spat on me. Instantly, my spirits buoyed. With her blood, we could track her, so if she did run back to Eisheth, she would lead us right to her. I began to jog—slowly. It hurt. A lot. So instead, I lumbered as fast as I could. I made it back to Kailani's place in Silver Lake just before dawn, tired and in considerable pain.

I am thirty-two hundred years old, and for the first time in my life, I'm feeling every day of it.

Chapter 28

Kailani opened the door before I could knock.

"Well, that was a special kind of clusterfuck, wasn't it?" she said, ushering me in with the wave of a hand. She was wearing a robe and showing a lot of leg.

"Yeah, well, this thing with Nemesis has got to end," I replied. "We can't fight on two fronts at the same time. But... all might not be lost." I waved my hand in front of my blue-stained waistcoat as though what I was thinking was obvious.

"Wow, that was fast," she said. "You ruined that in one night. No wonder you dress like you normally do. No point in wasting money on good clothes for you."

I shook my head and scrunched up my face. "No! Well, uh, yeah, but the point is it's Rebekah's blood. We can track her with it. If she runs back to Eisheth, then we'll know exactly where she is."

She gave me a pensive look and rocked her head back and forth for a moment as she thought. "Okay, so how does it work?"

"You don't know anybody that can track someone using a pendulum and their blood?" I asked.

Her face went blank, and she shrugged. "Not me. Hell, I'm not even the kind of vampire that *drinks* blood. And I have no earthly clue how to get Hulder blood out of clothing. That thing is ruined." She put her hands on her hips, shook her head, and sucked at her teeth.

"Enough with the damn waistcoat," I said, holding my hands up. "I know Duma can do it as long as it's fresh enough."

"Fresh? You smell like you've been swimming in a community pool," she said, wrinkling her nose. "You reek of chlorine."

I sighed heavily and sat down even more heavily in an armchair. Kailani immediately grabbed my arm and pulled me up, noticeably stronger.

"Uh-uh. You need to clean up first," she said, her grasp on my forearm strong and viselike without being rough.

That's when it hit me again. She was avoiding feeding to stay off the Moroi grid and regain some semblance of her former life. She'd given that up to help me. Part of me wanted to say her actions were stupid—I could handle myself, and three mundane gunmen presented very little threat to me, even as a mundane myself. But dozens of innocent bystanders had been there, and she'd saved many by acting. She wasn't just helping me. I pulled her close and hugged her, unsure what else I could do or say to thank her. Frankly, I was scared I would just screw it up if I opened my mouth. My action surprised her at first, but then she returned the gesture, and I allowed myself to wonder if that was what normal people did and felt. Somehow, I realized that, given all I had been through and seen in my life, if I didn't stop to thank those that helped and cared, then everything was for naught anyway.

The phone in my pocket rang.

"So, I saw you had a party at the Mondrian last night," Duma said, his grin audible. "I swear, I leave you alone for one day, and everything goes to hell."

"It was Nemesis," I replied, "but it gets worse."

"Worse?" Duma said with a laugh. "You're alive, so how bad could it have been? News reports say three of the gunmen were killed, one escaped, and one victim disappeared. Descriptions of the two still missing are totally off-the-wall crazy—short, tall, fat, skinny, blond, redhead. Was everyone there high or just drunk?"

"Neither. Fairy influence, thankfully. But trust me, I mean worse," I said.

"Well, thankfully, it wasn't my hotel this time," he said.

"Yeah, well, we ran into an old friend of yours."

"Aw hell, to be honest, I probably know most everyone who regularly goes to the Skybar at the Mondrian," he said.

"Rebekah."

"Rebekah, let me think..." he said. "Nope, not ringing any bells. You got a last name?"

"Your Hulder friend from Cocytus," I said softly.

The line was silent for a minute except for static.

"When you say 'ran into,' you mean repeatedly, with your car, right?" he asked, his voice flat over the phone.

"No, but we did grab her," I replied. "She got away when the gunmen started shooting."

Again, a long silence stretched over the line.

"She works with Eisheth," I said finally. "When we go after her, I bet anything we'll find Rebekah."

I heard him inhale sharply over the phone. "Whatever," he replied. "Meantime, I can tell you Eisheth is probably not here in Shanghai. Not enough security, although we can't be completely sure. I don't think she's in hiding, though."

"Okay, just see what you can find out then. Meantime, I have to deal with Nemesis first somehow. I can't risk having an Old One pop up in the middle of an assault on the Mother of the Moroi. Last time I tried something like that—"

"Yeah, well, last time you didn't have me and Ab with you," he said. "We'll recon and report until you say otherwise. But just so you know, if that Hulder bitch shows up, she's mine. And I won't argue with you about it."

The tone of his voice when he made that last statement sent shivers down my spine, and I actually felt sorry for Rebekah for a second.

Then I recalled seeing Duma wrapped in chains and beaten to within an inch of his life, Sarah in her comatose state, and Kailani's battered body dumped unceremoniously in the middle of the street—all, in part, thanks to her. My blood boiled, and I found myself wishing that my primal side had won out back at the Mondrian. *Even at my worst, I could never be as brutal as Duma. She is going to get what she deserves.*

"I won't," I said and went to hang up, but before I did, I heard Duma say one more thing.

"Hey, did you ever wonder how Nemesis keeps finding you in all these random locations?" Duma asked. "Food for thought." Then he hung up.

At first, I didn't think much about his comment, given that Nemesis was an Old One. I just chalked it up to her being super knowledgeable. The truth was she was a *weak* Old One, and while in her heyday, she might have known the hearts and intentions of every human, I had no idea what she was capable of at this point in time. *Could she locate me using some sort of telepathy, or is she relying on more mundane methods to do her dirty work like back at the Mondrian?* If it was the latter, then I wondered how—or *who*.

My eyes traveled to Kailani. *No. No way.* My head reeled, and I had to sit down again. The thought had me so off balance that I nearly missed the chair and had to reach for its arm to make sure I didn't fall.

"Are you okay?" Kailani asked me, quickly kneeling next to me rather than stopping me. "Who was that on the phone?"

I needed a moment to recompose myself. All I could do was think of all the times Nemesis had shown up. With the exception of the hospital in Pennsylvania, Nemesis and Kailani had always showed up at the same places. *No. It has to be a coincidence.* Thinking about it, I realized it was too obvious. I should have seen that possibility sooner—back in Hawaii, Moldova, and now here. Those places were too random for Nemesis to know about unless—

No.

"Diomedes, are you okay?"

I looked at her, but I couldn't focus. *Am I blissfully blind? Am I refusing to see what has been clearly right in front of me, or am I being paranoid?* I had to remind myself that I've survived for as long as I have because of my paranoia.

Kailani's face came into focus.

"Hey, are you okay?"

I had to find out, and if I was smart about it, I could find out in a way that I could use to my advantage. *And if I'm wrong, maybe she'll forgive me.*

"Yeah," I replied. "I'm okay. Just more bad news from Duma, and I haven't eaten in a while. Plus, I'm sore as hell. I'm sure that's all it is."

"So, that was Duma on the phone?" she asked. "What did he say that was so bad?"

"Um, oh, he said Eisheth wasn't there in Shanghai and that her place was a fortress," I said. And my brain went into overdrive trying to think of a way to expose Kailani if she was a mole. "We're going to have to meet up someplace safe to come up with a plan."

Phone still in hand, I texted Duma: "On second thought, Abu's Playground, in 48 hours. Expect company, so bring me some toys too."

"Who are you texting?" Kailani asked. I couldn't tell if she was concerned or just being nosy.

"Duma," I replied. "I told him I need to disappear for a bit, make a plan. I'm going to go to Gara Medouar and hole up for a day or two by myself. No one will find me there."

"Gara what?" she asked, shrugging.

"It's an abandoned fort in the Sahara outside of Erfoud in Morocco," I said.

"You want me to come too?" Kailani asked, holding out one hand, a look of genuine concern on her face. "You're starting to show your age now that you're mortal."

Her concern gave me pause. *Maybe I'm jumping to conclusions and being paranoid. Maybe she's just a good actress.*

"No, I'll contact you to let you know where to meet us," I said, trying to motivate myself into action. "I'll be fine."

Chapter 29

I left Kailani's house feeling numb, and I had no idea how I was going to get to the nearest pathway through the Ways—or through them, since I was mundane, for that matter. Halfway down the block my phone rang. It was Duma.

"Abu's Playground?" he asked. "Seriously?"

"Yeah."

"What about—"

"I can handle her," I said with a groan. My legs ached horribly, and I twisted myself around slowly, trying to stretch. Parts of me popped and snapped like a bag of popcorn in a microwave.

"You sure? 'Cause she's bad news," he said.

"I'm sure. Just bring me some firepower. I want to end this thing with Nemesis now."

"Done. See you in Morocco."

I hung up and began walking, continuing to work the kinks out. By the end of the block, I got the feeling I was being followed. *Just what I need—to be jumped by vampires.* In no mood—or condition—to deal with parasitic scum, I walked into the middle of the street. A dark-green Prius pulled up to me and stopped, but it couldn't have been going more than five miles an hour anyway. I ducked slightly, immediately wishing I hadn't, to see who—or what—was behind the wheel, and involuntarily jerked back upright when I saw it was Brey. *Ow, that really hurt.*

"Get in." Her voice was muffled through the closed windows as she waved me over. "Quickly, please."

I lumbered over to the passenger-side door with my hand on my lower back and *carefully* lowered myself into the seat, which was not as comfortable as the car's looks implied.

"I think Duma feeds his cars these things for breakfast," I said, looking at the austere interior.

"I chose it because it leaves less of an impact on the environment, Diomedes," she said, taking off with a surprising start. "Its looks were not a consideration."

I just cocked my head to one side and shrugged slightly at her comment. "Okay," I said with a groan. "So, you just happened to be driving around Kailani's neighborhood way the hell out of your way after a late night of clubbing?"

"No, I specifically came here to gather you," she said.

Seeing her at the Mondrian surprised me almost as much as seeing her speeding and blowing through stop signs despite her almost fanatical penchant for following rules.

"How did—"

"Athena texted me the address and told me you'd be on the sidewalk headed south," she said and swerved around a corner so tightly that the rear tire jumped the curb.

"Whoa, Andretti, take it easy," I said. "After three thousand years, I'd hate to die in a traffic accident. In a Prius."

"But there is no traffic," Brey replied. "I assume you mean in an automobile accident." She eventually merged onto the freeway, heading back toward San Diego, weaving around the cars we did encounter as if they were standing still.

"Well, I'll be," I said, holding firmly onto the handrail above the door. "I didn't think these things could go quite this fast."

"Oh, they are quite efficient and very peppy," she said. "They can go zero to sixty in ten seconds."

I had to focus on her driving because if I stopped to look at her, dressed like she was, I would have felt sicker. Once we settled into traffic, I was able to relax a bit. "Um, so why did Athena send you to pick me up?"

"I didn't ask," she replied. "I obviously incorrectly assumed you knew."

"All I know is I need to get to Gara Medouar, but I need to stop by Hart Island first."

"Well, that's easily enough done," she said, swerving into the far-right lane to take a rapidly approaching off-ramp.

While her driving skills were suspect, she clearly knew where she was headed. That made one of us. "Again, I hate to break your concentration when you're driving, but where are we headed now?"

"Ah, well if you need to get to Hart Island in New York, then the fastest way is through the Ways—obviously—and the nearest gateway is just east of LA. From there, you'll head to your usual spot in Mexico and then to upstate New York. And then back to the City. From there, I am sorry to say, you're on your own."

"I don't even have a Way Stone, and I'm not sure the Ways are going to work for me in my current state."

We swerved around two cars and cut between two more so quickly that I had to grab the handrail with both hands, nearly pulling it loose in the process.

"One piece, Brey! One piece!" I screamed. "I'd like to arrive in one piece!"

"I am in complete control, Diomedes. My reflexes are much quicker than a human's."

"Yeah, but your car isn't built for response and performance," I said, quickly bracing one hand on the dashboard as we cut between two more cars. I had to squeeze my eyes shut at the last second, preparing for a horrific crunch, but it never came. I warily opened one eye to see us still speeding along, fortunately in one piece.

"I am sorry to say I hadn't thought about the problem with you traveling through the Ways now," Brey said. "I cannot take you through myself. Perhaps an airport?"

My spirit sank at the mention of the word. I hadn't been on more than a dozen commercial flights since the Wright brothers flew at Kitty Hawk, and I was faced with taking my second transcontinental flight in just a few days. And to make matters more complicated, I'd left my fake passport at Kailani's. *This whole thing with Nemesis is going to get me killed if I don't get in front of it soon.*

"Get me home. I'll get to the airport in San Diego and figure it out from there."

She nodded and hit the gas as we headed south.

Chapter 30

Back at my house in Roseville on Point Loma, I showered, chewed a handful of ibuprofen, and drank about a gallon of water before packing a small duffel with a change of clothes. I couldn't bring weapons, not even knives, on board the plane, so I was counting on Duma to provide me with everything I needed. Plus, he still had most of my gear from Moldova anyway.

Throwing things into my bag, I heard a knock at the door, which threw me. The time was just about noon, so I knew it wasn't Strigoi, but they wouldn't knock anyway. I grabbed my Sig P226 off my dresser and walked over to peer out the peephole.

"It's me, Diomedes," St. Germain said, smiling broadly at the peephole like it was a camera. "I've come to help you get to Morocco."

I pulled the door open and shoved the Sig into my waistband in the small of my back. "How the hell—"

"Well, most of what they say about me isn't true," he said with a shrug. "But I am, in fact, an ascended master with access to the accumulated knowledge of the universe." His statement was off-the-cuff and without ego.

I stepped back and let him in. "So then, how are you going to help me get to Morocco? You know some arcane way to get me through the Ways?"

"Nah, simpler than that," he said with a smile. "I have a private jet over at Montgomery Field. I figured I have to get to Hart Island, too, then you can take the jet to Morocco from there."

Well, a private jet is a step up, at least.

"Oh. Well, let me grab my bag, and we can get moving, then."

"Excellent, I told the Uber driver to wait," he said, sitting on the arm of my couch.

We landed at La Guardia at seven in the evening, taxied around to a private area at the far western end of the runway, and walked down to a dock on Flushing Bay, where an old center console boat that had seen better days sat waiting for us.

"You're the experienced waterman," St. Germain said as we climbed aboard. He was carrying a small high-end aluminum briefcase. "Hart Island is a few miles that way." He pointed absently to the northeast as he sat in one of the rickety seats behind the console.

The run out to Hart Island took about an hour, and we made it to the dock on the west side of the island without incident. The walk to the hospital from there took only a few minutes.

Walking toward the hospital's entrance, I felt sick to my stomach but somewhat hopeful. Part of me wished I could walk in to find Sarah sitting up, grousing about wanting to leave already. The rest of me knew that wasn't likely. I had avoided coming before then for purely selfish reasons—I couldn't bear to see Sarah lying there comatose, her psyche damaged, possibly irreparably, because of her encounter with a fallen angel and my ineptitude. I got regular reports about her condition from newly named Brother Justicar Bartholomew, or Jonesy as I knew him first. No discernable change in her condition had been observed since they took her there months before.

St. Germain walked easily and carelessly beside me, carrying the briefcase. "I will need a few minutes alone with Sarah, if that's okay with you," he said as we approached the reception desk. I didn't respond.

The green-haired young woman behind the desk was dressed in white scrubs with a bright-red cross embroidered on the left side of the chest. Her entire left arm was covered in tribal tattoos. She seemed more than a little surprised by our presence, probably because the Holy Order tried to give the impression that the place was abandoned rather than a hospital for those affected by demonic influences.

"We're here to see—"

"Diomedes." A heavily accented male voice came from behind us. "So very good to see you again, my friend."

I turned to see the tall, lanky blond kid I'd met back when he was the coadjutor novice to Brother Justicar Bartholomew before we fought Ramiel at the Gates of Hell last year. He was dressed in a simple white cassock, his arms thrown wide in a genuinely friendly greeting, with his right arm in a cast from the elbow down.

"Oh, pay no attention to this," the kid I'd first met as Jonesy said with a dismissive smile. "I'm sure you can imagine where it came from."

I smiled back, but it was half-hearted. I was sincerely glad to see the kid who'd helped me kill the Watcher, Ramiel. Hell, he might even have saved my life. But I didn't like being there. I would rather have seen him in battle than at the hospital.

Before I could take a step forward, he was on me, hugging me like we were the oldest and dearest of friends. "So very good to see you again."

"Good to see you, too, Jonesy, or is it Brother Justicar Bartholomew?" I asked.

"For you, it will always be Jonesy," he replied, his smile wide and genuine. "You look different. Older, perhaps. Morose. Why, my friend? We are taking very good care of her."

"I know." I couldn't meet his gaze any longer, friendly though it was. I felt guilty—guilty Sarah was there at all and doubly guilty about my relationship with Kailani while she lay there comatose. I was unworthy of Sarah, unworthy of being Athena's emissary, and unworthy of the respect Jonesy showed me.

"Would you like to see her?" he asked.

I just nodded and stared at the ground. *I owe Sarah that much, at least.* "Oh, and this is, um..." I gestured toward St. Germain, unsure how to introduce him.

"My name is Dr. Michael Psellos, from the University of Constantinople," St. Germain said, shifting into an odd Eastern European accent, holding out his hand to Jonesy with a slight bow of his head.

"Psellos," Jonesy said, taking his hand. "Sounds familiar. Have we met before?"

"No, I do not believe we have," St. Germain said with a frown. "But I have heard of you and your exploits with the Order, good Knight."

"Well, I am only doing God's work," Jonesy replied. "And any friend of Diomedes is welcome here," Jonesy said, waving his unbroken hand at me. "It is an honor to meet you, and welcome to Hart Island. If you'll follow me, I will lead you to Ms. Wright's room."

So unworthy.

Chapter 31

Sarah's room was a spartan whitewashed hospital room with all the creature comforts of a monk's cell—down to the only decoration being a crucifix over the head of the bed. She didn't even have a window, just a fucking fluorescent light over the crucifix. A constant whooshing interspersed with an electronic beep were the only noises, which made the environment feel even more sterile.

Sarah lay on a bed at the center of the room, amid a host of machines, monitors, tubes, and wires. Her eyes were sunken and closed with dark rings around them. She had a tube taped into her mouth, her lips were pale, almost colorless, and her hair was significantly longer than I remembered. Someone had pulled it into a loose bundle and put it over her shoulder. At least the red color she'd changed it to back in New York had almost grown out—it was mostly back to her normal brunette. She had a pair of electrodes stuck to her temples, and a riot of colorful wires emerged from her gown at the sleeve and connected to several other machines. If not for the beeping monitor next to her showing her brain function, pulse, oxygen levels, blood pressure, and who knows what else, I wouldn't have believed she was even alive. *She's so still.*

My eyes welled up, and I didn't know where to look. I felt a hand on my shoulder.

"I'll give you some time," St. Germain said, patting my shoulder.

The door squeaked closed behind me.

I couldn't do anything but stare.

My fault.

I wanted to believe those beeps were telling me that, somewhere in her mind, she was fighting to get out. She was one of the strongest people I'd ever met. She would never give up.

And she wouldn't want me to, either.

There is no way I'm going to let her down again.

I wiped my eyes and nose with the back of my hand and went to find St. Germain. He was standing right outside the door, leaning on the wall.

"You can help her, right?" I asked, barely able to get the words out.

"I have a solution," he said with a consolatory smile. "*You* can help her. But it won't be easy."

"Fuck easy," I said, blinking tears away.

One of the nurses in the hall fumbled her paperwork at my statement.

"Give me a few minutes with her to set the vibration of these crystals to her frequency, and we can go," he said in a whisper, holding up the briefcase.

"Okay, I need to speak to Jonesy again anyway."

"There is no need," he said.

"Yeah, there is," I replied. "The Order has something I need."

"They have something you can *use*, but I'm telling you you don't need it," he said, shaking his head.

"How do you—"

"Must I explain it to you again?" he asked, rolling his eyes. "Repository of all human knowledge here. Trust me. You don't need it."

"Fine, I'll meet you at the front desk when you're done," I said, walking back up the hallway.

In the quiet stillness of the night, every room I passed held a scene similar to Sarah's, all just as bleak and hopeless. The only thing different was the person at the center: old, young, male, female.

Anyone who doubts the existence of evil in this world is insane.

I managed to find the front desk and a lone plastic-and-metal chair down the hall. I sat, hunched over, elbows on knees, trying desperately not to think about Sarah, but rather what was coming next to help her.

St. Germain had better be telling me the truth.

"Ah, Diomedes," Jonesy said, coming up the hallway toward me, hands behind his back and a smile on his face. "Is everything okay with Ms. Wright? Is there anything you would like us to do for her?"

I just shook my head. "I think I have a way to help her," I said. "I hope. Saint... um ... Dr. Psellos says he does anyway."

"Well, we will continue to do everything we can, especially praying for her," Jonesy said. "And you, of course."

"These days, I'll take all the help I can get," I replied.

"You look like a man who is desperate," Jonesy said. "Whatever you believe, Diomedes, do not forget to believe in yourself. And do not forget who you are. There is a poster in one of the break rooms here that says, 'Be the kind of person that when your feet hit the floor, the devil says, "Oh crap, they're up."' I've always felt that it was silly and maybe a little trite. Most of us fight little battles—important ones but little nonetheless. But you... Remember this world is a safer place for people because you are in it." His Scandinavian accent became thicker the more he spoke. "Don't be so rash in your actions that you make the devil laugh instead of cringe."

I raised my head enough to see him out of the corner of my eye. Part of me wanted to tell him to shut the fuck up, and part of me understood his not-so-subtle point. I just nodded and rubbed my hands as they hung between my knees. The scars, callouses, and thick knuckles made my hands feel and look old. For a moment, they didn't even feel like they were mine. *The damage they have caused over the millennia. How much of it made a real difference?*

"I am going to do something for you even the devil won't, my friend," Jonesy said. "I am going to leave you alone. Please take care of yourself." With that, he walked down the hall and disappeared around a corner.

I sat in silence for a while until I suddenly felt claustrophobic and needed some air, so I went outside and headed out to the dock where our boat was tied up. To my surprise, the sun was just breaking above the horizon at the far end of the Sound. I'd lost all track of time. Off in the distance in the fiery orange morning light, birds were diving at the water's surface as a few random splashes kicked up below them. Within a few seconds, the water erupted as fish, likely bluefish, began blitzing bait, sending the diving birds into a full-on frenzy. I watched, wishing I had a fly rod for just a second. But like so many things in this world, the likely bluefish blitz was over as fast as it had begun.

I just need to get Nemesis out of the way, then I can focus on going after Eisheth to help Sarah.

Chapter 32

I turned back to stare at the aging brick facade of the hospital, trying to determine where Sarah's room was, given her lack of a window. The truth was that I hadn't paid enough attention, but I could still hear the beeping of the machines and the whooshing of the ventilator in my head.

Whatever it takes, I am going to help her.

As the sun inched higher in the sky, I stood scouring the water for other signs of life—breaking fish, birds, maybe a dolphin—though I saw nothing but the pewter-gray water. At some point, the crunching of footfalls behind me drew my attention from the horizon.

"Did you do what you needed to with Sarah?" I asked.

"It's done," St. Germain replied. "So, if you're ready, we'll go back to the airport, and you can take the jet to Africa from there."

The ride back across the bay was quiet. I could tell St. Germain was giving me space. As we neared the old dock, I throttled back and kicked the steering wheel hard over and jammed the throttle briefly in reverse to slow our approach. I quickly moored the boat and hopped out—a maneuver that was harder than I expected since I was just a man again. St. Germain was right behind me.

"Back there, you said I didn't need what I wanted to get from *Pugnus Dei*. You said you had something instead?" I asked. I was doubtful and was sure that doubt was expressed on my face.

St. Germain cocked his head and held out the briefcase and nodded at it. I took it, once again marveling at how heavy everything felt since I was mundane. "I thought this was for the crystals."

"That's a big briefcase," he said with a smile. "I bet it could hold a bunch of stuff along with those crystals. You're going to have to trust me, Diomedes. It's the only way this works. Just tell the captain where you want to go, and he'll take care of everything."

"What about you?" I asked. "Don't you—"

"I'm good," he said with a wave of his hand. "I'm going to go see a friend in the City for a few days." He started to walk along the water's edge. "Oh, and you should listen to your friend Jonesy. Don't lose sight of who you are in all of this, Diomedes."

"How do you know—"

"Repository of all knowledge, Diomedes," he said without looking back. "I know everything."

I sighed heavily and headed to the jet.

After telling the pilot to head to Mohammad V International Airport in Morocco, I settled in and opened the case St. Germain had given me. Inside was a smaller watertight black plastic case and several file folders. One of the folders was labeled "What to do with these crystals," and the other simply read "Ttab'a," but it had a pink sticky note on its cover that read "Knowledge is always more powerful than objects." I placed the case on the seat next to me and opened the latter folder.

Inside was a sheaf of papers topped by a weathered old piece of parchment with faded writing on it. Much of it was hard to make out, but I could tell immediately that it was written in ancient Syriac. It was an account of the fallen angel Ttab'a as she was brought in front of King Solomon, directly followed by an account of her meeting with the Prophet of Islam. In both were long lists of names, but someone had long before made notations next to the ones spoken to the Prophet. I tried to make out as much of the text as I could, but my Syriac was rusty, and the writing was very faded. In frustration, I flipped to the pages that followed—modern lined paper like a schoolkid would use, covered with handwritten notes in black ink.

It began, "If you would have just flipped to this page first, you would have saved yourself a headache." And it was signed "El Sabelotodo." I couldn't help shaking my head. *Know-it-all. Smart-ass.* The rest of the note simply said that anyone that knew the following twelve names for Ttab'a would remain unharmed by her as per her agreement with the Prophet. They were: Lawlabun, Khal 'Asun, Dusun, Maltusun, Sayusun, Salmasun, Tuhun, Tusadun, Asra 'Un, Rabbun Qaruhun, 'Ayqudun, and Salmanun.

St. Germain was right. I had been planning to get one of the Seals of Solomon from *Pugnus Dei*, which I knew would grant me safe passage around Ttab'a, but I would have to return the small clay object at some point. According to the document, knowing her names ensured I would always be safe around her. In this case, knowledge was a lot more powerful than an object. And avoiding a confrontation with a creature who was known to eat flesh and drink blood and was called the "Mother of Sorrow" was far better than trying to fight her—or at least *me* trying to fight her. That piece of information was going to make my life infinitely easier at Gara Medouar.

Maybe using the crystals would be as easy. Maybe Athena would realize the importance of what I was doing and help me again too. I didn't feel like either one was very likely, but I opened the folder about the crystals. I was surprised to see the instructions were indeed short. However, the first step was nearly Herculean. But if that overdeveloped muscle head of a Guardian could do it, then so could I, mortal or not.

I popped open the small black plastic case and saw what resembled a crude crown or tiara of silver-white crystals woven together with a filament of silver wire as fine as thread. Between each crystal sat several other kinds of smaller, more colorful crystals, including some orange, pale-purple, metallic-silver, and black ones, all carefully placed and connected. The creation was elegant in its construction. Each crystal was in contact with at least two others, and I felt a slight vibration and a warming sensation in my hands as I held the device. Interestingly, the instant I touched it, I found myself picturing Sarah, vividly. I saw with utter clarity the first day we'd met outside the Met in New York, saw her focus and drive as we fought Medea in the witch's cave on Mt. Alvand, remembered the feeling when I kissed her for the first time in Miami, and felt the pain of the last time I saw her awake, leaving her dump of an SRO while she was working undercover to help me stop a fallen angel. The last images made me drop the crown, and for a few long minutes afterward, I felt sick to my stomach.

Unwilling to wade through those feelings again, I read over the list of instructions again, as simple as they were. The doozy of a first step was to subdue—but not kill—Eisheth. Then all I had to do was place the crystal crown on her head for no less than ten minutes. Ideally, that would be done on a new moon for maximum effect. Next, I had to get it to Sarah and place it on her head, ideally on the night of the following new moon. Once the crystals were charged, handling the crown would have to be kept to a minimum to keep any unintentional transference from occurring. Also, not keeping the crown on Eisheth for a full ten minutes could mean that the crystals were less than fully charged. Since they were set to Sarah's vibrational frequency—whatever the hell that meant—the energy that the crown would draw out of Eisheth should be mostly Sarah's. I wasn't sure I bought that part fully or even understood it, but at that point, it was my only solution for saving Sarah.

After figuring out how to connect to the jet's Wi-Fi, which, to me, was tantamount to wrestling a troll, I texted Duma about my arrival time in Casablanca just to make sure I wasn't standing around for hours. I hoped. I tried to sleep but found my mind wandering from Sarah to Kailani to Eisheth to Nemesis in a never-ending loop I wasn't able to break.

I tried to read the various magazines on the plane, only to find myself rereading the same paragraph over and over again without gleaning anything from it. I flipped through the channels on the satellite TV but couldn't find anything that could hold my attention there either.

Underlying everything was a gut-churning guilt about Sarah, caused by her current condition, my situation with Kailani, who may or may not be a mole that I've been blind to, and how that all fucked up my relationship with Athena. And I was becoming more and more aware of my limitations since I was mortal again. Even my knees popped and creaked when I stood up, and I was noticing things like the weight of a drink in my hand, along with a persistent weariness in my shoulders, arms, and legs. Everything whirled in my mind to the point that it was almost overwhelming.

Across the small cabin, over the well-appointed bar, the brightly lit crystal decanters filled with various shades of brown, golden, or clear liquids caught my eye. My head hurt, and I squeezed my eyes shut for a moment.

This is why so many people are driven to drink.

I walked over to the bar and perused the bottles. I was familiar with some of the names, but I really knew nothing about their taste, strength, or even if they were supposed to be mixed with other drinks or not. I grabbed one old black bottle with a worn and faded yellowed paper label, pulled the cork from it, and took a whiff. The alcohol made my nose crinkle involuntarily and my eyes water. *Yeah, that's pretty much all I remember about liquor.* That was the primary reason I didn't drink. I just didn't like the taste. I restoppered the bottle at arm's length and replaced it on the rack over the bar. Instead, I pulled a bottle of water from the small refrigerator underneath the bar, wishing I had aspirin to go with it.

Chapter 33

The remainder of the eight-hour flight was almost as fitful as the first hour. Apparently, I managed to pass out at some point, because I was startled awake by the pilot's voice over the intercom telling me we were about to land in Casablanca. While we taxied to the area for private planes near the freight terminal, I tried to go over my plan. Then I realized I didn't really have a plan. Even saying I was flying by the seat of my pants was being generous. The first thing Duma and Ab would do is ask me what my plan was, and unless inspiration hit me in the next few minutes, my only answer would have to be what I hoped was a winning smile.

Twenty minutes later, after clearing customs with papers provided by the captain, I was standing on a curb outside the freight terminal, overlooking a largely empty parking lot in the cool early-evening air. I checked my phone for messages from Duma but found none. I was about thirty minutes behind schedule, which should have given them more than enough time to meet me.

I absentmindedly checked my watch and phone without really paying attention as I became more and more irritated that Duma and Ab were late. After a half hour, I finally texted. Almost right on cue, a roaring engine split the quiet night air around the nearly deserted freight terminal. The sound increased in intensity until I finally saw the glow of what appeared to be searchlights bouncing off the buildings down the street.

The reflected glow turned into a blinding aura of light that I had to shield my eyes from with my hand, and within seconds, through heavily squinted eyes and the gaps between my fingers, I saw some sort of low-slung pale vehicle with giant wheels pull up in front of me, followed by a larger pale vehicle. My first impression was the former was some sort of overgrown remote-controlled dune buggy and the latter was an off-road armored car.

With a final rev of the engine, the dune buggy shut down, while the truck's massive diesel engine continued to chuff. Mercifully, when the engine shut down on the buggy, the light clicked off as well with a distinctive metallic *clink*. I was squinting hard, trying to overcome my night blindness, when I heard Duma's familiar voice.

"Well, don't just stand there. Get in. It's eight hours to Gara Medouar, and we have to stop in Erfoud for supplies first."

As my eyes adjusted to the darkness again, I could see the cars much better. Duma's vehicle did indeed resemble a real-life full-sized remote-control dune buggy built out of some sort of sports car, while Ab's monstrosity was an armored truck with oversized wheels and bars over the tiny windows in the doors. It even had an exhaust pipe that extended up in front of the driver's side door. Some sort of turret sat on the roof of the vehicle though I didn't see any armament at the moment.

"What the hell are these things?" I asked. "They look like kid's toys brought to life."

"Were you expecting a beat-up old Land Cruiser with extra gas tanks strapped to the roof? Just get in," Duma said, slapping the roof of his buggy.

Try as I might, I couldn't identify the door handle. "How do I get in this thing?"

"Oh for... just—" he replied, then the door hissed and popped open.

The inside was spartan to say the least, with just enough room behind the seat to put my briefcase without setting it on the engine, which was completely exposed inside the cabin.

"Um, is that safe?" I asked, hooking a thumb over my shoulder at the big motor.

Duma just grinned and fired up the engine to a deafening roar.

"Helmets are optional, sweet cheeks," he replied. "Seat belt harness is not. Put it on, or you'll get bounced all over the place. This thing is built for sand racing, not streets."

The streetlights and surrounding buildings provided enough light for me to notice the interior of the car wasn't just spartan. It was almost nonexistent. We were sitting inside something that resembled a metal cage, and the engine noise made conversation almost impossible without screaming. Truthfully, the lack of talking didn't bother me.

We headed southeast out of Casablanca and finally hit the N1 highway, which led to the N11, the A3, and a series of other highways and roads named as if they'd been pulled during a bingo game. After about four hours, we stopped at an oasis town called Ouaoumana on the N8 and fueled up.

"Put your helmet on, and we can talk through the two-way," Duma said as we got back on the road.

The moment I tightened the chin strap, the questions began.

"So, what's in the case?"

"St. Germain's plan for saving Sarah," I replied. "How much farther?"

"About four hours, but I have a shortcut for us," he said, smiling so wide that I could almost see the glow of his perfect white teeth in the scant moonlight. "Only downside is Ab can't keep up with us, and he has all the heavy gear."

"I'm not worried," I said.

"About what exactly?" he asked, the mirth suddenly gone from his voice. "Not worried about being a plain old human again, Nemesis, attacking Eisheth, saving Sarah, or what's waiting for us at Gara Medouar? You haven't forgotten about *her*, have you?"

"I know Ttab'a's names," I replied. "She can't hurt anyone who knows all her names."

"Seriously? Where the hell has this information been for the past five thousand years? I could have used it on more than one occasion," he said, pounding the steering wheel of the car with one hand. "She's been the bane of many North African campaigns for me, D."

I just shrugged. "Trust me, I didn't know either. St. Germain."

"St. Germain. Man, that dude knows everything," he said. "So, did he give you a plan for beating Eisheth and Nemesis too?"

"We're on our own for the rest of it."

"I'll be honest, D," he replied, "If it was us, including you as a Guardian, I still wouldn't like our odds very much. With you as, well... you, I like our odds even less. Nobody in their right mind would do what you want us to do."

"That's why it's going to work," I said. "She'll never expect it, and they still don't know I'm mortal. We'll have to rely on Violence of Action. We need to make her think we are more than we are. Hit her so hard she flinches and keep pounding."

"I'm familiar with the concept, D," Duma said. "I just ain't never had to rely on it being an illusion before."

With that, he stopped talking, but I could see his lips set tightly across his face. He probably thought I had more of a plan of attack, but I didn't at that point. Right then, all I wanted to do was draw out Nemesis and expose Kailani, if she was truly involved. With luck, we could then back off while the "Mother of Sorrow" beat the snot out of Nemesis for us. No one ever succeeded by trying to fight a war on multiple fronts.

Try as I might, I still couldn't get my brain in gear as we drove, once again in silence. We turned south on the N13, stopping once again in Erfoud for gas. While fueling up, Ab and Duma talked for just a moment, and Ab got in his truck and left without waiting for us. Duma pulled a pair of gloves out of his back pocket and began putting them on.

"He's going to meet us there."

"Isn't this thing faster than that armored truck?" I asked, slightly confused by our splitting up.

"Much, but we ain't taking the road, and in the sand, that truck makes only about thirty miles an hour," Duma said, pulling on his helmet. "He'll make better time on the highway. Plus, if we split up, we can make sure Gara Medouar is empty when we get there. Except for Ttab'a." He hopped in and started the buggy with a roar.

Within minutes, we were heading west through town, but when the roads ended at the edge of the oasis town, Duma just poked at a large touch screen in the middle of the dashboard, gunned the engine, and hit the sand, headed south by southwest, according to the screen.

"How far?" I asked, watching Duma work the steering wheel like he was trying to hold on to a squirming fish.

"Ten miles as the crow flies," he replied. "Wanna bet we can make it in less than ten minutes?"

Oh shit. I grabbed the metal roll cage with one hand and checked my harness with the other. *This is going to hurt.*

Duma made good on his bet, but I still bounced around like a ping-pong ball in a blender for seven very long minutes. Gara Medouar's black craterlike walls rose out of the desert landscape in front of us, shimmering in the heat of the new morning sun. The odd natural formation resembled something from the moon, and the black sandy walls stood in stark contrast to the various shades of tan of the surrounding countryside. Everything about it suggested it was entirely out of place. The closer we got, the more the crumbling structure's forbidding nature suggested nothing short of "go away."

"We'll approach from the north and head around to the west," Duma said.

Short of climbing over the dunes that made up the onetime fortress's walls, the only way inside was through the remnants of a wall and gate open to the southwest.

"I haven't been here in eighty years, but I'm guessing Ttab'a still holes up in the structures underneath," I said.

"Probably," Duma replied, taking a turn that was more of a controlled skid. "Only way in is through the ruins in the northwest corner, but it's a warren down there. Even if this names thing works, it'd be crazy to go down there. Wouldn't it be easier to wait till she comes up to us?"

"I was thinking you and Ab can take up positions along the east and north walls in some of the ruins if they're still standing," I said, hoping my made-up-on-the-fly idea sounded credible. "I'll wait down on the floor in view of the gate."

"Will Nemesis come through the gate?" Duma asked, throwing the sand racer into another controlled skid, clearly enjoying himself.

I slammed into the roll cage with my right side, unable to brace myself enough to avoid the impact. "Was that necessary, Duma?"

He did a deliberate double take at me. "Depends on what your definition of 'necessary' is." He pursed his lips into a thoughtful frown. "I'm going with yes. Yes, it was absolutely necessary. Hang on."

The sand racer went into a full-on slide as we passed from sand to loose gravel near the gate, putting us into a near 360-degree spin that Duma fed and then fought, then we came to a stop a few feet from the remnants of the wall. "Like a glove..." Duma said, glancing at me as though he expected applause.

Chapter 34

I unbuckled my harness, pushed open the door, and attempted to jump out, but my body wouldn't cooperate. I was sore and felt like every joint and bone in my body ached. Even my eyes hurt. I stumbled out of the vehicle, stooped over, hand on knee, then fought to stand up straight and stretch. My back popped and snapped like bubble wrap in the hands of a six-year-old.

From the other side of the car, Duma stared at me through squinted eyes, a grimace on his face. He winced at each noise my body made as he took off his helmet and fixed his hair.

"How old *are* you?" Duma asked.

"Just get my case out of that thing, will you?" I said, pointing at his sand racer.

"We're fucked," Duma said under his breath, shaking his head as he ducked into the dune buggy.

Off in the distance, toward the southeast, a dust cloud was growing.

"I'm guessing that's Ab," I said, rolling and stretching my shoulders as I took my helmet off.

"Be my guess unless you think Nemesis drives a truck," Duma replied, walking over to hand me the metal case very carefully by its leather-wrapped handle. "But I ain't going in there," he said, jerking his head back toward the ancient fort, "until Ab shows up with all our shit. You may have a magic list of names, but it'll just make me feel better if I have something I can stab someone with just in case." He sniffed and rubbed at his nose.

I pulled the list of names from the briefcase and tried to memorize them while we waited. I couldn't keep my mind from wandering—from Sarah to Kailani, to Nemesis, to St. Germain, to Athena, to a plain old normal mundane life. The last part kept sticking out. I didn't know how I could help Sarah if I was just *normal*. She needed me to be more than normal. I couldn't let her down again. *But she was mundane, and she entered my world without hesitation. Yeah, look where that got her…*

"D! Hey, D!" I finally heard Duma say.

When I realized he was trying to get my attention, I saw his reason. Ab was pulling up.

He got out of the truck, adjusted his pants, squinted at Gara Medouar for a moment, and frowned at me. "So, what exactly are we doing here again?"

"Yeah, I'd like to know that too," Duma said. "You keep giving me wishy-washy answers. What *is* the plan, D?"

"We can't fight Nemesis and Eisheth at the same time," I replied. "I'm hoping I can draw Nemesis out here and expose the mole that keeps ratting me out. I think it's Kailani, but I'm not sure."

"I knew I didn't trust that vampire," Ab said.

"Whatever," Duma replied, waving off his brother. "But why here? Couldn't we have drawn out Nemesis at, say, Disneyland instead of the prison of one of the nastiest creatures ever to walk the earth?"

"To be honest, I was hoping we could use Ttab'a to help with Nemesis," I said, looking at the ground as I said it. "If we're protected because we know her names, I was thinking we could piss her off so much that if Nemesis shows, Ttab'a will be so incensed she'll attack her. She might be powerful enough to do some damage to her and get her out of our hair long enough for us to go after Eisheth."

"That's fucked up," Ab said. "You want to piss off a hellspawn? Do you know how many ways that could go wrong? You sure my

RT-20 and those depleted-uranium high-explosive twenty-millimeter rounds I got won't knock Nemesis' ass to next Tuesday? I put a round through a Chinese Type-59 tank in Afghanistan with it a few years back. Not *into* but *through*," Ab said with a broad smile and a pointed gesture.

"Call that plan B, for if the Ttab'a thing doesn't work," I said.

"All I'm saying is that at least I can *control* the fucking RT-20," Ab said, shaking his head. "Maybe if I can hit Nemesis, then you and Duma can kick her while she's down. Or you can shoot her, and Duma and I can kick her. Hell, I even got my hammer in there. The *big* one." He pointed at the heavily armored truck he drove. "Get me a window, and I'll knock her into next year."

"Ab, are you forgetting the last time you tried to attack a D'ia?" Duma asked, his pale eyebrows raised high on his forehead.

"Yeah, well, he knew I was coming, and I still got a few shots in," he said.

"All up until he kicked your ass forty yards downrange," Duma said, trying to hide his amusement.

"Look, that'll be plan B," I said. "We'll put Duma on the RT-20 up in the ruin along the eastern edge. Ab, you'll be in the ruins on the northern edge with your hammer and one of your Jackhammer shotguns, if you brought one, and I'll distract Nemesis long enough for Ttab'a to come out. Then depending on how things go, you guys can unload on her then get your ass down to help me as fast as possible. It's the only shot we got to get Nemesis off our backs now that I'm—"

"Mortal. Yeah, got it. And this list of names you got will keep that monstrous wench Ttab'a off our backs in the process," Duma asked, holding up one hand, one eyebrow raised on his wrinkled forehead.

"According to St. Germain, yes," I replied, closing my eyes and cocking my head to one side with a heavy sigh. "It's the best plan I got."

"And it's all assuming Nemesis will even show up, because your current girlfriend is probably a blabbermouth snitch," Duma said.

Ab just planted his face in one hand. Several moments later, he clapped his hands and rubbed them together. "Well, should we get this show on the road?" the giant Peri asked, opening the back of his armored truck.

He reached in and threw a familiar black duffel bag at me, which I managed to catch and barely hold on to. It weighed a ton. Ab shook his head.

I went through the duffel, pulling out my tactical vest–covered cuirass, greaves, knives, my Glock, my Sig, and finally my swords. They were heavy, and when I pulled one partway from its sheath, the metal reminded me of an old bruise—the yellowish and black of tarnished silver. Part of me felt like I'd let *them* down too. I slid the weapon back into its sheath and geared up, feeling the weight. Rather than being the familiar comfort I was used to, my gear just felt clunky. I recalled a similar feeling from when I was a boy, putting on my father's armor, pretending I was him or some other hero.

A few short years later, he would be dead, and my friends and I would be fighting the largest war the world had ever seen to that point. *We were all just boys.*

I shifted my cuirass and walked over to the back of Ab's truck to see what other weapons he had. Duma was fiddling with one of the many knives he wore across his bandolier, picking at his fingernails. The massive RT-20 anti-tank rifle was next to him. His foot was on an ammo box.

"Can you carry that?" I asked, pointing at the heavy weapon.

"Probably better than you." He deftly slid the knife into a sheath on his chest then grabbed the big gun. He brought it to his shoulder and nearly dropped it trying to open the bolt.

"Dammit," Ab said. "That thing only weighs forty-five pounds or so. If you can't handle that, how are you going to carry that and those?" he asked, pointing at the ammo box. "Those weigh almost twice as much as the gun."

"I can help him," I said.

"I'll help him," Ab said, shaking his head. "I'll get him situated then get myself set. You do what you gotta do with Ttab'a. We'll keep in touch via radio." He nodded at another large duffel in the back of the truck. It had wires and other electronic equipment sticking out.

Ab slung his massive fully automatic shotgun over one shoulder, tossed his huge hammer onto his other, then bent down and palmed the eighty-pound ammo box like it was full of toothpicks and not six-inch-long quarter-pound high-explosive rounds. Duma threw the heavy anti-tank rifle over one shoulder, and he and Ab headed through the gaping hole in the wall that used to hold a heavily fortified gate.

I quickly grabbed a FN SCAR-H assault rifle and a few spare magazines. I checked the safety, inserted one, then checked the chamber. I grabbed the pages from the metal case St. Germain had given me, stuffed them in my vest, took a deep breath, and ran to catch up.

Chapter 35

The inside of the once-bustling fortress and trade center of Gara Medouar, often called a prison because of its connection to the slave trade, was as desolate as the surrounding landscape. It reminded me of standing in the crater of a meteor strike, with high, sandy black walls eroding all around the bowl-shaped geological structure. A few old mud brick structures poked out of the dark sediment here and there, reminders of what this place had once been.

When I closed my eyes, I could still see the brightly colored tents and stalls and smell the spices and exotic foods mixed with the barnyard smells of goats, camels, and even the occasional elephants, giraffes, and baboons. The sound was always a mixture of singing, crazy musical instruments, bellowing or bleating animals, raucous conversations, and blacksmiths pounding out various metal implements or chains. Most people were unaware that below ground was a warren of passageways and barracks for the garrisons that defended the trading post until it was abandoned in the late nineteenth century. That was when Ttab'a moved in, and the place became her prison. Now, all I smelled was the slightly musky aroma of hot earth, and the only sound came from the wind howling across the desert plain.

Here and there, remnants of pale mud structures jutted out from the dark sand inside the walls like broken teeth, but only two main footpaths were still visible. One meandered through a ravine between sand drifts that headed northeast up the eroded crater wall, while the other headed northwest past a decaying mud brick fence. At the end of the latter path, I could see the last remaining complete structure—a brick construction that resembled a mausoleum, complete with heavy wood and iron doors. That was the entrance to the catacombs below.

"I'll try to draw Ttab'a out to this open area," I said. "Duma, if you're up there"—I pointed at a decrepit structure along the eastern rise—"and Ab is up there"—I pointed at another structure sticking out from a dune in the middle of the caldera—"you should have clean shots at us. Hopefully, I will have pissed off Ttab'a enough that if Nemesis shows, she'll go right after her. That's when we open up on Nemesis. The second she's down, you guys get down here fast. Somehow, we'll have to hit her hard enough to damage her. That's the only way we're going to get her off our plane of existence and out of our hair long enough to deal with Eisheth without looking over our shoulders."

Ab and Duma both nodded solemnly, and they walked up the sandy, eroding slope toward the structure where Duma would take cover. They both walked over the shifting sands far too gracefully and easily, barely leaving footprints. *Fairies.*

I headed up the path to Ttab'a's hidey-hole. When I got to the crumbling remains of the fence, I pulled the sheaf of papers from my vest, making sure the list of names was on top. By the time I got to the massive doors on the mausoleum, my heart was pounding, and my hands were sweaty—far sweatier than they should have been—underneath the leather strips I used instead of gloves. The once-intricate decorations that adorned the heavy metal, stone, and wood doors had faded, and although I could no longer see the energy, I knew they were magically reinforced and warded to keep her imprisoned below. I was desperately hoping that once the doors were open, I could draw Ttab'a up to the surface. I had no desire to try to chase her down in the catacombs. No way could I outmaneuver a fallen angel, even a lesser one, on her own turf.

The enormous doors appeared ordinary enough, but I knew better. I ran my hand over the surface, hoping I could perhaps feel the energy the wards placed on the doors were giving off. With Athena's help, I'd always been able to see it. That was how I knew they were there in the first place. And it was the only way even the heaviest doors could keep a creature like Ttab'a within. Fortunately, as a human, the wards had no effect on me, nor could they stop me from opening the doors.

The lock on the doors was a rusted iron contraption that probably couldn't have functioned even if I'd had a key. Without thinking, I reached for one of my swords, but I managed to stop myself. Without my connection to Athena, they would likely break before the heavy lock would. For a second, I wondered if Ab might have a persuasion bar in the back of his truck. He had everything else in there. Then I figured, *Fuck it*. I pulled the Sig from its holster on my vest.

"We have movement on the top of the mausoleum," Duma said over the radio before I could pull the trigger.

I quickly replaced the Sig in its holster and brought the SCAR-H up to a combat high position. I slowly backed up, scanning the front edge of the structure above me through the aiming reticle on the rifle.

"Two more, moving to flank you, D," Ab said. "They don't appear armed. Possibly nomads or even looters."

"Looters would be armed and not stupid enough to raid this place anyway," I said. "Nomads avoid this place too. Whoever they are, expect hostile intent."

"*Tawqqaf*," someone said from above me.

I still couldn't see who said it. I'd been in the region enough times to know the voice was telling me to stop in Arabic.

"I can't do that," I replied.

A figure with a black turban wrapped around his entire face and head and draped over his shoulders, covering a tan padded tunic, appeared on the top of the mausoleum above me. He held a traditional butterfly-shaped Moorish Adarga shield in one hand and a massive cudgel in the other. He had several ornate Khoumya daggers on his belt, and the skin around his eyes and hands was a dark mahogany.

"Do not open these doors," the Moor said, that time in heavily accented English, his tone insistent.

Two more men dressed and armed in similar fashion appeared on either side of the mausoleum.

I wasn't expecting any kind of guards.

"Believe me, if I didn't have to, I wouldn't," I said, keeping the Moor on the roof of the structure in the center of my reticle while I continued to step backward slowly.

"We cannot let you," he said.

"Just back off, and let me do what I came to do," I said. "I know her names."

"How did you come by the true names of Um Sabyan?" the Moor asked.

"Doesn't matter," I replied. "But I can tell you something far worse is on its way here, and Ttab'a is my best hope at defeating it."

"You cannot defeat one evil with another," he said. "The risks are far too great."

"Well, we're going to find out. Look, I understand your concerns, but we are *wasting* time," I replied. "And I am not alone."

"We are aware of the two Peri that are with you," he said.

"Yeah, and tell him Ab and I are aware of the men he has circling us," Duma said over the comms. "Tell him to have them stand down. They're making me twitchy. They don't want me twitchy."

"Tell your men to stay where they are," I told the Moor. "Do it now, or this will get ugly."

"You come here intending to release Um Sabyan from her prison, and you bring two filthy Peri with you into this place, and *you* dare make demands of me and my men?"

"No demands," I replied. "I'm just asking. But I'm only asking once. Tell them to back off. Now."

"I cannot do that," he said.

"Last chance. Tell them to stand down, now!" I said, shouting.

"We will not."

"Fuck this. Duma, Ab, do what you gotta do," I said, feeling the snarl on my face as I said it.

The man in front of me and the pair flanking me remained still but kept their weapons at the ready. They watched me the way a male grizzly bear watches another male approach its territory. I remained steady, aiming at the man on the roof. The stalemate finally broke when a muffled scream erupted from behind us. I saw the eyes of the Moor above me widen at something going on behind me, but I couldn't risk taking my eyes off my targets to see what it was. Ab and Duma could take care of themselves.

"Tell him his men are dead," Duma said over the radio less than a minute later.

"All clear on my end too," Ab added.

Normally, the fact Duma and Ab had killed humans—especially humans trying to keep people from doing exactly what I was about to do—would have incensed me. I didn't care.

"Your men are dead," I replied. "While you're clearly familiar with Peri, you were obviously stupid enough to think your men could take them out. Now, you three leave, or you'll be right behind them. Last chance."

I kept backing up, slowly, trying to keep all three of the Moors in front of me as best I could.

"We cannot allow you to set her free," the Moor said.

I don't have the patience for this today.

I quickly swung the rifle down and to my left, centering on the Moor flanking me there. I pulled the trigger, sending a three-round burst into his chest. Without hesitation, I dropped to one knee and brought the rifle to bear on the man to my right. I fired, dropping that attacker as well.

I got back to my feet, trying to bring the rifle up to re-engage the Moor on the roof of the mausoleum. Just as I raised the weapon, I saw the last remaining Moor in midair, his cudgel stretched high overhead. My only choice was to parry the incoming blow with the rifle rather than fire. The force of the impact destroyed my rifle and knocked me on my ass, but it also clearly jarred the Moor too. I swept my leg beneath him just as he was regaining his balance. The attack knocked him flat on his back, giving me enough time to ditch the destroyed rifle, get to my feet, and pull my swords. They might not have been the weapons they were when I was connected to Athena, but they were still sharp swords.

The Moor flipped back to his feet, shield and cudgel still in hand, and he crouched, eyes darting around to assess the situation. I lowered the swords to my sides. "Just remember—you could have just left. This is on you," I said, shaking my head.

The Moor charged, leading with his shield then bringing the cudgel up and out from underneath it in a type of uppercut, forcing me to jump back to avoid the blow. The attack left him wide open, with his shield out to his left and his cudgel well to his right. I stepped in with both swords and shoved them hard into his chest. They met with some sort of armor I couldn't penetrate. The Moor brought his shield across to brush my swords aside, knocking me off balance. I was used to my swords cutting through anything and having the strength to make them. I had to reassess my techniques—fast.

I regained my footing just in time to jump back to avoid a crushing side sweep of the cudgel. The instant the cudgel passed me, I brought my right sword up across his arm then lunged forward to drive my other sword into his leg. Both drew blood and knocked him back. I pressed my attack. He blocked my next two attacks easily with his broad shield, but I had him on the defensive, forcing him back against the mausoleum doors.

Blood was pooling around his right foot, soaking through his tan tunic, turning it black. He made a desperate wild swing at me, and I stepped in and brought both swords up to parry the blow then continued to move in, bringing my right elbow up into his jaw. He fell back against the doors, lowering his shield and dropping the cudgel. I turned slightly and brought my right sword across his neck, sending a spray of crimson blood in a wide arc across the sand. The Moor fell to his knees, his eyes searching blankly before he finally collapsed.

Breathing heavily, I put my swords away then pulled the Sig from its holster on my vest and fired a single shot into the head of each man just to make sure they were dead.

"Did I just see what I thought I saw?" Ab asked over the radio.

"I warned them, Ab. And I don't have time for this shit," I said, feeling anger well up inside my chest.

"But—"

"Don't, Ab," Duma said, cutting him off. "Let's just do what we came to do and get the hell out of here before we're swarmed by the rest of Ttab'a's prison guards. Man, that was like watching a dance in slow motion. What'd that take, like three minutes?"

"Like you said, let's just do what we came here to do," I said.

Chapter 36

Sig still in hand, I pulled the dead Moor away from the doors by his arm then tossed his cudgel onto the sand. Once back in front of the doors, I put two rounds into the lock from three feet away. The old metal shattered, sending sparks and metal splinters everywhere. I pulled the hasp open and heaved the massive wooden door open with more effort than I'd expected. I pounded on the door with the side of my fist, sending an echo down the tunnel in front of me.

"Hello, anybody home?" I screamed at the top of my lungs.

I took a step just inside the threshold of the doorway, squinting hard to pierce the veil of darkness in front of me. Ttab'a could have been standing fifteen feet away and I couldn't have seen her.

"I know you're in there."

I reached inside my vest and grabbed the papers I'd stuffed there, finding the list of Ttab'a's names. "Come on, Ttab'a, where else you gonna go?" I asked. "By the way, you freakish, festering pile of worm shit, I know your names. All of them. All twelve. And most of them are as stupid as *Ttab'a*." I waited for a second, trying to hear something, but nothing came.

"Let's see... there's Lawlabun, which I assume is pronounced Law-la-bun and not Law-laybun, Khal 'Asun, which sounds like a *Game of Thrones* character or something. Then there's Dusun, Maltusun, Sayusun, Salmasun—what's with all the 'suns,' by the way?" I heard a heavy scraping noise echo up from somewhere down the tunnel. Because of the reverberation, I couldn't gauge the distance, however. "Oh well. Let's see, then there's Tuhun, Tusadun, Asra 'Un,

187

Rabbun Qaruhun—now we're on an 'un' kick. That only leaves 'Ayqudun and..."

From out of the darkness in front of me, a thick, dark log-like appendage broke the shadows. The limb ended in filthy eight-inch-long claws, which it walked on like a gorilla.

"How dare you disturb me." Its voice was high-pitched and breathy.

My skin grew cold, and the hair stood up on my arms and neck. I stepped back, outside the doorway, back out into the bright light of the sun. I tried to speak, but I suddenly had a lump in my throat.

"Who told you my names?" Ttab'a asked, placing a second giant log-like limb into the light. The stench of rotting flesh washed out of the tunnel and out into the dry heat, assaulting my nose to the point that my stomach turned. I had to fight not to throw up.

I stepped back even farther into the open, trying to draw her out.

"Oh, you know, I just asked around," I said, trying not to stammer. "One guy said your name was Dusun. Some other guy said it was Tuhun. I just figured one of them had to be the right one. I always thought it was just Ttab'a. You must have ghosted a lot of people in your day to need twelve names, huh?"

The two thick limbs extended tentatively past the threshold, and Ttab'a's head slowly emerged into the sun. She resembled a massive vampire bat, with four massive daggerlike teeth in her upper jaw, while the lower jaw had an extra pair of mandibles outside it, each topped with a single massive fang. Her nose was flat and leaflike, and her tiny eyes squinted in the light of day. Her ears were massive, and she had a dense black mane of matted hair. She continued to move out of the tunnel until she spied the dead Moors. Her short back legs were doglike with the exception of the ten-inch-long spike that stuck out from the back of the elongated heel. Several lengthy and sharp bony growths extended from the elbows of her long arms. Overall, she gave the impression of a wingless vampire bat. And it was sickening.

"But those are not all of my names," she said with a hiss.

"Oh, yeah—Salmanun," I replied, continuing to back up, constantly checking around my feet to make sure I didn't misstep and fall on my ass. "That should be all twelve, right? And as per the deal you made with the Prophet of Islam all those years ago, you cannot harm anyone who knows all of your names."

With that, she let out a screech that I felt in my skull as much as heard, and she charged me like a rabid baboon, shaking the ground as she galloped. She came to an abrupt halt, standing directly over the top of me. I was staring directly into her naked, pasty, but thickly muscled chest. I wish I could say I didn't move because I knew she would stop and I was just that brave, but the truth was I just couldn't react—not just fast enough, but at all. My legs were leaden and heavy. Even my arms felt stationary. It was everything I could do not to throw up at the intense, sickening smell of decay she gave off, but I finally managed to look up. She was staring down at me, our faces only a few feet apart. Her breathing was ragged, her breath even more rancid than her odor. When a rope of her hot, thick drool hit my cheek, I lost it. I vomited all over her.

She laughed a creepy, witchlike cackle and pushed past me, knocking me on my ass.

"Did you kill my captors?" she asked.

"Yeah." I wiped my mouth and got back to my feet. "No offense, but you really stink," I said. "Ugly as fuck too." I spat a few times, trying to get the bitter taste of bile out of my mouth.

Ttab'a ignored me, her head moving around in a twitchy, almost robotic way, her nose and giant ears vibrating. She stopped briefly when she focused in the directions where Duma and Ab were hiding.

"And who else is with you, human?" Ttab'a asked, turning her upper body to see me. "Two others, no?"

"Two others, yes," I replied. "But they also know your names."

"Ah, but they are not human, are they?" she asked, revealing way too many sharp teeth in what I assumed was meant to be a smile. "My deal with the Prophet only extends to humanity, not the other bastard children of this earth."

"Oh, fuck her," Duma said through the radio piece in my ear. "Bastard children? At least we're native."

"Well, let's not worry about them," I said, trying to ignore Duma. "Tell me, how exactly did you get so smelly?" I had to keep her attention on me because if she decided to go after Ab and Duma, my whole plan would turn to shit, fast. The only upside was that I was pretty sure the cannon Duma had would do a ton of damage to her.

"Seriously, did you always look like that, or was it part of your punishment for being such a douchebag?"

Ttab'a turned to face me. "Why do you insist on annoying me, human?" she asked. "I will not harm you. If you wished me to kill you, you should not have repeated my names. The other two, however, shall make for excellent feeding. Their kind is so much sweeter than human flesh." The second she said that, her head rose to focus on the entrance to the fort behind me, her massive ears and nose vibrating wildly.

"D, we got movement outside," Ab said over comms.

"So many visitors," she hissed as she turned her giant, awkward body to face the gate fully. I had to quickly jump out of the way to avoid her thick arm as she lumbered past.

"Can you see who—or what—it is?" I asked, pushing the talk button on my chest. "If it's more guards, just deal with them. We don't have time to screw around."

"I'll keep that in mind, but it looks like... Yeah, definitely. It's Kailani," Duma said.

"Confirm," Ab said. "Same woman from Transnistria."

Shit.

I ran to get in front of Ttab'a and made it just as Kailani approached the gateway. "Kailani, stop!" I screamed. "Do not come in."

The vampiress came to an abrupt halt the instant she saw Ttab'a, her look of surprise quickly changing to shock.

Ttab'a let out a screech that sounded like steam escaping from some sort of massive engine just before exploding. The bat-like creature threw her head back and shook her shaggy mane like a dog after a bath. "Bah," she said and turned around, trying to relocate Duma and Ab. "Filthy energy thief."

I was stuck. I needed to keep Ttab'a occupied while continuing to piss her off on the chance Kailani had tipped off Nemesis. More importantly, I needed to keep her from eating Duma and Ab. But I also needed to keep an eye on Kailani too. I turned to face Ttab'a but glanced back over my shoulder at Kailani. In the dusty, arid desert air, dark streaks were visible under her eyes and down her cheeks.

"Kailani, stay where you are!" I shouted. "Don't cross the gateway. Do you hear me?"

"I'm sorry, Steve," she replied. "I had to tell you something." She spoke just loudly enough that I could hear her. Then she crossed the threshold into the fort.

Ttab'a turned and squared herself to Kailani, her giant ears twitching as they rotated around toward Duma just up the ramparts to her left.

"Hey, Bat Face, you never did tell me how you got so ugly," I said, trying to distract her. "I have a theory you got hit with God's special ugly stick a few times more than necessary. But then anything ridiculous enough to choose the losing side in a monumental war is lucky that ugliness was its only curse. I mean, ugly and stupid—that's a real double threat."

With that, Ttab'a charged. Me. Again. In an elaborate threat display reminiscent of a gorilla's charge. Standing over me, she roared another high-pitched screech that physically hurt my ears and left me slightly deafened. She raised her right foreleg and swept it slowly and purposefully to catch me and shove me out of the way, picking me up slightly and throwing me just a few feet. It was a display of power, meant to let me know she could kill me if she wanted. *Only she can't.*

I landed on my ass, which hurt every already achy part of my body.

"Boy, the fact you can't kill me must really be eating at you," I said through clenched teeth, ears still ringing, as I pushed myself back to my feet.

Ttab'a let out a chuff that could have been intended as a laugh, and her head swung back around to Kailani.

"Duma, fire a warning shot," I said, pushing the talk button on my comms. "Between her and Kailani. Do you—"

An explosion erupted in the earth halfway between Kailani and Ttab'a, sending chunks of rock and sand ten feet into the air. It caught me off guard, and even Ttab'a reared up and shrieked. Kailani fell back against the wall behind her with a thud then fell limp. The moment the creature regained her composure, she changed direction and galloped up the hill toward Duma, screeching wildly as she ran. From up the hill to her left, Ab emerged from his hiding spot, the massive fully automatic Jackhammer shotgun in hand, and screamed a battle cry as he unloaded on Ttab'a.

Chapter 37

In the next instant, a figure appeared at the bottom of the decaying rampart wall. It was Duma. His speed, the unfolding chaos around me, and the sounds—even the thunderous report of Ab's gun inside the craterlike structure—reached me as if I had earmuffs on and made me feel as if I was in slow motion, barely able to move at all. Ttab'a stopped short and turned to face her new foe—Ab—whose speed was nowhere near his brother's.

My eyes traveled from Kailani's unconscious form lying against the wall to Duma, shouting something and gesturing wildly, his eyes fixed on his brother and the charging fallen angel, then Ab as the pale giant dropped the spent shotgun and pulled his massive hammer off his back, bracing for the oncoming charge, his face fixed in defiance as he roared. In the blink of an eye, Duma was gone again, and I still hadn't taken a single step. Everything felt like it was moving at hyper speed but me.

I need Ttab'a alive just in case Nemesis shows up.

I started running toward Ttab'a. A dust storm was rising around the bat-like creature, and I could just catch the occasional glimpse of Duma's form around her legs through the cloud. Ttab'a was lurching and rearing up, slamming her two thick pole-like arms down like a bucking horse. As she shifted, I caught sight of Ab blocking her wild attacks and swinging his giant hammer in return. Then with a swing of her foreleg, Ab went flying up the sandy embankment, and she charged after him.

"We need Ttab'a alive!" I screamed into my comm. "Stand down."

The fight raged on. I took a bead on Ttab'a's broad torso with my Sig, realizing that the nine-millimeter rounds would probably just bounce off her hide and further frustrated by the fact that I kept seeing Duma's blurry form move in and out of my line of sight. I couldn't shoot even if I wanted to, for fear of hitting him. And I didn't want to shoot because I needed her alive. But I couldn't just leave my friends fighting for their lives. And if I didn't do something fast, they were going to kill her.

Ttab'a bucked wildly, and Duma went cartwheeling off her back and through the air, landing hard twenty feet away. Without missing a beat, he got to his feet and disappeared again, no doubt heading back into the fray.

"Stand down!" I shouted again over the comm. "We need her alive, dammit!"

Just as I said that, a deafening crack split the air inside the crater-like structure, and Ttab'a reared up, her forelegs high overhead—her right one bent oddly—and she screeched a horrible wail that sounded like an engine running at high speed without lubrication. The massive bat-like monster spun around on her hind legs and galloped off, dragging her right foreleg alongside. The limb was bent like a telephone pole hit by a car, rent at an odd, almost grotesque angle. She loped past me and turned up toward her underground lair, breathing raggedly as she retreated. Her torso and legs were caked with sand and dust, clinging to areas soaked with her blood.

Back at the scene of the fight, Ab was down on one knee, breathing heavily, resting on his massive hammer. Duma appeared next to him, his chest heaving as well, as he slid his kukris back into their sheaths.

"Where the fuck were you?" Duma asked in between breaths.

"We needed her—"

"Stop," Duma said, holding up a hand. "She was charging at me. Fuck her. She's lucky we don't track her ass down and finish her right now. Besides, you don't even know if Nemesis is coming. This whole thing was fucked from the beginning." He flung his hand up in a dismissive gesture.

Duma approached me as Ab got to his feet and went back to collect his shotgun. "Where the hell were you, D?"

"We needed her alive and *unhurt*," I said, anger rising inside my chest. "She was our best shot at getting rid of Nemesis. Fuck."

"We could have used you, D," Ab said, his face fixed in a scowl. "When she came after me, there was no way I could outrun her like Duma. She had me cornered. Besides, I don't run from a fight anyway."

"Seriously, what the fuck, D?" Duma said. "This is us we're talking about here. Me and Ab. You know... friends?"

I just stared at him, getting more and more angry that they'd fucked up my plan. "Shit."

"Yeah, well, if that's all you got to say, then that about sums it up, doesn't it?" Duma said, walking past. "You sure wasted those human guards fast enough too. Is that what this is? Are we expendable too? Sacrifice everyone to save Sarah? Or is it more about your fragile ego? Ab and I are out of here. When you finally figure out what you're actually doing, let us know. Ab, let's go!" he shouted without looking back.

Ab slogged up the sandy embankment where Duma's hidey-hole was, grabbed the big rifle, threw it over his shoulder, and walked past without saying a word. I stood in the same spot until the dust from their cars was the only sign of them on the horizon.

Chapter 38

After a long few minutes of watching the dust cloud disperse over the desert landscape, a groan from Kailani, still unconscious, drew my attention momentarily. I glanced around absently, focusing on nothing in particular, and my eyes landed on the entrance to Ttab'a's underground prison. I was frustrated and feeling out of sorts, and the arid, dusty, earthy air caused my mind to wander to another time, another place not far from there, and another monster that wasn't really a monster at all.

1544 Rabat, Morocco

Coming into port after weeks at sea, chasing Arabic pirates attacking merchant ships along the North African coast of the Mediterranean, was a welcome respite, even a port that was mostly in ruins. The jagged, destroyed skyline of the city of Rabat resembled a distant crumbling mountain range, broken only by a single minaret towering over an incomplete mosque on the banks of the Bou Regreg. Counting the number of habitable structures still standing wouldn't have taken more than a few minutes. Across the river, the town of Sale stood in a similar dire condition. The dying twin cities were a perfect place for pirates to make port.

Within hours of disembarking into the decaying city, most of the few remaining residents had already swarmed the docks in the hopes that maybe a new ship full of sailors might bring some much-needed business. It also gave the Spanish Navy the opportunity to talk with them about pirate activity in the area.

Due to fear, information about pirates was always hard to come by, but stories about men disappearing farther north, along the Sebou River, supposedly taken by some sort of demon they called Aisha Qandisha, came freely. Humans were always more willing to talk about scary monsters they weren't quite sure were real than they were about real people they feared.

While I was supposed to be hunting pirates, chasing down demons was more in line with my role as a Guardian of Humanity, so I headed twenty miles farther up the coast to Mehdiya, where I borrowed a small dhow to head up the Sebou. After traveling upriver until it became little more than a shallow stream, I followed the river by foot for several days until I came across a fly-ridden, blood-soaked massacre.

Buzzing insects swarmed three heavily armed bodies on the bank and two more floating face down in the shallow river, washed into a calm eddy. The men on the beach had arrows in their chests, but despite carrying several swords and knives each, they had not drawn a single weapon among them. The two floating men in the river both carried bows but had the bloated features of people who had drowned. I'd seen enough war and participated in enough skirmishes to see not even the slightest bit of evidence of a fight remained on the sandy riverbank. It appeared as if they'd just stood there and let themselves get shot and the other two just drowned themselves afterward. And whatever occurred, it had happened no more than half a day previous at most. Jackals and hyenas hadn't even found the bodies yet.

The men weren't just random nomads, either. Their weapons, turbans and veils—similar to the tagelmust the Tuaregs wore except they were white instead of blue—and their lack of armor suggested they weren't proper soldiers but possibly some of the very pirates I was searching for.

As I searched the men for further signs of what had actually happened, I was surprised by what I first thought was a naked woman walking out of the forest. At least, she was in part a woman. She was, in fact, a strikingly beautiful brunette with the fine aquiline features and dark complexion that reminded me of Spanish nobility. Her lower half was something else entirely, however. She had the legs of some kind of horse or goat, with a small hoofed forefoot and an elongated and elevated heel and a thick, muscular thigh. She wandered out of the thick riverine woods and waded into the river as I was hunched near the water's edge.

"Am I not beautiful?" she asked after she submerged herself to her arms, skating her hands across the surface of the calm water.

I stood up, keeping a watchful eye on her. While she was clearly not human, she had to be the demon I was searching for. And while I had no idea exactly what she was capable of, I knew she'd killed five armed pirates before they could even react.

"All except your lower half," I replied.

Her reaction surprised me.

She jerked back slightly with a quizzical expression highlighted by a deep frown. "You can see my legs?" she asked, suddenly self-conscious, walking slowly out of the water and onto the riverbank a few yards downstream. "You can actually see me as I am?"

"Are you trying to hide your true nature from me?" I asked. "Because that won't work on me." I turned, staying square to her just in case. I didn't want to provoke her by reaching for my swords or even a knife, but I remained vigilant. "What exactly are you? Are you the one they call Aisha Qandisha?"

"I am Aisha La Condessa, yes," she replied with a slight bow of her head. "How is it you can see me as I am? How are you not vexed as other men are?"

"I am not like other men," I replied. "I am a Guardian, sworn to protect humanity from any that might harm it."

"So, are you here to kill me, then? You will not be the first to try. Since the Portuguese soldiers that invaded this country killed my family many years ago, I have been protecting myself."

"Portuguese soldiers killed your family?" I asked. "Were there others like you then?"

"No. I am... unique," she replied. "My mother was human—a Spanish woman of noble descent, but my father was something else. I never knew what he was. But I am..." She motioned to herself.

She was some sort of hybrid.

"You called yourself 'La Condessa,'" I said.

"Yes, my mother was nobility, so I would have inherited her title, but the locals pronounce the title slightly differently," she replied, eyeing me warily. "And they are convinced I am evil and that my blood has magical powers. I am constantly being hunted."

"It seemed almost the other way around," I said, kicking at the foot of one of the dead pirates. "These men didn't even have their weapons drawn."

She smiled and cocked her head to one side. "Of course they were hunting me. Fortunately, men are easily charmed and their wills just as easily bent. It allows me to subdue them before they can attack me. Despite my looks, I am not as monstrous as I may appear."

"That doesn't seem fair," I said.

"But five heavily armed men against one unarmed woman does? And I suppose you, Guardian with magical powers, were just out wandering in the forest miles from civilization for health reasons? Or maybe you were just lost?" She moved slowly farther away, closer to the forest.

"To be honest, I did come here for you," I said. "I cannot allow you to continue to enslave or kill men who encounter you."

Black and white. Right or wrong. I wish I could say that Aisha Qandisha was the real monster on that day, but I would be lying.

Chapter 39

My mind came back to the present when Kailani began to awaken. Almost instantly, with Ab and Duma gone, my anger shifted to her—the traitor working for Nemesis. I refused to approach her.

"You'll live," I said as she roused. I tried to locate the dust cloud on the horizon again but couldn't.

She squinted and rubbed at her head. "What the hell were you shooting at?" she replied. "And what was that... thing?"

"It wasn't me shooting. It was Duma, and relax, he wasn't shooting at you," I said. "He was trying to stop Ttab'a from attacking you. And that was Ttab'a." I jerked my head back toward the entrance to her underground lair.

"What the hell is a Ttab'a?" She sat upright, arms on her knees, blinking hard.

"She's one of the fallen, sentenced to remain here on earth for her transgressions," I said, taking a deep breath.

"Diomedes, we need to talk," she said, getting to her feet.

"No need," I replied, turning away. "I know all about it. That's why I'm here. This was all a trap for you and Nemesis."

"What?" she said. "What the hell are you talking about?"

"I know you've been selling me out to Nemesis these past few months, working with her."

"Are you crazy?" she said. "I'm not working with anyone. Especially not that *thing* you said was behind the attack at the Mondrian. Why would you even think that?"

I turned back to her. Her hands were in fists, her brow was heavily creased, and she stared at me sideways, through hooded eyes. Everything about her body language suggested she was confused and pissed off.

"I put two and two together," I said, feeling smug in my conclusion.

"And got what? Nine?" she said. "What exactly did you put together?"

"You're the only one who has known my every move," I replied, pointing at her. I walked over to look into her eyes up close. "Every time you showed up, Nemesis wasn't far behind. Every time. Hawaii, Transnistria, LA, here—"

"Nemesis was here too?" Kailani asked, her shoulders suddenly dropped, while her eyes grew wide and her brows climbed high on her forehead.

Her surprised reaction seemed genuine.

Maybe.

"Not yet, but I expect her at any moment, now that you've showed up," I said. The moment I said it, I realized my plan for dealing with Nemesis had totally fallen apart. Ttab'a was injured, and I had absolutely no backup and just two small-caliber pistols and a couple of tarnished swords. With no way to fight Nemesis, I was royally screwed.

"I'm sorry, but I'm still not following you," she said, shaking her head. "Look, I haven't fed in quite a while, and maybe I hit my head harder than I thought. You think I'm telling Nemesis where you are? That I am somehow her spy?"

"Sounds about right," I replied, frowning and jogging my head side to side.

"That's just ridiculous, Diomedes. Utterly ridiculous," she said with a dismissive wave of her hand. "You left my house so damn fast I came here to see if you needed help. And to tell you that some of my contacts say they saw Rebekah show up at a house outside Hidden Valley, just northwest of LA. I just wanted to help, Diomedes. Now, I guess I know why you were behaving so oddly before you left. You clearly aren't thinking straight."

For the first time since the fight with Ttab'a, I glanced around the inside of the old fort. Eight dark figures were sprawled around the sloped craterlike walls, arms and legs askew, some face down. Back by the entrance to the mausoleum were the three men I'd killed. *Men. Mundane humans.*

Kailani walked up next to me, hands on hips, taking in the carnage inside the fortress as well.

"What the hell happened here?" she asked, running a hand through her hair. "Was this all you guys, or was it that thing?"

If it isn't Kailani, then how is Nemesis finding me? Who else knew where I was?

I exhaled heavily. "Please tell me you drove here," I said.

"Of course," she replied. "The car is just outside."

"And you're sure Rebekah is at this house near Hidden Valley?" I asked. I needed to keep moving, both physically and mentally, or I felt I would crack apart.

Kailani shook her head and sucked at her teeth. "Yeah."

I headed out to her car. My duffel bag and the metal case St. Germain had given me were sitting in the sand next to an old beige Land Cruiser.

"So, you still sure I'm the leak?" she asked, walking slowly out of Gara Medouar.

She crossed her arms and fixed me intently with a gaze meant to wither me, but I was beyond caring. She did have a point, though. *Possibly.* And I needed a ride. And to find Rebekah. Mostly, I just need to be in motion.

I sighed heavily and let my head roll back. "I may have been wrong," I said, leaning back on the truck.

"That's not much in the way of an apology, Diomedes," she said, shifting her weight.

"I don't have time—"

Kailani held up a hand to cut me off. "Apologize, or you go nowhere." She jangled the keys. "Unless you think you can take them from me."

I stared hard at the ground for a moment. "I'm sorry for thinking you were working with Nemesis," I said, avoiding eye contact.

"That's almost as pathetic as the first one," she said. "But you're right. We need to get going if we're going to catch Rebekah."

Chapter 40

The trip back to California was painfully slow. Flying commercial really did stink. Honestly, traveling anywhere by any means other than the Telluric Pathways was a huge waste of time. Making the trip took the better part of twenty-four hours, made even worse by the fact that Kailani was upset with me and we barely spoke the entire time, even if it was justified.

I just couldn't bring myself to apologize.

All I could think is that if I could get to Rebekah, then I could find out where Eisheth was, which would get me one step closer to helping Sarah.

Momentum. One step. Just one step.

The problem was that each step I'd taken so far felt like I was going sideways or backward, not forward. And I was tired. I rubbed my eyes and pinched the bridge of my nose, feeling a headache set in behind my eyes as we stood outside the airport in the rideshare area, waiting for some stupid black sedan. I had to leave the guns behind in Morocco, but luckily, my swords and cuirass were so tarnished and weathered that the customs agents assumed they were cheap fakes bought as souvenirs.

"I really need to get more gear," I said. "You know anyone? Only guys I know up here in LA are from when I was with the Teams, but that was years ago. I don't even know if they're still in business."

"I know one guy. He's down off Concord Alley in Boyle Heights near the 60. He should be able to help."

"Boyle Heights?" I was worried about the neighborhood's reputation.

"It's either that, or you can go back to your house in San Diego," she replied. "This guy will be faster, but he is as sketchy as you'd expect in Boyle Heights." She shook her head. "It's your call. I'm not the one who's mortal. You got money?"

"No."

"That won't work. This guy won't sell on credit, Diomedes," Kailani said. "And you aren't superhuman anymore. People are shot in Boyle Heights all the time just for looking at people the wrong way. Can't you just call your gun-happy friends from Morocco? That would be a lot safer. Didn't you say one of them had a beef with Rebekah too?"

"Yeah, Duma," I replied. "I suppose I should. I told him I would if I found her. Let's go lay eyes on the place first and make sure she's there."

From LAX, we took just over two hours to get to Kailani's place in Silver Lake then out to Westlake Village along Highway 101 even though the town was only thirty miles northwest of LA. We turned off the 101 onto the 23 South, and the landscape quickly shifted from upscale and developed to rolling hills dotted with massive ranches and estates.

"Unfortunately, the house is fairly isolated on a large piece of property," Kailani said. "The owner is never there, but he has a full staff that maintains the house, the stables, and the other buildings. My contact is one of the stable hands."

"You trust him?" I asked as she drove.

"Yeah. He's, well, he's kind of in love with me."

"In love with you?"

"Well, sort of," she said, her shoulders creeping up around her ears sheepishly. "He's kind of, sort of, one of my thralls."

"Of course he is," I replied. "I should have expected as much from a vampire."

"Hey, that's not fair," she said, going from sheepish to pissed off in the span of a single heartbeat. "I only ever had two, and I've never abused mine. I only used them to stay informed. Lucky for you. The guy who owns this house is the managing partner for Cocytus and all its associated properties, along with a jillion shopping centers, a few buildings around the world, and some football team—European, not American. I felt it was a good idea to keep tabs on him."

"Nope, sounds like a great idea," I said. "Warp a man's mind, and trick him into risking his life and livelihood to do your bidding. Sure, I get it."

"Jerk."

"Pot. Kettle. Black," I said.

"Let's just not talk," she said, her eyes heavily hooded and her lips pressed tightly together when she wasn't speaking.

We drove into the Santa Monica mountains for fifteen minutes. The landscape became entirely undeveloped except for white fences and massive gates every few miles. Eventually, we drove past a massive forbidding gate with two stallions on it.

"This is it. The house is just over those hills. He's got a pretty sophisticated security system and private guards too. This is about as close as we can get without them noticing." She pulled off onto the side of the winding two-lane road.

"You wouldn't happen to have binoculars, would you?" I asked, trying hard not to be sarcastic.

"No."

"Well, can you contact your *thrall* and ask if she's still there, then?"

She pulled her cell phone from her back pocket and pressed a few buttons.

"Hey, is she still there?" Kailani asked, her voice husky. "Thanks, keep an eye on her for me, lover, please. I owe you." Then she hung up. She avoided making any sort of eye contact with me at all.

I nearly threw up.

"Yeah, she's still there. She's staying in the master suite," she said, putting the phone away, then she crossed her arms and leaned back on the car.

"Okay, then I'll call Duma and Ab and have them show up," I replied. "Then we'll figure out a way to go get her, and you can go pay back your thrall."

I walked a few yards away from the car before I pulled out my cell phone to make the call. I really didn't want to. Then I remembered the leather pouch inside my gear bag—the one containing my Roc-feather quill, parchment, and other implements that would allow me to send a message via *other* means.

While that was an infinitely more secure way to send messages, it was significantly more time-consuming and a far more inefficient process, and if I hadn't been so angry at Duma, I suppose I would have just called him. As I cut my thumb and spread my blood on the corner of the page and spoke the incantation I'd been taught, I felt drained and tired, something I'd never really noticed when doing that before. *Being human in this world is a truly tenuous existence. Everything is trying to kill you, including life itself.* When I was done, I took great care to burn the page and stomp it into the dirt on the side of the roadway.

"Let's head back to town, back to that shopping center up at the 101," I said, putting the messaging kit back into my gear bag. "I told them to meet us there as soon as possible."

"How long do you think that'll be?" she asked.

"I mentioned we found Rebekah, so I'm thinking somewhere between 'with all due haste' and 'damn fast.'"

She nodded and opened the driver's side door to get in. "Why don't we just wait for them here?"

"We need to head them off," I replied. "If Duma knows where this place is, he'll go in hot, straight for Rebekah, and I really need her alive. I need to find Eisheth, and I'm hoping that even if Rebekah doesn't know, she'll know who does."

Chapter 41

We drove back toward the 101 and parked in the parking lot of a shopping center just off the 23.

"How will we recognize them?" Kailani asked. "Or will they recognize us?"

In a quick glance around the supermarket parking lot, I saw two Bentleys—one Flying Spur and one Mulsanne—no fewer than a dozen white Teslas—including three Xs—two Rolls, an old Maybach, and even a McLaren of some kind or another. "Well, despite the affluence and the proliferation of exotic cars here, trust me when I say you will not have any trouble recognizing Duma's car when he pulls up. Whatever he's driving will make anything in this lot seem common by comparison, I promise you."

We sat in silence. Kailani was focused out across the parking lot at some point off in the distance. I wanted to be angry—at her, at Duma, at Sarah, at Eisheth, at Lilith, at Nemesis, and at the entire world, even at Athena. But if I was being honest, I was mostly angry at myself for failing, for being human, for breathing. And in the midst of my one-man pity party, something dawned on me: if Kailani wasn't the mole, I didn't know who was. And if we did get Rebekah and managed to find out where Eisheth was, I didn't know how I was going to do what I needed to when a brisk walk made me breathe heavily. *Sarah would be able to figure it out.*

Almost as if on cue, a matte-black SUV that appeared to be assembled from some sort of futuristic low-polygon design that would have given Mad Max nightmares pulled into the parking lot with a rumble so low that we could feel it long before we heard it. The black monstrosity was all angles without a single curve on it anywhere. The only color to break its monotone was a bright gold emblem on the dystopian zombie-killing grille. The beast of a vehicle made one pass around the periphery of the lot and parked in a mostly vacant area along Agoura Road.

"Told you," I said, pointing at the tanklike SUV.

Kailani's eyebrows rose high on her forehead, and she sucked at her teeth as she started the car and drove across the lot to get us closer.

"I thought that sand racer was crazy looking, but this thing is just..." I said, getting out of our car.

"He just got it, D," Ab said, holding up a hand to cut me off. "It's a Karlmann King."

"Where is she?" Duma asked. His voice was flat and cold, and he didn't even look in my direction.

"She's up the road at a large ranch house with a ton of private security," I replied. "I really need her alive, Duma. I'm serious this time. If she doesn't know where Eisheth is, she'll know someone who does. The second she gives me a name, she's yours, but until she does..."

"You gonna back us up this time, or you just want me and Ab to storm the place and take care of everything for you?" he asked, finally turning to look at me. "Like Gara Medouar. Just curious if we're going to have to watch our own backs."

"That's not fair, Duma," I said, walking over to him. "I told you we needed Ttab'a alive to go after Nemesis. You guys kicked the shit out of her."

"Yeah, well, did Nemesis show up?" he asked. "'Cause you don't look too bad if you had to fight her by yourself. For a pinky, I mean."

Duma hadn't used that derogatory term for a human with me in a very long time, and even in the past, I knew he was trying to be funny. This time, he put no humor into the statement at all.

"Hey, this is for Sarah," I said, stepping close enough to him that the toes of our boots touched. "You knew that, getting into this. Hell, you told me you wanted to help. You felt partly responsible for what happened."

"Yeah, but you don't see me sacrificing your dumb ass to try and save her, do you?"

"Nobody is sacrificing anybody for anyone," I said, stepping back from Duma and turning around. "We just have to play this smart."

"Then you need to get your head out of your ass," Duma said without missing a beat or even the tiniest hint of humor in his tone.

"Hear! Hear!" Kailani said.

"Gotta agree too," Ab added, leaning heavily on the SUV.

"Seriously, you guys are blaming me for all this shit going sideways?" I asked, hands on hips, feeling anger well up in my chest.

"Nah, D," Ab said, shaking his head slightly, his mouth fixed in a slight frown and his brow furrowed slightly. "Nobody's blaming you for anything. We're only saying you ain't thinking straight. And you know we got your back, man. Always have. But you aren't... you. And that shit's gonna get us killed." He slapped the roof of the odd-looking SUV.

"Watch the paint, Ab," Duma said. "Tell you what, D, why don't you let me and Ab go get Rebekah, and we'll meet you guys someplace?"

"No," I replied. "I'm going in with you. *We'll* get her. *We'll* find out where Eisheth is or at least who knows, and then *you* can have her."

"What about the vampire here?" Duma asked. "Aren't you still worried she's a mole?"

"No. Besides, she knows the house's layout inside and out," I said.

"I'm standing right here, guys," Kailani said, throwing her hands up. "And I am not working for anyone. At all."

The three of us stared at her blankly for a moment.

"Uh, if I get you something to draw with, can you sketch us the layout of the place?" I asked, finally breaking the awkward silence.

"Yeah, of course," she said, brushing her hair back.

Thinking quickly, I turned toward the grocery store at the end of the parking lot and headed toward it. I grabbed some butcher paper and markers in the nicest grocery store I had ever seen and headed back out to the group in the parking lot.

"See any movie stars in there?" Duma asked. "They all shop here, you know."

"What? No," I replied, confused. I regathered my thoughts and continued. "Kailani, we need to know all the entrances you know about, guard stations, cameras if you know where they are, and the basic layout, of course. Be as detailed as you can," I said, smoothing out a coil of heavy white paper. "Plus, if you can get your guy to estimate the number of people on-site, that would be helpful too."

"And give me the address," Duma said. "I want to pull it up on an online map to check the surrounding countryside for other access points."

"We got the drone, too, don't forget," Ab said.

Kailani took about thirty minutes to complete her drawing of the main house and stables, which also had some living quarters and an office in it.

"The main house has only eight bedrooms, all upstairs, but there are a large office, a theater, a massive kitchen, a formal dining room, living spaces, and a library downstairs. There is a private bedroom off the master suite, accessed through a hidden doorway. Just off the kitchen, there's a separate office for security with two small bunk rooms and two other small suites for a maid and a cook. The basement is mostly an indoor swimming pool, a gym, sauna, and bar. The private bedroom upstairs could double as a panic room, but it's not particularly heavily armored, I don't think. It's just hidden. All the weapons I ever saw were kept in the security room or carried. And security consisted of eight men at all times unless Constantin Roparos himself or some other dignitary was there. Then there would be at least four more personal bodyguards plus valets and attendants. And out in the stables, there are two full-time ranch hands and two more full-time security personnel who live on-site and two more that help as needed, depending on how many horses are present and whether there's breeding going on or not. Roparos takes his horses very seriously. There are also two more full-time groundskeepers who live out there, too, and over the course of the day, they could be almost anywhere on the property," Kailani said, pointing at the various spots on her map.

"That's nothing," Duma said with a snort. "Ten minutes tops."

Then Kailani exhaled heavily.

"That sounded ominous," I said.

"Well, that's just the human element," she replied. "There could be almost anything else there as well. And I mean anything. That place is neutral ground, just like the clubs. All types of vampires, all types of Fae, and who knows what else. I heard stories he once had a dragon there. Or some kind of wyrm anyway. It breathed fire is all I know." She waved a hand dismissively.

"Seriously?" Duma asked, his shoulders dropping, clearly more dejected than surprised. "How the hell come I never heard about this place, then?" His head canted slightly, and he mumbled to himself.

His brother slapped a meaty palm on his shoulder in consolation. The difference in size between the brothers and the entire context of the situation made the scene almost laughable. But I wasn't in a laughing mood.

"So, virtually anything?" I asked.

She shrugged and nodded. "I'd say a few Moroi at the least. But we could get lucky."

"Would your guy know?" I asked.

"He's a gardener," she said. "I doubt it unless it's very obvious they aren't human and they're out wandering around. Seriously, I can't imagine anything crazy is there unless there's a party or some sort of business meeting going on. If there is something there, whatever it is will be there by itself specifically because it wants to be isolated. That's been my experience."

Kailani gave Duma the address, and he promptly pulled it up on an online satellite mapping program. The property itself was reasonably isolated among the brown coastal hills and valleys south of the 101. In fact, the property was as close to isolated as it could get between the 101 and the Pacific Coast Highway. The nearest neighbor on any side was over half a mile away, but the nearest neighbor to the west—an equally large estate—was almost a mile away. The only access to the estate was off West Potrero Road, but satellite images showed lots of work roads within the property itself. To make matters worse, no flat land was anywhere in the area that wasn't man-made. Everything was rolling hills.

"Yeah, I'm definitely going to need to put the drone up," Duma said. "I don't even see a visible fence line except along the road, and if security is as tight as she says, that means they have vibration sensors, trip wires, or some kind of wards up. Likely all three. I may have to revise my earlier estimate."

Ab chuckled and crossed his massive arms over his chest, no small feat.

"Twenty minutes, tops," Duma said before snorting and wiping at his nose with the back of his hand. "In and out."

"I'm not interested in speed," I said. "Only that we get Rebekah out of there alive. Or at least we get out of there alive with the information."

"Killjoy," Duma said. "Besides, you're the limiting factor. Even if she's only one-tenth as good with a gun as you are, she's still twenty times faster than you." He pointed at Kailani.

"Thanks," Kailani said. "But I can hold my own with or without a gun."

"Woo-hoo," Duma said with a whistle. "Sarah two-point-oh."

"What's that supposed to mean?" I asked, feeling bile rise in my throat as my stomach churned.

"Yeah, what the fuck does that mean?" Kailani said, squinting, her eyes fixed hard on Duma, then she slowly turned toward me.

"Whoa, sorry," Duma said. "Tender topic. Duly noted. I didn't mean anything." He threw his hands up in mock surrender. "Seriously though, Kailani, let me get my drone, and you and I should head up to the estate. D, you and Ab stay here and try to come up with a good entry-and-egress plan."

Chapter 42

Duma and Kailani took off to do their recon while Ab and I went over the gear. The inside of the angular SUV was an odd conflation of spartan luxury. The car was obviously heavily armored, but it had only four individual seats inside, and all of them swiveled three hundred and sixty degrees. It was a first-class luxury tank, complete with gun ports, rocket launchers, roof-turret access, and heated cupholders.

"You really aren't yourself, D," Ab said matter-of-factly as he rammed shells into a special round magazine for his Pancor Jackhammer. He made it look easier than it was.

"I'm fine, Ab," I said, checking magazines, mostly out of habit.

"Bullshit, dude," Ab said.

Ab was simple—not simpleminded but simple. He never used more words than were necessary, and he never minced them. He had no concept of subtlety, but he was also never intentionally cruel. He just said what he saw. I chalked up his occasional lack of tact to the fact that he wasn't human and just didn't understand the nuances of human emotional diplomacy. So I tried not to take offense at his comment. I tried. I failed.

"Fuck you."

"See?" Ab said, stopping his magazine loading. He peered down his nose at me. "If you were you, you wouldn't have said that. But if you were you, I'd have crushed your fucking skull for saying it, D. You're a paradox. And I know this whole thing with Sarah has you all screwed up inside. I ain't never been in love, but I can imagine what

I would do if someone hurt you or Duma. Like this Hulder bitch. We're going to fix it, D. Just remember: me and Duma, we're on your side."

Ab and I continued to work in silence. It was awkward for me, but Ab worked on his weapons with unaffected precision. I found myself wishing I had his Fae lack of emotional depth. After an hour, I finally threw the gun I was working on down onto the map Kailani had drawn and leaned over it.

"What do you think?"

"About what?" Ab asked.

"In and out?" I replied.

"You're asking me, D?" The big Peri asked in return.

"Yeah, I am." I stood upright and crossed my arms over my chest.

"Well, way I see it, it's fucked," he said, finishing up loading a magazine before turning his full attention to me and the map. "There's one road in—two lanes. The place is surrounded by acres of open hillsides, no forests." He sniffed heavily and shrugged. "I'd prefer a helicopter insertion in the backyard, blow these doors, go in, get the target, get the hell out. But I'm guessing that's off the table."

"Unless you guys have access to a helicopter," I said.

"Only take a phone call. Maybe two," he said. "Our place in Vegas is just a few hours away."

I should've known they'd have a helicopter in Vegas. "Okay, so just in case that doesn't work out," I said, "the only thing I can think is we drop two downrange to come in through the hills from either the north or south or both. I'm thinking Kailani and Duma because they will move faster and lighter over the ground in case of security measures. I'm thinking you and I will take the two cars to the front. You take this thing through the front gate, right up to the door, through it if necessary, and I leave Kailani's car at the street to block the drive when we leave. We time it so we hit the house as a group, get Rebekah, and get her out the front into this tank, block the drive with the other car, blow it, and run like hell. That's plan B."

"Sounds reasonable," Ab said, raising his pale blond eyebrows, hands on hips. "How will Kailani feel about you blowing up her car?"

"Well, I hope you guys can get a helicopter, and I won't have to," I replied.

"Me too," he said. "Vampires can be scary when they're pissed off."

Just as the sun was setting behind the hills to the west of us, Kailani and Duma returned, laughing as they got out of the car.

"Give me some time to download these images to the computer to get a better look at things, and we can get moving," Duma said. "They had something going on with horses near the stables. Damnedest thing I ever saw. The horses seemed to be more aware of the drone than the trainers. Not spooked, but aware. Tracking it. Both of them."

"Yeah, those two horses are creepy," Kailani added. "They are Roparos's pride and joy. He never lets anyone near them, either."

"Duma, can we get the helicopter?" Ab asked.

"From Vegas? No. Maintenance. Why?" Duma asked. "Oh, damn, yeah, that would have made things easier, wouldn't it?"

"Well, D, you might as well tell her now, then," Ab said with a grimace.

"Tell me what?" Kailani asked.

"We need to blow up your car," I said.

Chapter 43

"What?" Her eyes went from wide to impossibly wide. "Did I hear you right? Why on earth—"

"We need it to block our exfil," I said. "I suppose we can steal one instead. Probably smarter if we do that. Some junker from somewhere that no one will miss."

Instantly, Duma's head perked up from staring down at his computer screen to swivel around, surveying the parking lot.

"Not here," I said, shaking my head. "These cars all have alarms, tracking systems, and owners that just ran into the store for a gallon of milk."

"So I'll find one down the road. There's a Lamborghini dealership—"

"No, if we steal one—especially one of those—it'll be missed. We've got to take one that's going to be from a part of humanity that won't miss it," I replied. "Where's the nearest gang-held territory?"

"Wait, you want me to go into some human gang territory and jack a car so we can blow it up?" he asked, tilting his head slightly, one eyebrow raised.

"Well, yeah," I said. "We need something to block our exit path—"

Duma held up his hands to stop me. "Dude, you had me at 'steal a car.'"

"Nearest gang territories I know of are west of here in Oxnard. Look for anything with a star, horseshoe, or a lightning-bolt logo from the pro football teams, and you'll know you're in one of the areas for the two biggest. Just be careful. They're not MS-13, but they're still ultraviolent," Kailani said.

Duma and Ab snorted at the same time at practically the same pitch, as if on cue. "At least MS-13 employs some Paran muscle. If there are gangs in Oxnard, I can tell you they aren't employing any inhuman hitters," Duma said. "Because that, I *would* have heard about."

"And if they ain't got nonhuman muscle to back them up," Ab said, interlacing his fingers and then stretching them until they popped, "I'm not worried."

"Oxnard's straight down the 101, right?" Duma asked, walking toward the driver's side of the angular SUV. He wasn't really waiting for an answer. "Computer's booted up and compiling the drone footage now. It'll beep when it's done. Last chance, D. Any specific requests for a car type? You want a truck, a van, something we can pack full of explosives? Or is a little sedan good enough?"

"Whatever is easy and inconspicuous and won't be missed," I said.

"Almost like us in Gara Medouar," Duma said as he closed the door with a heavy thump.

Ab climbed in the passenger side, and in a moment, I was left standing alone with Kailani.

"Blow up my car?" she said, her hands flying up and out. "Why didn't you just say we needed to steal a car? Passive-aggressive much?"

"I hadn't thought it through until Ab mentioned it, and I was just basing it on what we had in our inventory," I said. "We need Duma's tank to get out once it's done. To be honest, I was hoping we could get a helicopter. But these horses, are they going to be problematic?"

"I don't know," she replied. "The guy is very protective of them when he breeds them or when they are out. Duma said he saw two big horses, one black and one white. Zanidu and Bailiwick or something. I forget."

"Wait, what?" I said, my heart nearly stopping in my chest at her description and pathetic recall of their names. "A massive pitch-black horse named Xanthus and an identical horse *in every way*, except pure white, named Balius. Both males?"

"Yeah, that sounds about right," Kailani said.

"You've got to be kidding me," I said, mostly to myself. "Those were Achilles's horses, given to him by his father, who got them from Poseidon. They're not normal horses."

"Well, they're his prized possessions, and he breeds them for the right price," she said. "And they're better protected than the Pope."

If humans only knew what truly lives in the dark recesses and alley-ways of this world, let alone in some wealthy guy's stables...

The computer that Duma left running made a chiming noise then whirred softly. An image appeared on the screen, but it was far too small to make out any details. I hovered over it for a second, trying to make sense of the tiny blurs and pixels.

"Seriously?" Kailani asked incredulously next to me and snatched the computer off the hood of her car from in front of me. She cradled it in one hand while she ran a finger across a small space below the keyboard.

I really was a relic. I knew I needed to learn more about technology, but modern electronic technology changed terribly quickly compared to every previous technological advancement I had witnessed. In a handful of decades, we'd gone from skimming precariously through the sky over sand dunes into outer space, and computers went from the size of houses to the palm of your hand in half that time. The only constant was war. No matter the technology or its reason for development, man would find a way to apply it to war.

"Now, it should make more sense," Kailani said, setting the computer back down on the hood of her car. "Just touch here, and drag your finger around to move the image."

She pointed at the smooth square space below the keyboard. I was pretty sure it was called a touchpad, but that made too much sense.

The image on the screen was much larger, focused on the house at the moment. The overhead drone shots didn't reveal much of the house's facade. The only view was straight down. I moved the image around to reveal the expansive backyard, including the sprawling man-made ocean of a pool and palatial gardens leading to the stables and a few other outbuildings. But as Kailani said, the majority of the surrounding landscape was barren hillsides and valleys with a few stands of haunted old oak trees and scrub brush here and there, making for scattered and almost useless point-to-point cover. In fact, the terrain itself would be difficult crossing until we made it well onto the grounds of the estate.

Duma and Kailani could probably make the crossing, but that was too risky. They would be too exposed and have to cover too much ground before hitting the house. Duma could probably handle it. I didn't know how Kailani would do in a fight, and I didn't want to risk her not being up to the task. The truth was, with their speed, if we hit the house from the front, they could bail and circle around rapidly, using the landscaping as cover. All eyes would likely be focused on the big black battering ram of a vehicle barreling toward the house anyway. Ab and I would bear the brunt of the resistance.

It was going to be a full-on frontal assault straight in through the front door. It would lack style and stealth. We were going to have to rely on the element of surprise instead—and brute force. *At least Ab will be happy.*

"Isn't there a way to see this house in three dimensions or something?" I asked. "I know the early drone-mapping tech we tested when I was a SEAL was supposed to do that, and that was years ago. Surely that's a real thing by now?"

"I don't know Duma's computer," she said with a shrug. "Ask him when he gets back. What I can tell you is that the main doors are here." She pointed at the top of a multistepped stoop at the apex of the circular driveway. "There are large French doors here," she said, pointing at the outside wall to the right of the front doors, "that lead to the formal dining area inside, but I don't think they function. I've never seen them open—even at parties. Servant's entrance is here, and these are all garage bays." She swept her finger from the right side of the house past the main entrance all the way to the left side of the massive edifice. "The back has a main entrance as well, here, with additional doors here and here." Again, she pointed at the rear center of the house and then at its flanks. "The best news I can give you is that most of the doors are glass."

"Likely bulletproof Lexan or heavily reinforced at the very least," I said. "And Rebekah will most likely be where?"

"Well, during the day, she could be by the outdoor pool, I suppose, but otherwise, she'll most likely be here." She pointed at a turret-like structure on the back side of the house. "That's the master bedroom. It's actually an *en suite* of rooms the size of most houses."

I pulled out the butcher-paper map she'd drawn earlier just to refresh myself on the internal layout of the house. Part of me felt like I needed to do something about the horses, Xanthus and Balius. They should not be in the possession of a mortal, nor should they be bred for personal gain. I had to remind myself I was no longer a Guardian. I was way off the reservation.

"If you had to estimate, when would you say is the least active time of day at the house?"

"First thing in the morning, say around six," she said, one eyebrow raised thoughtfully as she tapped at a front tooth. "A lot of the guests are night owls, and daytime is when they deal with the horses, so it'll be between the two, when the owls are going to sleep and the daytimers haven't quite gotten going yet."

"Nothing to do but wait for Duma and Ab, then."

A few hours later, I heard the low rumble of Duma's angular SUV monstrosity as it pulled into the parking lot. Ab's crew cut was quickly visible behind the wheel. Behind the black behemoth was a relatively nondescript sedan. The only outstanding features were the massive silver wheels and the fact that it sat so low that the tires barely fit inside the wheel wells. Duma drove over the speed bumps in the parking lot with great care. He pulled up next to Ab and got out, a bandanna tied around his forehead and pulled down so that it almost covered his eyes. He had to tilt his head back to see us.

"So, we stopped and got a bunch of gas cans and some propane tanks too," Duma said finally taking the stupid bandanna off. "If I had the time, I'd rig a charge to split the car into large chunks to totally litter the driveway. Two cars would be better." His gaze traveled to Kailani.

"No, you *cannot* blow up my car," she said.

Duma shrugged. "So, did you come up with a plan, or do you need us to do that too?"

"I have a plan," I said.

"Lay it on us," Duma said, crossing his arms over his chest as he leaned on the low-slung sedan.

"We approach the front gate with the two cars, Ab driving that one with me"—I pointed at the big SUV—"You two are in this one. As soon as Ab hits the gate, you guys leave this car, rigged to blow just off the driveway, and hightail it up the drive and around the house to the doors on either side of the main back entrance. Ab and I will draw attention and drive right up to the front door, into it if necessary, then back out so it's ready to leave. Then we go in. We all meet at the base of the stairs leading up to the main bedroom here." I pointed at the drawing Kailani had made. "From there, Kailani will stand overwatch with Duma backing her up. Ab and I will go into the master suite to retrieve Rebekah, then you two will lead us out to the SUV, and we will run like hell, leaving the sedan here to explode in the driveway, blocking the exit for just a bit and buying us a few minutes."

"Those are garage bays over there, right?" Duma asked, pointing at the far-left side of the structure.

"Yes, four of them," I said.

Kailani nodded in agreement.

"I wonder if there's any way we can do something there to further slow them down?" Duma asked.

Ab laughed a deep bellow like an evil Santa Claus. "I brought an RPG. Pop the turret on the way out and let her rip. You don't even have to be that accurate."

Duma grinned a wolfish, toothy smile and nodded his head once. "That's why I bring him along."

Chapter 44

At half past five the next morning, we slowly drove down the road leading up to the house and parked fifty yards down the street. In the growing early-morning light, I could see through binoculars that only a few lights were on downstairs, but nothing moved inside as we drove up.

"Good a time as any," I said.

I opened my door and waved, letting Duma and Kailani know the time had come. Ab gunned the big SUV's engine and took off, turning straight toward the gate without slowing. The low-riding sedan was right behind us. We hit the gate going close to ninety, and the heavy SUV tore the reinforced gates off their hinges without slowing much. I watched Duma put the sedan into a slide in the side-view mirror, and by the time I turned my attention back, we were headed up the short stoop toward the front doors.

"Knock knock!" Ab screamed as we crashed into the heavily re-inforced doors. Instantly, an alarm blared, accompanied by flashing strobe lights from multiple sources. Ab gunned the big V-12 engine, but something in the structure held us from proceeding farther into the house. Ab's guttural growl matched the engines. Ab slammed the car into reverse and backed down the stairs, and I bolted out of the SUV, leaving the door open behind me. On the opposite side of the truck, Ab placed his skull-shaped helmet on his head, hefted his mas-sive hammer, and ran toward the door, stretching the hammer over-head and screaming. He hit the hinges like a fireman would, except with enough force to drive a steel rod straight through an engine block. The twisted structure fell free from its rent frame with a crash. I followed. I followed because I couldn't even keep up with Ab. In one fluid, practiced move Ab slid the massive hammer into a special sheath on his back and slid his Pancor fully automatic shotgun around as we headed toward the staircase.

If Kailani's assessment was accurate, the most likely direction for anyone to attack us was from our left. Sure enough, two men in suits came running into the marble-covered foyer from a hallway to our left. I stopped, trained my sights on the first one, and fired two quick shots into his chest and one into his head. Before I could swing my rifle toward the second guard, Ab's giant shotgun thundered next to me, and a hole the size of a grapefruit opened in the guard's chest.

Additional gunfire reverberated from farther inside the house. I pivoted, bringing my assault rifle to bear on the pathway under the sweeping staircase, but before I came to a stop, Duma was standing in front of me, blood dripping from his favored kukris.

"Clear back, there!" he shouted over the whooping claxon. He wasn't even breathing heavily.

"There'll be more, trust me." Kailani's voice rang out across the marbled entryway as she walked in, reloading a Glock. She had two bullet wounds—one in her abdomen and one in her thigh—but neither seemed to be bothering her. Both her hands were a bloody mess as well.

I ran up the stairs sensing but not hearing or feeling Ab beside me, despite his bulk. At the top of the stairs was a large, balcony-like walkway that led to a double door, which was currently closed. I nodded at it, and Ab charged like a rabid rhino, arms crossed over his head as he hit, sending one of the doors flying while the other buckled and twisted. They were not wood.

I entered right behind Ab and circled to my right, where I knew a closet would be. I kicked the door open but saw nothing but furniture and cabinetry within—no place for a person to hide. Another doorway sat on the opposite side of the room, and Ab lumbered toward it without hesitation. I ran to catch up and fall in behind him.

"Knock knock," Ab growled as he heel-kicked the door so hard that the frame splintered and the door flew from its hinges.

Gunfire erupted immediately, and I instinctively ducked in behind the giant Peri for cover. He was wearing his dragon-scale vest, which meant very little would ever be able to penetrate it. A bullet ricocheted off his helmet, and Ab roared but restrained himself.

"Stop fucking shooting at me with that fucking pea shooter, or I will blow you into next week, scrape your remains together, and tap dance on them—and I can't dance for shit, dammit!" he bellowed. "D, get up here and do something before I kill this bitch."

"Rebekah," I said, coming out from behind Ab, rifle leveled and tracking until she came into my sights. "Drop it. You're coming with us one way or the other."

The Hulder was a mess. Her hair was disheveled, her lipstick was smeared across her face, and her eyeshadow was caked up around her eyes like a deranged raccoon.

"You're Duma's brother, aren't you?" the Hulder asked, eyeing Ab skittishly.

"Yeah, you—"

I patted Ab on his shoulder as I passed around him. As I did, I lowered my weapon and raised my hands. "I just want to ask you some questions. Cooperate, and you might survive," I said. I lowered my hands to seem nonthreatening, but in truth I needed my hands close to the Glock on my hip. I was worried that if she felt cornered, she might try to do something stupid, and I didn't want to be caught flat-footed. I was already human in a room full of Fae, which was bad enough.

Her eyes were cast down, and she exhaled heavily, and I knew what she was about to do. I went for my Glock, but she was Fae. I felt a breeze blow past the left side of my head just as I brought the gun to a combat-ready position, prepared to fire to disable her and stop her from shooting herself as she raised the gun to her head. Before I could complete the maneuver—a span of less than a second—a knife struck Rebekah in the shoulder, and she dropped the gun with a clatter and a high-pitched yip.

"You don't get off that easy, love," Duma said, stepping out from behind his brother. His toothy grin was predatory and bloodthirsty and downright frightening.

"Okay, Duma, we got her. Now, back off, and go back up Kailani," I said.

Duma didn't move.

"Now, dammit!" I shouted. "Before we get fucked from behind. Ab, grab her, and let's get the hell out of here now."

I returned my Glock to its holster on my hip and pulled my rifle back into position on its sling, following Duma out of the bathroom. I had never seen him move so slowly. A moment later, Ab came out of the bathroom with Rebekah tossed over one shoulder. Duma glanced back and winked at her and was gone in the blink of an eye.

"Let's go, boys!" Kailani shouted from down below. "Backup is coming."

"I got 'em," Duma said. "Don't wait for me."

Once Ab and I made it to the stairs, I followed as Kailani took point straight out the front doors. To my surprise, we met no resistance exiting. As Ab threw Rebekah into the SUV and Kailani piled into the other side, a man fell limply from the roof and landed a few feet from the SUV. He had a gash in his back that went from buttocks to shoulder blade, which splayed his clothing and his skin wide open to the bone. Dark blood pooled around him instantly.

"Let's go!" I shouted, climbing into the free seat in the back. Rebekah was on the floor between Kailani and me.

Ab tossed his hammer and shotgun into the back and calmly—too calmly for my taste—walked back to the driver's side. As he climbed in, Duma landed next to the front passenger side fender with an easy, fluid move that suggested he'd jumped only a step or two rather than landing from thirty feet overhead. He was in the SUV with the door closed within the span of a breath. Ab slammed the SUV into reverse and spun it around while I pulled out the RPG.

I popped open the turret in the roof and braced myself in the opening, and Ab came to a skidding halt just inside the remains of the gate. Duma climbed out and headed for the bomb car, and I unleashed three grenades at the garages, sending shrapnel and debris from the structure and the cars inside up into the air and across the driveway. I dropped back into my seat, Ab pulled out, and Duma drove the bomb car across the destroyed gate mouth and walked back to the SUV with a detonator in his hand. A hundred feet down the road, he pressed the button, and the car exploded in three dull whumps and a fireball that sent a black cloud three hundred feet up.

"Where to?" Ab asked.

"Our place in Vegas," Duma said before I could answer. "Nonnegotiable." He turned to face me directly, slouched in the rotating seat. His gaze went from me to Rebekah's prone form on the floor next to me.

"Makes sense," I replied. "You remember what I told you, Duma. Interrogation first."

"No worries, D," he said, turning back around in his seat. "No worries."

Chapter 45

The bloodthirsty, revenge-seeking Peri behaved like a cat preparing to pounce on an unsuspecting bird for the entire five-hour drive to Vegas. He practically came unglued when traffic came to a complete standstill for almost forty-five minutes outside Baker. Duma twitched, spun around, fiddled, and stared intently at Rebekah, who remained still and quiet, trying her best to ignore him while he did his best to intimidate her. The entire ride was uncomfortable, to say the least.

Once we hit Vegas, Ab turned off Interstate 15 and headed west on Russell Road, on the opposite side of the interstate from the Four Seasons hotel and the Strip. The area stood in stark contrast to what people normally thought about Vegas. There was no glitz or neon. Low, metal industrial buildings and tall security fences took the place of the over-the-top glamour, activity, and glaring lights of the Strip just a few miles away. Other than the waves of heat rising off the asphalt streets, it could have been almost any other industrial park in any other city. The one feature that stood out to me most was the total lack of people. Perhaps because of the heat, or maybe for other reasons, no one was walking the streets.

We turned down several side roads then into an alleyway and stopped at a gate in a nondescript security fence that ran the entire block. Ab pushed a button on the touch screen embedded in the dashboard of the big SUV, and the gate slid open. The drab tan metal building inside the fence appeared to be a gigantic warehouse with a series of oversized garage doors along one side. Vehicles of all types occupied most of the open space inside the fence. Off to one side was a larger multistory building with a significantly larger rolling door in the middle of the facade facing the tarmac inside the fence. A large letter *H* within a circle took up most of the concrete in front of the building—a helipad.

As we came to a stop in front of the larger warehouse building, Ab hit another icon on the touch screen, and one of the smaller garage doors slid open. The cars in the lot struck me as pedestrian and commonplace—not the Ferraris, Lamborghinis, and other high-end cars I'd come to expect from Duma. In fact, many of them were junkers, most in a state of deconstruction, either with various parts missing or lifted on jacks. Once the door was fully opened, Ab slowly pulled inside, and the door closed behind us.

"Ah, Duma," I said, taking in the building's lackluster interior, "what the hell?"

I opened the door and lumbered out, immediately needing to stretch my aching back and legs from the long ride. Duma hopped out of the front passenger seat like a kid arriving at a theme park. Kailani stretched like a cat waking from a nap as she emerged from the opposite side of the car.

"What?" Duma asked, his brow knitted slightly.

"This place," I replied. "I don't see a single exotic car. I mean, that's a Toyota on that lift."

"This is a working shop, D," Duma said. "Legit."

"Mostly," Ab snorted. "Come on, chick, let's go. Don't make me drag you out of there." Ab leaned into the big SUV, his arms resting on the door frame as he peered inside.

"Then where is everyone?" Kailani asked.

"Told them all to take the afternoon off," he said, interlacing his fingers and stretching the palms out in front of himself. "I got work to do."

"Duma, promise me we'll get the information we need first." I could feel the bile and sourness rise into my throat at the thought of what was about to happen. I tried to focus on the fact that she'd nearly killed Duma and Kailani and had probably intended to finish the job, but I just couldn't get past the idea of torture. Kill her outright—she deserved it. But no one deserves torture, no one. I could feel the muscles tighten in my jaw and shoulders.

Rebekah clambered out of the SUV, and as Ab reached for her bound hands, she jerked them away. "Don't you touch me," she said defiantly.

"Oh, trust me, I won't be the one touching you," Ab said.

"Rebekah," I said, walking in front of her, trying to look her in the eye. She wouldn't make eye contact at all. "Tell us where Eisheth is, and I promise you I will make sure Duma goes easy on you."

"Don't you dare make that promise, D!" Duma shouted from across the garage. "Rebekah, babe, you will tell me what I want to know. And I am only too happy to make you tell me. In fact, I hope you try to be stubborn. Please be stubborn."

I watched him loading up a rolling cart full of tools. He would pick one up, examine it, rock his head back and forth for a moment, then throw it on the cart or back into the toolbox it came from.

Rebekah's face was slack. If possible, she appeared to have aged. Her eyes were droopy, and the corners of her mouth sank, and she stared vacantly at the ground or off into the middle distance.

"Karma's a bitch, ain't it?" Kailani said, clearly not bothered by the idea of what was about to happen.

"Karma's a crack whore meth head when I'm involved," Duma replied, shoving the cart full of tools over to an area with an engine hoist next to a subfloor workspace similar to what you see in an oil change shop. "Bring her over here. Those with weak constitutions need to leave now. D, I'm talking to you." He pointed at me without looking.

He was entirely too giddy, but I'd always known what he was really like. I would like to say it was because he wasn't human, but I've seen humans do things just as horrific.

Begging or arguing with him would prove futile. And as a milquetoast mundane, I couldn't intimidate him anymore. "Duma, please remember why we went after her in the first place," I pleaded.

"You mean why *you* went after her," he said. "I went after her for an entirely different reason," he said, picking up a cutting torch, an evil grin spreading across his face. His pale-white eyes seemed to darken.

Rebekah didn't move, so Ab pushed her slightly from behind. With preternatural speed, she spun around and spat at Ab. It caught him off guard, and he recoiled slightly. He wiped his face and stared at his wet palm, grinned, then backhanded her. She flew half the distance to Duma—a good fifteen feet—before she slid to a halt in a loose pile.

"Ab, what the fuck, dude!" Duma screamed. He raced over to the limp form, screwdriver in hand.

"Hey, she spat on me—"

"I don't care if she tried to rack you. She's mine," Duma said, kneeling over her. "Hey there, sweetheart. Wakey wakey." He lightly slapped her face.

Without warning, Rebekah kicked up, bringing her leg across Duma's shoulder and into his face, knocking him onto his back. In the span of an instant, I saw a blur of movement that I interpreted to be her getting to her feet and running, followed by an even faster move from Duma that resulted in Rebekah skidding face-first across the floor less than ten yards away with a screwdriver sticking out of her thigh. Duma got to his feet and shook the cobwebs loose from his head then wiped his mouth with the back of his hand.

Kailani and Ab exchanged surprised glances.

"I'm glad there's still some fight left in you, Rebekah," Duma said, licking at the butter-colored blood in the corner of his mouth while examining the blood pool on his hand.

I'd had enough, and I snapped.

"We really don't have time for this cat-and-mouse crap, Duma," I said, walking over to Rebekah's prone form. I pulled my gun and put it to the back of her head. "Yes, this is a gun, and if you don't tell me where Eisheth is by the count of three, I'm going to see how far a nine-millimeter bullet will penetrate concrete after passing through your skull." I knelt down next to her.

"Where who is?" Rebekah mumbled, trying to regain her composure.

"Wrong answer," I said, grabbing the screwdriver and wrenching it.

Rebekah howled in pain.

"Diomedes!" Kailani shouted from behind me.

"Whoa, D," Duma said from behind me. "She's mine."

"You were moving too slow. I don't have time for this drawn-out bullshit," I said, growling. "We need Eisheth's location, now."

Before I could blink, the gun fell apart in my hand, and Duma was dropping pieces of it slowly on the ground as he loomed over me. "Don't push me, D. She's mine."

"We need that location!" I screamed, rising to my feet to face Duma as quickly as I could.

"I. Will. Get. It," Duma said, squinting. "Now, back the fuck up."

I glared at him for a moment, realizing that in my mortal condition, I was no match for him. Feeling powerless, I turned and stomped away like a petulant child. Within a moment, I felt but did not hear Kailani appear next to me.

"What was that all about, Diomedes?" she asked.

"I'm tired of fucking around," I replied. "We are running out of time."

A guttural scream erupted from behind us, but I didn't look. I stormed out the nearest door into the blazing Las Vegas sun. I suddenly felt tired, hopeless, alone.

Behind me was the Vegas skyline—the garish hotels, the mock-ups of various famous landmarks in miniature, and I could hear the traffic. And more screams.

Chapter 46

I had no idea how long I'd been standing there, staring at the crazy cityscape, when one of the doors to the warehouse opened. Blinded by the sun, I couldn't see into the pervasive darkness within.

"Eisheth is in China, like we figured." Kailani's voice echoed from the doorway. "Apparently, she hasn't left in weeks."

"What's she afraid of?" I asked.

"What makes you think she's afraid and not simply waiting?" Kailani's response was flat and matter-of-fact.

Her statement hit me. "That would imply she knows we're coming after her."

I ran back into the warehouse, past Kailani. "Ask her if she knows we're coming after her!" I shouted.

As my eyes adjusted to the dark interior, I saw Ab carrying Rebekah's limp form down into the subbasement. Duma was wiping his hands on a rag, a pool of blue liquid around his feet.

"Yep. She knows," the bloodthirsty Peri said with a smug look on his face. "So what?"

"How? How does Eisheth know we are coming?"

He nodded slightly toward Kailani and shrugged.

That just didn't ring true. I spun on my heels to find Kailani, and she was immediately behind me, catching me by surprise.

"You got something you want to say to me?" she asked with a terse set to her jaw and a squint in her eyes.

"Tell me you aren't a mole," I said. "Right now."

"So you *don't* trust me," she said. "After all this? Then fuck you." With that, she turned and began to walk out.

"I swear if you betrayed me—"

"It wasn't me, Diomedes, but you can go fuck yourself all the same," she said with a flip of her hand as she walked out the door.

"Damn, you're just pissing off everyone there, buddy," Duma said, dropping the blood-soaked rag onto my shoulder.

"Well, if not her, then who?" I said grabbing the rag and tossing it.

"Beats me." He shrugged. "Who else knew what we were up to?"

"Athena, but she never would have said anything. Brey, but she never would have said anything," I replied, racking my brain.

"Yeah, there's no way those two would have said anything to Eisheth or any of her minions. Wasn't me or Ab."

"That only leaves your buddy St. Germain and that nutjob, Nemesis," I said, putting my hands on my hips.

Duma did a double take. "What would St. Germain have to gain? I mean, the dude is a bigger mercenary than I am, but without a real benefit to himself, he wouldn't move a muscle. Unless—"

"You're right," I replied in a sudden moment of clarity. "It has to be Nemesis. Who else could it be? She's shown up everywhere I've been. Somehow, she's been tracking me, and now she's working with Eisheth because I pissed her off by not killing St. Germain."

"Well, I suppose that could be possible," Duma said with a tilt of his head and a slight shrug, "but it's more likely that—"

"The problem is I can't go after Eisheth with Nemesis in the way too." I shook my head. "I've got to find some way to stop her *before* we go after Eisheth."

"Well, yeah, but what if she isn't the only problem?" Duma asked, though his question barely registered at all.

"Did you say something?" I asked, feeling the tension in my forehead from my furrowed brow.

"No, I guess not." Duma shook his head and pursed his lips.

"I wonder if Dvalinn could make a weapon capable of doing damage to one of the Old Ones?"

"Maybe, but don't you already owe him for using his cloak?" Duma asked, referring to the last time I asked for help from the leader of the Svartalfar.

"No. Well, yes, but not me. Athena," I said.

"You think he sees you two as separate?" Duma asked. "Besides, what could you, a mortal human, possibly offer him for his help?"

"I don't know... Information?" I suggested.

"Yeah, and last time he wanted... What was it?" Duma asked, tapping his lower lip. "Oh yeah, he wanted you to put a doodad onto a satellite for him. The greatest smith and craftsman this planet has ever seen wanted you to put one of his fucking machines into space. On a fucking spaceship, Diomedes." He raised his hand in a gesture imitating a rocket launch. "What are you going to tell this guy that he's going to care about? The whereabouts of some lost human treasure you think he doesn't already have? Your chicken soup recipe?"

"There has to be a way. You and Ab can use the Pelian Spear, right?"

"Use it? In theory, yes, but not like you can. Or could," Duma said with a slight shrug.

"Ab can throw it," I replied. "His range has to be several hundred yards. Mine was, and he's stronger than I ever was."

Duma laughed. "Ab has the worst aim past about fifteen feet. He just throws stuff so hard it hurts no matter what. But he's like me. We prefer to get up close and personal. That's not the problem."

"So you can't use it effectively against a Protogenoi?"

"Maybe not that weapon, but we have others. We've been fighting with the Old Ones a lot longer than you have, D. But me and Ab don't need a beef with any of them. You're the god-killer. They all expect hostility from you, but me and Ab are all that's left of the Peri. We can't afford to make enemies of any of those fuckers."

"If there are weapons you can use, is it possible I could use them too? Against Nemesis, I mean." I asked, suddenly buoyed with hope.

"Yeah, I'd guess. There's Lugh's spear, the one he used to kill Balor in the First Battle of Magh Tuired." Duma said, referencing the one-eyed Fomorian giant, who also happened to be Lugh's grandfather.

Lugh was a Fae hero from before my time, but I recalled stories of him being similar to a Guardian, working with an Old One they called Lugus, who I knew as Hermes. And he did possess several famous weapons, including a spear.

"Gae Assail? I thought Lugh killed Balor with a sling and a special tathlum stone," I said, trying to remember the specifics of Lugh's three legendary weapons: a sling, a sword, *and* his spear.

"That's one version, but no, it was actually with a spear named Areadbhair. I know this because he got it from King Pisear, who got it from *my* family as a gift about four millennia ago. Its name means 'Slaughterer.' We got it from Goibniu long before the schism. It must be kept immersed in a special container of liquid or it bursts into an intensely hot blue-white flame. It's some function of the material it's made from. I have no idea. Goibniu was all proud of it." He waved his hand dismissively as he talked.

"Where is it?"

"On Toraigh, inside Tor Mór."

"Ireland?"

"Yep. Protected by a Bánánach," his pale eyebrows rose high on his forehead as he said it.

"Damn. What about his sword... Fragarach?" I asked, suddenly remembering the weapon's name. "Supposedly it was as sharp as mine are... or were. Are supposed to be."

"For the same reason, D," he replied, tilting his head in a conciliatory fashion. "It was a gift from Lugus, an Old One. I forget what you call him."

"Hermes or Mercury, among other names," I said absently. "How bad is that Bánánach?"

"Those things are hideous and bloodthirsty spirits. You know that," he said, his face screwed up in disgust. "They thrive on carnage. The more blood, the better."

For him to say that was saying something.

"I know that, but can she be killed or somehow... subverted?" I asked hopefully, moving my hand as if avoiding an object for effect.

"Hell if I know," he said with a shrug. "What I *do* know is that Areadbhair has been there—safely—for thousands of years. Even *you* didn't know about it. Plus, even if you get it, how are you going to handle it? Nomex gloves won't be enough, D. It burns so hot Lugh could barely handle it. In fact, I don't even know how he did handle it. Even Ab and I couldn't figure out how to use the damn thing, and you know if we could have, we would have. And even if you do get it, transporting it is going to be a bitch. The special liquid that keeps it from bursting into flames weighs a ton and stinks like hell, and the spear is taller than me."

My mind raced. If I could get—and use—Areadbhair, I could get Nemesis off my back. And I might even be able to use it against Eisheth. But first, I had to get it from a bloodthirsty creature that thrived on carnage then, apparently, figure out how to transport it then figure out how to use it. *Simple.*

If the spear was made by Goibniu, it was most likely made from materials found naturally, which means that what might have seemed like magic back then had likely become easily explainable science stuff. And I knew a serious science nerd who probably knew everything about Areadbhair anyway: Will "Geek" Elmsmore, former British SBS operator, Royal Marine, technological genius, and super geek extraordinaire. But thanks to me, he was working for Athena, so getting him was going to be tricky.

"Geek," I said.

"I am not," Duma said in return.

"No, not you. Will Elmsmore. Geek," I replied.

"Oh yeah, he might be able to help with figuring out some way to move the damn thing," Duma said with a nod. "Assuming we can actually get it." He frowned and bobbed his head for emphasis.

I grabbed my phone and dialed the only phone number I knew by heart: The Metis Foundation.

Chapter 47

"The Metis Foundation. How may I direct your call?" asked a male with a husky voice on the other end of the line.

"IT, Will Elmsmore, please," I said as curtly and professionally as I could.

"May I ask who is calling?"

"Please tell him it's Mr. Tydides, with, um, Special Solutions Incorporated."

"Please hold..."

The Muzak was horrible, and I realized I'd never had to wait on hold before. *If I ever get back in Athena's good graces, I'll have to bring it up. Canned easy-listening versions of disco from the late 1970s. Ugh.*

After several minutes, Will's familiar British accent came on. "Oy, Special Solutions Incorporated? More like Problem Creators. Where you at, mate? You okay? Half the world seems to be looking for you right now. You really cocked things up, didn't you? Cocked 'em right up."

"Nice to talk to you, too, Geek," I said. "Look, I need your help. Do you know anything about a spear named Areadbhair, used by a Fae hero named Lugh?"

"Personally, only the legendary stuff about Lugh," he said over a keyboard clicking in the background. "He killed his grandfather as part of a prophecy, right? Balor, no?"

"Yes, that's him," I replied. "I never heard of the spear, and the only thing I found about it is connected to the Cathasach Clan of Peri Anseelie Fae. Hey, isn't that Duma and Abraxos?"

"Yeah, that's their family. They did own the spear at one point... Whoa. Says here that it bursts into flames if it's not submerged in some kind of liquid," he said with a drawn-out breath. "Frakkin' hell."

"Yeah, that's why I was calling. Duma says it was forged by Goibniu, so it has to be made from natural materials. If that's the case, then I'm thinking you might be able to help me figure out how to transport—"

"You know where this thing is?" he said, cutting me off again. "You *actually* know, *and* you're going to get it?"

"Yes, but it's complicated. Duma said the liquid is viscous and heavy, and the spear burns unbelievably hot outside the liquid," I said.

"Hmm, so it ignites either above a certain ambient temperature, which the liquid maintains, or it ignites in the presence of air, which means the liquid would be a saturated hydrocarbon," Geek began.

I could feel my brain shriveling in my skull.

"Only a few substances combust at standard temperature and pressure. Assuming it's truly a natural substance. Cripes. Can you ask Duma what the spear looks like? I mean, is it shiny or dull, golden or gray?"

"Um, hold on. I'll put you on speaker," I said, fumbling with the phone, trying to remember how to enable it. Duma sighed audibly, and though his eyes were solid white, I could tell he was rolling them as he walked over and pushed a symbol on my screen.

"How you survived this long is a mystery to me, D," he said. "Hi, Geek. This is Duma."

"Duma! Long time no see! How've you been, mate? How's Abraxos?" Geek gushed.

"We're both fine, as long as D here doesn't get us killed," he said.

"Enough with the reunion," I said. "What did you want to know again, Geek? About the spear..."

"Oh right." Geek shifted back into full geek mode. "What did the spear look like, color and appearance-wise? I mean was it shiny, golden, what?"

"I never really got to see it out of its storage vessel," he said. "I only remember it looked dull and gray, and the whole damn thing stank like a rotting fish on a beach at low tide."

"Dull and gray... and stank like rotting flotsam and jetsam," Geek said. Again, the sounds of a clicking keyboard filtered through the phone. Before I could even become impatient, Geek blurted out, "I bet the damn thing was made of some kind of cesium or a cesium alloy or perhaps some sort of carbon subnitride, and it's stored in a bath of spermaceti—whale oil! But neither of those materials can be forged into a weapon in and of themselves. Duma, what color did it burn?"

"Intensely blue white. They used to think it was lightning," he replied. "That's why I always wanted to use the damn thing."

"Well, if it burned blue white, it wasn't cesium. It was more likely carbon subnitride, which forms acetylene and burns at nearly five thousand degrees centigrade," Geek said, unable to contain his excitement. "I'd bet my copy of *Detective Comics* number forty on it. But how Goibniu created a spear out of it is incomprehensible."

I really didn't want to know what a *Detective Comics* number forty was or how incredible the construction of such a weapon would be. All I wanted to know was how I could move it and how I could safely use it.

"So then the obvious question is 'How can I wield it without setting myself on fire?'" I said.

"It wouldn't set you on fire so much as melt you," Geek said. "Just to be clear. Theoretically, you could wear a fire entry suit. That would give you a few minutes. If you could cover your hands in a thick hydrocarbon, that would help a bit too."

"Whale oil?"

"Well, no, you could use another hydrocarbon like, say, petroleum jelly," Geek replied, almost apologetically.

"Petroleum jelly?"

"Yes, if you kept it smeared in petroleum jelly, air couldn't get to it to ignite it," Geek explained. "Theoretically anyway. I mean, I don't know how it works, so I can't say for sure. Like I said, I don't even know how it's possible, but it makes the most sense based on what Duma said. Assuming it really *is* made from elements we're familiar with. Normally, you make acetylene by passing nitrogen gas over superheated graphite."

My head was hurting worse.

"But if I could see it—"

"Geek, that's not going to happen," I said. "If Athena found out you were helping me, we'd both be in big trouble. It's best that I just take your best guess and go from there. Besides, we may not even get past the Bánánach that's watching over it."

"Oh man, there's a Bánánach protecting it?" Geek gushed. "I remember stories of those when I was a kid... bloodthirsty female spirits roaming battlefields, searching for victims. Wicked."

"Ever hear of the one on Toraigh at Tor Mór?" Duma asked.

"No, never heard of a specific one anywhere. Never even read about one on any blogs," Geek said. "No battles in Ireland for a long time, I guess."

"They aren't limited to Ireland, Geek," I said. "Same thing as the Machai I grew up with. All I know is violence is not the best way to beat them. On a battlefield, they're all but unkillable. One-on-one, they are pretty tame unless you stupidly choose to fight."

"Hmm," Duma said with a tilt of his head. "That might actually work. If we show up peacefully to face a creature that thrives on violence—"

"Hey, yeah," Geek said. "Show up unarmed, with no intention of fighting!"

"Well, if it doesn't work, at least we'll be dead quickly," I said, walking outside.

Chapter 48

"So, Ireland," Duma said from the doorway behind me. "I'm guessing you want either me or Ab to go with you."

"It would be helpful, yeah," I replied. "I'd prefer Ab go with me because I need you to try to keep tabs on Eisheth."

"What about Nemesis?" he asked.

"She'll find me. She always has. I just need to be ready for her the next time she does," I said. "Do you guys have some sort of airtight container big enough for the spear? I mean, by chance we actually get it. And I gotta get a truckload of petroleum jelly and a fire suit."

"Gotcha covered," Duma said, cocking a finger at me with a wink.

"Which, the petroleum jelly or the suit?"

"Both," he said with a wave of his hand as he turned and headed back into the warehouse.

I stood for a moment, alone, in the heat of the intense afternoon Las Vegas sun. All I had to do was get a spear that burned hotter than the sun from the lair of a murderous spirit and find some way to transport it without it igniting, *then* came the hard part: using it—against a Protogenoi, something no mortal human had ever managed to do before, unaided. All while not melting my face off, somehow.

"Will this work?" Abraxos said in his deep voice behind me, catching me completely by surprise.

He wasn't as stealthy as Duma, but compared to the average human, he was pretty sneaky for a being that weighed close to four hundred pounds. He was holding a long, narrow, hard plastic case, similar to what hunters used to transport their rifles when flying. That one was particularly long, but in Ab's hands, it appeared to have familiar proportions until I reached for it and realized it was about a foot taller than I was.

"Is it waterproof?" I asked.

Ab actually managed to appear hurt.

"Seriously? You gotta ask me that?" he asked with his eyes heavily hooded. "We had these custom-made for our guys to transport anti-materiel rifles and anti-tank rifles. Not only is it waterproof, but I can create a vacuum within it with a special pump. It'll hold even on most nonpressurized air travel up to forty thousand feet or so."

"So can we fill this thing with petroleum jelly?" I asked, hopeful that such a simple solution might actually work.

"You want to what?" Ab asked, ripping the case from my hands and practically pulling me over in the process. "Duma just said to bring you the rifle case. He didn't tell me you wanted to fuck it all up and stuff."

"We need to put Areadbhair in it," I replied, regaining my balance and composure.

"Areadbhair? Why does that sound so familiar... Oh, wait, you mean the lightning spear thing Lugh used to kill Balor? Won't it melt this thing?" Ab said, holding it up like it weighed five pounds instead of the fifty it likely did.

"Not if we fill it with petroleum jelly," I replied. "Possibly."

"Possibly?"

"Definitely," I said with an authoritative nod. "Maybe."

He tossed the case to me, and I caught it, but the impact knocked me backward. It felt like it weighed far more than fifty pounds. "You carry it, then. If that spear ignites, it can burn your arms off to nubs. So, how we gettin' to Toraigh? And how are we getting it away from that bitch who guards it? I've tried twice. Unsuccessfully, obviously."

"Did you try by force?" I asked, knowing the answer. *Ab has only one speed.*

He didn't even answer. He just crossed his arms over his massive chest and glared down his nose at me as though I'd just insulted his mother.

"Yeah, I got a different idea," I said. "But you won't like it. Pick one weapon—something small and concealable—and leave everything else behind but this case." I handed the heavy molded plastic crate back to him.

"Yeah, you're right," Ab said with a frown. "This *is* gonna suck."

"It gets worse, Ab." I said as he shuffled off crestfallen, like a kid who'd just gotten told it was time to come inside at the end of the day. "You're going to have to drag me through the Ways."

"Yeah, yeah," he said with his head bowed. "Whatever."

"Let's leave as soon as we can fill that case with petroleum jelly, then."

Ab didn't respond beyond the dismissive wave of a pale, meaty hand the size of a baseball glove.

Chapter 49

My second trip through the Ways as a mortal was even more overwhelming than the first. I'd heard other mundanes who had traveled through them comparing the experience to ayahuasca, only magnified. Even though we took less than thirty minutes total, Ab had to carry me halfway through the first leg. There was too much light, sound, smell, and energy to comprehend, and everything felt like it was hitting me at once. Each step was like trying to stand against the surf during a rising tide—slammed head-on, with swirling vortexes pulling at you physically and mentally—from every other direction. Every step farther along our path magnified the feeling until I nearly passed out, almost unable to coordinate my movements at all.

We stepped out onto a narrow archipelago of green grass broken up by craggy rocks jutting randomly from the ground. The day was cold and windy, and the sky was the color of a deep bruise. Rain was imminent, and thunderous waves were crashing on the rocks below.

"Town is this way," Ab said, pointing farther along the island.

Based on previous trips there in the distant past, I knew we were at one end of Tory Island, along Ireland's northern coast in the North Atlantic. Settlements were on the southern central coast near the island's ferry dock and farther to the east. As my head cleared, I recalled that we should be close to the western edge of the island.

Then the rain began. Sheets of cold, wind-driven rain stung my face as we walked. Luckily, the storm was at our backs. Ab was largely unaffected by the weather. Neither the cold, the wind, nor the rain fazed him at all. He reached his large arm out, his hand pointing off to the horizon in front of us. In the distance, under his arm, I could make out a rocky point that resembled a lone canine tooth sticking out of a broken jaw. *Tor Mór.*

"There's no way I can make it in this rain, Ab," I shouted. "Not like I am now. Sorry, but we're going to have to stop and wait for the weather to clear."

Ab just shook his head and kept moving forward, the long, narrow plastic case strapped to his back and a heavy gear bag over one shoulder. I knew the island was only a few miles long and about a half mile wide at most, but the walk to the westernmost town, An Baile Thiar, took forever. Ab trudged steadily along the stone road that led into town and headed straight into a pub in the center of town, right across from the breakwater that served as the ferry dock. I was cold, wet, and worn out despite wearing heavy foul-weather gear and having walked less than a mile. Our trip through the Ways had hit me harder than expected, compounded by the weather and a lack of rest. We'd chosen to leave Las Vegas late at night to arrive midmorning at Tory Island. Even at ten in the morning, a few people were already in the pub. All eyes immediately turned to Ab as we walked in.

The giant Peri dropped the gear bag containing our climbing equipment and shrugged off the case and propped it against a wall.

"Here to do some climbing?" An older woman behind the bar asked in a heavy Irish lilt. She wore thick glasses and had a weathered but friendly face.

"You bet," Ab said, "Only the weather caught us."

"Just made it back in time, I see," the barmaid said. "When did you arrive? I don't believe I've seen you in here before?"

"We just got here," Ab said absently, his accent almost identical to the barmaid's.

"Just got here?" she asked, suddenly taken aback. "The ferry won't be here until tomorrow. How could you just have gotten here?"

"What he means is we've just gotten *here*," I said, pointing at the ground. "An Baile Thiar. We've been camping at the base of the ridge, but we've been staying in An Baile Thoir since we arrived the other day," I said, glaring at Ab.

"Oh, he sounds local, but you must be an American," she said with a big smile. "And you look cold. Grab a seat by the fire, and order when you're ready. We've still got breakfast on. We got bacon, black pudding, eggs, beans, and hash if you want it. Tea and coffee to drink, and Guinness, too, if you want it," she added with a wink.

With a nod, I made my way to the fireplace and sat down heavily. Ab made his way over, ducking under the low-hanging exposed beams, glaring back at the people watching him as he moved cautiously in the confined space of the pub. Faces turned away quickly as he made eye contact. He grunted as he sat down next to me on a bench. The seat groaned under his weight.

"I haven't been to this island in centuries," he said, one corner of his mouth ticked up in disdain.

"Relax," I replied. "We're out of here as soon as it stops raining."

"I could go now on my own, no problems, D," he said. "Beats sitting around in here, being stared at. These people think I'm strange, but they have no idea what occurred on this island thousands of years ago while their kind was still living like animals using stones for tools. The creatures and monsters that lived and fought here were gods to them. *Those* people wouldn't have stared at me like a freak. *They* would have revered me."

"Relax, Ab," I said. "You stand out, even among your own kind. And as much as I would love to send you to do this, I think it's going to take a bit more... finesse... than you are capable of, my friend. Face it: delicate, you ain't."

He huffed in response and pulled at his lower lip for a moment. "Guinness. Make it two and put 'em in one big glass!" he bellowed to no one in particular. Everyone immediately stopped and stared in surprise.

"I don't know if I have a glass big enough," the barmaid responded without missing a beat.

"Then fill a pitcher and bring me that," Ab replied.

The barmaid's eyebrows climbed high on her weathered forehead, and she shrugged and filled a pitcher from a tap at the bar. She set it down on the table behind Ab. "Now, don't you be getting drunk and causing problems, big fella," she said like a mother talking to a troublemaking child.

"You don't have enough alcohol here to get me drunk, miss," Ab said, grabbing the pitcher like a human would a pint glass. "And there's no one left on this island anymore that could go toe-to-toe with me anyway. You are all safe." Ab waved his free arm around the bar, addressing everyone present. He downed the pitcher in one long gulp, and I could hear murmurs from the few patrons watching in astonishment.

"How long is it supposed to rain?" I asked one of the incredulous male onlookers, who struck me as local mostly by the way he dressed: well-worn pants, a heavy sweater under a waxed canvas coat that had seen better days, and a tweed flat cap, rather than the refined clothes of someone on holiday.

"Pardon?" came his confused response. "Oh, the weather. I believe it's supposed to clear up this evening, right, Maeve?" He turned to address the barmaid.

"That's what the marine forecast said, Jack. This afternoon, it'd clear up for the next day," she said.

The conversation was tense, slightly forced. Clearly, Ab had everyone on edge.

"Oh good," I said. "So we should be able to get back out there tonight, then. We're here to climb Tor Mór."

"Foul place, if you ask me," the man named Jack said. "Be careful. There's more than slippery rocks to be wary of on that pinnacle. And some say that cairn up there is used for more than just protection for those that get up there."

"You have no idea," said Ab, mostly under his breath.

"I suppose a big lad like you has nothing to be worried about," Jack said, scoffing. "But strange things happen around the tower. Don't say I didn't warn you."

"I know exactly what's up there," Ab said.

"Yeah, one of the most technical climbs in the British Isles," I said, laughing, trying to defuse the tension a bit. "Does anyone know who first climbed it?" I asked Jack but then shifted to glance over at Maeve, who was back behind the bar.

"I don't know why anyone would want to climb that godforsaken rock," Jack mumbled just loudly enough to be heard.

"I don't," Maeve responded. "There might be someone over in East Town that does. Maybe ol' Cabhan. Not many come here to climb it. Just a few every great once in a while."

"I was just curious. Not a big concern, really," I replied. "Thanks, though. How about another round for my friend here?" I pointed at Ab.

"No, I don't want it," he grumbled. "Why don't we just head up now, D?"

I leaned in close to Ab. "Because I can't make the climb in these conditions, and your usual approach won't cut it with a Bánánach. We're waiting till it stops raining, then we'll go."

"I'll carry you," he said, resting his cheek on his hand as he leaned back on the table, which groaned in protest at the weight. "I carry everything else."

"Knock it off, Ab," I said, scolding him like the child he was be-having as. "Just a few more hours. I don't want to be here any longer than necessary either."

"So, what exactly is your plan, since we have limited weaponry?" Ab asked, his eyebrows tented high on his forehead. "All I know is you keep saying I won't like it."

"I'm going in on my own, unarmed, with peaceful intentions."

"Are you insane?" Ab practically spat out, sitting bolt upright. "Are you going to bring her flowers too? You're going in unarmed—"

"Keep your voice down."

"You're going in unarmed against a Bánánach?" Ab whispered, leaning in. "You'll be lucky if I can recover your body." He sat back for emphasis, and the table behind him slid noisily across the wood-en floor.

"Listen, they are spirits of violence, and everyone she has ever en-countered has come at her ready to fight, which is exactly what she feeds on," I said.

"So you're saying you're going to beat her by not trying to kill her," Ab replied, cocking his head and pursing his lips, thinking about it. "Sounds crazy to me. But then, she's kicked my ass every time I've tried."

"I'm saying I'm going to avoid violence with her. If I don't act ag-gressive, she'll have nothing to feed off, and she'll remain weak. If she stays in the tower to protect the spear, she can't have had many visi-tors in a while."

"You're assuming she stays in the tower," Ab said.

"Well, if she doesn't, then maybe we can draw her out, and I can sneak in and steal it," I responded. "But I'm thinking that'd be too easy. If that were possible, it would have been stolen by now."

"You don't even know if it's still there."

"No, but I'm pretty sure I would've heard about Areadbhair be-fore now if someone had managed to get it already," I said. "Besides,

I'm the only one going in there, Ab. If it doesn't work, then all this mess is over with, and you and Duma can go on with your lives without worrying about me anymore."

"Got news for you, D," Ab said. "Me and Duma don't worry about you that much anyway. All this," he said, waving his hand around, "is for Sarah. Cuz, frankly, you've been a real douche lately."

"What do you think *I'm* doing this for, Ab?"

"Oh, it's clear you're on some personal mission," Ab replied. "At the expense of everyone around you."

"What do you know? Sarah's in this condition because of me, Ab. Not you, not Duma, but me."

"I think she'd tell you she's in this condition because of a choice *she* made," Ab said with a shrug.

"She made that decision because I promised I'd keep her safe. And I didn't. This is all my fault."

"So you're going to get everyone else involved killed in the process of saving Sarah?" he asked in a simple, matter-of-fact manner that was totally characteristic for Ab. "I *know* what she'd say about that."

"Screw you," I said, getting to my feet. For a moment, I thought about turning a table over or smashing a chair, but I realized picking up a chair was about the best I could do as a mortal. My hands struck me as being old and weak, so I stormed out of the pub, back into the rain.

Chapter 50

I had no idea where I was headed or why I really marched out of there like that or even why what Ab said made me so angry. I stood in the rain, and I could swear I heard Sarah's voice calling to me for help among the sounds of the rain falling. I shook my head to clear it and nearly fell over when I suddenly realized Ab was standing right in front of me.

"You're an idiot," Ab said over the rain. "And if you're going to stand out here in this crap, we might as well head to Tor Mór."

He headed down the road. Only one road led into and out of town, the only road on the island in fact, and I watched as Ab passed the few remaining buildings and houses that made up the small town. Finally, I ran to catch up. The sound of rain on the hood of my rain jacket gave way to the pounding surf against the cliffs on the island's northern shore. Just outside of West Town and less than half a mile from East Town, the island was barely a few hundred yards wide. And other than the dark, forbidding craggy cliffs and outcroppings, the island was brilliantly verdant, even under the sunless slate-gray sky.

As we neared East Town, the road split, but barely. And just near the center of town, the road split again, with one fork leading east and the other toward the southern shore. Ab never even slowed or hesitated at the forks. In better conditions, I'm sure Tor Mór would have been easily visible, but with the steady rain and cloud cover, visibility was only a few hundred yards at best. We passed close to the cliff's edge near another fork in the road that led to a few isolated houses only visible because of the lights in the windows. The roar of the surf against the cliffs drowned out everything, and in the windy conditions of the storm, saltwater spray was as abundant as the rain. My face became tight with salt, even under my hood. The road began to descend, and I could see the rocky ridge that led to "The Anvil," Tor Mór.

The road ended at the base of a peninsula, where there were the remnants of the destroyed tower. Most of the land in front of us was flat and easily passable, but the closer we got to the base of the ridge, the more uneven the ground became. Once we reached the base of the ridge, I could just make out Tor Mór, about a quarter of a mile in front of us, between bands of wind-driven sea spray and rain, juxtaposed against the darkening North Atlantic sky. All that was missing was a bolt of lightning and an ominous peal of thunder.

Ab turned to face me, dropping the gear bag on the ground. "Time to rig up a safety line," he said, pulling rope and harnesses out of the bag. "We'll tether to each other. The eastern slope of the ridge is grassy but steep in places. We'll make faster time moving on that, though, than across the western side, trust me."

"Just remember I can't move as fast as you can on even ground anymore, so I'll be moving very slowly on that ridge. Especially in this weather," I replied.

"I'm aware," Ab said, tossing me a harness. "Why do you think it took us so long to get here? And why do you think I'm having you tether to me?"

We took six hours to traverse the quarter-mile span to the base of Tor Mór. Though the rain had ended, the sun had set, forcing us to move painfully slowly in the darkness because I slipped and lost my footing about every tenth step, even on the more navigable parts of the ridge. Several times, we had to all but crawl along the very spine of the ridge and ascend three steep pitches that would have been a challenge on a dry, sunlit day. The final pitch up to the summit was completely vertical. The only thing that kept me safe was being leashed to Ab. His preternatural Fae ability to navigate any terrain with ease, combined with his size and strength, kept him from being pulled along with me when I stumbled and fell.

In the darkness, standing on the summit of Tor Mór, Ab coiled rope as the wind whipped around us. It felt precarious even though the summit was quite large and relatively flat. *Now that I'm mortal, everything feels precarious.* I began to unhook my harness, but Ab shook his head.

"Nope," he said, pointing down the north face. "You still need that. The entrance is down there about thirty feet. It's a spider hole about four feet in diameter. It'll lead you to a staircase. Follow the stairs all the way down. And don't forget that." He nodded toward the heavy black plastic case.

"You going to lower me?" I asked.

"Probably faster and safer than letting you descend on belay," he replied. "We ain't here for sport."

I nodded and reached under my jacket to grab my Sig Sauer P226, glanced at it for a second while I reassessed my plan of nonviolence toward a creature of bloodshed and aggression, decided that was indeed the right way to go, and handed the weapon to Ab. He took it and tucked it into a pocket on the side of his pants. He grabbed the rope tied to my harness with one hand, ran it around his back and held it with the other hand, and braced himself.

"Whenever, D," he said, his face hard and unreadable. "When you're ready to come back up, just give it a few tugs. If I don't hear from you by dawn, I may or may not come down after you. I haven't decided yet."

I rechecked my harness and the bowline knot then tried to pull the case onto my back using the straps Ab had used. Filled with petroleum jelly, it easily weighed 150 pounds, and I quickly realized that was a bad idea. I snapped a carabiner onto the case's straps and created a loop in my line using a figure-9 loop knot and clipped the case to that so that the rope would bear the weight rather than my back.

When I was finally ready, Ab controlled my descent, making it easy and quick. I found the hole, shoved the case through, and made my way in without issue and shrugged out of the harness.

My pocket knife.

I grabbed the small folding knife I always carried from the side pocket of my pants and clipped it to the harness. The knife was always more of a tool than a weapon, but any blade could be used offensively in a pinch, and I didn't want to take the chance.

Chapter 51

In the light of my headlamp, I could see the passage was large, larger than expected. Easily over twelve feet high and wider than my reach, it stretched only a few steps before turning into a narrow spiral stairway carved from the rock of the pinnacle itself. The stairs descended into pitch blackness. I shrugged the case onto my back and made it as comfortable as I could, given the makeshift shoulder straps, and began the descent.

The stairs themselves were in pristine condition—not a single broken edge or chipped surface, and they were completely dry despite the air inside the tower being cold and wet. The air tasted stale and earthy. I heard no sounds beyond my breathing and footfalls on the stone stairs, which echoed incessantly through the chamber. I couldn't have sneaked into the place even if I wanted to, especially not with this case on my back.

Climbing back up is going to be a bitch.

I slowly descended the stairs for a solid five minutes before they leveled off and turned into a narrow path that wound through a sizable natural passage in the rock. An eerie green light shone through the cleft in the rock. On the other side, the cavern opened into a large space with a floor and walls so smooth and flat that it had to have been created. The space spread some thirty yards wide, but I had no way of telling how tall it was. My light just disappeared into the chasm overhead. Set in a square around the center of the room, four torches gave off the dim green glow of some sort of unnatural flame. A jet-black sarcophagus sat in the center of the four torches.

I unstrapped the case from my back and carefully laid it on the floor and stood up, putting my hands on my hips, trying to appear as nonthreatening as possible. I was scared to speak, so much so that when I tried, nothing came out. I ended up clearing my throat. The inky blackness at the back of the cavern gave the illusion of movement at the sound. Still, the only sound was my breathing, which remained a bit ragged from the long descent. Then I noticed the movement within the blackness again.

All at once, part of the shadows seemed to cleave off and form a small sphere that coalesced into a humanoid shape. By the time it had traveled a few feet, the shape was walking, soundlessly and languidly, across the floor. Within the span of several steps, the shape took on the features of a woman. By the time it passed the torches, it had a fully formed face and body, shrouded by wisps of stygian blackness. The shadowy face was strikingly attractive though pale and gaunt—not at all horrific, like I'd expected.

It's probably what she wants me to see rather than what she looks like.

A cold chill ran down my spine, and I held my hands up, trying to demonstrate that I was no threat.

"Why have you come to this place?" she asked, weaving between the two closest torches at the foot of the sarcophagus. She had no discernable accent when she spoke.

"I need Areadbhair," I said, hoping directness would be more effective than idle banter.

The moment I said the spear's name, the being stopped, turned to face me, and roared so loudly that the rock structure shook around us. The sound knocked me to my knees, and her visage transformed from pleasant to utterly horrific—a mass of twisted and broken bone, broken teeth, torn flesh, a distended jaw, and matted hair—projected at me to within inches of my face. My first instinct was to roar back, but that was precisely the type of response I wanted to avoid. Instead, I bowed my head and covered my ears.

"To take the spear, you will need to deal with me first, mortal," the creature said. "Are you prepared for us?"

"I will not fight you," I said, keeping my head bowed.

She was definitely the Bánánach, but I had no idea who or what the other part of the "us" she spoke of was.

The smell in the chamber became fetid and dank, like long-rotted flesh and mold.

"How do you expect to take such an object, then?" she asked. "You bring nothing to fight with, save your skills, warrior."

"I have come in peace, without a weapon, to ask for it."

Again, the Bánánach roared, physically knocking me back onto my butt, where I rolled into a ball, covering my head and ears as best I could. That time when she roared, the green-flame torches intensified and lit up the room in a sickly green glow.

But she still hasn't touched me.

I sat up slowly. The Bánánach was weaving around the sarcophagus and torches, walking slowly, indifferently. When she noticed I was sitting up again, she watched me out of the corner of her eye as she walked.

"No weapon? Surely, a warrior knows that spears and swords are merely tools. The warrior is the weapon. We are here for the taking," she said. "If you want us, come... Take the spear." She waved her arm toward the obsidian crypt.

"I will not fight you for the spear," I said, getting to my feet.

The spirit instantaneously appeared inches in front of me, causing me to step back. Again, she didn't touch me. "We are an instrument of death and destruction, and only a true warrior can wield us. If you will not fight, you are not worthy of us."

"The deadliest armament a true warrior possesses is their mind," I replied. "What you guard is just a means to realize the intention. Any tool can be used to do good or evil, depending on the hands that use it. The spear is incredibly powerful, but aren't you concerned about the intentions of one who would use Areadbhair? I assure you my intentions are noble."

"What do I care for intentions?" she said, cocking her head a bit too far to one side. "I only care that we are used."

"As I understand it, Areadbhair hasn't been used in millennia," I said. "I have need of it. I can put it to good use, fighting an Old One like Balor—the one this spear last killed here on *this* island so long ago."

The Bánánach's head shot back upright then jutted forward in a stilted, mechanical movement.

"I will use it to protect humanity, but I will not fight unless I need to," I said. "And I know enough to know that even with all my skills, I cannot best you as I am, without the spear. So, I choose not to fight. I will not fight in a battle I have no chance to win. But I *must* have the spear."

She laughed. "You know nothing. You could not beat me even with the spear, fool," the spirit said without mirth. "You can take the spear. I am bound to it and it to me. But we were not placed here to keep us safe from those who would use us. We are imprisoned here to keep the world safe from us."

Again, she roared as if in frustration, and I covered my ears and had no choice but to fall to one knee to keep from falling over completely.

"If you will not fight me like all the others, then take the spear and use us. Turn us loose on the world once again. Free us from this prison. Use us."

The green-flame torches burst into an intense firestorm that converged overhead in a sudden thunderous boom, and the Bánánach disappeared. The torches went out, and the green flame overhead suddenly descended like a falling bomb, hitting the black sarcophagus with such force that the resultant shockwave threw me back against the wall. The collision of the flame with the stone container caused a sonic boom–like crack that deafened me and caused me to black out. When I came to, my ears were ringing as I gathered my wits and tried to make sense of what had just happened. In a daze, I saw the bright beam of my headlamp on the ground a few feet away and crawled to get it since the cavern was completely dark. Sitting on the floor, I shone the light around the space to see what exactly had happened. As the light fell on the sarcophagus, I could see the stone casing was shattered into several large pieces, revealing a large, narrow storage container within. The light reflected off whatever was inside. The Bánánach was nowhere to be seen—or heard.

Huh, that was easy...

After a long moment spent waiting to see if the Bánánach was going to suddenly reappear and rip my intestines out, I slowly approached the ruined sarcophagus, continuing to shine the light around as I did, just in case. Then the smell of rotted meat mixed with a sunbaked beach at low tide hit me like a fist in the stomach. I had to suppress a gag. *Whale oil. Geek would be happy to know he was right.*

Once I got close enough, I could see into the container. At the bottom of the surprisingly clear yellowish liquid was the dark shape of a rod the length of the sarcophagus, nearly seven feet. Again, I shined the light around the room, checking to make sure the Bánánach wasn't hiding somewhere, tricking me somehow.

If the Bánánach really is tethered to the spear, I'll be able to control her too. I won't need Athena's help to go after Nemesis or Eisheth. Or anyone else for that matter. Ever.

I ran back to find the case full of petroleum jelly and brought it over to the sarcophagus. I had to be very careful in the transfer from one case to the other because I still didn't really know how the thing actually worked. Geek was right about the whale oil—I'd smelled it many times before in the past and even worked on whaling ships a few times a century and a half before. Given that, I guessed he would also be right about the spear combusting when exposed to air. The trick was getting it out of the whale oil and into the case quickly, without letting the weapon dry off in any way.

It'll only take me a few seconds to transfer it, so how hard could it be?

Except I'm not as fast or as strong as I used to be, dummy.

I set the case on the edge of the sarcophagus. The whale oil wasn't particularly deep, maybe a foot at most, so I just decided to reach in, grab the spear, and drop it into the case. Disturbing the oil made the foul, stale odor even more pungent, especially with my face mere inches away. I gagged and hesitated briefly. The spear was lighter than expected, so I pulled it up, and as quickly as I could, I dropped it into the case full of petroleum jelly, where it sank into the viscous goo with a *splort*. Then I quickly closed the lid and snapped the heavy latches in place to secure it. When I got topside again, I would use the pump to create a vacuum inside just to be safe.

I shrugged the case onto my back, and I could hear and feel the spear shifting in the case. I stood motionless for a long minute, half expecting it to poke through the case, burst into flames, and melt my legs off. Then I started to breathe again. When I was sure nothing was going to happen, I took the path back to the stairs slowly and cautiously. When I got to the bottom of the staircase, I fixed the headlamp back on my head and began the long slog up.

What took me five minutes heading down took me nearly three times as long going up. I had to stop several times along the way. The spear didn't add that much weight to the case, and even though I was still in great shape, the climb was grueling with the load on my back. The waning adrenaline rush wasn't helping either.

I forced myself to keep moving back to the entrance. Once there, breathing heavily, I shimmied into the harness, shoved the knife I'd clipped to it back into my pocket, then secured the case to the cara-biner and headed out the entrance hole. I gave the rope a few sharp tugs as I sat in the entrance, still breathing heavily in the fresh, cool sea air.

At least it's not raining anymore.

The rope pulled taut, and I maneuvered the case awkwardly out of the hole then began to walk up the cliff face as Ab raised me.

Once at the top, rather than offering me a hand to get back onto the summit, Ab lifted me and dangled me like a fish on the end of a line. "Did you actually get it? Because that didn't take very long, and you don't look beat up at all."

"Yes, I got it," I said, getting irritated at dangling like a piece of bait. "Put me down. We need to make sure the case is vacuum sealed."

"Damn, that's impressive," he said, the corners of his mouth dropping deeply and his pale brows climbing high as he bobbed his head in disbelief. "She kicked my ass every time. Looks like your plan of being a wimp worked." He set me down on the rocky summit.

I unbuckled the harness and scrambled to our gear bag to find the vacuum pump for the case. Ab just watched as I retrieved the small device, connected it to the valve on the case, and switched it on. The pump made a low humming noise like the purring of a cat for a few seconds before its pitch increased.

"That's it," Ab said. "Vacuum achieved. Just tighten the valve screw then disconnect the hose, and you're all good."

I did as Ab said and wound the hose back up to store the small pump.

"So, tell me, what did the spear look like?" Ab asked.

"Nothing special, actually, but I didn't look at it very long for fear it would burst into flames," I replied. "Dull gray, not very heavy, but simple and javelin-like. And it was definitely stored in whale oil."

"And the Bánánach just *gave* it to you because you wouldn't fight her?" he asked, incredulous.

"Basically. Ab, if *you* couldn't beat her, do you really think I could have in my current state? And without any weapons at all?" I pointed from Ab to myself for emphasis. "It's in there. Trust me. And yes, I got it without fighting her."

"Well, where is she then?" he asked. "Is she packing for a vacation now that she doesn't have to guard that thing anymore? Did she vanish into thin air when you wouldn't fight? Oh, wait... no, no, no! I got it! She wasn't even there, was she? You walked in, the place was empty, and you just took it, didn't you?" He gave me a suspicious, squinty side-eye.

I rolled my eyes. "Does it matter? Didn't you feel this place shake when she screamed? Let's just get going, okay?"

"Oh shit, that's what that was," he replied. "I just figured it was a big wave hitting Tor Mór or something."

I shot him a dirty look. "Can we just leave?"

He shrugged and threw his hands up in supplication then grabbed the case, pretended to assess its weight for a second, then put it on his back. I coiled up the ropes and reattached the safety lines between us for the climb down and the hike back, and we set off.

We stayed quiet until somewhere between East and West Town.

"You never did say what happened to the Bánánach, D," Ab finally said after letting out a huge sigh.

"I honestly have no idea," I said, telling half the truth. "She screamed, and then green flame shot up and fell back down on the sarcophagus, it shattered, and she was gone. That's how I was able to get the spear without your help. The outer casing broke apart when the flame hit it. But the Bánánach was gone."

"She didn't do or say anything? She just vanished?"

"She screamed and ranted and wanted me to fight her, but when I said I wouldn't, like I said, she screamed, the green-flame torches flared and cracked the case, and she was gone. That simple," I said, feeling it was best to leave out the specifics of her statements about being connected to the spear.

Ab whipped around, squinting into the darkness as though looking for something. His speed and reaction startled me.

"What the fuck, Ab?"

"Just making sure she isn't following us," the big Peri said, being theatrical. "Because that sounds way too easy, D."

"She isn't following us," I replied. "Let's just get home so I can figure out how to use the spear without killing myself."

We didn't speak for the rest of the trip back to the warehouse in Vegas.

Chapter 52

Back in Vegas, Ab and Duma spent a fair amount of time talking in low, hushed tones in one corner of the warehouse while I waited. I really didn't care about their conversations. I wanted the fire entry suit, or at least the gloves, so that I could work on handling the spear. Finally, after nearly ten minutes, Duma walked over to me.

"So, she just let you take it?" He asked. "The Bánánach, I mean."

"Pretty much," I replied. "How else would I have gotten it without carrying a single weapon? I either stole it, or she gave it to me. Either way, does it matter?"

"Stealing it wouldn't bother me in the least," he said. "But just giving it to you makes no sense. And then, according to Ab, you said she just disappeared?"

"What's the problem here, Duma? Does it bother you that I figured out how to get the spear—*without fighting her for it*—and you guys couldn't for thousands of years?"

"It just seems too easy, D," he said, shaking his head. "That Bánánach ripped apart hundreds of beings over the years to protect that thing, and you just waltz in and waltz out. An ordinary mortal human? Something's off."

"I don't know what to tell you two, but there it is, and here I stand without a scratch," I said, stretching both arms toward the case, sitting on a rolling tool cart. "I just need the fire suit. Call me crazy, but I don't want to open that case without *some* precautions."

"It's really in there?" Duma asked, his pale blond eyebrows shooting up with interest. "Areadbhair?"

271

"Yes, but I have no idea how to use it."

"Well, we need to figure it out, then," Duma said, rubbing his hands together. "One fire entry suit, coming up."

Across the building, Ab threw his hands up, and his jaw dropped open. He shook his head and sighed heavily then walked off mumbling to himself, gesturing in random motions with his hands.

A few minutes later, Duma walked up dressed in a silver fire suit with the hood thrown back, carrying another suit over one arm, and holding a pair of matching boots in the other hand. He dropped them in a pile on the floor. "Suit weighs over sixty pounds. You gotta go get your own breathing apparatus. Over in that closet," he said, pointing with one mitt-covered hand at a storage closet along the back wall. "What are we waiting for?" Then he slapped his gloved hands together with a dull *whump*.

I could see the violent gleam in his white eyes.

I grabbed the scuba tank–like breathing apparatus from the closet and pulled it on as I walked back to Duma. Shrugging into the shiny aluminized suit was more like pulling on a dry suit to go diving than putting on armor. The suit was heavy and thick and reeked of sweat inside, but once I pulled the mask on, that wouldn't matter.

"Suits are good up to about two thousand degrees," Duma said. "But from what I remember of this thing, it burns way beyond that. But it's the best we got."

"What?" I stopped what I was doing. "Hotter than two thousand degrees?"

"Easily," Duma said with a shrug. "I watched shit burst into flames just because it was within twenty feet of the spear. You could feel its heat a hundred feet away, no problem. Handheld lightning, my friend. Let's open this puppy up!" He ran his hand over the case almost reverently.

Ab walked into view but kept his distance, clearly curious. "First thing you gotta do is open the valve on the end to equalize the pressure in the case, or it won't open even if its unlatched," the big, sullen Peri said, shouting a bit. "Oh, wait..." He reached into his pocket and pulled out sunglasses. He crossed his massive arms over his chest and leaned back against the wall.

With renewed caution, I unscrewed the knurled knob at the end of the case, and a low hiss began but was done within another half-turn. The case popped slightly, and Duma and I both jumped back, Duma slightly farther than me. After my heart started beating again, I unsnapped the four heavy latches along the case's long side. Duma pulled his breathing mask on over his head then pulled the suit's hood into place. I did the same.

Through the smoked glass lens of the hood, everything was dark, and the heavy three-fingered gloves made me feel even more clumsy. I could feel my discomfort, fear, and irritation at that fear rising by the second. Every one of my senses and movements was dulled except my hearing, but the only thing I could hear inside the massive protective hood was my breathing. I slowly opened the case, revealing the dull sheen of the spear sitting in the pale-yellow petroleum jelly. Neither of us moved, and I didn't even breathe. Duma finally back-handed my shoulder, which jarred me. Once he had my attention, he pointed at the spear and raised both hands insistently.

I would have flipped him off, but that was impossible with three-fingered gloves. I couldn't even shake my head because he wouldn't see that either, under the hood. I reached over and closed the case, but didn't latch it, then I pulled my hood and mask off and took a solid breath of fresh air. I was sweaty as hell, and I hadn't moved more than a step.

Duma followed suit. "Dude, what the hell?" he said the instant his hood came off. His pale blond hair was barely messed up.

"I gotta talk to Geek," I replied. "If I pull that thing out and it flames up, I have no idea how to turn it off again. If it burns hotter than two thousand degrees, I won't be able to pick it up even with these damned gloves," I said, raising my gloved hands. "And it'll melt through anything, even the ground, in seconds."

"I know, right?" Duma said excitedly. "Oh yeah, that could all be bad. I get what you're saying. At this point, it could be a one-shot deal." He pursed out his lower lip. "Good luck with that. And let me know what Geek says." He slapped me on the shoulder and walked over to Ab, peeling out of the metallic suit as he went.

I got out of my suit then grabbed my phone and dialed Geek. He answered on the first ring.

"Was I right?" he asked without saying hello. "About the acetylene and such?"

"You're assuming I got it."

"Well yeah, why else would you call me, mate?" he replied. "Turn the camera on your phone on and point it at the spear. I want to see it."

"Yeah, well I need your help with it," I said. "How do I—"

"For the love of everything holy, mate, where the bloody fuck are you?" he demanded, suddenly losing patience with me. "It'll just be easier if I come to you. Unless you're off in some backward boondocks somewhere."

I sighed heavily. I didn't want to get Geek involved because of his connection to Athena. But I needed his help. He's the only one whose debt I could easily pay back under the current circumstances. "Okay, fine," I finally said. "I'm in Vegas."

"Be there in four hours, two if I can wrangle a helicopter out of you-know-who," he replied.

"Don't you fucking dare tell her you're helping me or even where you are going, Geek. Not a word. Promise me, or so help me—"

"Right, right, of course. Not a word, I swear," he said. "I'll call as soon as I'm close so you can tell me the address."

Chapter 53

Geek pulled up in front of the warehouse and honked his horn just after midnight. Duma made it outside before I could, but to my surprise, he returned a few moments later and opened one of the garage bays to let Geek drive straight inside. Then he promptly closed the garage door behind his car.

Geek got out and peered around for a second and spotted me. "Help me with the gear," he said and slapped the top of his generic black sedan.

"Gear?" I asked. "What gear? I just need your help figuring this thing out."

"No kidding, mate," he said, opening the trunk. "Hence the gear." He waved a hand in the air and fixed me with a glare that suggested I was an idiot. "I don't have magic or the ability to divine energy. I rely on machines. You better get used to that too: simple, old-fashioned mortal human technology."

"Yeah, well, if we can figure that thing out"—I pointed at the case on the rolling cart—"Then even as a mortal man, I'll still have a leg up."

"Well, that's why I'm here." He took three rugged suitcase-sized bright-yellow plastic cases out of the trunk, similar in construction to the case for the spear. "I need some place to set those up." The last thing he took out of the trunk was his messenger bag–style laptop case.

"Duma, where can we set up?" I shouted across the warehouse so that he could hear me while he and Ab lounged in a sitting area near what served as an office.

Without getting up, he waved in a movement that encompassed the entire warehouse. "Wherever. Let me know when you're going to start. I wanna watch."

"Hey, Duma, what can you and Ab tell me about this spear, Areadbhair?" Geek asked as he lugged one of the yellow cases toward the spear.

"Not much beyond stories," he answered from his prone position on the couch, scrolling through something on a smartphone. "It was given to our family by Goibniu as a gift from Queen Mab. We were always told that the fat tub actually made it. Our family, in turn, gave it to a human king, Pisear, about four thousand years ago for services rendered to our family—"

"And because it was too dangerous to use," Ab interrupted.

Duma shot him a dirty look. "Pisear apparently gave it to Lugh, who is the only one I've ever heard of using it. And he killed his grandfather, Balor, with it. An impossible shot, right through the bastard's armored eye." He poked his finger at his own eye and clucked his tongue loudly for effect. "It's been in protective custody inside Tor Mór ever since, guarded by a Bánánach that *recently* got cabin fever *apparently*. And then..." He gestured toward us and the case with one hand. "That's all I know."

"And it burned blue-white fire so hot that stuff within fifty feet of it would burst into flames sometimes too," Ab added.

"Right. What he said," Duma said. "Lightning. Hot as fuck."

"Helpful," Geek said, rolling his eyes. "I already knew that part."

"So what'd you ask for, then?" Duma asked.

Geek just shook his head. "I'm going to try to take some samples and figure out what it's made of. If I can ascertain its makeup, then I might be able to figure out how it works." He wheeled over another tool cart to open the plastic suitcases. Inside each was a different set of equipment, with a small LED screen embedded in the lid and wires connecting all manner of devices nestled in gray foam. He quickly plugged various colored cords into the individual devices and connected them, in series, to each other. Then he plugged an electrical cord into each case and held up all three to me. "Outlet?" he asked.

I found a multiheaded extension cord on a retractable pulley in one corner and pulled it out while Geek finished setting up. As he plugged them in, each case whirred and beeped. He pressed a few buttons and tapped the screens in each case then pulled on a pair of Nomex work gloves and grabbed a test tube and scalpel. "Whenever you're ready," Geek said.

"What exactly do you want me to do?"

"Open the case so I can take a look and get a scraping of the material to see what it is," he said, his eyebrows raised high.

I opened the case, and within an instant, Duma was standing at my side. "Should we suit up?" he asked, eyes wide with anticipation.

"Won't do any good, I suspect," Geek said. "If it's any form of acetylene, it burns far hotter than any protective suit I know of can withstand. But if you have a Class B fire extinguisher, that could help just in case."

"The whole place is rigged with FM-200," Duma said. "If something ignites, the whole place gets flooded with the chemical."

Geek frowned and bobbed his head in approval. "Excellent. Well then, shall we?"

Geek and Duma leaned in, and I leaned back. Geek set the scalpel down and pulled a magnifying glass out of a pocket and did his best to examine the spear through the petroleum jelly. He stuck a finger in to touch it a few times and made a few random noises to himself. "Well, it's obvious that the tip and the shaft are two different materials," he said after a few moments. "Does the entire thing burst into flames or just one part of it?"

Duma shrugged. "Beats the hell out of me."

Geek shook his head. "I'll start by testing the shaft since that would be least likely to ignite just from the standpoint of practical usability."

Duma crossed his arms and leaned in close to Geek as the would-be scientist worked. Again, I took a step back just in case. Using the scalpel, Geek scratched at the shaft of the spear inside the petroleum jelly then scraped the side of the blade on the edge of a test tube. "I'll wash off the jelly with a sterile solution and run it through the spectrometers to see what it is, but the shaft appears to be wood."

"Makes sense," Duma said, trying to appear studious.

Geek stopped and did a double take at Duma's comment before continuing. He took a few minutes to wash and rewash the scrapings inside the test tube, but once he was finished, he placed the small glass vial into a slot in a machine in one of the cases then hit a few buttons. "Now, we wait."

"How long?" I asked.

"Few minutes, maybe more if it's truly exotic," he said. "It's definitely some sort of wood, though."

The machines barely made any noise at all, and we all stood and watched, except Ab. "Want to know how this all works?" Geek asked, nodding at his digital setup.

"No" was the instantaneous and unanimous answer.

"Sheesh," Geek replied. "Uneducated cretins."

"And damn proud of it," Ab said from his spot on the couches across the warehouse. "I'll guarantee you Goibniu didn't have that fancy machinery, and he made the damned thing. Humans always overthink everything."

"Maybe, but we're late to the game compared to you Fae," Geek replied. "We're doing the best we can."

"You guys came on the scene, and ever since, the world has gone to shit," Ab said. "Global warming, extinction rates, pollution, deforestation all have increased dramatically even in the last hundred years. At what cost does your knowledge and understanding need to come?"

"He's got us there," I told Geek.

"Maybe, but given our species has gotten from the functional stone age to the moon and beyond in such a short time, I think we're doing pretty well," Geek said with pride.

"What has going to the moon gotten you?" Ab asked. "Seriously, is your life any different because your kind went to the moon?"

"The technology we developed in the process has changed our lives immeasurably," Geek said but was interrupted by the machine beeping before he could continue.

Duma and I exchanged thankful glances and sighed in relief.

"Ah, ready." Geek put on a pair of glasses and stared at one of the small LED screens for a moment. "Looks like *Taxus baccata*, commonly known as yew. But there are all kinds of other compounds impregnated into the wood. All are ridiculously complex and none that I am familiar with, nor is my limited database. But I can send them to friends for further analysis. My guess is whatever those compounds are is the reason the wood doesn't burn."

"Great, so the shaft doesn't burn," I said, half in question.

"And has *never* burned," Geek added. "It's not charred at all."

"So, what about the tip?" I asked.

"Let's find out," Geek said, changing out the scalpel blade for a new one. "This could be a bit trickier. I may have to just keep the jelly on it so it doesn't ignite."

Duma and I glanced at each other then back at Geek. "So?" we both asked, almost simultaneously.

He sighed heavily and rolled his eyes. "Never mind. Just let me work."

Duma and I both backed off, and even Geek moved more slowly than he had previously. He mopped at his forehead with his sleeve several times during the procedure.

"Hmm, very peculiar," he said, finally snapping the lid on a small vial after scraping the edge of the scalpel on it. He placed the scalpel on the tool cart next to one of his cases, and within seconds, the thin metal instrument burst into an intense blue-white flame and melted through the cart and onto the cement floor, where it quickly burned itself out. Everyone jumped back, but it was over before anyone—including Duma—could really react.

"Damn!" Duma said. "What the hell?"

"I'm guessing the particles of the material remaining on the scalpel got exposed to air and combusted," Geek said. "It's a peculiar material. Not like a metal at all, but it's softish."

All that was left on the floor where the scalpel fell was a molten blackened blob. The hole on the cart where the scalpel melted through was still glowing white hot and dripping around the edges.

"Damn. That was an aluminum alloy cart," Duma said.

"Probably melts at about fifteen hundred degrees or so, I'd guess," Geek said, impressed. "And this went through it instantaneously. I'd guess it burned at least at three thousand degrees."

No one said anything as Geek put the sample into the machine and let it run. I kept staring at the blackened blob on the ground. Duma was poking at the now red-hot edges of the hole in the cart with a pair of needle-nose pliers.

This had better work.

When the machine beeped, we all stopped and stared. Geek was the only one animated and upbeat, driven by his innate and insatiable curiosity. He stared hard at the screen for a few minutes then scrunched up his face in confusion.

"Give me a second, guys," he said. He pulled his computer from his bag, hooked it up to the machine that beeped, and typed furiously with one hand while he cradled his laptop with the other. "Just want to email this to a friend for his perusal."

He can type faster one-handed than I can with both.

Windows popped up on his computer screen, and he continued to type furiously as his computer began dinging almost as fast as he was typing.

"No fucking way," Geek said with a wide smile and a chuckle. "That would be so cool."

"What?" I said, curious.

"My friend is double- and triple-checking, but he's pretty sure it's dicyanoacetylene in its solid form. It's the hottest burning substance we know of, but most of the time, it's in gaseous or liquid form. Scientists have only theorized about its solid form based on observations on Titan, Saturn's largest moon. This would be incredible if it was. And if it is, then it burns at *over nine thousand degrees Fahrenheit*. Woohoo! That's just slightly cooler than the surface of the sun!"

Ab sat straight up, and Duma went rigid. I suddenly wanted to throw up.

"The sun?" I asked, feeling a slight breeze on the back of my neck that made my hair stand on end.

"Its surface, yeah, definitely not its core," Geek replied. "If it's dicyanoacetylene in solid form. Where would Goibniu even get this stuff from?"

I heard and felt a woman whisper in my ear: "Use the weapon. Set us free." I whipped around, but no one was there. I felt all eyes in the room focus on me as I turned back.

"You okay there, mate?" Geek asked.

"Yeah, bug or something," I said, trying to sound close to reasonable. "So, um, how does it work, exactly?"

"Well, based on what we just saw, I think you just need to expose the blade of the spear to air, and it will ignite on its own. But to put it out, you'll have to douse it in this stuff," he said, pointing at the case full of petroleum jelly.

"All you need to do is pick us up. We will do the rest," the female said, this time not in a whisper. Again, I spun around to find the source. Again, everyone stared.

"You guys didn't hear that?"

"Hear what?" Duma asked with a shrug. "The part about the spear igniting or shoving it back in that goo to put it out? Of course we heard that."

"Use us," the voice said more insistently.

"You okay, D?" Geek asked, his brow heavily knitted.

"Yeah, I'm fine," I replied, trying to shake the odd feeling I was hallucinating. "Go on with your analysis." I awkwardly pointed at the spear, feeling myself blink hard.

"Right, right," Geek said, turning back to his computer screen. "As soon as my friend replies, I'll know for sure. How it hasn't reduced the shaft to ash, I have no idea." He shook his head, shrugged slightly, and raised his eyebrows in wonderment.

"If you wield us, we will protect you from our rage," the voice said from over my left shoulder.

Instinctively, I jerked my head around.

"Do not fear us. You will be part of us."

"Well, um, if the blade is made from a strange material, maybe the wood is treated somehow too," I said, trying not to appear as disconcerted as I felt.

"I'll keep on the analysis of the wood to identify the other chemical compounds present in it, because whatever they are, it would be incredible!" Geek said, his volume increasing as he spoke. "Can you imagine a retardant that is resistant to almost ten thousand degrees?"

"Pick us up," the voice said insistently.

Without thinking, I just grabbed for the spear and pulled it free from the jelly. It felt light, even in my mortal condition.

I heard a sound like the purr of a contented cat.

The spear began to vibrate ever so slightly in my hand. As the jelly dripped from the blade, motes of intense blue sparks flew from it, but it could not ignite. I rolled the spear around and, with a sudden violent jerk, flicked the jelly off the spear. Instantly, the blade burst into flames. Duma and Geek both jumped back.

"Dude, what the fuck?" Duma screamed.

"Be careful, D," Geek said with a tremor in his voice, holding one hand out. "We don't know much about that thing yet."

The glow of the blade became too intense to look at, and my vision was filled with black spots.

"Ah, much better," said the woman.

Out of the corner of my eye, I saw the Bánánach standing next to me, and I flinched.

"Holy shit, watch that thing, would you?" Duma said, backing up even farther.

No one reacted to the Bánánach standing next to me.

Duma and Geek both held their hands up to shield their faces as they continued to back away. "Damn, that's hot," Duma said. "Put that thing down, would you? Before you burn the place down."

Then the metal tool cart buckled from the mere proximity of the heat, and a chorus of protests went up. I felt nothing, not even a warm breeze.

"D! Put. That. Thing. Down. Now," Duma said, pointing at the case from fifty feet away.

"Ignore them. Use us," the Bánánach said defiantly.

"Fuck," Duma said then disappeared.

In the blink of an eye, I was on my butt on the ground—without the spear—and the case was sitting on the ground next to me, closed.

Black blotches marred my vision, and my hands hurt. They weren't burnt but rather sore, like after a day of trophy fishing.

"What the actual fuck, D?" Duma said from a few feet away.

"Oh, thank God," Geek said, pressing the heels of his palms into his eyes.

Ab was standing behind Geek, flexing his gloved hands. "I was about to see just how tough dragon scales really are," the big Fae said, flexing his fingers. "Duma's way was more delicate than I would have been." Ab fixed me with a withering stare.

As the blotches in my vision began to abate, I noticed Geek was sweating profusely, but I wasn't even hot. Ab and Duma weren't human—they didn't sweat. I didn't know if the reason was the heat of the spear or just the intensity of the situation, but everyone was on edge. Then I noticed that, in addition to the partially melted tool cart, the entire front end of the car we were working next to was warped and buckled, and the paint had blackened and cracked along the hood, and the windshield had shattered.

I pushed to my feet. "Um, is everyone okay?" I asked.

"Oh, now you're concerned?" Duma asked. "Screw you, D. You've gone off the rails with this whole thing. Pulling that damn spear out inside this building. Man, I got flammable liquids and gases all over this place, and you fucking melted that cart," he said, pointing at the metal tool cart that had warped and bent. "And that damn car. You're lucky the fire-retardant system didn't go off or nothing worse happened. We all could have suffocated, you dipshit."

"A little warning would have been nice, D," Geek added. "Seriously. That thing is hot as Hades. Well, maybe, I mean, I don't know." He looked at Ab and Duma, who both just ignored him. "You should get your fire-retardant system checked 'cause that definitely should have triggered it."

"Sorry," I said, only partially meaning it. "I needed to see if I could wield it without melting my face off."

"Well, obviously you can, so don't do that in here or around me again," Duma said. "And no more fucking experiments without warning us, you got it?" He pointed a finger at me. "Man, you are definitely pissing me off." He walked away mumbling to himself while gesticulating wildly.

Whatever. All I have to do now is figure out how to get Nemesis to show up where I want her, and the easiest way to do that is to set up an altar.

Chapter 54

"I need a yardstick, a scale, and a scourge," I said to no one in particular. "And where's the nearest police station?"

At that, both Ab and Geek glared at me. Their confusion was clear.

"What on earth for?" Geek asked. "And I don't think you should go near a police station right now. You're still wanted for that thing in LA."

"Yeah, well, the easiest way to get Nemesis to show is to set up an altar to her," I said. "In order to exist on this plane, the Protogenoi all gather strength from the energy created by belief in them. If I build it, she will come. And I'll be there waiting, with that." I pointed at the case the spear was in.

"We probably have a yardstick and a scale of some kind around here, but what makes you think we'd have a scourge?" Ab asked.

I canted my head and put my hands on my hips in incredulity. "Seriously?" I asked. "Duma's probably using it on whatshername right now."

"Point," Ab replied, raising his eyebrows. "That'd be downstairs, then. Help yourself."

Geek joined me while I was searching the shop. "What's with the treasure hunt, D?" he asked. "I mean, that's a pretty bizarre set of tools you want."

"Nemesis is a goddess of retribution, the punisher of hubris," I replied, pulling a metal yardstick from behind a workbench. "She's ancient. Older than Zeus, even. And she was always depicted with a measuring stick, balance scales, and some sort of weapon, like a sword, a dagger, or a scourge. I need to represent some of those. Hence…" I held up the yardstick. "And since she was an avenger of crime, the best place to set up an altar to her would be near a police station."

"Wouldn't a courthouse be better?" he asked. "And how about a digital scale? I have a small one for weighing material for the spectrometer." He pointed back at his gear.

"That'll work," I replied, walking back over to Geek's hard-sided cases. "Now to find that scourge."

"I've got a knife," Geek said.

"So do I," I said. "The yardstick and the digital scale are a reach. I need to find something more traditional to add to it to make sure it gets her attention. A dagger and a sword are just too generic. Duma probably has one somewhere in one of his collections. I just don't want to walk in on him using it."

"Using it?" Geek said with a start. "Where? Here? On who?"

"You wanted to come, Geek," I said. "You're probably better off just focusing on Areadbhair. Worrying about what Ab and Duma are up to at any given time is likely to give you issues you won't be able to resolve."

"I heard that!" Ab shouted from across the shop. "And I'm just lying here, trying to rest after nearly having my face melted off, thank you very much." He held up a middle finger.

Ignoring Ab and leaving Geek with his computers and equipment, I headed to the stairway that led down to the basement or whatever was below ground level. At the top of the stairs, rather than heading down, I felt it was prudent to just shout.

"Hey, Duma! If you aren't too busy, could I get you to bring me up a scourge when you have time?" I called, trying to be straightforward so that I wouldn't have to go farther down the stairs and try again.

After a minute of no response, I was just about to shout again when Duma popped up on the bottom step, wiping his hands with a rag. When he finished, he pulled a scourge from under one arm and tossed it up to me. "I need that back," he said nonchalantly. "And don't worry, you can't catch anything from the fluids on there. There aren't any human ones."

The scourge was black leather with thirteen straps, each tipped with what appeared to be small rusty iron claws, some of which were covered in chunks of bluish matter and fluid. My stomach went queasy. Forcing myself to think of anything else but the blue goo on the end of the straps, I began to wonder if Geek could be right. Maybe the courthouse would be a better place to set up the altar. *Tonight.*

Chapter 55

Just after one in the morning, I had Ab drop me off near the Saint Joan of Arc Church on the corner of East Bridger and South Casino Center Boulevard, just across the corner from the old Golden Nugget hotel. The Bridger Building, where the courthouse was, sat just behind the church. Construction was going on around the courthouse, so I would create the small altar within the enclosed workspace then hide and wait.

The Bridger Building was old and dated, with shiny black marble tile walls surrounding the first floor and columns of white marble for the next two. The smaller tower above that was a faded sky blue on the eastern and western facades, while the northern and southern ones were dotted with uniformly spaced windows. That part of town was deserted at that hour, unlike the Strip to the south.

My first reaction was simply to jump over the screened fence to get into the parking lot on the building's south side, but I had to settle instead for climbing it clumsily with the heavy and awkwardly long spear case. Once inside the open lot, I scrambled to the covered scaffolding that lined the rear of the building, cut a slit in the plastic sheeting, and slipped inside with the case and my bag of items for the altar.

It took the work of just a few minutes to lay out the yardstick, the scale, and the scourge. Then I placed a small votive candle among the objects and lit it. The last thing I did was conduct an invocation.

"Nemesis, winged balancer of life, dark-faced goddess, daughter of Justice, avenger of crime and punisher of hubris, we desperately need your help," I said in a whisper. "Please bring us the justice we deserve, and castigate those who believe they have gotten away with crimes unpunished. We are in need of your retribution. Only you can help us. Please, Nemesis, Goddess of Rhamnous, come."

I felt I could be most sincere by being generic rather than specific because I was concerned that making up a situation would come across as disingenuous and therefore more likely to be ignored. My little ritual needed will and belief to give it power to attract her. The biggest hurdle was, for me, that I was well beyond belief. I *knew* she existed, and I *knew* what she did to those she felt deserved her justice. I was hoping my anger would substitute for will and belief.

I would just have to wait and see.

After the summoning, I found the darkest corner in the construction zone, popped open the case, leaving the spear immersed in the jelly, and waited.

I was startled awake two hours later, according to my watch. The small candle had long since burned out, and I couldn't see anything in the scant light filtering through the sheeting, but I could *feel* something—not the way I was used to feeling the presence of an Old One or some other magical creature but just a gut instinct. I closed my eyes and tried to listen. I heard nothing but the occasional car or truck pass by outside and random drips from some leaky piping overhead. Trying not to focus on any one spot, I scanned the area for anything. Out of the corner of my eye, across the space, I saw something move through the shadows off to my right. I stuck my hand into the jelly and grabbed the spear, keeping it immersed until I was sure it was her.

I'll have only one shot at this.

"Use us." The Bánánach's voice spoke in my ear. "Your target is there. I will guide you. Trust us."

The voice surprised me at first, making me think it came from somewhere in the darkness nearby. I jerked back reflexively and landed hard on my right elbow, jarring my shoulder as well. I muffled a scream, but I couldn't muffle the sound of me falling over. It wasn't loud, but it was enough.

Heavy-duty work lights on stands began to pop on one by one around the space. The instant the first one came on, I could see Nemesis in her winged form, slowly peering into the darkness around her.

"Whoever you are, I mean you no harm," she said, her voice and visage as beautiful as always. "If you are the one who invoked me, I have come to help. Show yourself." Lights continued to pop on with sharp snaps and cracks.

"Throw us! Your target lies before you. Strike now!" the Bánánach said in my head that time.

Nemesis was less than ten yards away from me, but the pain in my elbow and shoulder of my throwing arm was intense, and my hand and fingers were numb. *There's nothing funny about the funny bone.* Not to mention, my back and knees were stiff as well. I tried to stretch and move them and decided that after thousands of years of training, my best chance was to get in close if I could.

Just as a light popped on, revealing my position, I stuck my hand into the goo again and grabbed the spear.

"Yes!" cried the Bánánach.

I shook the spear hard to throw off the residual jelly, and the tip instantly burst into a blue-white flame.

"Yes!"

Nemesis laughed. "Oh, it *is* you, Diomedes," she said. "I thought as much. But you know, if you wanted to see me, you only needed to ask," she said. "It's easy for me to find you. I just follow the trail of your carnage." She walked her fingers through the air.

I knew better than to get drawn into a conversation. I didn't have my speed or strength, so I needed to act decisively. I stepped toward her cautiously, crouching and holding the spear low with both hands.

Nemesis walked confidently and nonchalantly to my right, seemingly unconcerned about the glowing spear. I kept closing the distance cautiously.

"I'm not sure what you expect to do with that, Diomedes," Nemesis said with a slight shrug of one shoulder. "You cannot escape your fate. You have abused and flaunted your rewards at the expense of countless mortals, and for that you will pay the consequences."

"Yes, let her become complacent, let her disregard us." The Bánánach's voice echoed in my head.

I continued to move toward her as she circled me in return, taunting me as she moved.

"You mortals never seem to realize there are consequences to all of your actions," Nemesis said. "You *all* think you can get away with it, but there is always *retribution*."

"Now, attack!" howled the Bánánach.

Once I closed to within ten feet of her, I quickly slid the spear toward her in a thrust that she easily evaded, but I wasn't done. From my fully extended position, with the butt of the intensely burning spear in one hand, I began to spin the weapon overhead in complete arcs, lunging toward her with each pass. The Bánánach laughed maniacally as I focused my attack, ignoring my surroundings until something fell behind me, and I felt heat pressing in on my back.

"Consequences, Diomedes," Nemesis said as I noticed her white gown was reflecting a flickering yellow-orange glow.

I stopped spinning the weapon, holding it at shoulder height, pointed at Nemesis, and quickly glanced behind me to see the empty workspace on fire and part of the internal scaffolding melted and collapsed on itself. Ignoring the fire and trying to block out the constant cackling of the Bánánach, I lunged at Nemesis again. In a fraction of a second, she stopped, drew her short sword, and attempted to parry the blow. Her maneuver was only partly successful. She directed my attack to her side, but the intense heat of Areadbhair melted and warped her sword in the instant the blades connected, and the blue-white flame singed the goddess of retribution, causing her to flinch. The result took us both by surprise.

She moved across the space, farther away from me in an instant, putting as much distance between us as she could, clearly confused and concerned.

"Sometimes, the punisher should be held accountable too," I said, snarling. I could feel the heat on my back increasing, and the light in the space continued to brighten, casting everything in an eerie flickering orange light. I had her on the defensive, and I had a chance.

I reared back and threw the spear as hard as I could. From less than ten yards there was no way I could miss. But Nemesis was able to sidestep the blazing weapon thrown at the speed of a mere mortal. Areadbhair sailed past and stuck into the masonry wall behind Nemesis with a solid *thunk*, and within the span of a heartbeat, the cement wall burst into flames and began to crack. The infernal heat from the spear caused the cinder blocks to shatter and fall apart until an eight-foot-wide hole opened up and the spear dropped to the ground, continuing to burn with sunlike intensity. The floor cracked, and an acrid, penetratingly dry smell hit me.

Crazy maniacal laughter echoed through my skull, and I couldn't think straight to determine what I should do next. The fire continued to spread to the plastic sheeting securing the construction site, which instantly curled and melted, billowing black smoke, and everything flammable in the space started to burn. The smell and heat started to become overwhelming. Everything was happening at once, and the damn laughter in my head wouldn't stop.

"Pick us up!" the Bánánach said in between fits of laughter. "We are not done yet. Your foe still lives."

My foe. I was sweating in the intense and growing heat of the enclosed space as I watched the wood flooring of the scaffolding burst into flames as the metal structure buckled then collapsed.

Then something struck me, and my feet left the ground. No sooner had I landed—hard on my right side—than I felt myself being thrown again, through a wall of fire. I hit something very hard, and the world went black for a moment. A loud crack and deep rumble brought me to my senses, and through the flames, I could just focus on a massive figure facing off against Nemesis' winged form.

I blinked hard several times, focusing through the waves of heat and flames.

It's Ab.

"We are here. Pick us up," the Bánánach said as I slowly got to my feet. I could feel the draw of Areadbhair and saw it shift—as luck would have it—less than arm's length away as the rubble it lay on disintegrated into ash and dust beneath it. Without thinking, I grabbed the weapon.

Ab wielded an axe in each hand. For most beings of normal stature, each weapon would have been a two-handed device, but Ab handled each easily in a single hand. He swung and lunged with tremendous speed and power but was unable to connect with the vengeful would-be deity.

"Now is your chance. Your foe is preoccupied," the Bánánach said. "Strike."

I watched the pair through the rapidly spreading tongues of flame, making the air almost unbreathable and painfully dry. My lungs were burning with each breath.

"We will guide you," the demon in the spear said. "Trust us."

The giant Peri and the Old One continued to face each other, with Nemesis avoiding every attack, though some only barely. As they fought, Ab moved into my line of sight, his broad back almost completely obscuring my view of Nemesis. The only part of her I could see was just under his left arm when he swung. My window was minuscule at best, and even though she was less than thirty feet away, my chance of not hitting Ab and hitting her was infinitesimally small.

"Trust us," the Bánánach said. "We will tell you when to throw."

Some part of my brain believed the bloodthirsty spirit.

I reared back, crouched, and waited. Ab moved, Nemesis moved, the building burned and fell apart around us, and I could barely breathe or see. My eyes watered, and I began to cough, and my vision began to narrow.

"Now!" the Bánánach screamed in my head.

Without thinking, I threw as hard as I could then fell over into blackness.

Chapter 56

Water poured over my face and head and into my mouth, choking me. I coughed as I woke in a startled fit.

"Wake the fuck up, D. It's me," I heard Ab say. "You're fine."

In the background, I heard sirens blaring. I opened my eyes and saw Ab pulling off his dragonskin gloves. I was lying in the bed of Ab's giant pickup. I painfully pulled myself up on one elbow.

Ab wiped at his face with a wet bandana, poured more water on it from a bottle, and dabbed at a blackened and blistered part of his rib cage. "Helluva throw, but it was a bit too close for my liking." He winced. A yellowish substance was oozing from the wound.

"Did I hit her?" I asked with a croak.

Something crashed off to my right, and I could hear the roar of flames as my senses came back to me.

"Yeah, you got the bitch," Ab said, still tending to his wound. "Right fucking past me... Thunk... Right into her chest." He pointed at a spot under his right collarbone. "Her, ah, evaporation knocked all the flames out around us for a few seconds so that I could see where you were. I thought about leaving your ass for this." He held up his left arm and glared down at the nasty wound.

"You won't scar," I said. "What about the spear?"

He pointed back into the burning building behind me. "Thanks for your concern. And screw you. I may not scar, but it still fucking hurts. That thing was like a hundred thousand degrees or something. Dick."

"We gotta get the spear back," I said, trying to sit up. My lungs burned, and I began to cough uncontrollably.

"That whole place is on fire," Ab said while tending to his burn. "There's no way."

"We can't leave it," I replied between coughs.

Ab sighed heavily then winced. "You're right. That thing is way too dangerous to leave for human firefighters to find," he said with his face screwed up in pain.

"I need it," I said trying to take a slow, deep breath and control my coughing.

"What?" Ab replied, his face a mask of incredulity. "Are you kidding me? That's why we have to get it back? You see what you did with that thing, right? The whole fucking Bridger Building is on fire. It could easily jump to the church over there or that crazy wedding place back there. The *whole* block could go up if the wind shifts or picks up. But no, let me go back into the blazes of hell to get your spear for you."

"Ab, you're right," I said, trying to backtrack. "We can't let mundanes find that thing."

He shook his head, his blond hair and pale skin stained black with soot. "Fine." He wrapped the wet bandana around his face and pulled on his dragonskin gloves.

More crashing and popping along with a small explosion came from the conflagration behind us.

"Fuck." He ran back toward the building, shielding his face from the heat with his gloved palm, holding his other arm over his burned rib cage as he loped. More crashing and collapsing occurred within the building, and I could see flames in the upstairs windows. The entire building was going to be destroyed.

I lay back, trying to breathe without pain. My eyes felt dry and crusty, even when closed. I just lay there in the bed of the truck, listening to the sound of the burning building, trying to figure out how I was going to kill Eisheth without that spear if Ab couldn't get it.

Something large collapsed inside the building as windows began to blow out of the upper floors, and the sound of sirens became deafening from almost every direction, echoing off buildings. I could hear people screaming and yelling and the beating of a helicopter somewhere overhead.

At least Nemesis is gone. For now.

The reflection of flashing red lights bounced off the windows of the surrounding buildings and illuminated the streets around me, made even more ominous by the flickering orange glow from the fire. Muffled whumps and explosions of glass became regular. I pulled myself up to peer over the bed of the truck, back toward the Bridger Building.

The lower three floors were entirely engulfed in flames, and flames were shooting out windows on the sixth floor. People were gathering on the street to film and photograph the event as more and more fire trucks, police, and ambulances clogged the streets.

Over the din of the first responders, a series of dull thumps caught my attention. I had to focus to hear them, but they were coming from the corner of the building closest to where I was. Then the cement wall of the lowest floor of the Bridger building bulged and cracked. Then a cement block dislodged and fell to the ground, followed by several more. Then the wall gave way, and Ab came running out, spear in hand. Once he hit the fresh air, he stopped and coughed and wheezed for a moment, Areadbhair burning white hot in his hand.

"Start..." Ab screamed and caught his breath. "Start the damn car!"

I pulled myself up and lumbered out of the truck's bed to the driver's side, opened the door, and pushed the button on the dash, and the big truck roared to life.

"Move," he said, motioning me to slide over. "You gotta hold this somehow. I couldn't find the case." He held up the spear as he stumbled to the car. He was coughing and wheezing uncontrollably, and most of his visible skin was blackened or at least covered with soot. I tumbled out of the truck and limped over to grab the spear as Ab pulled himself into the driver's side. I crawled back into the bed of the truck, holding the spear with both hands, like a flag, as Ab spun the tires on the big truck and tore out of the parking lot and onto the street, barely missing onlookers watching the fire burn.

We drove past the Clark County Government Center and under the 15 Freeway and, much to my surprise, into a parking lot at the University Medical Center. Then I heard Ab's voice.

"Parking lot at University Med Center... corner of Shadow and West Charleston," he said in brief bursts, clearly in intense pain. "Bring... case for the spear..."

Then I heard something drop as his voice tailed off. I pushed myself up to peer into the rear window of the truck. Ab was slumped across the seat. I couldn't figure out what to do to help him because I couldn't put the spear down safely.

"Use us," the Bánánach said in my head, her voice strong and clear, even forceful. "We can end his misery quickly. He is too badly injured to survive."

I slid out of the bed of the truck and walked around to the driver's-side door to check on Ab. The cab of the truck stank like charred meat, and wisps of smoke rose from Ab's massive flank. Wet blotches of pale yellow, dripping a waxy butter-colored fluid from between cracks in his blackened skin, covered his arm, his torso, and his legs where the pants had burned away. I couldn't see his chest moving or hear him breathing.

"Ab, you okay?" I asked, trying not to touch him for fear it would hurt him. I leaned hard on the spear for support as I tried to listen for sounds of his breathing. "Ab, grunt, groan, or fart—I don't care—just let me know if you're still alive."

I heard a raspy breath followed by a very weak cough.

At least he's still alive.

"He will not survive," the demon in the spear said. "He is suffering. Ease his passing. I told you to trust us in the building, and we succeeded. Trust us now."

I shook my head. *He's a tough sonofabitch. He'll survive.*

"His body is too badly damaged," she said. "I have seen this before. Trust us."

The inside of the cab was dark, so I tilted the spear a bit to cast more light into the truck to get a better view, and the doorframe buckled and sagged within seconds.

"Aw hell no," Duma said from behind me. "I know you aren't about to jab him with that damn thing. Get the fuck away from Ab with that."

Duma caught me by surprise. I stood up, and he snatched the spear from my hand before I knew what had happened. I was too weak to fight him. He took the weapon back around to the rear of his giant SUV, shielding his face with his free arm. The intense white glow at the back of the car died instantly, and I could hear the snapping of the clips on a case. I leaned heavily against the door of the truck. The parking lot was so full that even at that hour, the closest he could get to the truck was on the road behind us.

"Pull it together, buttercup," he said, walking back over to me. "You gotta help me move him. And he weighs more than he looks. While we're doing that, you can explain to me what the fuck happened and why he's hurt so badly."

We took a solid five minutes to drag Ab's enormous bulk from the cab of the truck. His skin cracked and crunched every place we touched him, but Ab never made a sound, nor did he even seem to be conscious.

"Is he still alive?" I asked.

"He better be," Duma said, "or your damn story of how he got this way better be epically heroic. Now, get ready because we got to walk him to the back of the SUV."

The ten-yard walk took forever. Ab was dead weight, and dragging him took everything Duma and I had, each of us under one of his massive arms. We nearly fell twice, and I was too winded to talk while we trudged. We got him to the back of the crazy SUV and somehow managed to shove him far enough in to close the rear gate. I was wheezing to catch my breath, hands on both knees, fighting to remain standing.

Duma slapped me painfully on the back. "Now, talk."

"We eliminated Nemesis," I said, my voice cracking. "The spear worked. Ab distracted her, and I was able to hit her."

"How the fuck did the building catch on fire?" Duma asked as he sprayed a stream of fluid over the pickup truck, including inside the cab.

Whatever the liquid was smelled like a men's urinal on a hot day at a concert, magnified a hundred times. My eyes watered, and I began to choke.

"Get in the car," Duma said. "This will go up fast."

I limped up to the front passenger-side door of the SUV and dragged myself into the seat. Through the driver's side window, I watched Duma drop a match in the bed of Ab's pickup. In the instant it took the match to fall, Duma was behind the wheel. The fire exploded, quickly engulfing the truck with a *whoof*—startling me even though I was watching—and we were speeding off through the parking lot, going faster than I would have thought possible with such a large vehicle in tight quarters.

I'd had enough of fire.

"So, how did the building catch fire?" he asked, rolling his hand at the wrist to prompt me to talk as he jumped a curb and skidded onto a deserted street.

"The spear," I said, exhausted. I glanced back at Ab's still smoldering form in the back of the truck. All I could smell was the oily, acrid odor of burnt flesh. "Is Ab going to be okay?"

"Funny you're concerned now, D," Duma said. "He should be okay. I saw him take worse from a fire wyrm he wanted to get scales from. It took him a few months to recover, but this isn't as bad. How *exactly* did he get caught in the damn fire?"

"My fight with Nemesis wasn't going well," I said with a cough. "He showed up and distracted her long enough for me to hit her. We got out, and then we realized we couldn't leave the spear behind for first responders to find. I couldn't, so he went back in."

"When you say 'we,' you really mean 'you,' don't you?" he asked pointedly. "Doesn't matter. I'll ask Ab what happened when he wakes up. But whatever the plan was going forward, Diomedes, you can rule us out. This whole thing"—he waved his hand around—"to save Sarah is bullshit, and we are done with it. You understand?"

"I can't do this alone, Duma, and you know that," I replied.

He sighed heavily and was silent for a long moment, the anger evident in his face and posture. "Yeah, well, you're going to have to 'cause at this rate, you're going to get us killed anyway," he said.

"You owe—"

"Do. Not. Go. There," he said, holding a hand up. "Don't fucking say it. We've risked our lives with you for hundreds of years now and done some sketchy shit. But this? This is beyond any of that. You've thrown us into shit like we're expendable. We have nearly been killed multiple times, and we've gotten nowhere all on some fucked-up quest to save the first woman you had sex with in years. All because you blame yourself for circumstances way beyond your control and you barely survived yourself. The all-powerful Diomedes, Guardian of Humanity," he said waving his free hand in the air. He gave a derisive snort as we pulled up to the garage. "Fucking humans, I swear," he said just loudly enough for me to hear.

"Help me get him inside, then I think it's best you leave," he said.

"I can't do this without your help, Duma," I said as we struggled to get Ab's massive limp form out of the SUV and into the garage. Geek came to help the second he realized we were there.

"Bloody hell," Geek said when he saw us. "What happened? And do what?" Geek asked me. "Can I help?"

"Not if you know what's good for you, Geek," Duma said. "Probably best if you leave too."

"Wait, what's going on here?" Geek asked, confused.

"Have Diomedes explain it to you while you guys are leaving," Duma said.

"Let's get Ab settled inside, and then we'll go," I said. "I'll explain everything to you on the way back to San Diego, Geek."

"And take that fucking spear with you," Duma said.

Chapter 57

"So, what are you going to do now?" Geek asked as he pulled up to my house in the Roseville area of Point Loma, just across the bay from downtown San Diego.

I hadn't been home in months.

"I'm headed to Shanghai to get to Eisheth," I replied matter-of-factly.

"Oh, yeah, sure," Geek said. "Of course you are. Are you bloody nuts, mate? With what backup? Did you forget you're mortal now? And you have no support of any kind."

"I've got Areadbhair," I replied, hooking a thumb back at the case that held the spear.

"That thing burned down a building and nearly killed you and Ab in the process."

"Yeah, but it took out Nemesis too," I said. "It'll take out Eisheth."

"And half of Shanghai in the process, no doubt," he replied. "You've got to figure out how to control that thing better, or it's going to kill you too."

"I'll be fine, and at this point, I don't care if I burn down half the world," I replied, getting out of Geek's car.

Geek stayed outside my house for about thirty minutes before he finally drove off. I sorted through several garbage bags of mail left on my kitchen counter, presumably by Ned—mostly trash and fishing catalogs.

Fishing. Where had my life gone?

I sat on my couch, staring for a long time at the heavy case that held the spear, sitting on my coffee table, unable to move but not really thinking either. The front door opened, and Ned walked in, holding the head of two Strigoi. I realized it was dark outside.

"Don't go out there alone, boy," Ned said, dropping the heads on the kitchen counter and wiping his hands on his violently colorful shirt.

I had all but forgotten about the blood war Lilith had declared on me. No way would I be able to defend myself as a mortal against the regular onslaught of mindless Strigoi she continued to send against me, even with the spear. And I couldn't conceive of a way to attack Eisheth either.

"Dude, you look like a man about to make a really stupid decision," Ned said, pulling a beer from my refrigerator, popping it open, and sitting down heavily in my leather armchair. "Piece of advice from someone who's watched you make lots of dumb decisions in the past: Don't. But I know you won't listen to me." He shook his head and wiped spilled beer from his beard then belched loudly. "Shit, boy, you don't listen to anyone these days. Not that you ever really did, but lately—"

"Why should I? I took care of Nemesis by myself," I replied.

"Yeah, boy, you did," he said. "Burned down two buildings in the process. Three firefighters got hurt, one still in critical condition. Bravo, dude, bravo."

"Fuck you, Ned," I replied. "Is it easy for you to judge me, sitting on the sidelines?"

"Sidelines, you say?" Ned asked. "You have no idea how many times I have saved your butt, boy. None. And not just me, but lots of others, including your uptight benefactor."

"Former benefactor," I said pointedly.

"Former. Fine," Ned said. "I'd like to see things from your point of view, boy, I really would, but I ain't flexible enough to get my head that far up my ass."

"You can leave any time you want," I said, standing up. "Now that I have that, I don't need your help anymore anyway." I pointed at the case.

"You don't know what you're messing with," Ned said. "That thing is all bad news. Cursed. There ain't nothing you can do with it that won't come back to bite you in the ass. The monster that's stuck inside that thing is evil and twisted and only wants to cause death and destruction. It'll help you, alright, but to its own end, guaranteed. You ain't gotta believe me about anything, but trust me when I tell you to dump that thing. Drop it in a volcano somewhere, bury it under a hundred tons of concrete, whatever, but don't drop it in my ocean. Just get rid of it."

I stared at the case. Geek and Ned were right about the spear, but it was the only chance I had at helping Sarah. And I needed it. Clearly, my expression conveyed my thoughts.

Ned slapped his thighs. "Well then, I guess I'll just go fuck myself, then," he said, standing. "Take care of yourself, boy," he said from the door, letting himself out.

My mind went into overdrive once Ned left. I knew Eisheth was on the top floors of one of the three towers in the Riverside Triumphal Arch complex in Shanghai. She would be guarded by a virtual army of supernatural creatures and humans alike. On top of that, she was the Mother of the Moroi and a lesser fallen angel. And I needed her unconscious long enough to put a crown of special stones on her head for a few minutes in order to save Sarah.

All I had to do was get past Eisheth's security, subdue her, and get out safely—all with no money, no backup, no allies, and no real resources except a dangerous flaming spear possessed by a vengeful spirit.

What could possibly go wrong?

I turned on the TV only to see footage of the burning Bridger Building in Las Vegas. And the fire gave me an idea. If I could isolate Eisheth away from her army, she'd be an easier target, but I would still need to drop a bomb on her to knock her out. But maybe I could find a way to make her the bomb I was dropping.

If I triggered a fire alarm in her building, she would likely be evacuated and probably by helicopter off the roof of the building to another safe house. If I could be within range of that helicopter, I could hit it with the spear and bring it down. I'm pretty sure that falling from well over a thousand feet, encased in a burning hunk of metal, would incapacitate even a being like Eisheth for at least a few minutes upon impact. *Unless she can fly.* It wasn't just my best option, it was my only option short of knocking on the front door, posing as an Amway flaming-spear salesman.

The more immediate issues were getting out of San Diego without being attacked by Lilith's bloodthirsty hordes and getting to Shanghai expediently while carrying a weapon capable of burning hotter than the surface of the sun.

Maybe St. Germain would know a way. After all, I didn't kill him when I could have, so he owed me.

Someone knocked on the door.

I went back into my loadout room and grabbed a Sig Sauer P320 XCompact, checked the slide to make sure there was a round in the chamber, and went to the door. The nine-millimeter rounds wouldn't kill a Strigoi, but enough bullets to the head might slow it down enough that I could kill it some other way.

"Rest assured I am not a vampire, Diomedes," St. Germain said through the door. "You won't need the gun."

I cracked open the door to see the ascended master and his perfect white smile, holding a small leather messenger bag in one hand.

"You do have quite the vampire problem in this neighborhood, though, don't you?" he said. "There are at least three dozen within fifty yards of us right now." He grimaced. "So please let me in. And yes, I do believe I can help you."

I let the alchemist in and closed the door behind him, tucking the gun into the back of my pants rather than putting it away. I just felt safer with it on me.

"So, how exactly can you help me?" I asked.

"Well, given that it's just you now, I think I can level the playing field a bit," he replied. "Not entirely, mind you, but a bit." He held up a hand with his thumb and index finger less than an inch apart.

"Again, how exactly?"

"Information. How else?" he replied.

Chapter 58

"Information about what, exactly?" I asked, not sure why I was feeling uneasy about him suddenly. I definitely didn't like the fact that he'd shown up unannounced just as I was thinking about him. As an ascended master, I knew he supposedly had access to all of mankind's knowledge, but reading minds was something else. And in my experience, those that had telepathy always abused it.

"Well, I know you need to get to Eisheth in her fortress condo in Shanghai, and I know you are pretty much on your own now," he said, shrugging. He set the messenger bag on my coffee table. "I also know you need to get to China quickly while carrying Areadbhair, which means you can't exactly travel regular commercial airlines."

"Not exactly, no," I replied, crossing my arms over my chest and squinting at him.

"So, I bring you this," he waved a hand at the bag on the table. "And information about Eisheth's building and condo."

"What's in the bag?"

"See for yourself, Diomedes," St. Germain said, flopping onto the couch with practiced ease, crossing one leg over the other knee.

Skeptically, I went to the bag and dumped its contents onto the table: some sort of ID badge on a lanyard, an Italian passport, a flight itinerary, folded commercial blueprints and papers bound by a heavy rubber band, a large manila envelope labeled "Travel Docs," and a fat letter-sized envelope spilled out. The ID badge was an access pass to the Shanghai International Circuit racetrack with my photo on it and the name "Giuseppe Rossi," the Italian version of John Smith.

The Italian passport bore the same photo and name. The large envelope labeled "Travel Docs" contained a sheaf of documents including technical drawings and forms in several languages, while the small envelope contained a thick stack of five-hundred-Euro notes, a stack of Chinese ten-thousand-yuan notes, and a small stack of US one-hundred-dollar bills with a band around it.

"There's a large wheeled metal container at the LAX cargo terminal, waiting for you to load it up with whatever gear you'll need," St Germain said while focusing on his fingernails. "The cash is for payments to specific individuals set up to help you clear customs. You'll be going as a specialized Italian car mechanic for the upcoming Touring Car Championship races. With all your tools and equipment, of course. I can get you there. The rest is up to you."

I bent over and picked up the blueprints and papers. In one corner, the blueprint read "Riverside Triumphal Arch, Building 1, penthouse remodel, 2014." I stared at St. Germain. After a moment, he simply smiled, still examining his fingernails.

"I told you I could help, and I owe you," the alchemist said. "I understand you managed to take care of Nemesis too. Which gives us both a little more breathing room for now. So I doubly owe you." He bowed his head slightly. "Consider this my thanks." With that, he stood up and walked to the door. "You have a flight to catch, and I should be going. Good luck, Diomedes. Contact me when you have the charged crystals."

His statement about catching a flight spurred me to check the flight details. To my surprise, the flight would leave at just after noon the next day. I had to move quickly. According to the documents in the manila envelope, the shipping crate was at the LAX cargo terminal, just down the street from the main airport. I had to contact someone named José once I got there, but the crate needed to be loaded and sealed five hours before the cargo flight, which was scheduled for 11:00 a.m. the following day, and the current time was just after 10:00 p.m. That left me less than four hours to organize and pack before I had to drive the three or four hours to LA. And that was assuming I didn't hit traffic on the 405.

What are the odds of that? Long but still far better than the odds of me succeeding.

I ran to my loadout room and pulled several more sidearms from the racks, including my standard Sig Sauer P226, two Glocks, an FN-SCAR-H, and enough ammunition and magazines to outfit a small militia. Probably the safest way to bring down the helicopter would be with a heavy sniper rifle, but I didn't have one, and I doubted I could get one on such short notice since I wasn't working with Athena or Duma. I would have to make do with what I had. At least the spear could kill Eisheth if I absolutely needed to.

I threw some clothes and toiletries into a small duffel, put all the papers and documents back into the messenger bag, and grabbed my phone and the spear and packed up the rear seat of my truck, which was parked in the garage, fortunately. I knew the minute I opened the garage door, I would be under siege from the vampires hunting me. Not only did I not have time for that, I didn't know if I could survive being attacked by even one of the creatures.

I got in, started the truck, turned on the lights, and opened the garage door. I took a deep breath, let it out, then jammed the gas pedal to the floor. The tires screeched on the smooth concrete of the garage and then the driveway before I spun the car around onto the road, narrowly missing a neighbor's car parked along the curb. The first vampire hit the truck before I could shift out of reverse and into drive. The crew cab truck rocked as the gangly creature broadsided the vehicle like a cornerback tackling a wide receiver. The truck suddenly lurched back in the opposite direction as one hit me from the passenger side, and in my headlights, I could see several more blood-suckers loping awkwardly on all fours, coming at me down the street. At least one leech landed in the bed of my truck, and I floored it, hitting both creatures in front of me head-on, spraying black gore everywhere. In my rearview, I could see two vampires pursuing me and catching up fast. The one in the bed of the truck was trying to hang on as I fishtailed and weaved down the street.

The narrow, car-lined residential street and the truck, meant for power, not speed, kept me from outrunning the creatures right away. I was sure vampires virtually surrounded me as I sped down the road at fifty miles an hour. I couldn't see much around me beyond what appeared in my headlights except shadows, but every time one of the creatures got close enough, they slammed into the side of the truck, making it lurch and skid. As long as my tires held, I would be okay. I just needed to make it down to Rosecrans and onto the 5. I skidded around every corner and flew through every light and stop sign until I hit the intersection of Rosecrans and Lytton near the old Naval Training Center turned modern shopping center.

Once I hit the major intersection at Rosecrans and Midway a few blocks farther along, the number of creatures following me decreased dramatically. While I could see two Strigoi still scrabbling along behind me in the rearview mirror, the collisions had stopped. I raced along Rosecrans past the shopping centers at Midway and Sports Arena, running yellow and red lights and racing past the few cars plodding along as I approached the on-ramp for the interstate.

Taking the loop onto the freeway a little too fast caused the truck to lurch a bit, and I heard something roll around in the bed of the truck behind me. As the vehicle leveled out onto the 5, I reached for the gun still in my waistband. The rear window shattered behind me, spraying safety glass everywhere. I swerved hard, almost turning the truck sideways on the road, barely managing to regain control as the creature tried to shove its body through the opening in the glass. I slammed on the brakes, sending the creature flying through the large cab and into the front windshield. Luckily, no cars were behind me, though one car in the lane to my left swerved wide as I skidded to a halt. Unfortunately, as the creature flew past, an ungainly arm hit my face.

Blinking hard and shaking my head to refocus, I pulled the gun up and unloaded the magazine at the creature's bony and bulbous head less than five inches from the barrel, with the bloodsucker jammed between the dashboard and the shattered windshield, still stunned from the impact. Sixteen nine-millimeter rounds obliterated the monster's head, along with the remains of my windshield and dashboard.

Fortunately, none of the rounds deflected into my engine block or any other vital parts of the truck. I dropped the gun to the floorboard, grabbed the vampire by its arm, and heaved it out the driver's side door as other cars swerved around me. The limp creature, far from dead, landed on the concrete freeway with a dull *splat*, and I pulled the door shut with a heavy creak due to the bent metal and floored it. The rear tires spun freely for a moment as they came into contact with the creature and burst its blood sac, spraying its slick black blood everywhere. The destroyed vampire resembled a bag of discarded garbage strewn across the road in my rearview mirror. I swear I saw an arm move in the oncoming headlights of cars behind it, but no way was I going back to check.

My jaw and cheek ached, and my ears rang from firing the gun in such close quarters in an enclosed space, and the adrenaline had my heart racing, but I was still alive—so far. The drive through LA to the airport could prove deadlier than the Strigoi.

I made it to the air freight terminal just off the 105 and Aviation Boulevard near LAX a little after three in the morning. I pulled into the parking lot and gathered my documents and the cash and the gear I needed to ship, including the spear and all my weapons. That was the first time ever I could remember not bringing my swords or my cuirass. I felt naked, like part of me was missing, a significant part. But as a mortal human, if I got close enough to any nonhuman beings to use my swords—which were just sharp blades in my hands now anyway—I would not be fast or strong enough to last very long. And my cuirass was just added weight that might stop a few errant rounds from a small-caliber weapon, but that was it. Once I had everything gathered, I called José as instructed, and he arranged for me to pull my truck around while they brought the metal shipping crate out to me by forklift. Technically, the freight handler didn't open until five, but I was "expected." The only other person there was a man preparing to send his dog across country by plane, and he was not happy.

I took less than thirty minutes to pack and arrange all my gear safely within the padded container. Inside were straps and tie-downs to help me secure everything, and I locked the case and put the key on my keyring. When I was done, I waved José over. He rolled security tape over the joints and secured the lock with US Customs stamps marked "Inspected." He took longer to prepare the crate than I'd taken to pack it.

"Okay, it's good to go"—he glanced at the bill of lading—"Mr. Rossi." He pronounced it "rose-ee." Then he stood there.

I took a moment to realize he was waiting for his payment. Awkwardly, I pulled the cash from my pocket and peeled off several one-hundred-dollar bills. José shook his head and waved his fingers. I peeled off several more, and he nodded curtly then craned his neck to glance at my beat-to-hell truck then back at me, and he shook his head. I peeled off one more, handed him the five hundred dollars, gathered my paperwork, and climbed back in my truck. The guy with the dog was still sitting there, petting the animal, which was clearly agitated and upset. Even with what I was about to do, I didn't envy him.

I got back in my beat-up truck and drove around to long-term parking for the airport, set an alarm on my phone for five hours, and lay back to take a nap, which proved harder than I'd expected, since I had no rear or front window anymore and LAX is never not crowded. I would sleep on the twelve-hour flight to Shanghai.

Chapter 59

The packed flight was full of business travelers but otherwise uneventful, and I used the time to study the plans and blueprints St. Germain had provided for me. Clearing customs in Shanghai took several hours due to the massive influx of passengers, but it was easier than expected. I spoke Italian long before I spoke English, so playing the part of Italian mechanic Giuseppe Rossi was easy. The cargo terminals were just on the other side of the airport, but navigating the queue and the counter proved more difficult due to the language barrier. Of all the languages I've learned over my lifetime, the many dialects of Chinese, including the local Shanghainese, were never ones I picked up.

I tried multiple languages I could speak before I was finally referred to a clerk who spoke English well enough that we could communicate. Inside her glass enclosure, the instant she entered my name into the computer, she flew into a fit of motion and screamed into a handheld radio in Shanghainese. The response was so garbled that I had no idea how anyone could understand it even if they spoke the dialect, but the clerk nodded, acknowledged what she'd heard, then pointed me around a corner.

"You meet Zhu around corner, down hall, at next door," the clerk said in broken but passable English. "She take care of you."

"Choo? Around the corner and down the hall?" I asked, trying to clarify the name. My question got me a nasty glare and a stern gesture pointing toward the corner of the windowed office, abruptly followed by her waving up the next person in line.

I proceeded according to the clerk's directions and found a gray-haired woman whose face was a dour mask of wrinkles, standing in the first doorway I came across. She held a clipboard of papers in front of her.

"Choo?" I asked, trying to be polite.

"Signore Rossi?" she replied with an impeccable Italian accent.

"*Si*" was my response, and I fished my passport out of my pocket just in case. She examined the document briefly and waved me to follow her as she walked farther down the hall. At the end of it was a gated metal cage that led out onto the main warehouse floor. I could see my metal shipping crate being dropped off in an area demarcated by a bright-yellow square on the otherwise dark cement floor. That area was almost completely devoid of people, but the sounds of shouting people, forklifts and other vehicles, an incessant beeping, and the *clang* and *clunk* of heavy objects moving rattled through the open building.

"Can you store the crate for me?" I asked in Italian. "The contents are portable, but I'll need to ship them back once I'm finished here."

She rolled her eyes and sighed heavily. "Yes, I can arrange to store it, but not for more than a week. And you must see me when you need to repack it," she said, her Italian indeed near flawless. We finished the paperwork, and I went through an awkward process of determining the correct denomination for the bribe identical to what I'd done back in California with José. Zhu handed me a business card, turned, and left the way we'd come. I could not read anything on the card though I did see a string of numbers I assumed to be her direct phone line.

I fished through the messenger bag to find my keys, unlocked the crate, and pulled my duffel and the case out and left the way I'd entered. I headed back to the passenger terminals to catch a cab. By the time I'd made the half-mile trek, I was exhausted from walking and carrying all my gear.

After resting for a solid ten minutes, I hailed a cab and told the driver to take me to the Riverside Triumphal Arch condos in Pudong. He understood me well enough to do a double take and give me a complete once-over, clearly unconvinced I belonged there. I figured it would be easier to get there and find a hotel close by on my own rather than trying to communicate I wanted to go to a hotel near there and see what happened.

The area around the three-building complex where I was headed was a bustling high-end business-and-shopping district with countless malls, shops, restaurants, museums, and other tourist attractions on every corner. Given Shanghai was the second most populous city in the world, it made perfect sense that the progenitor of the vampires that live off human energy would live there. The streets and sidewalks were swamped with tourists, businesspeople from around the world, and locals alike. From the information, blueprints, and photos St. Germain had given me, I recognized the three towers, particularly the taller twin towers, among the myriad of high-rises along that stretch of the Huangpu River. The Pudong riverside skyline was dominated by the massive Shanghai World Financial Center Building, the Shanghai Tower, and the Oriental Pearl Radio and TV Tower. The area reminded me a bit of a cross between New York City and Las Vegas, except very new.

"Hotel?" I asked as we got closer to the condos, deciding to risk confusion and turmoil.

The driver shook his head and pointed at the buildings just in front of us then said something else that rambled on for a few seconds. Just past the Oriental Pearl Tower, I saw a hotel called the Shangri-La.

"Stop, hotel," I said, pointing at the brown stone building. "Shangri-La."

He glanced in his rearview then pulled into the driveway for the hotel. Again, he said something that I had no chance of understanding. He pointed at the condos just up the road in front of us then at the meter on the dashboard, still talking. The fee on the meter read 150 yuan, about twelve bucks, not including tip. I handed the cabbie two one-hundred yuan bills and got out, and before I was completely out, the bellhops for the hotel had already unloaded the trunk and put my gear onto a trolley for check-in.

Behind me and just down the busy street, I could see the Riverside Triumphal Arch complex. The tan stone facades and the bright blue-green glass that covered the top two floors of each high-rise as well as the riverside faces were designed to resemble water cascading over a waterfall.

I checked in to the hotel on a floor as high up as I could get with a riverside view without being in some sort of presidential or penthouse suite. The room on the thirty-fifth floor was nondescript and could have been in any moderately priced large-chain hotel anywhere in the world. The earth-tone colors were simple and felt clean when washed with daylight through the large picture window overlooking the river and Shanghai proper to the north. Despite the ever-present haze, I could see the condos clearly in the midafternoon sun.

I knew from the blueprints that the condos were each fifty-two stories tall and that Eisheth's remodel occupied the top two floors of building one, which included a helipad on the roof. The buildings were far narrower than they were wide and were laid out so that one narrow end faced the river, providing river views from all but the opposite windows. The top three floors were stepped, with each upper floor smaller than the one below. Eisheth had a pool on the deck of her lower level. Unlike the levels below her, no other tenants were on her floors.

According to the blueprints, the only public space on her floors was the elevator shaft and mechanical structure on the roof, accessed by a stairway from the floor below and added at the remodel. The stairway and elevator had no outside access, even from the roof, just vents and fans for the machinery. Because the penthouse had its own roof, it also had its own air-conditioning and heating units separate from the rest of the building. Every floor below Eisheth's unit had four trash chutes that fed all the way to the subbasement, but those had been eliminated on her floors.

The third floor from the top consisted of four units of roughly equal size, but the two on the riverside edge had balconies that extended out from under the floors above. Theoretically, someone could stand on one of those balconies and look up to see Eisheth's pool and deck. I had very little doubt that whoever lived there did so at Eisheth's behest, willingly or not.

The penthouse itself consisted of public spaces down-stairs—massive living room, den, media room, office space, kitchen, small servant's quarters, and several bathrooms, in addition to the pool and deck. The upper floor was composed of one massive room and a smaller space broken into four other rooms, two on each side of a hallway leading from the stairs to the large open space. According to the plans, two bathrooms were just at the top of the stairs to the upper floor, and none were in any of the other rooms on that floor. The stairs then continued up to the roof and helipad.

In the event of a fire, I speculated that Eisheth would just go up to her private helicopter and evacuate, especially since the elevators would likely be locked down anyway. And the blueprints showed she had no stair access, either. From what I could see from my hotel win-dow, she had a black-and-gray Airbus H225 Super Puma helicopter on her helipad. It was a commercial-grade helicopter often used as transport for oil rigs or for long-range search-and-rescue operations by the Coast Guard. It could easily seat up to twenty people with two pilots, depending on how it was configured.

In an ideal world, I would have a sniper take out the tail rotor, gear casing, or a pilot with a .50-caliber Raufoss round from an adjacent building while I waited to see where it crashed and then dragged Eisheth from the burning wreckage.

I would have to do that with the spear instead of a sniper rifle then get down to the crash site as quickly as possible to get to Eisheth. Given I would have to be in throwing range—mortal throwing range—that meant the floor below Eisheth's at farthest. To get down quickly, I would never be able to use the stairs or elevator because of the fire alarm and the crowd of people descending it or firemen climbing it. At maybe five hundred feet, it would be a very low BASE jump, and while I was an experienced jumper, it would be risky on a good day, and I lacked the specialized equipment. The only other choice I had was to rappel down the side of the building. Again, I was experienced at both climbing and abseiling, but I'd never done it on a building over ten stories high and never as a mortal human. It still seemed the more reasonable option to BASE jumping.

I was going to need a harness, a lot of rope, and a way to get Eisheth's downstairs neighbor out of the way. In a truly ideal world, I would have done this with backup and in an area that wasn't so populated, but that was the hand I'd been dealt, so that was where I would have to play it.

The problem I had at the moment was getting the gear I needed. I'd always relied on Athena or Duma for equipment or connections, and I didn't know anyone or anything in Shanghai that I could ask for help. The truth was that all I really needed was about seven hundred feet of seven-sixteenths-inch poly rope. In a pinch, I could use twenty feet or so of the extra rope to make a "Swiss seat" harness. With no other options, I went down to the lobby and asked the concierge if she could tell me where I might find a marine equipment supplier or an outdoor outfitter. I didn't want to be so specific that I stood out as suspicious after they found a few hundred feet of cordage dangling from the side of a building after a helicopter fell out of the sky.

Luckily, the concierge was able to refer me to a marine salvage yard a few miles upriver, and a massive sporting goods store was just across the river as well.

The next day, I took a cab to the marine salvage yard and picked up two coils of two hundred feet of rope. I was astounded at how much they weighed—something that would never fail to surprise me now that I had to pay attention to such things. Carrying six hundred feet of this stuff up to the fiftieth floor was going to be a nightmare, especially carrying other gear too. And no way would I be able to take the elevator. My back started to hurt just thinking about it. I shoved the rope into two pillowcases from my hotel room and caught a cab to the sporting goods store to get two hundred more feet of rope.

It turned out that the store, named Decathlon, carried not only the rope I needed but every piece of climbing gear in the known universe, including descenders and harnesses. They even had a practice wall to test gear out on. I was hopeful I wouldn't stand out, buying that kind of equipment once news got around that somebody had rappelled down a building there in town. That was part of the reason I split up the rope purchases. I also bought a large duffel bag with shoulder straps to carry everything up fifty flights of stairs, along with a pair of binoculars. I wanted to keep my cash just in case, so my one credit card was going to melt from overuse. Being mortal and entirely on my own really stank. At least the credit card was linked to a fictitious identity.

Back in my room, I did the best I could to surveil Eisheth's penthouse. I was too far away to see anything useful beyond a few random people walking around the pool deck from time to time. *If they are people.* The helicopter took off once and returned within an hour, but I couldn't see who—or what—got on or off. And I knew that the helicopter wouldn't stay there unless it was needed. Most likely, it was housed in a nearby airport hangar or private field. I watched the unit below Eisheth's but never saw anyone or anything, which didn't mean much.

I spent time walking around the three towers that made up the Riverside Triumphal Arch complex, trying to get a feel for where I would have to rappel down and what I would land on, where the nearest road access was, and what security looked like in general.

Building 1 was heavily landscaped all the way around except for a covered driveway at the entrance. At least three valets were waiting to take cars as residents drove up or to have them ready when needed. One main entrance lay beyond the lobby, and you had to pass a concierge/security desk to get to the bank of six gold-colored elevators. Some sort of an office was behind the desk, and the people working it acknowledged every resident by name. Half a dozen security cameras were watching the double door entrance, which was opened for guests by a uniformed doorman. Cars seemed to be housed in a subterranean garage under the building complex. One other entrance was on the backside of the building, labeled as a fire exit. Residential floors began at the fifth level above ground.

Six cameras appeared to be a bit much for the only entrance, but given that they covered the doorway from every angle imaginable, I was sure they were involved in facial recognition. They were also likely the reason the security personnel behind the counter knew everyone's names. It was a simple system, really, hard to fool. *So how am I going to get up to the unit on the fiftieth floor?*

Since I had no way to just walk in and take the place over, my options were either to fake some sort of service appointment or to ingratiate myself to a resident and get invited up. I had a feeling that appointments were logged and that those that weren't simply were not allowed access. Posing as a potential buyer might have worked, but no units were currently available in the building. The entire process made me feel like I was spinning my wheels. I just wasn't used to working like that. And it was looking like I was going to have to dust off my charm.

It would be easier to just take the place over.

Quite a few bars and restaurants were within easy walking distance of the towers, so I planted myself as nonchalantly as I could in a nearby park and watched for any residents that might make a pilgrimage to one of them. Over the course of the afternoon, only a few residents came out without getting directly into a vehicle. Of the few that didn't immediately drive off, one young blonde non-Asian woman went for a run, and the other, a middle-aged non-Asian man, took two Shiba Inus out for a walk. Over the next twenty-four hours, I saw two slender men go out for a run together very late at night and the young female runner and the dog walker again. People came and went by car on a regular basis at all hours, but only those three ever left the building on foot.

Everything about that building was strange. I saw no children and no elderly residents either. And everyone was fit or slight of build and attractive. Though I couldn't tell by seeing energy signatures or their true forms anymore, I had to wonder how many of them were actually mundane humans. I guessed not many.

I began doing research on Shiba Inus so I could strike up a conversation with the dog walker. At that point, he appeared the most normal of any of the residents I'd seen so far. While I was scrolling through a web page about dog breeds, someone quietly sat down next to me—too quietly. I moved to put a hand on the gun in my jacket pocket.

"Knock it off, D. You ain't fast enough," Duma said. "And you ain't as sneaky as you think either. You are, in fact, predictable."

I couldn't mask my surprise.

"Look, whatever the fuck is going on in your head, I know you aren't yourself, and you're likely to get killed on your own," he said with a heavy sigh. "Hell, you're likely to get killed even with my help. But if you think I'm going to let you go into that place"—he pointed at the literal fortress of a tower rising in front of us where Eisheth lived—"alone, then you're not only stupid but crazy too. Besides, who wouldn't want to be part of a half-assed raid on the Mother of all Moroi? I mean, come on. That's epic shit, right there. Like storming-a-castle epic. And we've done that a few times, right? Besides, I can get into that building, which, I can only imagine, is what you are trying to figure out how to do."

"I didn't think you'd—"

"Nope, this is to honor my blood oath," he said, pointing at the building again. His expression held no humor. "And for Sarah."

I nodded in understanding. "How's Ab?" I asked.

"He'll be okay in a few months," he replied. "He still can't really speak, and he can barely open his eyes, but he'll be okay. Oh, I brought backup too. Geek and Kailani are in my condo up there." He raised his chin at the second tower. "Geek does not shut up, does he? Kailani had to drain him to knock him out on the flight over. And whatever your plan is, it's trash, and I have a better one."

Chapter 60

I quietly followed Duma up to his apartment in the neighboring tower. Neither of us spoke. Duma appeared as disaffected as always, and I hated the fact that I couldn't tell if he really was okay with everything that had happened to that point or if the Fae simply had no true human emotions. Either way, it was an awkward silence for me.

I watched the numbers climb until the elevator reached PH1, just above the fifty-fifth floor. The finely finished wood-paneled doors opened into a completely furnished room looking out upon a wall of floor-to-ceiling windows. The floor was a dark-tan marble, and every piece of furniture I could see was black leather and dark wood, making the space feel warmer than the stone-covered abode it actually was. Duma strolled out of the elevator as casually as ever, but I took two tremulous steps, leaning forward to get a better view while staying in close proximity to the elevator just in case.

"As soon as I get this thermal-imaging camera set up, we'll get a better idea of how many people or, um, things are inside that unit." Geek's unmistakable excitement echoed through the cavernous space. His enthusiastic lilt instantly caused me to relax. "It's the top two floors, yeah?" he asked.

"Top three actually," Duma replied pulling a can of something from a minifridge under a marble-topped bar farther down the enormous space.

Typical for Duma and Ab, the apartment was over-the-top. The unit had to stretch the width and breadth of the building, surrounded by windows on all sides I could see. We were in a room over-looking the other tower, but just to our right was the river. The view was spectacular and uninterrupted, assuming one liked cityscapes, which I did not. Duma flopped down onto a long black leather sofa in an easy manner gymnasts practice long and hard to achieve. Along the wall of windows near the building's southwest corner, Geek was busy connecting cables to a tripod-mounted camera system next to a wooden cart covered in computers and other electronics. On the floor all around him were half a dozen opened heavy-duty black plas-tic storage cases.

"So, he was able to find you," Kailani said from behind me. She sounded not only incredulous, but also disappointed.

Before I could say anything in response, Geek chimed in.

"D! This is great, innit?" he said, his voice booming, throwing his hands wide at the view. "Duma and Ab have the coolest places."

"Sit down, D," Duma said. "Rest a minute, then we'll go get your gear from whatever hovel you have it stored in. Kitchen is around that corner behind the bar if you're hungry, and bedrooms and bath-rooms are back that way." He pointed behind me toward Kailani.

Kailani brushed past me and headed straight to Geek.

I noticed, despite the fact that we were walking on stone floors and surrounded by glass walls, nothing echoed or reverberated in the massive open space, easily two hundred yards across and twenty feet high. The austere space lacked any decoration and appeared to be made so that it could be cleaned with a hose. I walked closer to Geek's workspace and watched him work for a moment. Geek glanced back at me over his shoulder.

"Aw, mate, this is nothing yet. As soon as I get this all set up, I can start calibrating it," he said, winding up for the overly complicated monologue that was about to spew forth. "All these windows are spe-cially treated to reduce UV penetration *and* thermal scans, as well as being multipaned to reduce vibration," he said, pointing at the glass panels in front of him. "So basically, we can't see through them or hear through them from the outside under normal conditions. But I have a mate back at the Defense Science and Technology Lab's CBR division in Oxfordshire, and he's been working on a special radioisotopic signature reader algorithm that can piece together dampened or even blocked thermal radiation and put it back together in a way that makes sense. And it can do it in real time, no less. Assuming you have the computing power. Which I am borrowing from Metis at the moment. She designed the system to track shielded nuclear material, but in theory, it'll work just as well on any energy source, including heat given off by people! Freakin' awesome, right?"

Kailani shook her head and rolled her eyes. I smiled in acknowledgment, and her visage turned stony, and the temperature in the room seemed to drop by twenty degrees.

"Here's what I'm thinking," Duma said, leaning forward, putting his elbows on his knees. "Fire alarm."

"That's exactly what I was thinking," I replied, pointing at him.

"And yet my idea is still better," Duma replied, spreading his hands out as if he expected some sort of accolade.

"Am I supposed to know what any of that means?" Kailani asked without trying to mask the irritation in her voice.

"It means we trigger a fire alarm in her building," Duma said, waggling his head as if it was obvious. "Even Eisheth will have to evacuate, and then boom!" He slapped one hand into the other.

"Surely the Mother of the Moroi wouldn't come down the elevator like the rest of the common folk," Geek said, sitting on his heels as he plugged another cord into some machine.

Duma replied, "Nah, she has her own elevator straight down to the garage, but—"

"But she'd take the damn helicopter rather than deal with traffic on the street." I pointed at the helicopter on the pad of the building across from us.

Duma pointed at me for emphasis. "Bingo."

"What kind of firepower do you have on hand?" I asked.

"I told you I got everything we need." He picked up a large touch screen remote-control unit off the couch next to him and poked at it.

With a soft whirring, the wall halfway down the enormous space slid open.

I walked toward it and peered into the dark, cavernous hole, only to see a storehouse of weapons an army would swoon over. Everything from small arms to RPGs lined the walls and sat in stacked wooden munitions crates. All of it was neat and orderly.

"The RPGs are too much, and they leave a trail from where they are fired," I said scanning through the weapons and thinking aloud. "What we need is an anti-tank rifle." Then I saw just the thing: a KSVK 12.7 antimateriel rifle. "Perfect."

"Let me guess, the KSVK?" Duma asked before he appeared at the door. "Yep. Those 12.7mm rounds will go right through the rotor housing, no problem."

"Can you shoot it?" I asked.

"Yeah, but..."

"I need you to shoot the helicopter down while Kailani and I chase it down on the ground so we can be there wherever it crashes," I said, staring at the rifle.

"You know the crash won't kill Eisheth or any other Moroi she has with her," he said, leaning on the doorframe.

"Nope, but falling out of the sky in a whirling, burning hunk of flaming metal and crashing uncontrolled into the ground should incapacitate them long enough for me to get to her and let the crystals do their thing. So, you need to shoot it down, and I need to be on the ground."

"Not exactly what I was thinking. You're a better shot than me and a lot less mobile now, remember?" he said.

"Yeah, but I've already put you in harm's way too many times through this mess," I replied. "And even you can hit a helicopter at three hundred yards. And with this thing," I said, patting the big rifle, "you don't even need to be that accurate."

"And just what exactly is my role in all of this?" Kailani asked, hands on hips as she walked up to the weapons locker and peered inside.

"If you're up for it, you'll drive me to the crash site," I said. "As fast as possible."

"Can you shoot?" Duma asked over his shoulder, "'Cause maybe I should drive?"

"Can I shoot a gun? Yes. And well, too. Can I shoot that thing? No. Not at all." She cocked her head at the rifle before shaking it slowly for emphasis.

Outside the room, Geek's lopsided limping step sounded on the marble floor as he approached.

"And what, beyond sitting here and setting up all this electronic equipment, is my role in all this?" he asked. Once he could see into the room, his eyes widened, and a smile broke out across his face. He wasn't just a tech expert, but also a former SBS and Royal Marine though that was easy to forget. "Damn, is that an ASVK? Whoa, no. It's a KSVK SVN-98, the prototype, right?"

Duma and I glanced at each other then back at Geek as he walked up to the rifle.

"Yeah, it is. You know, the issue with these damn things is the Russians couldn't make the 12.7-millimeter round worth a shite, so it never really took off," Geek said.

"No kidding." Duma laughed. "That's why I have all the rounds for it custom-made. She's accurate to at least fifteen hundred yards in the right hands."

"Nice. My PB was a tad over eleven hundred with an old AI L96A1, but it was harassing fire, not lethal range," Geek said, trying to be humble.

"So, maybe Geek should fire the rifle from here, while Kailani and I drive the chase vehicles, and you can pick who you ride along with," Duma said.

"He can ride with you in that case," Kailani added, pointing from me to Duma, and turned on her heel and left.

"Oh yeah, I can easily hit that helicopter from here," Geek beamed. "Just give me a few hours to sight her in and get used to it, and Bob's your uncle. Besides, I won't be very good to you on the ground." He patted his artificial leg.

It made sense.

"Okay, Geek, you're the shooter up here. Duma and Kailani, you're driving chase, and I'm riding with Duma and carrying the crystals," I said. "I'm assuming you have two fast cars on site or nearby, Duma?"

"Really dumb question, D," he replied. "Spectacularly stupid. Hey, Kailani," he shouted, turning to leave the weapons locker, "can you ride a bike?"

"All I need to figure out now is how to set the fire alarm off in that building in a convincing manner," I said. "From a logical, tactical standpoint, to guarantee the upper floors will evacuate, the fire alarm needs to be triggered as high up as possible."

"Yeah, but to keep collateral damage to a minimum, it really should be limited to her floors, unless we rig a false alarm," Geek said.

"Ideally, yeah, but we can't afford Eisheth not reacting to a false alarm," I replied. "We need a fire or an explosion."

"Yeah, but what if some unfortunate tenant gets hurt?"

"I'd guess most of the residents of that building, and this one for that matter, are far from human," I replied.

"Yeah, but they are still innocent bystanders, human or not," Geek said, his eyebrows tented high on his forehead.

"We don't have time to figure out which residents are home and which aren't. So, what can we rig that will set the alarms off?" I asked.

"Well, once I get the thermal scanner set up, it should, in theory, tell us which units are vacant. And if we can somehow get a smoke grenade in one of those empty units on the upper floors, then that should give all appearances of a fire, trigger the alarms, and get Eisheth into her chopper. Or I can try to hack the building's computer system and trigger it remotely."

"Too dicey," I said. "It's got to be real. Eisheth will not react to anything short of catastrophe, and only then because she'll want to avoid scrutiny."

"I was thinking bomb in a box," Duma said.

"An incendiary device delivered to an upper floor unit and remotely detonated could work. But I'm thinking incendiary round fired into one of the lower units. A vacant one."

"You really want to set that building on fire, mate?" Geek asked. "After what happened in Vegas?"

"No, but it's the only way to get Eisheth isolated," I replied. "We can't lay siege to her castle, so we need her to come out of it where we can get to her. We can't starve her out, so we have to burn her out."

"Seems dangerous. A high potential for collateral damage," Geek said. "I mean, what if that chopper comes down into another building, a shopping mall, or a crowd of people?"

"We will have to do our best to mitigate the potential problems, but collateral damage is always an issue. You know that, Geek," I said.

"What we did for the military was surgical," Geek said, pointing between the two of us. "Precise small-unit tactics. This is... using a sledgehammer instead of a scalpel."

"The only way to get to these beings, Geek, is by using a sledgehammer. You realize even being shot out of the sky and crashing in a helicopter will not kill Eisheth or any of her cohort, right? If we're lucky, it'll do enough damage to her to weaken her for a few minutes. All of this for a few *minutes*, Geek. And if it would save Sarah, yeah, I'd blow that building up."

Geek nodded, his face a grim mask.

"So get that thermal imager up and running so we can figure out who's home and who's not," I said, putting my hand on his shoulder as I walked past him. "Duma, let's go get my gear."

Chapter 61

In the time Duma and I took to retrieve my gear and return, Geek had gotten all the equipment up and running.

"Well, it seems to be working as far as I can tell," he said in a somber tone rather than the boisterous one I'd expected. "I mean, I can see what I assume are rodents moving in gray spaces, birds nesting in the crevices on the outside of the building, and a few residents that give off human-range thermal signatures. But there are a lot of humanoids that are either way warmer or way colder than you'd expect. I calibrated it off creatures and figures I could ID positively. Known quantities, so to speak. Based on that, on the top three floors—Eisheth's penthouse—I get no human readings whatsoever but twenty-one figures far colder than the surroundings, which the computer suggests are in the mid-eighties. One of them, I'm guessing, is Eisheth."

"More than likely," Duma said.

"And it looks like most of the floor under the penthouse is currently vacant, unless there are creatures that can mask their heat signatures. Even then, if they moved at all, the computer should be able to see the disturbance in the surrounding environment and map it. So, I'm reasonably confident in saying that all but this one unit are empty at the moment." Geek pointed at a blueprint.

"We need to do this in the middle of the night, around three a.m. because traffic around the area will be minimal on the streets," I said.

"Yeah, but everyone is more likely to be home then too," Geek said. "There's a greater risk for collateral damage."

Neither Duma nor Kailani expressed any concern. "Not if they aren't human," the female vampire added.

"Human or not, it is our best shot, Geek," I said. "If this bothers you, you can leave. We'll understand."

Geek squinted hard, swallowed, then shook his head, and he lowered his eyes to the floor.

"Tomorrow night at three a.m., then," I said. "And I can end all this crap and save Sarah."

"At the cost of yourself," Kailani said, mostly under her breath.

I ignored it.

"Wait, why tomorrow night?" Duma asked. "Why are we rushing this?"

"New moon," I replied. "St. Germain said it had to be done on a new moon to be most effective. And do I need to ask if you have incendiary rounds for a weapon capable of piercing that glass?" I asked.

"Yeah," he replied, lounging on the couch, affectless. "I have Raufoss Mark 211 rounds for the AX50 in there." He hooked a thumb over his shoulder toward the armory.

"Perfect," I said. "Geek, put a few rounds into an empty unit under the penthouse with the fifty. Once you can confirm a fire and the alarms go off, then switch over to the KVSK. We'll be down on the street. You tell us when you see her board the chopper, and I'll tell you when to take the shot. We'll get to the crash site as fast as possible, and I'll put the crystals around Eisheth's head, and we get out as fast as we can."

"Hopefully, it'll be that simple," Kailani said.

"Not likely," Duma replied with a snort. "Not in my experience."

Everyone except Duma just stared at each other for a long, tense moment.

Duma appeared to be checking his cuticles. "Yeah, definitely no way it goes that easy," Duma said, shaking his head.

"If anyone else has any better ideas, I'm all ears," I said.

No one responded.

"Then until I hear a better idea, this is the plan. And we aim for it tomorrow night because I don't want to wait another month to try to pull this off. The sooner we can end this, the better."

"Amen," Duma said, leaning forward and slapping his thighs before standing to leave the room.

I went to the armory to find the high-explosive armor-piercing rounds we needed and the fifty-caliber rifle required to fire them. All at once, I was struck at the heft of the box of rounds and the massive rifle that fired them. Until that moment, I'd never known how much they actually weighed for the mundane snipers I worked with when I was a SEAL. I had renewed respect for my friend Frigate, who did everything the rest of my SEAL platoon did, all while carrying the added weight of the ungainly weapon and ammunition.

I carried the equipment back to the seating area, where Geek was busy once again, clicking away on his computers while muttering to himself about algorithms and coding or some such.

"You want me to bring out the KSVK, or do you want to get it yourself?" I asked. "You'll need to start sighting them in before dark."

"Huh?" Geek replied absently, finally doing a double take at me over his shoulder. "Oh, right, yeah, yeah," he said seeing the rifle in my hand. He turned back to his computers just as quickly. His actions held a palpable tension, as if he was trying to appear preoccupied.

For all the concern I placed on Duma and Ab's lack of empathy and emotion, I found that the longer I lived, the more I lost the ability to identify with and understand mundane humans on multiple levels.

Feelings and misgivings aside, we had a mission to carry out, so all that crap needed to be put on hold.

Out of frustration and irritation, I went back to my gear. The familiarity of going over my equipment not only occupied my mind but brought me a sense of peace. Normally, I understood my weapons, but the fact that they no longer felt the same in my mortal hands caused me no small concern. They felt heavy and clunky as I cleaned them—unwieldy. Geek's concerns about innocent bystanders kept creeping into the corner of my mind between images of Sarah's comatose form. I couldn't get past breaking my promise to keep her safe, and anger once again crept in and erased all concern. I went back to cleaning my Glock and Sig on autopilot, becoming more and more agitated at everyone's attitude.

Is one life worth more than any other? Is my plan really that dicey? Isn't danger a part of our lives? Eisheth is a monster in her own right, so taking her and her entourage out is part of my job description. So what if this is an unprovoked action? Don't they understand what's at stake? Don't they get why we're doing this? If they have problems with my plan, then they can fucking leave.

In my annoyance, a bullet slipped from my fingers as I pressed it into the magazine, and it skittered across the table. I tried to catch it, but I moved clumsily and, in what felt like slow motion, knocked over the box of ammunition in the process. Rounds went flying everywhere. Incensed, I threw the magazine against the wall and shoved everything across the table and onto the floor in a resounding clatter, then I roared.

Kailani and Geek both appeared outside the door to the armory, peering in cautiously.

"What?" I asked with a growl, breathing heavily from the sudden exertion.

Kailani shook her head and walked away with a dismissive hand gesture, while Geek held up both hands and slowly retreated.

Fuck 'em. Either they're with me, or I'll do it on my own.

Duma came in with his hands in his pockets and took a long, slow look at the mess I'd created, pursed his lips, and dropped his head. "You need to clean this mess up and get your head on straight,

D," he said. "I have no intention of dying because you're too caught up in your own head to think straight. You nearly got Ab and me killed a few times already. You got Ab deep-fried and crispy."

"I'm fine."

By the time I finished the statement, Duma was standing at my shoulder, leaning in to speak in my ear.

"Not even fucking close, Diomedes," he whispered. "You're only fooling yourself. You want to kill yourself, go ahead, but I won't let you take us with you. Oh, and some elf chick brought this for you before we left. Maybe it'll help you remember who you are."

Before I could respond, he was gone.

"I'm fucking fine," I said under my breath, and I began to pick up the mess I'd created. I kicked the bag absently to get it out of my way, and I realized it was familiar. It was the bag I'd left behind with my cuirass and swords in it—and the damn crystals too.

Fuck. Maybe Duma is right.

Thanks, Brey.

Chapter 62

Everyone avoided me for the rest of the afternoon and evening. At one in the morning, I walked out to see Kailani standing next to Geek and pointing at something on the thermal imaging screen. Duma was stretched out on one of the couches, playing on his phone.

"Any changes to Eisheth's place?" I asked.

"Not really, no," Geek said. "A few more beings have come and gone, but it averaged twenty or so since this afternoon. I can't say if it's the same twenty or not with any real certainty."

"Anyone come up with a better plan?" I asked.

No one responded.

"Then I say it's time to get ready."

Duma got up from the couch in a single sweeping movement that would've been impossible for a human. Reaching into his pocket, he pulled out a small case similar to something fine jewelry would come in. "Earwigs," he said, shaking the case. "Only Diomedes will be able to speak, using a throat mike. The rest of us can acknowledge by pressing on the earpiece. It'll beep. Usually once for yes, two for no, unless you guys want to get fancy with it."

"Let's keep it simple. Once for yes, twice for no is fine," I replied.

"Simple, he says," Kailani snorted.

I stared hard at her, but she ignored me.

"Unless everything goes sideways, the only thing I will say is to direct Geek when to shoot, understood?"

Geek nodded.

"Duma, you got the keys to the bike?" Kailani asked with a heavy sigh.

"Key rack on the wall just inside the butler's pantry on the other side of the kitchen," he said, pointing nonchalantly toward the kitchen. "Grab the Ducati or the Ecosse keys. They'll be the easiest to find in my garage area. Garage level three, bay four. Helmets are down there, too, if you want."

"Geek, are you ready? All sighted in?" I asked.

"In theory, yeah, but it shouldn't be hard to hit a helicopter at a few hundred yards," he replied. "Especially since I don't have to hit a specific spot, given that even the crash isn't likely to kill anything on the bird anyway."

"Hopefully, the crash will weaken them enough for us to do what we need to," I said. "I'll make the call on when to shoot. If you don't think she's on board, just buzz back twice, and I'll call abort."

Geek nodded.

"Okay, Duma, let's go."

I pulled on my vest, including the cuirass that served as little more than an extra layer in my current condition, and strapped on my greaves, shin guards, and elbow and knee pads. I found myself staring at the plastic case Areadbhair was stored in, and I pictured myself using the spear to bring down the helicopter. Something in the back of my mind caught the absurdity of the idea, and I suddenly found myself scoffing at the idea of using the weapon. When I snapped back to what I was doing, I noticed I had the Sig Sauer in my hand. Somehow, the gun seemed just as absurd, given what I was about to do. Even so, I placed my sidearms in their holsters on my hip and vest and grabbed the FN SCAR-H fitted with a suppressor. Lastly, I slid my swords into their scabbards on my back and stuffed the crystals into a pocket on my vest. None of it felt familiar anymore, but at least the action and preparation were. Everything felt like I was about to fight a losing battle.

"No swords," Duma said from behind me. "Not enough room in the car I want to take, with those on your back. And you damn sure aren't bringing that fucking spear!"

"Trust me—I'm not. But can't we take something bigger, then? I'd rather keep the swords at the ready. Especially since I'm not as fast as I used to be," I said.

"No shit." Duma laughed. "Fine, we'll take the Tank."

Duma grabbed a brace of knives on a bandolier and draped it over his shoulder. It held his two favored kukris in scabbards on the back. He chose to wear no armor. It would only slow him down and probably not do much to protect him against Moroi anyway.

We descended in the private elevator in silence. When the door opened, I followed Duma to the side of an odd-looking bright-red satin-finished SUV. The only marking was "Rezvani" in black on the rear of the vehicle. We drove out of the garage and out onto the deserted streets. I saw Kailani on a black motorcycle with a helmet resting on the gas tank, not far down the block. She was dressed in a black motorcycle jacket and jeans. Duma flashed his lights at her, and she waved back. I placed the throat mike around my neck and attached it to a transmitter on my vest then put the small listening device into my ear. I switched it on.

"All stations report," I said, holding down the transmit button. I got two different single tones in response, and I could see Kailani reach for her ear in conjunction with one of the sounds.

"I can hear you fine," Duma said. "Now's as good a time as any." He shrugged.

"Geek, let's start a fire," I said. I got a single tone in response.

We watched up through the windshield at the building across the small green space. Surprisingly, I heard nothing of the shots, but within a few minutes, smoke was pouring from a window on one of the upper floors. Moments later, an alarm erupted from the building, and klaxons went off, along with rapidly flashing intense bright-white lights. Lights in various units on lower floors came on, but not many. Within a few minutes, people were gathering at the front desk in the lobby of the building, no doubt asking about the alarm, while security ushered people out the front door.

"Any movement up there?" I asked into the mike. I got two tones in response. "Dammit, she needs to move before this place gets too crowded with fire trucks and gawkers."

"Let's move up the street," Duma said. "Her helicopter will be hard to miss, even from down the street."

He started the car, and Kailani fell in behind us as we drove a few blocks upriver. No sooner did Duma pull over than we could hear the rotor of a helicopter, even over the sirens and alarms. The second I saw it clear the building, I radioed for Geek to fire.

"Hit it," I said.

In the tight confines of the buildings, the shot from the heavy rifle thundered a split second before an explosion rocked the helicopter, knocking it off-kilter and nearly sending it into a spiral.

"Hit it again!" I screamed. I got two tones in response. "Geek, hit it again, dammit!" After a few seconds of silence, again, the rifle thundered, this time sending the helicopter into a full spin as it descended quickly.

The falling bird burst into flames and barely missed an apartment building as it spun out of control and careened inland, away from the riverfront. Duma floored the red SUV, and the vehicle's massive engine roared. Kailani shot ahead of us on the motorcycle, following the trajectory of the crashing fireball. Falling and spinning, the helicopter barely missed the twin towers of another skyscraping apartment complex before crashing hard on a major thoroughfare and rolling into a city park. Debris spread in every direction as the rotor came into contact with the ground and shattered. Several small *whumps* preceded the intact fuselage finally bursting into flames. Duma sped up, jumped a divider in the road, and hopped a curb into the park. Kailani was already on foot, running toward the burning wreckage.

A massive explosion went off behind us, but we were all too focused on the helicopter in front of us. Sirens filled the air from the streets around us, echoing off the buildings and making it impossible to determine their direction. Duma and I got out of the SUV, and I ran as fast as I could toward the flaming pile of wreckage.

Something was off. I didn't need Athena's help to sense it.

Kailani glanced back at us, her face a mask of confusion, her arms dangling at her sides and her shoulders dropped. Then she shook her head. Duma moved so fast around the wreckage that he just appeared at various places around the fuselage. In the fire's ghostly orange glow, I could see the creases on his forehead. He screamed something, but I couldn't hear what he said over the growing din around us. I shook my head as I ran closer, and he just shook his head and shrugged.

In the few seconds it took me to get there, breathing heavily, my heart pounding in my chest, even I could see the reason for their concern. While the fuselage was mostly intact, the doors had been ripped off. The only being inside was the pilot, who was clearly dead. I could see no blood, not even the pilot's, and no body parts or carnage—definitely no Eisheth.

"Geek, did you see more than one figure get on the helicopter?" I asked, pressing the mike button.

Kailani jerked slightly at the feedback then reached up to her ear and tossed her listening device into the fire.

I got no response.

"Geek, I repeat, did you see more than one figure get on the helicopter?" I asked.

Still no response.

I turned back to the buildings behind us, deafened by the number of sirens and alarms now going off, only to see Duma's building billowing smoke. Not just his building, but his floor.

"Geek, respond!" I screamed into the mike.

Nothing.

Duma's face went from me to his building then quickly back to me. He pulled a phone out of his pocket and poked at it furiously. Kailani's eyes grew wider as she saw what we saw, then she went rigid. A cold shiver passed through me like an electrical shock. From behind Duma, a bat-winged figure appeared out of the shadows of the trees at the far end of the park. In the blink of an eye, Duma bolted at the figure, only to end up knocked back, cartwheeling across the grass like a rag doll. Kailani fell to one knee, her head bowed.

Fuck.

I pulled the heavy assault rifle to my shoulder and fired, not because I thought it would do anything to Eisheth but because I could do nothing else. I ran through the magazine, ejected it, and slammed in another one. Eisheth continued her approach unfazed. When she got to the burning wreckage, she flew over it, landing lightly in front of me.

"Did you really think I need to leave by helicopter, Diomedes?" Eisheth practically purred. "In fact, did you really think I would evacuate at all?"

"Clearly, I was hoping, yes," I said, backing up carefully but keeping the rifle in a combat high firing position.

"Coming after me directly took serious balls, Diomedes, even for you," she said as she stopped, hands on hips. She had a bestial face, a cross between a feline and one of those odd bats with a snub nose, made even more ghastly backlit by the burning helicopter. Her body was muscular and as chimeric as her face, down to her doglike legs. She moved with a fluid grace despite the awkward nature of her physique.

"I assumed there was no reason to hide from you," she said, clearly aware I was noting her appearance. "Though there is something very different about you, Diomedes. Very different, indeed."

"Same old me," I said, hoping she couldn't tell I was mundane and currently without Athena's help or powers. "And the same old you, I see."

She held out her arms and made the slightest bow of her head.

"Given all that's transpired between us in the last year or so and all that you've done to my sister," she said, glancing over at Kailani, who was unmoving, "why on earth would you come after me so directly? Do you have a death wish?"

"Actually, just the contrary," I replied.

Behind her, I could see Duma getting to one knee. He pulled his two kukris and nodded at me. I glanced over at Kailani, who remained unmoving, head still bowed. Duma had one shot. I had to distract Eisheth.

"Honestly, I brought you a gift, some jewelry. Want it?" I asked, hoping to catch her off guard.

"Please, Diomedes, stop," she said, stepping forward.

"No, seriously," I said, reaching into the pocket on my vest for the crystals bound in copper wire. I held them out in my left hand, keeping my right hand on the grip, finger on the trigger. *Firing the automatic rifle one-handed as a mundane would not be easy.*

Eisheth's brow creased slightly, making her face even more grotesque. "Oh, not those damn things from St. Germain again?" She laughed. "He's been trying to get some poor fool to put those on me for eons. I can't believe you let him dupe you. Or did she put you up to this?" She pointed at Kailani and laughed but with no humor in it. "Did he tell you that you can transfer my energy with them?"

"I have no idea what you're talking about," I said, trying not to think too much about her goading. "I was just out shopping and saw them and thought, 'I bet Eisheth would just *love* these.'"

That time, she laughed with amusement.

"You know, you've really caused my sister a lot of trouble in the last few years," she said. "She'd be thrilled to death if I broke your neck right now and ended her vexation."

Duma was on his feet on the other side of the helicopter, and the air was filled with the smell of burning aviation fuel and the sounds of sirens and alarms. I could even see the reflections of flashing lights off the glass building fronts though none came near us or the park. The Peri lowered his gaze and snarled—a gesture made grotesque by the flames. He spun his curved knives then gave me a nod.

"Nah, let's not do that," I said. I opened fire on her, emptying the magazine of heavy 7.62mm rounds at her at less than twenty yards.

She didn't even flinch as the rounds hit her, and Duma disappeared behind her. Just as quickly, Eisheth's right arm shot out, and suddenly she had Duma by the neck. She turned toward me, cocked her head, and shook it in disappointment.

"First, your friend up in his flat," she said, lifting her chin slightly from Duma to his building behind me. "Now, your greatest ally and friend. Oh, and that one too." She jerked her head toward Kailani, who fell limp to the ground, unmoving.

Duma struggled in her grip, hacking at her arm with his kukris to no avail—not even a raised welt where the blades crossed her mottled skin. I watched him twisting and hacking impotently. I had nothing, nothing left to hit her with.

Then a thought crept in: *What if St. Germain was playing me?*

I realized I was holding my breath as my heart pounded in my chest. Watching Duma's feeble and futile actions, everything hit me at once. *Ab, Duma, Kailani, and Geek. And Sarah. All for Sarah. I sacrificed everything I am—was—and everyone loyal to me, to help her. Everyone. Without so much as a second thought. I even gave Athena reason to question my actions, and I never thought twice about it.*

I was instantly haunted by a vision of my father, mortally wounded in the battle at Thebes, eating the brain of an enemy out of sheer selfish pettiness and spite. I hated my father for betraying Athena like that. Yet here I was, all but doing the same exact thing.

My rifle felt heavy in my hands. I lowered the weapon slightly at first then dropped it altogether and held up my hands, dropping the crystals as well. "Stop," I said. "Wait."

"You have nothing to bargain with, Diomedes," she said flatly. She wasn't taunting me. She was simply stating a fact.

"Let them go," I said, sinking to my knees. "I caused the trouble, not them. I'm the one who's been a thorn in your and your sister's side for millennia. I'm the one you want."

"But I have you, Diomedes," she said with a snarl. "But hurting you deeply begins with hurting the ones closest to you." She turned toward Kailani, who began to screech and gurgle as she writhed uncontrollably on the ground amid a cloud of blue lightning-like energy.

My stomach dropped as I watched her thrash.

Eisheth then turned to face Duma, who had never ceased his useless attacks. Without much effort, she reached out to grab one of the Fae's kukris by the blade, turned it over, and stabbed him in the chest, full to the hilt. He went rigid, and everything I ever was fell away, and something inside me broke. Then she tossed him away.

"We'll find his brother, too, rest assured," Eisheth said, turning back to me. "But... there is something different about you, Diomedes." She cocked her head. "It's not like you to just give up like this." She hesitated.

I couldn't move.

Chapter 63

Then something crept into the back of my mind. I recalled the prayer I'd uttered on the battlefield at Troy that day over three thousand years ago.

Athena... If you ever loved my father, stood by his side in murderous combat, be my friend now...

I didn't give up then and hadn't since—not once.

Not with the fighting spirit still in me...

But I wasn't sure I still had the fighting spirit. *So much death. So much of it at my hands and because of me. Friends, teammates, fellow soldiers, loved ones.* My eyes traveled from Kailani's writhing form to Duma's lifeless body sprawled on the grass. *Geek.* I couldn't breathe.

The next thing I knew, Eisheth had me by the vest, lifted off the ground, feet dangling. She was closely scrutinizing my face the way a scientist examines a specimen on a dissecting table. Then she drew her head back in surprise.

"You are mortal," she said, blinking in obvious confusion. "Athena has forsaken her warrior. Humanity's greatest protector is now an impotent menace."

She dropped me, and I fell to my knees again. Eisheth turned, contemplating her next move in light of my situation.

"Maybe you would make a good pet for my sister," she said. "Or maybe for me," she said, smiling over her shoulder at me.

My friends didn't all die for me to become a slave. I was a soldier. If I can't die in service to my fellow man, I will die in memory of those who died for me. But I will die fighting, not as a plaything. Pain is acceptable. Tears are acceptable. Quitting is not.

I pulled my swords, knowing they were currently all but useless in my hands against Eisheth, and drove myself to my feet. She turned to face me and laughed.

"How cute," she said.

She moved so quickly to grab me that I couldn't react. Dangling in her viselike grip, I stabbed at her, but it was like poking cement with a stick.

"Then again, maybe not," she said.

Smiling a wicked smile, she hit me with the palm of her other hand, full in the chest, and I went flying backward into a flopping roll. When I came to a stop, I realized that somehow, I'd managed to keep my swords in hand. Catching my breath and fighting through the pain of what were surely broken ribs, I pushed myself back to my feet.

I felt the roar as it grew in my chest—defiance and desperation all in one. Eisheth's head jerked back slightly at the wail. Then her face changed, and she bared her teeth and charged.

The world slowed down.

Eisheth came at me in an attempt to hit my chest once again, but her attack came slow. I easily sidestepped it, batted her arm farther away with one sword, knocking her off balance, and swung hard and wild with the other blade. I connected with part of her right wing, the sword slicing it off cleanly midway through the appendage with ease. The Queen of the Moroi hissed and spun around to face me.

I roared again, hearing the cry echo off the buildings around the park, and I pressed the attack. She moved quickly, but not as quickly as I expected—perhaps because she was toying with me. Still, she was easily able to avoid my thrusts. I fell back to reassess, and Eisheth attacked in a sweeping blow with a clawed hand. Knowing I couldn't move fast enough to avoid the attack, my only option was to parry the blow with both swords, catching her arm just below the wrist. To the surprise of both of us, the end of her arm fell away where it met my blades, and it pinwheeled across the grass. The Moroi reared up and fell back in abject fear, clutching the stump of her arm.

"When you fight for the protection of others rather than selfish gain, I will be with you, warrior," Athena said in the familiar voice that echoed in my head once again.

Eisheth screeched then bellowed, "How could you have done that? You are mortal!"

"Yeah, well, I'm just as surprised as you are," I replied, spinning the swords in my hands, feeling their familiar lightness once more.

I needed to bide my time. I could not beat Eisheth in a straight one-on-one fight. The Mother of the Moroi, a fallen minor angel, was faster and far stronger and could heal in minutes. Taking her arm and wing was pure dumb luck. I'd been hoping that knocking her out of the sky and crashing her in a flaming helicopter would knock her senseless for a mere few minutes.

A cry of anguish and anger drew our attention to Kailani, who was standing up, her face twisted with rage and pain. "You look like shit, Mother," she said, wiping her mouth with the back of her hand.

"You are not my child," Eisheth said, snarling. "My children would never have turned against me. They could not. But surely you know this?"

"What are you talking about?" Kailani asked, clearly confused.

"You mean you don't know?" Eisheth asked, turning slightly to face her. "Oh, we are connected, just not how you think. You are an experiment by that damned alchemist St. Germain. An abomination. A creation of the very thing this one came to try"—she gestured at me—"only this time, using me instead of a dozen of my oldest off-spring."

"What are you talking about?" Kailani asked, more angry than inquisitive. "I'm one of your wretched offspring, cursed to feed on other people's life force for eternity." She spat on the ground.

"That was the result, yes, but not because I or one of my children turned you—"

With Eisheth distracted, I attacked.

Rather than running at her, I thought I would be more successful throwing the swords. They both hit home, striking her in the chest and abdomen. The impact of the two swords knocked her sideways, and she tripped and staggered backward into the burning wreckage with an inhuman shriek. The second Eisheth faltered, Kailani shouted, took a few steps, and lunged, like a cheetah on an impala. The impact sent them both fully into the wreckage. Again, an ungodly inhuman wail arose, comingled with a scream of agony.

Within the flames, Kailani's clothing had caught fire. I needed to get her out of the conflagration quickly. The only thing I could think to do was what she had done, so I charged and tackled her, knocking her well out of the fire as we rolled and bounced over the wreckage. Just as I came to a stop in the cool grass, rolling onto my back, Eisheth stretched out her wings—the one I'd hacked off had already healed—and took off straight into the sky. In the eerie yellow-orange glow of the flames, the face of the Mother of the Moroi appeared misshapen and mangled as she disappeared into the darkness overhead.

Breathing heavily, I scrambled over to Kailani and tried to pat out the flames and rip off the smoldering clothing where I could and roll her on the damp grass. She moaned but said nothing as she shivered uncontrollably as shock set in, then she went totally still.

"Kailani, listen to me," I said, "I need you to feed. Use my energy. I need your help with Duma."

She barely shook her head. "No, I won't," she said, her voice barely audible. "Not you."

"Dammit," I muttered, looking around at the situation.

No emergency vehicles were yet pulling up to the park to check on the helicopter crash, but a few people were stopping along the roadside in cars to see what was happening. I saw Duma, lying on his side a few yards away. I scrambled over to him only to find he had removed the knife from his chest.

"Duma," I said, kneeling close to his face to check on him.

"Fuck, that shit hurts," he groaned.

Suddenly, my spirits buoyed. "You're alive?"

"I suppose if I'm talking to you, I am," he said.

"I gotta get you and Kailani out of here, now," I said. "Hold tight."

The bright-red SUV was about a hundred yards off across the park, doors still open. Kailani's motorcycle was lying in the grass near it.

I ran back over to Kailani, who had somehow and for some reason crawled around the wreckage. Her skin was black and charred, and her hair was smoldering. Without asking or preparing her, I grabbed her arm and hauled her over one shoulder. She tried to protest, but nothing came out but a slight squeak. I ran across the park to the SUV, rolled her into the cargo area in the back of the vehicle, and went back as fast as I could for Duma. I repeated the process with him, except he groaned the entire way, which I took to be a good sign.

"You got first aid in here somewhere?" I asked, tearing the cargo area apart, looking for storage compartments.

"Condo," Duma said through wheezes.

"Can't go back. The condo is gone," I said. I quickly pulled my vest off and wrenched the cuirass out from under it. "I'm going to pull this vest onto you, Duma, then stuff the front and back with my shirt to staunch the bleeding, got it?"

"I know the condo is gone. Geek," Duma said with a croak. Then he coughed, spitting up yellow goo, which was never a good sign. "What about Geek?" Duma spat out between coughing fits.

"No response. I think he's gone with the condo," I said, pulling the vest onto Duma. "Brace yourself while I tighten the straps." I suddenly realized I needed to be gentle because I had my strength back. Still, Duma shouted. Kailani was shivering next to him. I pulled my cuirass back on. "Okay, we're moving. Any suggestions where to go that's safe?"

"Fuck. Yeah, get on the road... and just drive out of the city... in any direction," Duma said. "When we're clear of this mess, I'll figure it out. Need to rest... And what about the damn spear..."

I had completely forgotten about Areadbhair. *Fuck.* I didn't have time to worry about that right then. I had to save my friends. I slammed the car doors shut and took off across the park, trying to make sense of the nav system in the car. In the process, I somehow flipped a switch that turned the windshield into a thermal-imaging screen. The wreckage suddenly lit up the pane of glass with a brilliant orange that all but blinded me, so I floored the SUV and drove straight through the destroyed fuselage, bouncing and pinballing across the park, through a small grove of trees, across some sort of sandy area, a small playground, and a parking lot with more than a few parked cars and people gawking at us, until I finally hit a street. The thermal imaging flare-up faded as soon as the flaming wreckage was behind me, allowing me to see where I was headed. I jerked the wheel hard, slammed the gas pedal all the way to the floor and skidded onto the road. I merged onto Century Road, and I didn't slow until I hit Century Park a few miles later.

Chapter 64

No one followed us, but my guess was that Eisheth managed to keep the area cleared for her own purposes. Even so, we were going to attract attention to ourselves soon, especially in a bright-red SUV that was entirely out of place on city streets. I didn't have much choice, so I just kept on, heading southeast.

Every minute or so, I tried to raise Geek again, just in case, even after I knew we were well out of range. I never got even the slightest hint of static in response. And I could only imagine what would happen with Areadbhair if it fell into the hands of Eisheth's offspring. I wanted to rip the steering wheel apart and go back and finish off Eisheth. Sarah would have told me the whole mission on her behalf was far too costly *before* we lost Geek. Now, in a futile and misbegotten attempt at saving her, I'd lost another good man—a good friend—on top of everything else. I'd almost lost all my friends over it. They weren't just lost but had willingly sacrificed themselves. And one of the most dangerous weapons on the planet was possibly back in the world for who knew who... or what... to use. No words were strong enough to describe the lack of respect I'd shown them or the dishonorable way I'd treated them.

Some hero.

Outside the SUV, the landscape changed from heavy urban to suburban to a mixture of rural farmland and villages quicker than I would have guessed near Shanghai. As the eastern sky lightened with the rising sun, I pulled over onto the side of the road to check on Duma and Kailani.

Kailani was comatose or at least in some sort of stasis—hard to tell. I knew as a Moroi, she was far from dead, though. I hopped in to check on Duma. Incredibly, he appeared far better than I expected.

"How you feeling?" I asked.

"Peachy," he said. "Except for the gaping hole in my chest. Eisheth nuked the condo, but did we win? Did you get it? The crystal thingy?"

"No," I replied, checking the shirt packed under the vest I'd put on Duma as a pressure bandage. I knew Duma's internal organs, whatever they were, were not the same as mine, and the ones he had were in different places as well. A gaping chest wound for him could be either the equivalent of a gut shot or a simple flesh wound. Even after hundreds of years fighting alongside him, I didn't know.

"'No' what?" Duma asked. "'No' you didn't kill her, 'no' you didn't get the crystals you needed, what?"

"No to all of it," I said. "It wasn't worth it. It wasn't worth risking any more lives for. Whatever happened, it was clear she knew we were coming for her. We lost Geek. I was lucky to get you guys out of there alive. But I did manage to take her hand and part of a wing."

"That explosion. That was definitely my place," he said matter-of-factly. "And Geek..." he said quietly. "Oh, and what about that fucking spear?" he asked, coughing and wincing after a long moment of silence. I just shook my head, unable to meet his gaze. "Well, you managed to take her hand and part of her wing, though?" he added, a little more upbeat after another wracking cough and groan. "How'd you manage that? I couldn't even scratch her."

"Apparently, I managed to find favor in Athena's eyes again," I replied.

His pale blond eyebrows rose high on his forehead, and his eyes widened.

"Not sure I deserve it, though, the way I treated you guys."

All at once, I felt tired—very weary—as if I'd been running all day without stopping—not sleepy, but exhausted. I shook my head and sighed heavily. I felt Kailani shift behind me.

"She's feeding," Duma said with a moan. "She'll be fine. She's a vampire. Fuckers don't die easily."

"She's something, but I'm not sure she's a vampire exactly," I said. "At least Eisheth didn't seem to think so."

Suddenly, Kailani shouted and scrambled upright in the back of the SUV. Her blackened and charred skin was starting to appear less crispy, though still covered in oily soot. I jumped out of the back to avoid being smacked or worse.

"Fuck," she said with a start and tossed something down in the back of the SUV next to her that landed with a weighty, wet splat.

What Kailani had thrown was a meaty blob that, on second glance, I recognized as an eyeball and a hunk of flesh.

"Holy shit," I said, leaning in for a better look and glancing from Duma to Kailani and back to the eyeball staring up at me.

Duma craned his neck between me, Kailani, and the pile of flesh next to us. "Wait... is that one of Eisheth's eyes?"

"Well, it's not one of mine or yours or hers," I said, checking her face just to make sure I hadn't missed a grievous injury.

"Son of a bitch," Duma said, staring at Kailani with respect and concern. He surreptitiously tried to push himself a little farther away from her. "She ripped part of Eisheth's face off?"

She was breathing rapidly and erratically, her bright eyes wild in her smoke-stained face and wild, burnt hair. Most of her clothing had burned away, except part of her leather motorcycle jacket, and I became acutely aware of the smell of burnt flesh and hair in the enclosed space. She screamed again, but that was a different kind of agony—more confusion than pain. Then she began to kick and punch, first the air, then the roof of the SUV.

Duma's eyebrows arched high on his forehead, and he tried to shift even farther away from her as she thrashed.

"Oh, that bitch!" she screamed with one final volley on the roof of the SUV, denting it and nearly putting a hole through it.

Duma winced.

"And you?" She kicked at me.

Instinctively, I jumped back to avoid the blow, and since the adrenaline was wearing off, my ribs ached again at the quick movement.

"Ow," I said. "What'd I do? I was just trying to drag you out of the fire and away from Eisheth before she killed you."

"I had her," she replied. "Why'd you pull me out?"

"Had her? You couldn't have killed the Queen of the Moroi even if you aren't exactly one of her offspring—whatever the hell that means, by the way. And besides, you were on fire," I said, trying to breathe more shallowly to control the spasms of pain brought about by moving so quickly. "Sorry, I don't have any extra clothing, Kailani," I said, motioning erratically at her nearly naked form.

"You didn't get it, did you?" she asked, not really wanting an answer. "And did I hear you say Geek is—"

"Yeah," I replied, averting my eyes to stare at the ground. "Eisheth knew we were coming. That explosion... and I couldn't—can't—raise him."

"Motherfucker," Kailani said.

Again, a long silence passed among us.

I cleared my throat. "Duma, where are we going?"

"Help me to the passenger seat, and I'll look at the GPS."

I slowly helped Duma to the passenger-side door and walked back around the SUV, jammed the tailgate closed again and immediately felt the all-too-familiar sensation of Athena's presence behind me.

I turned slowly, ashamed to face her.

"I hope I can live up to a second chance," I said, head bowed.

"I wouldn't have given it to you if I didn't think you could," Athena said. She was dressed in a simple white robe, her red hair flowing down over one shoulder and her blue eyes burning brightly. "But now is not the time. You need to move."

"But Geek," I said, "I mean, Will Elmsmore—"

"You needed his help," she said in a tone that conveyed both understanding and deep sorrow. "He chose to help you. Free will. He believed in you, Diomedes. Do not dishonor his sacrifice or his belief in you. Or mine. There will be time to mourn him, but now, you need to get moving."

My throat was so tight that I couldn't have said anything if I wanted to, so I nodded.

"Oh, you'll need these," she said, turning to walk away. "And you will recover Areadbhair with all due haste."

On the ground where she stood were my swords, topped by a stone that caught the morning light and glittered in every color imaginable—a Way Stone.

I coughed to clear my throat. "Duma, screw the GPS. Get us to the nearest Waypoint on the Telluric Pathways," I said, picking up my gear.

Chapter 65

We made it to one of Duma and Ab's many safe houses, one in Kenya on Mombasa Island in a heavily walled compound on the water, next to the Mombasa Club and Fort Jesus. The equatorial heat and humidity felt good on my skin, though the day was not particularly sunny. Staring out across the stone wall topped with broken glass and concertina wire at the remnants of the old fort, I recalled when King Philip I of Portugal ordered the fort's construction in an attempt to control trading in the Indian Ocean—a simple but futile idea.

A few days after we arrived, Ab showed up. The pale hulk was barely mobile but upright, nonetheless. As we were all convalescing, I noticed the distinct lack of a boat at the compound, despite it being on the water. Duma strolled up behind me, wearing pajama bottoms and a long gauzy robe, drink in hand. His entire torso was heavily taped, as was mine.

"Duma, you and Ab need a boat," I said. "How can you live on the water like this and not have a skiff at least?"

"Easy," he replied. "I hate the water."

"But this is an island. It's surrounded by water," I said.

"Sorry, but I won't say it," Duma said. "I hated that movie."

I laughed. "How're you doing?" I asked.

"I'm fine. The only advantage of being the last of your kind is that no one seems to know where your vital parts are," he said. "She got me good but not good enough," he said with a wink and held out his glass of amber liquid.

"Hey, Duma, I'm really sorry," I said.

"For?"

"For everything," I replied, holding out my arms wide, a painful gesture in my current state. "Being an ass, nearly getting you and Ab killed, not listening to you, ignoring you, taking you and Ab for granted. All of it. I'm an asshole. A dick."

"Yeah"—he rolled his hand—"keep going..."

"I lost sight of the big picture. Of who I am," I said. "I needlessly put you and Ab and everyone I knew and trusted in mortal danger to save Sarah, who would have told me not to if she could have. I let my feelings get in the way."

"Humans," he said with a laugh. "Your biggest gift is your greatest weakness. Your emotions. We Fae, and pretty much every other being on this planet, play on them constantly to manipulate your species. But they are what defines you. It's what makes you human, Diomedes, no matter how removed from *them* you think you are. And you can't be other than what you are. Why the hell would you want to anyway?" he asked, holding his drink up in a mock toast. "Apology accepted. Ab might be a tougher sell. You did almost drop a burning building on his head."

"Athena told me that her people managed to recover Geek's body from your condo. He is going to be given a full military veteran's burial with special honors near his home in Herefordshire. Should be next week if you guys want to go," I said.

Duma pursed his lips and nodded. "Geek was a good man," he said. "Ab would never admit it, but he was intimidated by him. We'll be there."

"I'm going to leave tomorrow and go visit Sarah one last time," I said. "To say goodbye."

Duma waggled his head side to side slightly as if weighing my statement. "You do what you need to, D. Put this all behind you and move on." He turned on his heel and walked off.

I thought about what he'd said and went back to staring out the window.

I heard Duma talking with Kailani somewhere in the distance then heard shoes clacking on the tile floor behind me.

"Kailani, I'm sorry," I said.

"Skip it," she replied, walking up next to me, arms crossed over her chest.

She had no signs of the burns—not even pink skin though she'd cut her hair very short because it was all but destroyed by the fire. She was wearing jeans and a tank top.

"I'm trying to apologize for all I did and said," I said, turning toward her. "And for how I treated you."

"No need," she said with a dismissive wave of her hand.

As I was about to say something else, she held up a hand to stop me. I turned back toward the window.

"Geek's funeral is next week in Herefordshire if you wanted to attend," I said a few minutes later, putting my hands behind my back while staring out the window.

I could see her shrug and nod in the reflection in the window. Then she reached into her back pocket and held out the crystals wrapped in wire. They were glowing greenish white ever so slightly in the hazy morning light.

"How did you...?" I asked, wide-eyed in disbelief.

"Heck, I ripped part of her face off," she said with a grin.

"Thank you," I said, reaching for the crystals but stopping short. "I... don't know. I'm not sure I trust St. Germain after what Eisheth said."

"But you trust Eisheth?" she asked with a snort. "Suit yourself. I'm leaving, by the way. So this is goodbye, Diomedes. I hope you get your closure and move on."

"Thank you, Kailani," I said. "If you ever need my help, for any reason, just ask. I owe you."

"Yes, you do," she said.

As she walked away, in the window's reflection, I could see her place the crystals on a side table.

"Hey, what was all that stuff about you and St. Germain and those crystals?" I asked with a shout, turning toward her.

"That's what I'm going to go figure out," she said, hips swaying confidently as she walked away.

And I thought St. Germain had something to worry about with me going after him.

Chapter 66

Several weeks after Geek's funeral, I finally headed back to San Diego to check on my boat and my house and to generally put things back together. I needed to find Ned and apologize to him, too, but he wasn't around his usual haunts, and none of the bartenders at Rocky's Pub or down at the bars on Mission Beach had seen him in weeks. I made a point of leaving the house well after sunrise and returning well before sunset to avoid the Strigoi I knew were still tracking me.

My boat was a mess. Even though I'd left it covered in dry dock, boats are meant to be used, not left sitting. Gaskets and seals crack and leak when left to dry out, and hoses and wires crack and kink. Getting my twenty-six-foot Jones Brothers running right took me a week of solid work. Every captain on the dock insisted on telling me that I had missed a hell of a season on big bluefin tuna.

"We ain't never seen it like this before," the captain of the boat next to mine was saying as I reconnected the fuel lines.

I could hear the young guns on the skiff behind mine jabbering about using rubber flying-fish-shaped lures a hundred yards back under kites and other crazy techniques to get the spooky giants to eat.

It was all a welcome distraction, but the truth was I didn't want the distraction. I wanted to work. I needed to work. I needed to earn my honor back for Sarah, for Geek, and for myself.

Just as I was finishing up, I heard a commotion across the marina at the fuel dock. People were pointing toward my boat but not at me. I stood up, wiping my hands on a rag, to see what was going on. Next to my boat, the big resident bull sea lion we called Elvis was floating, staring up at me. The instant he saw me, he barked and splashed me with water with his big flippers as he rolled over and effectively mooned me. Everyone on the fuel dock laughed at his antics.

"Very funny, you big turd blossom," I said, wiping my sunglasses off.

"It was pretty damn funny if I do say so myself." The deep voice came from the dock behind me.

Ned.

"I guess I deserved that, then?" I asked, turning around and leaning on the gunnel to face him.

His full gray beard hung halfway down his chest, and his belly wasn't any smaller than I'd remembered. As usual, his shirt was something out of a nightmare: greens and purples with what appeared to be silhouettes of a bigfoot holding a fish.

"Where in the hell do you find your clothes?" I asked.

"You can find anything on the interwebs these days," he replied. "Heck, I even got one with flamingoes having sex on it." He laughed so deeply that I could feel it through the hull. It made me smile.

"Ned, it's good to see you," I said.

He peered at me, squinting hard.

"What's wrong?"

"I'm just trying to see whether you got your damn head screwed on straight yet or not," he said.

"It's on straight," I replied with a sigh. "Well, straightish. I'm sorry for the way I treated you the past few months. I have no excuse."

"Ah, it's okay, boy," he replied, stepping onto the boat from the dock. "Hey, you wouldn't happen to have any beer in them coolers, would ya?"

"In fact, I do." I opened the built-in cooler nearest me and threw him one. "Just in case you stopped by."

"In that case, apology accepted," he beamed and opened the can, which foamed all over his beard. Before he took a sip, he fixed me with a glare, and the sea breeze went dead calm.

"These people depend on you to have your head on straight, boy. I don't mean nothing to any of them anymore, but you... You matter whether they know it or not. You need to go sow your oats, fine, go do it. You want to tell *me* to fuck off, that's okay too. I'm a relic who don't belong here anyway. But these people..." He gestured around us and specifically at the people across the dock watching Elvis, with the beer in his hand. "These people need you and the very few others like you, to protect them. And I know that's a big responsibility, and it takes a lot of sacrifices, but that means you can't just go off half-cocked and use your abilities to do whatever you please. I know you know this, boy, and that's part of the reason I stick around—to keep an eye on you. You and me," he said, gesturing between us with his beer, "*We're* good as long as *you're* good."

I nodded. "So, what's the other reason you stick around?" I asked.

"Mostly 'cause I like you, boy," he smiled. "And the free beer don't hurt either." He let out a belch that caused a small wake around the boat, and we both laughed.

My cell phone twittered in my pocket. I pulled it out to see a message from one of the brothers at the Pugnus Dei hospital tending to Sarah. "Call immediately." I hadn't been back to see her. I couldn't bring myself to say goodbye quite yet.

I dialed the only number I had and told them who I was.

"Please hold," said the woman, who immediately sounded harried and flustered when I told her who I was.

Within a few seconds, a more familiar male voice came on.

"Diomedes, this is Brother Doctor Cosmas, one of the two physicians attending to Sarah," he said.

Some sort of ruckus and alarms were going off in the background.

"I recall," I said. "What's so urgent?"

"Well, the specialist you sent came a few weeks back—"

"What specialist?" I replied. "I didn't send anyone."

"But you did," the doctor replied. "Said he had an ancient relic you found that he was supposed to use in an attempt to bring Sarah back around. He was the physician you brought with you the last time you came."

"Uh, you mean Michael, um, Sellers?" I asked, trying to remember how St. Germain had introduced himself, while becoming increasingly irritated by the background noise on the phone.

"No, it was, ah, Dr. Michael Psellos." He was flipping through papers.

"Right, right. Psellos. What did he do?"

"He placed some sort of crown of crystals around her head and said to leave them there for at least forty-eight hours. And we did as he asked, but nothing happened at first."

"What do you mean 'at first'?" I asked, growing impatient and excited at the same time. My heart sped up in my chest.

"It took a few weeks, but... she woke up," he replied.

"What? I'll be there as fast as I can," I said, instantly buoyed by the statement.

"Wait! Before you come, there's something you need to know," he replied.

I held my breath as everything around me fell away and my throat constricted.

"What?" I finally managed to ask, though it came out more like a croak.

"We currently have no idea where she is," he replied sheepishly, but he clearly had more he needed to tell me.

"How do you not know where she is?" I asked, almost not wanting an answer.

"Well, when she woke up, she killed two orderlies, broke one guard's femur, and ripped the arm off another before breaking *through* two walls and fleeing."

I knew I didn't want to know…

About the Author

Brian S. Leon is truly a jack-of-all-trades and a master of none. He began writing in order to do something with all the useless degrees, knowledge and skills--most of which have no practical application in civilized society--he accumulated over the years.

His varied interests include, most notably, mythology of all kinds and fishing, and he has spent time in jungles and museums all over the world studying and oceans and seas across the globe chasing fish, sometimes even catching them. He has also spent time in various locations around the world doing other things that may or may not have ever happened.

Inspired by stories of classical masters like Homer and Jules Verne, as well as modern writers like J.R.R. Tolkien, David Morrell, and Jim Butcher, combined with an inordinate amount of free time, Mr. Leon finally decided to come up with tales of his own.

Brian currently resides just north of Los Angeles, CA. You can visit his Web site at www.BrianSLeon.com.

About the Publisher

Dear Reader,

We hope you enjoyed this book. Please consider leaving a review on your favorite book site.

Visit our site to find more quality books!

Read more at https://RedAdeptPublishing.com.